Lady of Steel

by

Mary Gillgannon

Medieval Ladies Series

Lady of Steel

Cover Art by *Debbie Taylor*

The Wild Rose Press, Inc.
PO Box 708
Adams Basin, NY 14410-0708
Visit us at www.thewildrosepress.com

Publishing History
First Tea Rose Edition, 2018
Print ISBN 978-1-5092-1833-2
Digital ISBN 978-1-5092-1834-9

Medieval Ladies Series
Published in the United States of America

His expression softened.

His dark eyes again flared with violent emotion. "You forget. I knew Mortimer. He tried more than once to kill me. I have no sympathy for him. None at all."

She let out her breath. Perhaps now they could begin again, and he would stop playing this game of cat and mouse with her. She nodded. "I'm very grateful you understand. I'd worried you might have heard tales of me, stories meant to portray me as wicked and manipulative."

He watched her intently. "Aye, I have heard tales. 'Tis good you saw fit to reassure me. Perhaps now, perhaps we can..." He let his words trail off and the atmosphere between them shifted. His dark eyes no longer seemed stern and implacable, but smoldered with frank sexual desire. The tension between them changed, erupting with blazing arousal.

Fire started in her loins and spread outward, making her skin ache for his touch. She tilted her head, awaiting his kiss.

He hesitated, as if even now he feared to take this final step and give into what his body obviously desired. Observing his forbearance, she thought for the dozenth time of how different he was from Mortimer. Mortimer had been a slave to his emotions. This man sought control at all times.

But at last he brought his lips to hers. The blaze took them both.

Dedication

To my beloved knight and hero, Patrick.

Chapter One

Valmar Castle, May, 1189

"Useless slut! When the squire comes to this chamber, you will lie there willingly while he does his business. You will do as I bid, or I will beat you senseless." Walter Mortimer's handsome features twisted in a grotesque mockery of a smile. "I would have liked to send you a peasant from the fields. But I had trouble finding one with your devil-black hair. The babe must look like you lest anyone guess the truth."

"Hah!" Nicola matched her husband's arrogant tone. "Think you that no one at Valmar knows what you are? That you prefer young boys to women?"

The blow came so quickly she didn't have a chance to turn her head. She staggered, hand pressed to her bleeding mouth.

"Aye, they know what I am," Mortimer said, softly. "I am their lord. And the child you give birth to will be my heir. If the matter is spoken of otherwise, I will accuse you of adultery and have you beaten to death." He put his face close to hers. "Remember that, bitch. Remember to be convincing."

Nicola struggled to take a breath. It wasn't fear that choked her but rage. How had she come to be married to this man, this monster? She'd been raised an heiress, coddled and loved. But when her father died, her life

1

abruptly changed. She was made a ward of the king, and the rich lands to which she was heir became the means for King Richard to raise money for his Crusade. He'd wasted no time in offering her and her dowry to the most ruthless lords in the land.

She'd feared to be wed to a man who was old, crude, or ill-visaged. It had been a relief when she first glimpsed Mortimer. With his fair hair and fine features, she'd thought him as comely as an angel. What a jest! A demon was more like it. She had been too naive to understand his hostility at first, too stupid to guess that he did not respond to her attempts to please him, not because he disliked her, but because he disliked all women.

As if guessing her thoughts, Mortimer smiled. He touched her face. "A pity your charms are wasted on me. The serving women tell me you are fair, but all I see is your witch's black hair and icy eyes." His hand fell away and his gaze moved downward. "They also say you are too narrow-hipped to give birth easily. I pray they are wrong. Should you die in childbirth, your dower lands will revert to the king. Damn Richard, he's such a greedy bastard, he'd probably make me pay for them a second time." Mortimer started for the door. "You will obey me in this, Nicola, or I will make you very sorry."

As the door slammed shut, Nicola released a pent-up breath. She wanted to pray, but she dare not. Her thoughts were too vengeful and wicked. She wished Mortimer would trip on the tower stairs and break his neck. That he would die in battle and his slayer cut out his heart and feed it to a dog!

She went to the window and stared out at the fields

beyond the castle. Hatred had kept her alive these past weeks. It allowed her to endure the despair of being locked in her bedchamber and subject to her husband's mocking taunts. Now she must survive another humiliation. To lie willingly while a man chosen by Mortimer mounted her and spilled his seed inside her body.

Somehow, she would do it. She would not allow herself to be crushed beneath Walter Mortimer's boots. She would survive and find a way to defeat him.

****

Fawkes reached the top of the stairs and hesitated before the wooden door. Inside was a lady, his lord's wife. The thought made him taut with nerves. What would the woman think of him? Would she shrink in revulsion? Although scrubbed as clean as lye soap and water could make him, he still looked like a common soldier.

"Would that I was young and virile myself, that I might have this plum of a task," the sergeant had told him, his grizzled face split with a grin. "A right honor it is."

For certes it was. But why had Lord Mortimer chosen him? Fawkes could not help thinking of his old nurse's words. *If you fancy that something sounds too good to be true, 'tis probably so.*

Too late. He had already agreed. Had he a choice? Even couched in fine words, an order was an order.

He looked down at his plain leather boots as his stomach fluttered. What if she laughed at him? *Jesu, you can't think like that. 'Tis not the woman who will unman you, but your own thoughts.*

What did she look like? He'd never seen Lady

Mortimer, but in the few weeks he'd been in the garrison, he'd learned she was a great heiress. A woman who brought as her dowry the castles of Valmar and Mordeaux scarce needed to be comely.

What if her limbs were misshapen or she smelled foul?

He could close his eyes and hold his breath. His shaft had never before failed to rise when presented with a willing woman.

But was she willing? He took a breath, trying to calm himself. If he didn't master his fears, he would never earn his spurs as a knight. He must have courage. A mere woman was nothing to a warrior.

He rapped sharply on the door. There was a sound, but he couldn't tell if she bid him enter. He shoved the door open. The one window was shuttered, sealing out all but a tiny sliver of the afternoon sunlight. He made his way to the bed. "Lady?"

He could smell her rich perfume. Never had he bedded a woman like this, pampered and refined. For a short while, she would be his. He would not think about why. He shucked his clothing. The ropes supporting the bed groaned as he climbed in. He reached out and felt warm, smooth skin. Her shoulder was silk, her arm lithe and gracefully shaped. With cautious fingers, he groped upward and grasped a thick braid.

"By the saints!" Her voice was a taut whisper. "Will you get on with it!"

He went rigid. She clearly dreaded what was to come. Disappointment shafted through him. Very well. He would do his duty. Then he would leave.

He released her hair and moved his hand lower. The feel of a lush, pliant breast made his breathing quicken.

He caressed her nipple.

"Don't," she murmured. When he ignored her, she tensed as if she would push him away. But then she arched upward and the nipple he was fondling peaked tight and firm against his fingers.

He was intrigued by this woman. Her scent. Her sleek body and rose-petal soft skin. His cock was aching hard, but there was so much yet to explore. He touched her face. Fine features. Delicate bones. He wondered what color her eyes were. He had to know. Had to see her.

Rising from the bed, he went to the window. "Nay!" she cried as he threw open the shutter.

He turned. "Why not?"

"'Tis a business best accomplished in darkness!"

"I wish to see you."

"Well, I wish otherwise!" Her voice echoed sullenly.

He approached the bed and the breath seemed to leave his body. She was a soldier's wet-dream. Hair like black silk. Skin like fresh cream. Her face a perfect oval with wide-set gray eyes and a rosebud mouth. The thin linen chemise revealed a body as finely made and lovely as he had imagined.

She crossed her arms over her breasts and glared at him. "There will be no kissing. And no more touching except as required. You will not dally. You will not gainsay me or give me orders."

It took a moment, but he finally found his voice. "My name is Fawkes de Cressy. Your husband bid me get you with child. He didn't explain the details. "

"I won't lay silent while you handle me as if I am a mare to be gentled! I'm a lady and mistress of Valmar!"

He went to the bed. Leaning near, he touched her cheek. "So you are. I have not forgotten." He climbed onto the bed and brought his mouth to hers.

****

His mouth felt hot and wet. His kisses made her gasp, and when she parted her lips he thrust his tongue inside, like a sweet, spiced plum. Nicola went rigid at the invasion, but a moment later her body filled with aching heat.

She wanted to fight him, but oh! His tongue moved in a tantalizing rhythm, mimicking what was to come. He grasped her braid and worked it loose, then smoothed the strands over her body. His strong, callused fingers cupped one of her breasts, playing expertly with her nipple. She fought back a moan. He moved his mouth to where his hand had been, suckling. Gentle at first and then more roughly. A ripple of sensation spread through her body and struck lightning between her thighs. Her hips arched upwards, wanting, wanting.

His fingers slid down her belly and teased the soft hair of her mound before moving lower. He explored her as if he was a blind man memorizing her flesh. His fingers discovered that secret place she hardly understood herself, possessed of mysterious folds and contours and a damp slit between that grew wetter still when touched.

He opened her like unfurling the petals of a flower and dipped one finger in the center of the blossom. Her body clenched and tightened, then melted to allow him entrance. He left his finger inside her, pressing slightly upward, and kissed her again. Pressure built, turned to ache, then undeniable need. She arched her hips seeking something more. He moved his hand to her cleft and struck sparks when his fingers reached a spot hidden deep. She burst into flame and a wild cry echoed in her ears—her own voice.

He adjusted his body over hers and she felt something different. Something bigger than a finger. His shaft. He brushed her belly with it and traced a path downward, stroking softly. As if she had no control, her body opened. Her legs splayed wide. Hips lifted. Without thought, her body sought his.

A stinging thrust of pressure. Followed by a startling moment of pain. She clutched his shoulders and clawed him with her nails. But the time for turning back was over. He was almost inside her. She panted, undone by the sense of being torn apart.

"Shhhh. I didn't know you were a virgin. I'll take it slow."

He moved his hand between them, to where taut skin stretched around solid flesh. Expert fingers stroked, coaxed, soothed. Her body responded, appeased into surrender. More pressure and he was inside her.

Pain, but it subsided. He began to move and the wrenching ache returned. She let out a cry. He responded by kissing her. First her lips, then nibbling her neck and ears. Gradually she relaxed.

He moved again. She tensed at each thrust. He halted and once again slid his fingers between them, searching for some precise hidden spot. He found it and like a door opened by a key, her body yielded and caught fire. Fierce sensation coursed through her. Her hips locked with his, drawing him deeper as she strained for some elusive, desperate satisfaction.

Finding it, she bucked upwards and keened wildly. The fire inside her exploded and drenched them both.

For a moment, she was senseless, blinded and deafened by waves of pleasure. Then the room tilted back into place again, and she became aware of a pounding that was not the blood throbbing in her ears.

She could not heed it, so disoriented she was. He shook her gently and whispered, "Answer. I dare not."

Weakly, she called, "Who is it?"

"Walter, your husband."

Fawkes jerked away and started to get up from the bed. She grabbed his arm. "Nay, don't let him in!"

He gave her a desperate look. "I must. He is my lord."

Nicola watched helplessly as Fawkes got out of bed, pulled up his chausses and rearranged the rest of his clothing. He went to the door and opened it. "Milord?"

"You must be the boy Warmond found." Mortimer thrust his bulk through the doorway, forcing Fawkes aside. "I came to see how my wife fared. From the caterwauling, I feared you did not do right by her." He looked toward the bed, the familiar sneering expression distorting his features. "I see I was mistaken. She looks well enough."

"My lord, I—" Fawkes said.

Mortimer silenced him with a shake of his head. "Nay, do not explain. The truth is obvious. In the right hands, my wife is clearly a lusty creature, a veritable bitch in heat."

Fawkes stared at Mortimer in stunned silence. Nicola tightened the blanket she held around her body. "We were attempting to do as you bid, milord." She fixed him with an icy look. "To beget an heir to secure *your* lands."

Mortimer smirked at Fawkes. "Did you plant your crop well?"

Fawkes looked stricken. Nicola answered quickly. "Aye, milord. We are finished."

Fawkes finally found his voice. "Mayhaps we should let the lady rest, milord. I've heard the seed takes better if the woman lies down after."

"I was told you were a good soldier." Mortimer's tone was deep and mocking. "One who would do his duty well. Warmond's faith in you was not misplaced."

Mortimer approached the bed, and Nicola held her breath. "I can't imagine how you managed it. Do you not find her overly pale? And that ugly black hair..." He glanced at Fawkes and laughed. "Of course. Yours is the same, so you would not notice." Mortimer turned back to Nicola. "I feel nothing for my wife, of a certes. All I've had of her these weeks since we've wed is her sharp tongue and peevish temper."

"My lord, I..." Fawkes took a step forward.

Mortimer turned. "My lord...what?"

Nicola felt a wave of pity for Fawkes. She sensed the battle going on inside him. A less controlled man might have struck out, but Fawkes merely went rigid and looked as if he might choke.

Mortimer smiled. "That's right, boy. I am your lord, and it's me you obey, not your randy loins or"— he jerked his head toward Nicola—"this cunning slut." He looked back at Fawkes. "You have spilled your seed, but it will be weeks before we know if it takes. In the meantime, I go to London and you go with me."

Fawkes's eyes widened. He shot Nicola a startled

look. She wanted to say something, to bid him farewell. But she dare not. If she showed him a hint of warmth, she would seal his doom. As it was, she feared Mortimer meant to be rid of him as soon as possible.

Fawkes hesitated a second, then awkwardly bowed. "My lady." He turned and went out the door.

Nicola's heart jumped into her throat. While Fawkes was in the room, she'd some hope Mortimer would not abuse her. Now, he was gone, and she was alone with her husband. Although she'd vowed never to let him see her fear, it grew more and more difficult to conceal her dread. The memory of the pain he'd already inflicted made her stomach lurch.

Mortimer gazed after Fawkes for a moment before turning back to her. A slight smile touched his features. "All that youthful lust wasted on a whey-faced bitch like you." He grabbed her chemise. Nicola struggled to jerk away, but he pinned her against the bed with his body.

"Get away!" she screamed. She reached up to claw his face.

He twisted from her attack, brutally squeezing her arm. Then he laughed.

Nicola went still. All she wanted was for him to leave her alone. After a moment he released her, dumping her against the bed. "Ugh." He backed away. "You smell like a well-used harlot. I soil my hands by touching you." He started toward the door.

"Where are you going?" Nicola whispered. Despite her dread, she wanted to know his plans.

"To London. I can't delay any longer." His blue eyes flicked over her. "If I were you, madam, I would get down on my knees and pray my lover was successful in his plowing. If your belly is still flat when I return, I vow I will find a raven-haired serf to finish the task."

The door thudded as he left. Nicola sat on edge of the bed feeling stunned. In the space of half an hour, one man had taken her to heaven, another to hell. Even now, her body thrummed with the echoes of her climax. She could feel Fawkes' seed dribbling down her thighs.

The thought of him made her wince. She imagined the young man lying dead beside the road to London. Anger rose inside her, hot and choking. How she hated Mortimer! She would do anything to thwart him. One way would be to have Old Emma to go to the healer and fetch a potion to kill Fawkes' seed. She could make certain Mortimer never had the heir he so desired.

In the weeks while Mortimer was in London she could try to gain allies. If the men of the garrison knew how cruelly her husband treated her, what a perverted beast he was, some of them might agree to defy him when he returned. Nay, she thought with disgust. The garrison had sworn their allegiance to Mortimer, and they would not go back on it. Even for her. The most she could hope for was that they would help her escape Valmar.

But where could she go? As soon as he returned, Mortimer would hunt her down. No one would give her shelter. No one would risk his wrath.

Her anger turned to despair. There was no way out. Unless Mortimer died. For a moment, she imagined Fawkes riding down Mortimer and killing him. She could see Fawkes's face, proud and defiant, as he thrust his sword into Mortimer's belly. "This is for Nicola," he would say.

But there would never be such a meeting. Mortimer would pay someone to murder Fawkes. To spill his blood quickly and quietly before they reached London. Nicola touched her belly. If Fawkes had gotten her with a babe, the child would be all that was left of him in this world. How could she kill it?

She wrenched her fingers from her body and clutched her hands together. Such thoughts were soft and womanly. To defeat Mortimer, she must be as ruthless as he was.

Hurrying to the door, Nicola leaned down the stairs and called for Old Emma to attend her.

Chapter Two

"Have you lost your wits, Fawkes? Sir Alan will be back from gaming at any moment. If you don't have his armor finished, he'll flay you alive!"

Fawkes looked up from the soiled helm in his lap to see his fellow squire regarding him with a mixture of aggravation and dread.

"I mean it, Fawkes." Reynard raked a hand through his thick hair, making it stand up even more. In the firelight outside Sir Alan Wazelin's tent, Reynard's tresses gleamed a fox-like red. "I don't know what ails you these days. I thought you'd be thrilled to go to London and see the king. But ever since we left Valmar, you've walked around like a man in a daze."

"I've much on my mind." Fawkes grabbed a handful of wet sand and rubbed it over the helm.

"Seems to me you scarce have a mind left," Reynard said. "Did you get hit during quintain practice?"

Fawkes scrubbed harder. "Nay, I am well. And I'm pleased to see London, 'tis only that..." He'd spent less than an hour with Nicola, but the experience had changed his life forever.

"Well, you might think of the rest of us," Reynard muttered. "If you anger Sir Alan, he'll grumble to Mortimer, and Lord Walter is already foul-tempered. I don't understand. If he's in such a hurry to see the king before he sails, why did he wait so long to go to London? I admit that being barely wed and all, he had to spend some time with his new wife. Get her with child, if possible, so his claim to the lands is secured." Reynard rubbed his face. "But even bedding a woman night and day does not assure a babe will come of it. Not that I think Mortimer was very diligent in his efforts. The woman must be a toothless harridan the way he keeps her hidden away."

"Jesu, Reynard, will you shut your flapping mouth!" Fawkes lobbed the helmet in his direction. "I'm sick of all this crude talk of Lady Nicola. As if she was a broken-down mare Mortimer kept for breeding stock!"

Reynard stepped back, his skin pale beneath the splatter of ruddy freckles. "Lady Nicola? How do you know her Christian name?"

Fawkes stiffened. "Sir Alan sent me with a message for Mortimer. She was in the solar, sewing." His voice rose. "And I vow the reason her husband keeps her hidden away is not because she is ugly but because she is surpassing fair, and he has no wish for his men to besmirch her name with crude gossip!"

Fawkes felt himself flushing. Speaking of Nicola's beauty aroused mind-numbing memories.

"I didn't know you were ever in the upper parts of the castle," Reynard said. "You never spoke of it."

"Lackwit! 'Twas meant to be a secret! I don't go babbling my lord's private business!"

Reynard's plain face twisted with perplexity. "I never dreamed you were so well-regarded by Sir Alan. Or Mortimer either. I've labored this past week thinking I must save you from their wrath. I was even going to offer to help you with Sir Alan's armor." He went to pick up the helm, which shone gold in the firelight. "God's feet, Fawkes. It's dented. How are you going to get that out?"

"You're going to fetch me a hammer from the smith." Fawkes grabbed his friend's tunic sleeve and propelled him toward the opening between Sir Alan's and another knight's tent. "Many thanks, Reynard. I'm grateful to have such a fine, loyal friend."

Reynard made sounds of protest but he allowed Fawkes to shove him off. As soon as he was gone, Fawkes sank down on his knees beside the pile of armor. Sweet Mary, Queen of Heaven, what was he to do! Reynard was right; he'd lost all reason. Since that day, he'd been able to think of nothing but Nicola. Of her beauty, the feel of her body close to his. And of the terrible way Lord Mortimer used her. The man was a wretch, a slimy snake, a black-hearted demon! He should be drawn and quartered for his treatment of his wife!

Fawkes' hands clenched reflexively on the cold metal as he imagined closing them around Mortimer's thick neck. He'd plotted a dozen ways to kill his nemesis. Poison in his food. A knife in his ribs while he slept. An arrow between his shoulder blades while he rode at the head of the army train.

None of the means he'd thought of aided his other goal—saving Lady Mortimer. Nay, not Lady *Mortimer*. He refused to think of her in connection with that filthy swine! The Lady of Valmar, she was. Beautiful beyond compare. With skin scented of flowers. A mouth as sweet and intoxicating as mead. A body as lithe and graceful as a willow branch. And a quim of silken fire.

15

He was hard again. Endlessly aching from the memory of the most perfect sex he could imagine. The only way to fight the consuming desire was to remember his anger and hatred. And his plan for revenge.

Reynard was right. He must get control of himself. Remain clear-headed. It would not be easy to kill Mortimer. But somehow he would do it. Then he would earn his spurs as a knight and seek a boon of the king. He would not ask for Valmar but only the woman herself. And her child, if there was one.

A shudder passed down his body. To think that her body and his, joined together, might have created a babe. A son or daughter. Better if it was a girl child. That way, it would be more tolerable if some believed the offspring was Mortimer's.

He frowned. According to law, the babe would be recognized as Mortimer's, even if everyone knew the man had never lain with his wife. Unless Mortimer died before the truth of the babe were known.

But he got ahead of himself. He didn't even know if his seed had taken. If Nicola's womb was fertile. If she was hardy enough to bear a living child. She was so fine and delicate.

Cold fingers gripped his heart. What if she died in childbirth? What if his crude rutting killed her! He closed his eyes, praying. "Dear God, let her be well. Let her live. I'll ask for nothing else…"

And he would not. The rest he would do himself. Somehow.

A shadow loomed large in the firelight. "Ah, the dutiful squire, working his fingers raw, polishing my armor." Sir Alan's voice rang out.

Fawkes stood, tense but not fearful. Sir Alan was a harsh man but generally fair. And Fawkes had never given his master cause for complaint. Until now.

"I can't credit it, de Cressy. You've never been over half a fool before. What's addled your brains? Some slut take your fancy? Pshaw! Don't let a wench under your skin. They're all the same. Part their legs for any man."

Sir Alan bent down, his hawk-like face split by a wicked-looking grin. "Tell me her name, and I'll prove it to you. Offer her some silver and she'll be flat on her back, faster than a fly on dung, screaming my name instead of yours." Sir Alan straightened and guffawed, then belched loudly.

He appeared to be very drunk, which surprised Fawkes. The crusty Wazelin was not one for over-imbibing.

"Reynard went to get a hammer, sir. I found a dent in your helm." Fawkes picked it up and turned it so the firelight shone on the flaw.

Sir Alan waved his hand impatiently. "Dented or not, if it serves to protect my balding pate, I'm satisfied. But my mail... You can't leave it there in the mud to rust. Finish it up, boy."

"But, sir, don't you wish me to help you to bed first?"

Sir Alan grunted and moved toward the tent, swaying slightly. Fawkes followed, wondering how Wazelin felt about his liege, Walter Mortimer. If he meant to bring down a lord, he must enlist powerful men to aid him. "Were you meeting with Lord Mortimer?" he asked.

The knight grunted as he took a seat on a stool and

raised his arms so Fawkes could pull off his surcote. Taking that for an assent, Fawkes pressed on. "I suppose all the talk is of London and the king. Have you ever met King Richard, sir?"

"Aye, but never in this country. Fought beside him in Poitou and at Chinon before Old Henry died. The Lionheart is a good soldier."

"And Lord Mortimer," Fawkes continued, "I hear he is well-acquainted with the king."

Sir Alan made a snorting sound. "Mortimer knows how to flatter royalty, that's all."

"So, the king is off on Crusade," Fawkes said after a moment. "I hear that freeing Jerusalem, despite Richard's optimism, might take years. In the meantime, Prince John will stir up trouble. They say he is already looking for barons willing to sell their loyalty. I wonder if Mortimer—"

"I say, boy, your tongue is running off dangerously tonight." Sir Alan, now freed of his surcote and gambeson, regarded Fawkes with a baleful stare. "This talk of Mortimer and the king. Prince John. 'Tis not seemly. Or healthy. Besides, it probably doesn't matter what happens here in England. You and I will be deep in the domain of the Saracens by next Lenten. Probably die there, too."

"What do you mean?" Fawkes asked. His mouth was suddenly dry. His heart hammering.

"We're to go with the king. Mortimer is sending us on the Crusade. Since he can't go himself. Since he is so busy with his new lands and wife and all." Sir Alan's voice dripped scorn, but Fawkes scarcely heard it.

He was to go on Crusade. He would earn his spurs and might even be knighted by the king himself. It was

Richard's dream to free Jerusalem. He had beggared England to equip his army and buy mercenaries to reach his goal and he would reward all who aided him.

Fawkes saw himself returning to England as a knight and seasoned fighting man. A hero and in the king's debt. When Richard asked what reward he wished, there could be but one answer, the Lady of Valmar.

"They say there are fevers that make your eyes and mouth bleed," Sir Alan said. "Deserts so hot your blood boils. Vicious Saracens who cut off your ballocks and stuff them in your mouth so you can't scream while they torture you to death." He sighed heavily. Fawkes did not note it.

****

December 1090, Valmar Castle

"Christ save me!" Nicola shrieked. "Oh, let me die! Let me die now, I beg you!"

The pain came in waves. Hideous, wrenching waves. Nicola felt her body being torn asunder and at this moment, she hated the man who had caused her such agony. "Damn him. Damn his wretched, black-hearted soul!"

Nay, she thought as the contraction subsided, she should not blame Fawkes. 'Twas her evil wretch of a husband she should curse. Fawkes had a least given her pleasure when he bedded her.

She sought to recall the memory, a distraction from the pain clawing her belly. His dark eyes like burning coals as he gazed at her. His tanned skin and striking features. The gentleness of his mouth as he kissed her ears, her neck, her breasts. His hands caressing her with expert care. As if he was a blind man memorizing her flesh.

The memory shattered as the pain came again. "She screamed.

"Shush, lady," Emma crooned as she wiped Nicola's brow. "I've put a knife beneath the bed to cut the pain. Your lying-in progresses well. The babe is placed right. Your womb has opened. Now, 'tis only the matter of pushing the child out into the world."

The next bout of crushing misery. "Arghhh. Ahhhh. Ohhhh." The babe bursting through her flesh. The pain cresting like a huge beast devouring her. She screamed again. And again.

"'Tis a boy, lady. Hear how lustily he cries!"

Nicola roused herself from the darkness of the pain. "Make him stop," she whispered. "What if Mortimer hears?"

"Whist now, little one," Emma cooed. The cries ceased.

Nicola felt a weight on her chest, feather-light after the soul-searing pressure of the birth. Despite her weariness, she forced her eyes open, longing to see this thing she'd fought so hard for. It lay crumpled against her breast, a reddish, swollen creature with bruised eyes and a tiny, puckering mouth.

"Oh," she gasped, "Oh."

The delicate mouth opened. Closed. A primeval longing swept through her, the bone-deep ache of love.

"Lady, I must take him," Emma murmured. "Now, while he is quiet."

The thought of it brought crushing pain, as agonizing as the labor pangs. Nicola choked on a sob. Tears stung her eyes. Her babe. All this struggle and pain and now she must give him up.

****

Acre, July 1091

Fawkes de Cressy crouched in near darkness, inching forward like a worm. The tunnel was as hot as a forge, and each time he inhaled, his lungs filled with smoke from the horn lantern. He used his pick to strike another chunk from the rocky earth ahead of him. Again. Steady. Careful.

He paused and sought to tamp down the dread that clawed at him each time he struck a blow. Nay, he refused to think about what would happen if the tunnel collapsed. Instead he would concentrate on the reward King Richard promised. To any man brave enough to dig underneath the Accursed Tower, he offered ten gold pieces. Not enough for Fawkes to fulfill his dream, but a start. And if he could acquit himself well in the fighting when the tower came down, he might acquire even greater riches. With luck, he might rise high enough in the king's favor to ask for the ultimate prize—the demesne of Valmar and the woman who came with it.

Thinking of Lady Nicola banished his fatigue and fear, and filled him with new determination. He'd spent a bare candle hour with her, but it was enough to keep him going through all the misery and struggle of the past two years. She was a thing of dreams, a shining vision lighting the way ahead of him.

A sound interrupted his reverie. Was another sapper working parallel to him? He'd heard nothing before this. The sound came again. A slippery, whispery noise, followed by a shower of stones. Then a torrent. He gasped in horror as the tunnel behind him collapsed. Everything turned to darkness.

****

Valmar Castle, December, 1192

"King Richard's ship went down at Aquileia, forcing the crusaders to travel by land. He was then taken prisoner by Duke Leopold, who blames Richard for the murder of his cousin, Conrad of Montferrat."

Although Father FitzAlan delivered his news in an appropriately solemn voice, there could be no mistaking that edge of gloating in his expression. Seated across from the cleric, Nicola experienced a similar sense of elation. This might be it, her chance to free herself from her wretched husband. Mortimer, slumped over his wine cup, scarcely seemed to take note of FitzAlan's words.

Nicola poked at the boiled mutton on her trencher and sought to make her voice cool and noncommital. "What will happen to Richard now?"

The cleric shrugged. "Who knows? Perhaps Leopold will leave Richard to rot in his dungeon. Or mayhaps he will turn him over to one of his other enemies. Either way, it's likely Richard will never return to England."

Mortimer suddenly raised his blood-shot eyes and glared at FitzAlan. "Richard will find a way to get free. Mark my words."

"Perhaps…" FitzAlan's voice remained smooth and non-committal. "But it seems to me a wise man might reconsider his alliances. I'm certain Prince John would be willing to let you keep Valmar and your other properties if you—"

Mortimer rose, the speed of his movement belying his body's bloated form. He pounded the table. "'Tis treason you suggest, and I'll not have it in my hall!

Cease your wicked innuendos or I'll have you thrown out of the castle!"

Father FitzAlan's face blanched. "My lord, I meant nothing traitorous. I'm simply pointing out the peril of the Lionheart's situation. He's imprisoned far from home, in the hands of his enemies."

Mortimer twisted his features into a hideous snarl, and FitzAlan drew back, looking horrified.

Now. Now is your chance. Nicola reached across the table to touch the priest's sleeve. "Father, if you would come with me to the solar, I would like to make confession now."

FitzAlan nodded and rose, looking very relieved. Nicola led him through the crowded hall. Along the way, her heart raced with excitement and her hands grew clammy. Did she really dare to do this? Plot with John while Richard was yet alive? It was, as Mortimer had said, *treason.*

But it might be her only chance. Mortimer was Richard's man. If the king never returned to England, Prince John would seize power. And from what she'd heard of John, he was a man who remembered those who sought his favor.

They reached the solar and she motioned to a cushioned chair near the hearth. Too nervous to sit, Nicola stood a respectful distance away. She clutched her hands together to keep them from shaking. "Before I confess Father, I must speak with you of another matter. My husband was granted Valmar and my other properties by King Richard. Now you tell us the king is imprisoned by men who despise him. If something terrible befalls Richard, and John becomes king, I fear Prince John might take retribution against Valmar for my husband's stubborn allegiance to Richard." She lowered her gaze. "I beg you, Father. If you have any influence with the prince, please convey to him *my* support for his cause."

FitzAlan regarded her steadily. "The prince has no *cause*. Other than hoping, as does all England, that the king comes home safely."

Nicola repressed a shudder of nerves. This was it. Once said, there was no going back. "I may be a woman, but I'm not naive, Father. I'm well aware of the harsh realities of English politics. I'm certain Prince John prays hourly that his brother never returns to England. He wants the crown for himself, and I think he is clever enough that he will eventually have it. To that end, I'm pledging him my support, and that of Valmar, Rosebrook, Mordeaux, and the other properties I am heiress to."

Something glinted in FitzAlan's brown eyes. "I mean no disrespect, madam, but the fact is, you offer what is not yours to give. Your husband is the one who controls your dower lands."

"My husband has not roused himself to even hold a lance these past two years. If John were to send a force here, I doubt there would be much resistance."

"And what would be your gain in this?" FitzAlan's expression grew wolfish.

"My husband is a drunkard and a sodomite. Can you blame me for wishing to be free of him?"

"I had heard rumors of such things. Now you have confirmed it. I will carry your message to court. If and when John decides it is time to act, I will be in contact with you." He stood and bowed. "I thank you for your candidness."

FitzAlan left the solar, and Nicola considered how far she had come. Before Simon was born, she would never have dared such a thing. Her concern for her son was so great that she was capable of many things, including, apparently, plotting treason.

A moment later, she turned at the sound of Old Emma's heavy tread on the hides covering the solar floor. The old woman's rheumy blue eyes regarded her with concern. "Whist, lady, what are you up to?"

"I'm safeguarding my son's heritage."

Old Emma darted a glance at the doorway. "What if someone should overhear? I fear you are too bold, milady."

"King Richard is leagues and leagues away, while John is here in England. If I am to have any property to pass on to my son, I must play the prince's game."

"'Tis not fitting. A woman should defer to her husband in these matters."

"My husband? You mean that monster I'm wed to?" Nicola shook her head. "I'll not let Mortimer bring us all down. I will choose my own destiny."

"What of your son? If you choose ill, he will suffer."

Nicola closed her eyes and clenched her hands into fists. *Simon. How was she to protect him?*

Old Emma came and patted her arm. "At least your son lives, and thrives. The reports from Mordeaux say Simon grows bonny and tall. He'll make a fine knight someday."

Nicola jerked away. "I don't want him to be a knight! If he never takes up arms, I would die a happy woman. Think of all the suffering that would be prevented if men would cease their constant warring!"

Old Emma gazed at her sadly. "'Tis the way men are, and I fear only God can alter such things."

Chapter Three

Mordeaux Castle, July, 1193

Fawkes de Cressy pushed back his helm and stared across the valley at the gray bulk of Mordeaux Castle. Rather than weathered stone, his vision was filled with another image, Lady Nicola. Perfect, milk-white skin. A fall of hair like liquid night. Eyes like moonstones. A mouth of petal-like softness.

The odors of sweat and horse and oiled armor also vanished, replaced by a scent so rich and intoxicating, it took his breath away. He'd never been able to decide what sort of flowers and spices comprised her rare perfume. Perhaps it was the sublime essence of the woman herself, mysterious, untouchable, offering the promise of almost unbearable delights.

But soon, very soon, he would have a chance to breathe the exalted air that surrounded her exquisite flesh. To touch her, to hold her, to—

"Why are we stopping here?" Reynard pulled his destrier up next to Fawkes's mount. "I thought the plan was to show them the writ from the king, then take control of the castle. We can use Mordeaux as a base to attack Valmar if Mortimer decides to fight."

"What if something goes wrong?" Fawkes asked. "Will they honor the writ? With Richard imprisoned and John trying to seize power—"

"Jesu, Fawkes, you can't get cold feet now! There's likely no more than a handful of men garrisoned here. And I can't believe they feel that much loyalty to Mortimer. He wasn't well liked when he first took control. By now they surely know what a fiend he is."

Fawkes nodded. Reynard was right. After all he'd endured, he must not lose faith. Besides, there was more than his own dream at stake. He'd promised the knights arrayed behind him a chance at a new life. For their sake, he must remain bold and confident.

He raised his arm and brought it down. The troop of knights surged forward, down the slope and into the valley. A cloud of dust surrounded them and the clink and clatter of their heavy armor rattled in their ears.

Fawkes knew a sense of relief as his body reacted with the familiar energy and excitement. The will to survive and triumph had taken him this far. He thought of the very walls of Acre collapsing upon him, the only tunnel leading to air and life blocked by an assassin sent by Mortimer. He thought of watching men die of fever, moaning and out of their wits. Of the long march down the coast of Palestine, when men roasted to death in their armor and fell prey to the devil Saracens, who flayed their victims alive.

He had survived those things, by the grace of God. Now there was only this, one last confrontation, the final link in the chain that would render unto him all that he had dreamed of. Valmar Castle claimed as his own. Mortimer, dead. Lady Nicola, in his arms, safe forever.

"God's teeth! Look at that!" Reynard called.

Alarm prickled along Fawkes's spine. Knights poured through the castle's portcullis. He slowed his mount and motioned for the men behind him to do the same. "Jesu," he breathed. "Have they been warned? Did they know we were coming?"

"It would seem so," Reynard responded. "The information we had when we were in London was that Mortimer never leaves Valmar. And yet, that is surely him."

The knight leading the force wore a green surcote emblazoned with a gold lion rampant. The familiar device aroused Fawkes's fury and hatred. This was his enemy. The man who had tried to kill him. The man who had humiliated and abused Nicola. Mixed with the fury was a grim satisfaction. How shocked Mortimer would be when he discovered King Richard had given Mordeaux Castle to Fawkes.

"What should we do?" Reynard sounded panicky. "Do we charge? Or wait for them to come to us?"

"We wait," Fawkes said. "Mortimer hasn't fought a battle in years, perhaps never. He'll want to negotiate."

Fawkes's prediction was confirmed when the troop of knights halted a few paces away and their leader raised his helm. Although he immediately recognized the hated face, Fawkes knew a moment of shock. Mortimer's face was puffy and red, and his eyes appeared as mere slits in the bloated flesh. He looked little like the youthful and vigorous man Fawkes recalled.

"It's you!" Mortimer bellowed. His eyes were wide with shock.

"Yea, it is I, Fawkes de Cressy. Your assassin failed. I left his body to rot beneath the walls of Acre." He took a step forward and drew his sword. "Now I have returned to repay you for your treachery."

Mortimer made a hoarse, derisive sound. "You're

naught but a lowly squire, a stableboy. You're not worth the effort of killing."

Fawkes fought the urge to forget the rules of combat and rush forward for the kill. He forced himself to speak with calm. "I'm a knight now, exalted by the King of England himself. Richard also gave me the writ to Mordeaux. I challenge you to a fight to the death. For Mordeaux and Valmar, and for the lady who rightfully possesses the two castles."

"You're still mooning over my bitch of a wife?" Mortimer's smile widened, giving his face a grotesque, toad-like appearance. "The slut hardly recalls you with fondness. She's the one who warned me of your arrival."

For a moment, Fawkes stood stunned, disbelieving the words he heard. Then reason returned. He smiled back. "Nay. She wouldn't. Even if she cares naught for me, she hates you enough that she would never try to save you."

"You think not? Do these words sound familiar?" Mortimer clasped his hands and quoted in a gleeful falsetto, "My dearest lady. At last I've come to save you. My forces will reach Mordeaux Castle in a fortnight…"

Fawkes's gut wrenched as his own words rang out mockingly. *No. She wouldn't.* It was a trick. Somehow Mortimer had found the missive. He might have intercepted it before it even reached Nicola.

"Ah, it's gratifying to see the poisonous viper strike another victim." Mortimer's voice rang out, rich and mocking. "For too long she has reserved her torments solely for me. I vow, my wife is the devil's handmaiden, an evil, cunning Eve, a witch from hell. I would give her to you gladly, with my blessing, but unfortunately, the lands are hers. To maintain my claim, I must endure her foul presence in my household." Mortimer straightened. "I accept your challenge. I will kill you and carry your heart back to my wife. Perhaps the sight of it will please her, heathen sorceress that she is."

Fawkes sought to recover himself. It was a trick. The bastard meant to demoralize him. He would not succumb.

They dismounted and handed off their horses, and then drew their swords. Mortimer moved toward Fawkes with a stealth and ease that belied his corpulent form. They circled and parried, assessing. Fawkes felt the battle fever surge through him. He'd waited nearly four years for this moment. Every man he'd killed, every opponent he'd struck down, had worn Mortimer's ugly visage. Now, at last, he faced his true enemy. Mortimer had tried to murder him. He'd humiliated him and mocked him. Even worse, this man had hurt and debased Nicola.

He lunged. His blade caught Mortimer's arm. Mortimer retreated and parried the next blow. Again and again, cold steel grated against cold steel. Fawkes felt no fatigue, no fear, nothing but exhilaration. His body, honed in a dozen battles, sang with speed and strength. His legs easily carried him out of reach of Mortimer's blade, and his sword arm struck out with deadly precision.

His opponent was weakening, the movements of his bulky body growing sluggish. Mortimer's breath came in harsh rasps. As if watching it from far away, Fawkes observed his blade striking nearer and nearer to Mortimer's mail-clad body. Blood dripped from a wound on Mortimer's left arm and another at his hip. Any moment he would falter and Fawkes would land the killing blow. Victory was so near he could almost taste it.

"Is she worth it, you fool?" Mortimer panted. "If you kill me, you'll have to face Richard someday and tell him why. Do you think he'll be pleased you took my life over a woman, and a perfidious, scheming slut at that?"

"She was never a slut, you bastard!" Fawkes pressed his advantage, feeling his hatred grow fiercer and more consuming. "*You* sent me to her! *You* used her like a piece of livestock!"

Mortimer lost his balance and fell. Fawkes loomed over him, panting in rage. "Whatever she's done, you'll never defame or degrade her again." With a savage thrust he drove his sword into Mortimer's neck.

Mortimer's blue eyes bore a look of surprise as the wound spouted blood. Watching the red liquid flow out, Fawkes was reminded of other deaths, so many deaths. He felt vaguely queasy. He leaned over and cleaned the blade of his sword on the grass. Behind him he could hear his soldiers cheering. He had waited for this moment for so long, but now that it was here, it didn't seem real.

Someone clapped him on back. Reynard spoke, "It's over, Fawkes. You've done it. Now all that is left is to claim everything that was Mortimer's. First, Mordeaux, then Valmar and your new wife. How does it feel, my friend? You're a wealthy man now. A real lord. Mordeaux appears prosperous, and Valmar was always a rich demesne. You'll have to pay some sort of fine to the king, I'm guessing. That is, if Richard ever makes it back to England."

Fawkes pulled off his helm and looked down at his blood-spattered hands. "I need to wash. There must be a well in the castle." He started off.

Reynard grabbed his surcote. "What are you doing? Aren't you going to speak to your men? They're all waiting to congratulate you. What's wrong? Are you wounded?"

Fawkes shook his head. "None of the blood is mine."

"Then, what's the matter with you? You aren't acting like a man who's won two castles and the right to wed the woman he loves."

Nicola was his now. Nothing stood in the way of claiming her. He should be jubilant. So, why was there a cold emptiness in the pit of his stomach? Mortimer's taunts. What if it was true? What if she hadn't wanted him to prevail?

"What's wrong?" Reynard asked again, his voice harsh with impatience.

"I'm well enough."

"Well, then, act like it!" Reynard slapped him hard on the shoulder. "Smile. Acknowledge your men."

Fawkes turned and saw his knights cheering. This was their dream as well as his. As knights in the garrison of a prosperous keep, they would have a roof over their head at night, food in their belly, mayhaps a serving maid to warm their bed. After the miseries of the Crusade, it sounded very like paradise.

He raised his arm in a gesture of victory. These men were his brothers, his comrades. They'd been through so much together. To hell and back.

The men cheered more loudly. Fawkes took a deep breath. He'd won Mordeaux and Valmar Castles, but the real prize was not yet his. Nicola.

Would she even remember him? Making love to her

had been the most splendid stirring experience of his life. He'd recalled every detail of their coupling a thousand times. But he had no idea what it meant to her. When he'd had doubts in the past, he'd told himself she would be grateful to him for saving her, and that would be enough to make her wed him willingly. Then, once he got her in bed, he would make her feel for him what he did for her.

But now... Though he fought to dismiss Mortimer's taunts, they gnawed at him. For the first time, he realized his dream was simply that, a dream. He'd forged his whole life around a woman he knew almost nothing about. Now it was time to find out the truth. Who was Lady Nicola? Was she a true damsel in distress, the helpless victim of Mortimer's sick scheming? Or did something darker and more sinister lay behind that stunning countenance, those beautiful features he could not forget?

****

Nicola stared out the narrow tower window, gripping her hands tightly together. Old Emma was right. She should never have meddled. Her scheming had brought about her worst nightmare. Mordeaux was under attack. *Please don't let Simon be in danger. Please!*

She turned from the window and paced across the only open space in the tiny chamber. It had been almost six months since she spoke to Father FitzAlan, having heard nothing since, she'd decided John must not have any interest in Valmar. Perhaps the prince had been waiting until he was more certain King Richard wouldn't return. Now that Richard was in the hands of Henry VI, the Holy Roman Emperor, and Henry was demanding a ransom of 150,000 marks, John may have felt it was safe to act.

If only she were a man. She might have been able to convince Mortimer to surrender Mordeaux and fall back to Valmar. After all, it truly was the soundest strategy. Valmar would be much easier to defend.

Of course, she didn't *want* Mortimer to defend Valmar. The whole point was to have Prince John's forces seize control with as little conflict and bloodshed as possible.

Bloodshed. She shivered. She'd felt certain Mortimer was too far gone to defend his lands. But unbelievably, when the news came that an enemy force was headed for Mordeaux, Mortimer had roused himself from his usual drunken lethargy, donned his armor and ridden out with his knights to confront the threat. All she could do now was hope Mortimer had arrived at Mordeaux before John's forces. If either army gained access to the castle, there would be a battle for control of the keep and Simon would be at risk.

Nicola whirled at a sound on the stairs. The latch to the door rattled and Old Emma waddled in, her plump cheeks flushed as red as apples. "There's news," she panted.

Nicola waited as her serving woman recovered herself. After long unbearable moments, Old Emma finally spoke. "The two armies met at Mordeaux, but they didn't engage. The enemy knight leading the other force challenged Mortimer. They fought in single combat and your husband was killed."

Nicola sank down on the bed, faint with relief. Mortimer was dead. Her foul tormentor would never trouble her again. Everything had turned out as she hoped. "Thank goodness. Prince John will no doubt insist I be wed quickly. But with luck, he'll give me some sort of choice. Even if he doesn't, I can't imagine the man he chooses will be worse than Mortimer."

"You don't understand," Old Emma said. "It wasn't one of King John's barons who killed Mortimer. It was some crusader knight who fought beside King Richard at Acre. He claims to have a writ from King Richard giving him Mordeaux."

Nicola frowned at the maidservant. "Mordeaux is part of my dowry. How can Richard award it to another man when he already gave it to Mortimer?"

"Perhaps news of what a worthless tosspot Mortimer has become spread as far as the Holy Land, and Richard decided to put another man in his place. Although, I suppose I shouldn't speak ill of Mortimer now that he is dead." Old Emma crossed herself. "This crusader knight, whoever he is, will insist on wedding you to seal his claim. Whether his allegiance is to Richard or John is of no consequence."

"But it *is* of consequence!" Nicola responded. "If Richard is never freed by the Emperor, John will end up being king. Then John might well give my lands to yet another man."

Nicola sank down on the stool where she sat when Old Emma dressed her hair. She was very weary of being a pawn in the power struggles of kings and princes. But at least for now, Simon was safe. That is what mattered.

She turned to the maidservant. "Is there any word when this crusader knight will arrive at Valmar?"

"The man who came with news of Mortimer's death didn't know much about the knight who killed him. Although he did mention he was surprisingly young. At least you'll not find yourself wed to hoary old goat."

"I don't care if the man is old, or hopelessly ill-favored, as long as he treats me with respect and allows me to run the household as I see fit."

"If that's what you wish for, then I would advise you to seek your new husband's favor, and behave as a dutiful wife should. Try to appear meek and compliant, at least at first. Few noblemen desire a wife who speaks her mind or who meddles in affairs best left to men."

Nicola gave Old Emma a bitter look. "You think I'm too proud and bold to make a good wife. Is that it?"

"I'm simply telling you what I've learned in my years upon this earth. 'Twould not go amiss if you sought to appear as a demure and modest gentlewoman."

Nicola exhaled in disgust. "A demure and modest gentlewoman would have been ground beneath Mortimer's boots long ago. The only reason I survived is because I'm not some weak and helpless maiden who depends on others to rescue her. If I hadn't been bold and daring, I would be dead by now, and my son as well!" Anger and outrage raced through her veins. She would not apologize for doing what was necessary to save herself and her son.

"Of course, milady. I didn't mean to make you fret. I'm sure you'll fare much better with this man than you did with Mortimer. Unless he is blind, the new lord will appreciate your beauty, and you'll be able to use your looks to bend him to your will." Nicola frowned at the servant, and Old Emma shook her head. "I'd forgotten how sheltered you've been. Most of the serving wenches in the kitchen below know more about getting their way with a man than you do. Perhaps we should fetch one and have her teach you." She gave a cackling laugh.

"I don't want to learn to flirt and entice a man. I only want to protect Simon."

"Those two things may be one and the same, milady."

Nicola closed her eyes and contemplated Old Emma's words. If she had to make a fool of herself to win over this new man, what of it? Would that be any worse than some of the other things she'd done to protect her son?

As Old Emma waddled from the room, Nicola considered her advice. Like Mortimer, this conquering knight sought land, wealth and power. She was merely the woman that came with the demesne—the heiress. It was likely she would once again end up being a broodmare, a vessel to beget the conquering lord's heir. At least this unknown man was unlikely to do as Mortimer had done and send a squire to sire a son on her. Few men were as strange and twisted as Mortimer. Nay, the new lord would undoubtedly bed her himself. Although it was very unlikely he would take as much care as her first lover had.

Her mind slipped back to that afternoon so indelibly imprinted on her mind. Fawkes de Cressy had loved her with skill and tenderness. Although she'd urged him to finish quickly, he'd used his fingers and mouth to turn her body pliant and yielding. She'd wondered more than once where he'd learned his tricks. Even now, the memory of what he'd done to her made heat rise to her face. Fawkes had loved her until she was gasping and writhing.

She shook her head to banish the beguiling memories. Thinking of Fawkes would hardly help her get through her next wedding night. She moved away from the window and paced around the small chamber, her thoughts returning to the result of her and Fawkes's coupling. She'd seen Simon a month ago. He'd looked like an angel, with his tousle of golden curls and sweet cherub's face. By now his flaxen hair would have darkened slightly. His face grown thinner, his chubby legs, straighter and more agile. He would soon be a little boy, and leave the innocent perfection of babyhood behind. How could she protect him?

****

"How long?" Reynard demanded. "How long before you decide Mordeaux is secure and go to claim Valmar, the true prize?"

"There are things to do here," Fawkes retorted. The two men sat eating bread and drinking ale in Mordeaux's hall. "I must make certain the people have truly accepted me as lord. And my men need a rest, to have a full belly and sleep on a bench in a warm keep for a few nights."

"Lame excuses, both of them. Everyone at Mordeaux appears delighted you have killed Mortimer. The man was not well liked. Of course the fact he spent the last two years in a state of near constant drunkenness did not aid his reputation. I wondered what happened to the bastard. I recall Mortimer as a vigorous leader and a decent fighter. He was also shrewd and cunning. The Walter Mortimer we left in London would never have been so foolish as to accept your challenge."

"I don't give a damn what happened to Mortimer. I'm only glad he's dead and I finally have my revenge."

"Does it feel as sweet as you'd hoped?"

"Yea, it's all I've dreamed of." Fawkes paused before taking another bite. Not true. It had all happened too quickly. He'd never had a chance to say the things to

Mortimer he'd wanted to say. To make him suffer for what he'd done. To make him beg for mercy.

"Then why don't we go to Valmar immediately so you can savor the fruits of your success? You could share Lady Nicola's bed this very night."

What if she doesn't want me? The thought popped up, unbidden and unwelcome. He knew so little about the woman who played such a large part in his dream. They were strangers of everything but each other's bodies.

Fawkes clenched his jaw. "We'll stay here this night and go to Valmar on the morrow. We'll wear full battle attire and be prepared to fight. It's possible the garrison there will refuse to open the gates."

"And who would order the gates closed?" Reynard asked. "Do you truly believe any of Mortimer's men remain loyal now that he's dead? You saw how they received us here at Mordeaux. Most people appeared relieved to see you take command."

Should he tell Reynard of Mortimer's taunts? If Nicola *had* warned Mortimer, she might refuse to surrender the castle. Nay. He would not repeat the foul bastard's lies. He set his pewter cup down with a clatter. "Tomorrow. We'll go tomorrow."

Chapter Four

Adam FitzSaer, Valmar's castellan, entered the solar. He gave a faint bow and approached Nicola where she sat sewing by the glazed green window. "My lady. If I could speak with you a moment."

Nicola's stomach clenched. She put aside the altar cloth she was embroidering. "What is it?"

"The man who killed your husband and seized control of Mordeaux has sent word he means to claim Valmar. He will arrive in a few candle notches. How do you wish us to proceed? Do we draw up the bridge and man the walls? Or welcome him and his army?"

If only she knew more about this man who had turned her life upside down. Even as she told herself he could not possibly be worse than Mortimer, a part of her was terrified.

But she dare not let FitzSaer see that. He'd always disliked her and thought she overstepped her authority. Indeed, she was surprised he was even asking her opinion. Of course, with Mortimer dead, he probably had no choice. He might be castellan of Valmar, but she was the heiress of the property and the only person with any legal claim.

"My lady?"

FitzSaer glared at her. She sought to focus her thoughts and speak confidently. "I see no reason not to admit this man and his men. After all, he has a writ from the king."

"But that writ is for Mordeaux, not Valmar."

"The two properties have always been connected. Besides, I see no purpose in fighting. We might hold him off for a few months, but if he's survived the Crusade, he's likely to be skilled at warfare. We'd probably end up surrendering anyway."

"This knight might have fought beside Richard at Acre, but that doesn't mean he's a skilled battle commander. From what I've heard of de Cressy, he's quite young. Indeed, Richard knighted him only a year ago."

Nicola's heart seemed to freeze in her chest. "De Cressy? You said the man is named de Cressy. What is his given name?"

"I don't remember. Why? Does the name mean something to you?"

It could not be him. Fawkes was too young to have risen so high. To go from lowly squire to commanding an army—it took more than four years to accomplish that.

"So, knowing the usurper is young and untried," FitzSaer persisted. "Have you changed your mind about defying him?"

She heard the excitement in the castellan's voice. He clearly wanted her to order the gates closed. Like so many men, he was eager to fight, never considering the cost to others. She fixed him with a stern look. "Go now and tell the garrison to open the gate and bid this man and his army enter."

FitzSaer gazed at her with an expression of resentment and almost hatred. Then he bowed stiffly and left the solar.

Nicola remained sitting. She felt so dazed and stunned she feared her legs would not hold if she tried to stand. Could it really be true? That her incredibly tender and skilled lover was to be her husband? It did not seem possible that her circumstances might be reversed so completely.

The de Cressy name was not common. And he was the right age. She'd been so certain Mortimer was going to kill him, and erase any trace of the man who had impregnated her. Somehow he had not only survived, but thrived.

With effort, she forced herself to stand. She must seek out Old Emma. She must get ready to face this man. He'd once conquered her body; now he seized control of all else she possessed.

****

"Here now." Old Emma approached Nicola. "Come away from the window. We need to get you ready."

Nicola let Old Emma help her out of her serviceable wool kirtle and into her best court gown. Old Emma fastened the laces underneath her arms, then stepped back and squinted at the effect. The rose silk bliaut fit snugly through the bodice and sleeves before widening to a long, full skirt with a train. Silver embroidery glistened at the neck and along the trailing sleeves.

Emma grunted in satisfaction. "Your breasts are fuller from bearing the babe, but it fits tolerably well. Now for your hair. I think you should wear it down."

"Unbound hair is for maidens. I'm a maid no longer, as everyone knows."

"You're also a widow, but it would be a shame to dress you in mourning attire. No one here will care about how you wear your hair, and you might as well make use of every advantage you have with the new lord."

"Fawkes liked me well enough years ago." Too late, Nicola pressed her lips together. She had not meant to speak of what had happened between the two of them in the past.

Old Emma chuckled. "Aye, so he did. So he did." The serving woman sobered. "But he was a young, untried squire back then. Now he's a hardened knight. They say no man comes back from Crusade unchanged."

Nicola sat on the stool so the servant could dress her hair. Old Emma was right. She shouldn't expect Fawkes to be the same as he was four years ago. Although she hadn't gone to war or fought in any battles, *she* was certainly much changed. No longer was she a pampered, naïve girl. She'd learned to be wary and calculating. Otherwise, she'd never have survived.

How ironic this all was. When Fawkes had left her bedchamber that day, she'd feared for his life. Now he returned in triumph. He meant to claim Valmar and the rest of her dowry.

But he didn't need to claim her body. He'd already done that.

She suppressed a shiver of desire as she remembered the feel of his hands on her, the near unbearable sensation of his shaft inside her. His smell, so male and alive. The silky feel of his hair as she sought to hold onto his shoulders as he thrust into her. Would it be like that this time? Would he banish all her resolve and bend her to his will in other ways, even as he had in the bedchamber?

And what of Simon? Dare she tell Fawkes that he had a son? A son no one knew about. Would he be pleased? Or would he doubt he was Simon's father, since the boy looked nothing like him?

As if reading her thoughts, Old Emma said, "When will you tell him about Simon?"

"I think...I think I must wait. Until I'm more certain of the man." She flashed the serving woman a helpless look. "Given how my marriage turned out, you can hardly blame me for being cautious."

"But Simon is Fawkes's son."

"Will he believe that? Everyone at Valmar will tell him the babe I gave birth to three years ago was stillborn. For me to suddenly produce a child now, a child that looks nothing like him, and then claim the boy is his..." She shook her head. "I need to know what Fawkes is like now. I knew very little of him then. One candle-hour with someone is scarce long enough to take their measure. Especially since we barely conversed."

Old Emma smothered a laugh. Then she grew serious. "I think you should tell Fawkes everything right away. Tell him about Mortimer's madness. How you feared your husband's hatred of you was greater than his desire for an heir. How you showed Mortimer the dead baby so you could hide Simon away and save his life. I vow, you'll be able to convince Fawkes. He knew Mortimer and what he was capable of. Why should he doubt you when you tell him you thought Mortimer deranged enough to kill an innocent babe?"

The way Old Emma explained it, it sounded perfectly reasonable. But Nicola wasn't the only one at Valmar who would have the new lord's ear. Mortimer might be a monster who raped children, and a drunken lout, but he hadn't abused those who were loyal to him. The knights of Valmar and Mordeaux had been disgusted with Mortimer, but they hadn't suffered under him. If they told Fawkes some of the things she knew were spoken about her, he might well believe them. Men were much more likely to believe another man than a woman.

"I will tell Fawkes about Simon. But not yet."

Old Emma let out a sigh. "Very good, milady. Now, to decide on jewelry."

****

The day was dazzling. Sunlight winked and glinted off the knights' armor as they approached Valmar castle. Sweat soaked the linen shirt beneath Fawkes's gambeson. The heat was stifling, but even worse was the tension building inside him. He'd dreamed of this day for so long; now he worried it would all go awry. He glanced up at the castle wall, searching for archers. Although the portcullis was raised, that didn't mean they would be allowed safe entry.

Fool, he told himself, there was no treachery here. He'd become too suspicious, too wary. Years of warfare did that to a man.

The castle seemed smaller than he remembered. Probably because he'd seen much grander fortresses. Whole walled cities. The splendid palace of King Tancred of Sicily. But Valmar was a fine enough castle. It had stout walls, solid defenses, and four turreted towers that added a touch of grace to the sprawling structure.

The tower to the right of the gatehouse was Nicola's bedchamber. For so long he'd seen it as a rare and exalted place. Now that he knew the tower belonged to him, it had lost part of its magic. Would the same thing happen with Nicola? Could any mortal woman live up to his impassioned dreams?

His memory of her had become a kind of grail, a shining vision of beauty and perfection in a world of atrocity and evil. He'd built up such expectations. Now he worried the reality would disappoint him. It had been four years. What if Mortimer's abuse had damaged her beauty? What if she was no longer slender, elegant and perfect? Worse yet, what if Mortimer's words were true? Was it possible she was so embittered that she'd betrayed him even as he sought to rescue her?

Cruelty and abuse could alter anyone. And even though he'd coupled with Nicola, he'd known little of her thoughts. She was the lady of Valmar. So far, the people he'd encountered spoke of her with respect, and muttered disapprovingly of Mortimer's treatment of her. But that didn't mean she was some paragon of goodness. Over the years, he'd idealized her until she'd become almost a goddess in his mind. But the real Nicola might well have flaws, terrible flaws.

Fawkes set his jaw and urged his destrier onto the bridge. There was nothing to do but pass through the gates and find out what awaited him.

****

Nicola watched from the ramparts as Fawkes and his army swarmed into the bailey. She was surprised at how many knights there were, how well equipped, how fine their horses. She'd heard tales of warriors who went off on Crusade in hopes of winning glory and wealth, only to die ignominiously of the fevers that ran rampant in the hellish climate of the East, or to be killed in battle with the Saracens. For every man who returned in triumph, two or more had perished. Yet Fawkes had prospered. Thinking of the sum required to pay this many knights, she was impressed anew. Not only had

Fawkes earned his spurs, he must have won an enormous amount of booty. How many men had he killed to amass this fortune?

Anxiety made her breathless and tightened like a band around her chest as she caught sight of the army's leader. Fawkes seemed bigger than she remembered. Perhaps that was due to his chain mail or the huge, glossy chestnut destrier he rode. Over his mail he wore a crimson surcote, emblazoned with the white cross of a crusader. He wore no helm, and his long black hair riffled in the breeze.

Fawkes's coloring was the reason Mortimer had chosen him to impregnate her, believing any child Fawkes sired would look enough like her to stifle gossip. She'd always found it satisfyingly ironic that Simon was as blond as a Saxon. Now the jest had turned sour. If Simon's hair had been dark, it would be far easier to convince Fawkes he'd fathered the boy.

In the bailey, servants shouted. Dogs barked. Knights cursed as they struggled to dismount in close quarters. She finally caught sight of Fawkes again. He was on foot now. And there was Adam FitzSaer hurrying to meet him. Valmar's castellan bowed low, formally relinquishing the castle to the new lord. Fawkes motioned for FitzSaer to rise. Then he glanced around, as if looking for someone.

Apprehension squeezed Nicola's chest so tight she could hardly breathe. Fawkes had expected her to be there to greet him. Was he offended by her failure to do so? Had she already got off on the wrong foot with the man who was to be her husband and lord?

Old Emma had urged her to rush out to meet him and throw herself at Fawkes's mercy, to wring her hands and weep to show her fear and sense of helplessness. But Nicola couldn't bring herself to do it. Although defiance had earned her more than a few bruises, standing up to Mortimer had ultimately worked better than trying to please him.

The knot of tension in her chest tightened. She told herself she could delay no longer. If she didn't go down and greet Fawkes soon, he'd grow angry.

With more than a little trepidation, she started down the stairs.

****

Where was she? Fawkes scanned the castle yard, his agitation increasing by the moment. Was Nicola deliberately avoiding him? Did she consider him unworthy of her? His jaw clenched at the thought.

Reynard came up beside him. "She's probably in the hall waiting for you. Or maybe she's seeing to the preparations for the evening meal." Fawkes shot him an incredulous look. Reynard shrugged. "If she doesn't appear soon, we'll ask someone to fetch her." He turned. The next moment he said, "Fawkes."

The knights and servants drew back as Lady Nicola walked across the yard. She was a vision in a rose-hued gown. Her face was a perfect oval and her eyes shone like raindrops glimmering in the sun. Her slender figure had ripened; her exquisite features refined with maturity. Fawkes exhaled a breath of wonderment. Four years ago, he'd coupled with a maid. This was a woman.

But what sort of woman? Her face revealed not a hint of her feelings, as if her features were carved of marble. He should say something. A loathsome weakness rendered him unable to speak. When she was a few feet away she bowed. Her raven-black tresses, secured by a ruby-studded silver circlet, fell forward, concealing her face. "My lord."

She straightened. The scent of her perfume reached him at the same moment. It curled around him, rubbing against his senses like a languorous, silky cat. Heat and woman, rare crushed flowers, wild herbs. His balls tightened and his cock grew hard, even as the rest of him seemed to grow weak.

"Lady Nicola." His voice sounded harsh, but at least it was not the adolescent croak he feared it would be.

The tension between them seemed to make the very air vibrate. Everyone in the yard was watching. His men. The garrison knights. Servants and squires. Even the kitchen knaves and pages. Jesu! If they guessed at how nervous he was, none of them would ever respect him! He could not let them see what she did to him, how she turned him into a callow, adoring squire, ready to kiss the hem of her skirts and beg for the honor of being her champion.

He took a steadying breath and spoke in a commanding voice that rang up to bailey walls. "I claim Valmar castle and all the surrounding lands by right of conquest. And I claim you, Lady Nicola, as my wife."

"My lord." She bowed again. "I've had the bathing chamber prepared. Thomas will direct you there." She motioned to a young, golden-haired page and looked back at Fawkes. "After you have refreshed yourself, we'll celebrate your arrival with a banquet."

Fawkes started after the page, feeling stunned. Nicola's response to his announcement seemed very odd. He'd told her he intended to make her his wife, and she coolly sent him off to bathe.

She was probably still in a state of shock. In less

than two days, her circumstances had completely changed. Her husband was dead. No matter what she thought of Mortimer, being widowed probably took some getting used to. And now she was to wed another man, a man she didn't know. Nicola was probably unnerved, and so, good chatelaine that she was, she fell back on the formal gesture of offering a noble guest the opportunity to bathe.

But usually the lady of the household helped with the bathing, and he saw no sign she intended to do so. Did she consider him beneath her personal attention? Was he still no more than a squire to her?

The muscles in his jaw tightened as he followed the boy into the bathing chamber. A fire burned in the hearth, despite the summer heat, and buckets for fetching water were stacked nearby. In the center of the chamber stood a large tub, with sweet scents wafting from its steaming depths. Two giggling maids waited with towels and a bowl of soap.

Nicola's absence meant nothing. She was probably busy seeing to the banquet, as Reynard had said.

The two maidservants put down the bathing supplies and sought to divest him of his armor and garments. Fawkes finally had to call a squire to help, as his height and the weight of his mail made it an impossible task for a woman, or even two, to accomplish. Once his armor and gambeson were off, he dismissed the squire and the maidservants. The young women looked disappointed, but he was firm. He didn't want any woman's hands on him except Nicola's.

He climbed into the tub and sighed as his body relaxed in the heated water. What luxury. In his life he'd had few baths in a proper bathing tub. Usually it was a cold wash by the castle well, or a dip in a river or stream. The fragrant scent of the bathwater reminded him of Nicola and her exotic perfume. It was the first memory he had of her. The bewitching odor he'd smelled as soon as he'd entered her bedchamber. But even the haunting promise of her scent had not prepared him for the woman waiting in the bed. She'd been more arousing than his wildest fantasies.

She still was. He thought of how Nicola had looked in the bailey. The elegant contours of her face. Her body—as slender and fine as reed, but with a woman's charms. Her breasts seemed fuller, but her stomach remained flat as a maid's. His seed had never quickened in her. Nor had any other man's. At least he *hoped* Mortimer had sent no other man to service her.

More than once, he'd considered that Mortimer might have decided to try again. If he had, then the man sent that time had also failed. Which suggested she might be barren.

"Don't fall asleep, you worthless whoreson! I'm next in the bathing tub and I don't want the water to be freezing."

Fawkes jerked open his eyes. Reynard stood nearby, his perpetually ruddy face split with a grin. "Jesu! You startled me," Fawkes said.

"What were you dreaming of, I wonder. Could it be the fair Lady Nicola?"

"None of your business." Fawkes ducked his head to rinse his hair and started to rise from the tub. Curse it! The serving maids had returned. Worse yet, he had an erection. Merely thinking about Nicola had been enough to arouse him.

"Fetch me a towel," he growled at Reynard, before

sinking down into the tub.

Smirking, Reynard stepped back and gestured to the serving maids, waiting near the hearth. "Milord requires your services."

Fawkes shot Reynard a furious glance as the two serving women approached carrying towels. Damn Reynard! There was no way he could stand without them seeing he was aroused!

He tried to turn away as he climbed over edge of the tub, but they saw anyway. "My lord, your lance is a fearsome thing," one of them tittered.

"Aye," the other responded. "I would surrender easily to such a show of might."

Fawkes seized the towel and covered himself. The women left giggling at his glowering expression.

"Milord is saving himself for his lady wife," Reynard said, as he removed his own clothing. "Don't you think that is noble of him? He hasn't had a woman in almost four years. Can you believe—"

"Shut your wretched mouth," Fawkes growled. "Or I'll drown you here and now."

Reynard's grin widened as he settled himself on the seat in the tub. "As monk-like and pure as milord is, I more than make up for him." He motioned for the serving maids to approach.

With coos of delight, they soaped him.

Fawkes dried himself, wondering how Reynard did it. No one would call the man attractive. His hair was red as the fox he was named for, and he had an overlarge nose and mouth. But despite his lack of pulchritude, his friend always managed to have a woman, or two or three, eager to bed him.

Fawkes looked around for his clothes. When he

didn't see them, he called to the women. "Where are the garments I took off?"

"Thomas carried them to the laundry," one of them answered.

"What am I supposed to wear?"

"I brought your saddle pack." Reynard gestured. "It's by the door. You might as well don your court tunic. Since you're to be married."

"You think I should marry her now? Today?"

Reynard gave him a look of exasperation. "If you want to have the lawful right to take Lady Nicola to bed tonight, the ceremony has to be performed right away."

"But I—" Fawkes stopped. Why was he protesting? Marrying Nicola as soon as possible was the logical thing to do. But somehow he didn't feel prepared. What if she didn't want to marry him? Shouldn't she have some say in the matter? She obviously wasn't consulted when she was forced to wed Mortimer. He wanted things to be different this time. But even if she didn't wish to wed him, how did that change anything? Would it not be better to wed her and *then* seek to win her affections?

But what if there was no hope of that? What if Mortimer's words were true and she was so hardened that she was incapable for caring for any man?

He would not accept that. Somehow he would win her over, no matter what it took.

He grabbed his saddle pack. "I suppose the damned tunic is hopelessly crushed," he muttered.

****

The chapel was stifling. Knights, villagers and servants filled the small church and spilled out into the yard. Everyone was eager to catch a glimpse of the new lord as he said his vows with the heiress of Valmar.

Fawkes sweated in his tunic of blue samite and wondered why he'd even bothered to bathe. But the heat didn't seem to affect the woman beside him. She looked cool and regal. Her hair, held away from her face with the ruby and silver circlet, flowed over her shoulders like a blue-black river. Her skin was the palest, finest alabaster. Against its creamy purity, her lips appeared as rich and red as the rubies in her headpiece. In the soft light filtering in through the chapel's rose-tinted windows, her eyes were silver.

He must stop thinking about the way she looked and concentrate on the woman herself. So cool and aloof, she was. An icy princess, regal and self-contained. He had absolutely no idea what was going on in her mind.

The thought dampened his desire, which he decided was a good thing. He needed to rein in his emotions and reason things through. Take Nicola's measure as if she was a man and he was evaluating her as an ally. Or an enemy. If there was any truth to Mortimer's mocking words, he must discover it and deal with her accordingly.

He should have dealt with the matter before he pledged his troth with her. But, as Reynard said, everyone expected him to wed Nicola immediately. With Richard imprisoned, his hold on Valmar and Mordeaux was tenuous. Prince John was already taking advantage of his brother's situation and trying to seize power. Fawkes knew his only real claim to the demesne was if he put a babe in Nicola's belly.

What if she was barren? How would he hold onto the demesne then? And what if she didn't want to be married to him? According to Mortimer, she'd already betrayed him. What else might she do to be rid of her new husband?

But it was ludicrous to think she preferred Mortimer to him. If only he knew more about this woman. For the past four years he'd seen her as a victim. But what if she wasn't? What if she'd actually been content with her lot as Mortimer's wife?

Mortimer had called her a viper, a cunning witch, as if she was the one who had manipulated him. Maybe that was the way things had ended up. Perhaps when she found herself married to a drunken lout—which all agreed Mortimer had become—Nicola had seen a chance to seize power and live her life the way she wished. Under those circumstances, she might have no desire to see Mortimer killed. He must discover the truth. And soon.

Fawkes looked up and saw the priest was prompting them to move toward the altar. The mass was finished. Now it was time for them to exchange their vows.

Nicola said hers in a soft, refined voice, promising to love, honor and obey. He responded that he would love, honor, keep and guard her.

The priest pronounced them wed, and everyone left the chapel. Outside in the sunlight, the women showered them with flower petals and the men shouted crude innuendos regarding Lady Nicola's fertility and his sexual prowess. Fawkes endured the bawdy remarks, wishing Nicola didn't have to be subjected to such coarseness. She was a lady and shouldn't have to endure leering comments.

They started toward the hall. Fawkes felt a tug on his arm. He turned and saw a plainly dressed woman with a scattering of freckles on her cheeks and coppery brown eyes that matched her ruddy curls. "I'm pleased for you, milord." She dipped into a deep curtsy. Fawkes nodded and prepared to move away, but the woman caught his arm again. "Don't you remember me?" she asked breathily. "It's Alys." She winked, and Fawkes suddenly recalled the feel of her plump, full-breasted body beneath his.

Aly's full lips curved in a teasing smirk. "I must say, I barely recognized you. You've changed so much, Fawkes. Now you're a fine knight and ruler of the keep where once you were merely a squire, albeit a very handsome one." She winked again, and her voice dipped to a smoky whisper. "Do you still remember what you did to make me scream?"

He exhaled sharply and looked around to see who might be watching. He was horrified when he saw Nicola looking at them. She was probably too far away to hear, but even so…

He removed Alys hand from his arm. "Things have changed. I'm now married to Lady Nicola."

"Hah, to the biggest bitch in creation, you mean. You won't get any good of her. She poisoned Mortimer, you know. Fed him something to make his ballocks wither and his cock shrivel."

Fawkes nodded numbly, then turned to look for Nicola. She was walking away, not toward the hall, but the opposite direction.

Chapter Five

Nicola's head ached as she made her way across the bailey. The wedding ceremony had reminded her far too much of her marriage to Mortimer. That day she'd also stood next to a handsome, imposing knight and said her vows. She remembered feeling pleased that Mortimer was young and comely. So often when a woman was married by the king's decree, her new husband was some ancient, battered warrior, with a thick belly and breath that stank. Although he was massively muscled, Mortimer had not been fat when they wed, and his teeth were white and strong.

But her enchantment with her fair-haired, muscular bridegroom hadn't lasted. All too soon, he'd revealed what a devil he truly was. She wondered as she approached the kitchen, would Fawkes be any different? No longer was he the boyish squire who had loved her well. Now he was a powerful knight who had survived untold horrors to return to England and defeat Mortimer. Only a man who was very ruthless and determined could have risen so far so fast.

Nicola reached the crowded and chaotic kitchen and approached the burly Saxon cook. Movement to her right distracted her. A bunch of pages were gathered around the wine tuns. Instead of filling pitchers, they were watching one of the squires as he gestured wildly with a kitchen knife, holding it like a sword. "You should have seen him," the youth, Will, crowed. "Fast as lightning he was. Feinting this way and that. Fat old Mortimer couldn't keep up with him. Fought hard, Mortimer did, but he was overmatched. And then de Cressy got him down and thrust his sword clean through Mortimer's throat. I vow, the bastard bled like a pig at butchering time." Will paused and gazed around at his audience with bright, excited eyes. "I've never seen a knight fight so fiercely and with so much skill."

"They say he was a hero in the Holy Land and admired by even the king himself," someone chimed in.

"I heard he killed a hundred men at Acre," another exclaimed. "That's why Richard knighted him."

"A hundred men?" The kitchen wench Berta gave a snort of disgust. "That's not possible."

"Yea, it is," the squire protested. "They were Saracen prisoners. They were all lined up, bound and trussed. The king commanded they be killed to show Saladin how we deal with men who fail to honor their oaths. The knights moved down the line of Saracens, cutting their throats one by one. I heard there was so much blood it reached up to the knights' ankles."

Nicola's gorge rose at the image painted in her mind. One of the other squires, a youth named Robbie, grabbed her by the arm. "Milady, are you well? Let me help you to a bench."

Aided by Robbie, Nicola made it to the bench by the bread ovens and sat down. The cold savagery of the tale she'd heard made her stomach roil. What sort of man had she wed?

"Milady?" She looked up to see Agelwulf. The cook was holding out a wooden dipper of water. "Drink. And don't worry about the food, milady. Everything is well in hand. Go to the hall and sit beside your husband. I promise he'll be pleased with the banquet we've prepared."

Nicola took a drink of the water and thanked Agelwulf. She got to her feet. The pages had returned to their duties and were filling baskets with dried cheat bread to be used as trenchers. After smoothing her veil and skirts, Nicola left the kitchen.

****

Fawkes gazed around the great hall of Valmar with satisfaction. The whitewashed walls were hung with bright weavings of hunting scenes and religious vignettes. Snowy linen cloths covered all the trestle tables, and the high table was set with jeweled plates, cups, bowls, and candlesticks

Reynard came up beside him. His admiring words echoed Fawkes's thoughts. "I've not seen such splendor since King Richard's coronation banquet in London. Certainly when we served as squires here, Mortimer never put on such a spread. This must be Lady Nicola's doing."

"I have no complaint about how the keep is run," Fawkes said.

"Ah, but skill in managing a castle is not the reason you wed Lady Nicola." Reynard poked him playfully in the ribs. "How do you bear it, to know you must endure a tedious formal banquet before taking her to bed?"

"It would be good of me to talk to her a little first, don't you think? It may be my right to bed her, but I'd like to share at least a few pleasantries before I pursue such intimacy."

Reynard shrugged. "You sound more patient than I would be. If you'd slaked your lust with a whore or serving wench once in a while, I could better understand. But you've gone years without—"

"There are other ways to relieve lust," Fawkes interrupted. "The Church may abhor onanism, but most men have done it under some circumstances."

Reynard shook his head. "I don't see the point, if there is a willing woman available."

"You don't understand. I didn't want *any* woman, I only wanted Nicola."

"Of course, there was the one dancing girl…" Reynard smirked.

"Yea, there was." Fawkes had not bedded her either, but he wouldn't tell Reynard that.

"At last your long wait is over," Reynard said. "Here she comes."

Nicola entered the hall. She looked even paler than during the wedding, but her spine was as straight as an arrow. Indeed, her whole bearing was so queenly and composed it took Fawkes's breath away. He could hardly believe that soon he would have the right to touch such perfection. To hold her exquisite body in his arms and kiss those rose-petal lips.

He told himself he must get over being awestruck by this woman. He was now a lord, and Lady Nicola's equal. And this night he almost looked the part in his court tunic.

****

Nicola let Fawkes help her take her seat at the raised table. He sat beside her in the lord's chair. The carved back bore the silhouette of a hawk, the device of Valmar castle. She thought how fitting it was that Fawkes had earned the right to carry that bold symbol on a banner. He reminded her of a fierce, unpredictable bird of prey.

She perused him from under her lashes, observing the way his hair shone like polished ebony and the hard shape of his freshly shaven jaw. He wore a tunic of deep blue velvet banded with gold, but even the sumptuous fabric failed to soften the hard lines of his body. Like a wild animal, his lean form mixed grace with deadliness.

Potent emotions churned inside her. Her body remembered this man. It recalled the feel of his mouth, the touch of his callused fingers, the fullness of his shaft inside her. The memory made her flesh sing with longing.

But even if her body desired this man, she could not let those thrilling memories muddle her wits. Her thoughts went back to what she'd heard in the kitchen. A man capable of killing dozens of people would clearly do whatever else he thought necessary to maintain his position and power. If Fawkes discovered Simon and thought the boy was his enemy's son, he might decide to eliminate his potential rival's claim. Nicola swallowed a sip of wine, then took a deep breath to keep it down.

The servants brought out the food: whole boar's head, roast duck and capon, platters of trout and eel in sauce, trays of cheeses, baskets of freshly baked bread, berry tarts and spiced pasties. They poured more wine, the finest vintage in Valmar's cellars. A warm, lazy murmur filled the hall, the sounds of people eating and drinking, smacking their lips and making contented comments to their companions.

Nicola ate carefully, all her concentration on the man beside her. As her husband, Fawkes had complete power over her. He could beat her or imprison her, as Mortimer had done. She had endured that and would do so again if she had to. Anything to keep Simon safe.

Fawkes turned toward her. "The food is delicious. My compliments to you and to your cook."

"Thank you, milord."

"Valmar seems like a prosperous, well-defended keep. I'm pleased with what I've seen here." He put down the goblet with a thud, despite the linen tablecloth. "Now Mordeaux—I have to say that Valmar's sister castle appears much less secure. In fact, I was thinking of sending some of my men back there in a day or two."

Nicola tensed. Why did he mention Mordeaux? Had the garrison resisted him in some way? Ridiculous. Gilbert de Vescy, the Mordeaux seneschal, would not be so foolish as to defy a man like Fawkes, who had an army of crusader-trained knights at his back.

She told herself to relax. As long as no one knew who he was, Simon was in no danger. And who would betray her son? Not Gilbert's wife, Hilary, who was raising him as her own. Not Old Emma. The serving woman had been with Nicola ever since she could remember. Although meddlesome and outspoken, Old Emma was utterly loyal.

"In a few days, I'll tour all the lands attached to the two castles," Fawkes said. "As well as the castles themselves. Although the defenses look solid, you never can tell. I want to find out how deep the main wells are, if we could survive a siege."

"Do you expect Mordeaux to be attacked?"

"A good commander always expects attack. I'm always prepared for treachery."

Nicola recalled the conversation she'd had with Father FitzAlan over six months ago. If Prince John had decided to act upon her hints that Mordeaux and Valmar were ripe for the taking, surely he would have done so by now. Instead it was this man, one of Richard's supporters, who'd seized control. John would have spies; he would soon learn her lands were now controlled by an experienced Crusader knight, a man who had the skill and the fortitude to hold on to what he'd seized.

She dared a glance at Fawkes. He seemed restless. Why? There was no reason for him to be uneasy. He had all the power. She was the one who must walk a narrow parapet, carefully weighing everything she said, everything she did.

****

He was bungling things. Bungling them badly. Here he was at their wedding banquet, talking about defenses and battle tactics. She probably thought him a crude fighting man, little different than her first husband. When had he lost the skill of cosseting a woman? He'd once done it a half dozen times a day. Cajoling the kitchen wenches to give him a fresh loaf or a drink of buttermilk. Stealing a kiss from one of the dairymaids. Enticing a village girl into a hay mound for a quick, exuberant tumble.

But none of them had been anything like Nicola, a lady, born and bred, with the manners and the aloofness of a queen. Only in the bedchamber had he known what to do with Nicola, how to win her over. He didn't want to wait until then. Or rely on lovemaking to thaw the ice between them. He must find a way to reach out to her now.

"I apologize for the abruptness of our wedding," he said. "I had to wed you quickly to seal my claim. In all the haste, I forgot to give you this." He reached for the gilt money pouch on his belt and withdrew the ring he'd carried all the way from Jaffa. Although she didn't know it, he'd had it made especially for her, guessing at the size.

He motioned and she held out her right hand. "Nay, the other one." He took her left hand in his and slid the ring onto the third finger. "They say that the blood in this hand flows directly to the heart."

The ring fit perfectly, gold filigree and rubies glinting in the candlelight. Fawkes stared at her hand resting in his. The hand of a lady. Smooth, unblemished skin. Long slender fingers. Perfect fingernails. The contrast with his tanned and battle-scarred hand was startling.

"Thank you. It's beautiful."

Fawkes took a deep draught of wine, feeling better. She liked the ring. He'd seen surprise and pleasure flare in her eyes. For a moment, he'd almost thought he'd glimpsed a hint of the passion he knew was behind the demure mask. He would arouse that passion once again. But first, he must find a garderobe. He rose. "Pray, excuse me, madam. I will return anon."

There was a spring in his step as he started toward the back of the hall, and he had to quell the urge to grin like a fool. Then he encountered Reynard, and the troubled look on his captain's face instantly soured his cheerful mood. "What's wrong?"

Reynard shook his head before shooting a glance at the high table. "Let's go out in the bailey."

"God's teeth, spit it out!" Fawkes said, as soon as they were away from the hall.

Reynard shook his head again. "It's hard to believe, but I heard the same thing from two different men, and Adam FitzSaer, Mortimer's castellan, confirmed the story. So it seems likely it's true."

"What is true?"

"You remember when we arrived at Mordeaux and Mortimer rode out to meet us, like he'd known we were coming? Remember when we speculated who could have warned him? Well, it was Lady Nicola. Mortimer knew by heart the message you'd sent her. He quoted it repeatedly to show what a lovesick, ball-less whelp you are."

Fawkes fought the fury that engulfed him. Even dead, Mortimer had the power to provoke him into a murderous rage. "I'm certain Mortimer had servants who spied on her," he said, curtly. "They probably found the message and took it to him. For that matter, the message may never have reached Nicola. If she was Mortimer's prisoner..."

Reynard shook his head. "That's the thing. The helpless damsel you thought to rescue does not exist. For the past three years, Lady Nicola has roamed freely about Valmar, directing the household."

"Well, I'm pleased Mortimer finally came to his senses and released her. I was half afraid she might have lost her wits from his mistreatment."

Reynard cocked a brow. "It seems it was Mortimer who lost his wits. There are tales that Nicola poisoned him, cursed him, or maybe both. At any rate, she did something to him to cause him to change from a strong virile man to a worthless tosspot muttering to himself in a corner of the hall."

Fawkes recalled Mortimer from two days before, the puffiness of his face, the glazed, bloodshot eyes. "If she cursed or poisoned him, then it was with good reason. Mortimer treated her most cruelly. I have no sympathy for him."

"Don't you understand what I'm trying to tell you? The fact is, Lady Nicola is no meek, helpless victim. Mortimer may have deserved whatever fate befell him. But if she is capable of such things, you need to be aware. And the fact that she warned Mortimer makes it likely she has no fondness for you. What I'm trying to say—" Reynard put his hand on Fawkes's arm. "You have made this woman into a saintly creature worthy of any sacrifice. But what if she is all too mortal and flawed? I don't want to see you ruined as Mortimer was."

"Mortimer was a corrupt, hateful bastard! He deserved the fate that befell him! "

"Yea, but you do not."

Fawkes let out his breath. The idea that Nicola had poisoned or cursed, or otherwise done something to Mortimer didn't distress him. But if she'd seen fit to warn his deadly enemy of his arrival at Mordeaux, that was another matter. He'd sought to block out Mortimer's words, to believe they were lies meant to demoralize him. But someone had warned Mortimer and it was logical to think it was Nicola.

He saw pity in Reynard's eyes, so he turned away and strode swiftly across the bailey. He found the stairs leading to the ramparts and climbed.

What if it's true? What if she cares naught for you, even though for almost four years your every waking moment has been consumed with rescuing her? He felt like weeping. As if he were a small child who has waited for what seemed like an endless time for a precious treat and then when the time comes, is cruelly denied the promised pleasure.

Standing on the battlements, he gazed out at the

landscape spread out under the purple-edged sky. Come morning, the hills would be dotted with creamy white sheep. The valley would glow green and gold with ripening grain, rich meadows and stands of beech and oak. Below the castle mound he could almost make out the village, several dozen daub-and-wattle houses, with neat vegetable gardens behind them.

There was more to Valmar than Nicola. This demesne was his now. He'd earned it. Paid for it with blood, suffering and struggle. Rising far, far higher than his poor, landless knight father could ever have imagined. Even if it turned out Mortimer's terrible words were true, he had to remember there was more to his dream than simply rescuing Lady Nicola. He'd accomplished what he'd vowed he would accomplish. Having done so, he would not let sly, hideous rumors steal from him this night of triumph.

He leaned his head back so the evening breeze wafted soothingly over his face. Inhaling deeply, he breathed in the sweet scent of summer: Hawthorn in the hedgerows. Meadowsweet and ripening grasses in the fields. A sound from the bailey below drew him back to the present. He must go down. They were probably already looking for him, and sharing ribald jests about the bedding.

The bedding. For four years he'd dreamed of this night. For the moment when he would have the right to touch Nicola. To kiss her rosy lips and caress her silken, ivory-skinned body. Now the magic moment was here and instead of anticipation and longing, a shard of foreboding seemed lodged in his gut.

Curse Mortimer! And curse this FitzSaer fellow and the whole lot of them! Now instead of pleasuring Nicola and picking up where they'd left off, he was going to have talk to her and question her about this business of warning Mortimer. It was infuriating, to have the sublime, thrilling experience he'd anticipated so tainted. It almost made him want to forego the bedding altogether. It would be easier to deal with the rumors—and with Nicola—in the morning.

But nay, he could not. As Reynard had reminded him, he must remember his men, and what his defeat of Mortimer meant to them. They were celebrating, living through his triumph and envying him his upcoming wedding night with the beautiful Lady Nicola. He couldn't disappoint them. And there was another consideration. It wasn't enough to wed Nicola; to seal his claim on Valmar, he must bed her.

Or at least pretend to. Since she wasn't a virgin, he need show no proof that he'd taken her maidenhead. All he had to do was go through the motions, and everyone would assume the deed was done.

The realization relieved him. He headed to the battlement stairs and started down.

Chapter Six

Something was wrong. Nicola realized it as soon as Fawkes returned to the hall. The harsh-miened knight who strode in wasn't the same man who'd left earlier. *That* Fawkes had given her a beautiful ring, his dark eyes lit with boyish enthusiasm. The man who rejoined her on the dais was guarded and wary. He didn't even glance her direction as he said, "Milady, if it pleases you, I think we should go up now."

She got to her feet, unsettled by his abrupt, formal tone. What had happened while he was gone from the hall? He'd been away less than half a candle-hour. Someone had engaged him in conversation, probably one of the garrison knights. What had they told him?

Cold emptiness invaded the pit of her stomach as she followed Fawkes from the hall. The crowd began to cheer and call out ribald comments. She drew up beside her new husband and saw a muscle tense in his jaw. If only she knew why he looked so wroth.

He stopped to take a cresset torch from a wall bracket. Turning toward her, he said, "Is your bedchamber still in the east tower?"

"Aye." Her throat was as dry as dust.

The torch illuminated the hard planes of his face and the scar near one of his deep-set eyes. "Is that where you wish to go? Or is there another bedchamber you prefer?"

She matched his terse mood. "This way, milord."

****

Milord. Coming from her, Fawkes found the word jarring. He was already struggling to forget the difference in their statuses. She'd been born a lady while he was the son of a landless knight. He told himself he'd earned the title of lord. Fought and struggled and suffered for the honor. Even so, deep down, there was a part of him that did not feel worthy. Of the title, or of the woman.

Or course, if she was the treacherous viper the rumors implied, it hardly mattered if he was her equal in status. If she was capable of such perfidy, he had no reason to feel overawed by her.

He should have found out if Mortimer's words were true before he married her. Yet even if he'd known for certain she had betrayed him, what could he have done differently? He would still have had to wed her. Only a fool would fail to validate his control over such rich properties.

A fool. Is that what he'd been all these years as he focused his whole life on rescuing this woman? This woman, who if the tales were true, did not wish to be rescued.

His already gloomy mood declined further. He wanted this wretched night over. They could begin again on the morrow. Curse it! He needed more wine. Why had he not thought to bring a flacon?

He halted on the stairs. "Would you like some wine? Should I go back and ask a servant to fetch some?"

"Old Emma will be waiting in the tower. We can send her."

Old Emma. He had a vague recollection of passing an ancient maidservant on the way down the stairs as he

71

left Nicola's chamber years ago. That memory brought back others. Blindingly intense ones. Instantly, he was aroused.

His treacherous body responded to this woman, even if his mind told him he must ignore all the feelings she evoked. Nay, he would not let her tempt him. He must keep his wits about him and remain in control.

He still hadn't decided on a course of action. If he broached the subject of Nicola's betrayal, there was every chance she would lie. She'd obviously believed her husband would prevail. Since he hadn't, she likely feared the consequences.

With a man, he would feel confident in his ability to get at the truth. But women were so much trickier, especially this one. Nicola had been used as a pawn by men all her life. She'd obviously developed skills of subterfuge and deception. The only way she could have gotten the better of Mortimer was by being cleverer and more ruthless than he was. Now she might well use those traits against *him*. Especially if she had betrayed him and feared he meant to punish her for her treachery.

They reached the top of the stairs. He hesitated a moment, recognizing the oaken door as the same one he'd stood agonizing before on that fateful afternoon. Nay, he would not think about that day. Would not let his memories cloud his judgment. He jerked the door open and moved aside to let her in ahead of him.

As Nicola had said, the old maidservant was there, preparing for them. The bedclothes were pulled back and lighted beeswax candles were arranged around the room.

The plump elderly servant gave a stiff bow. "Milord." She straightened and gestured to a pitcher and two silver cups on a table by the bed. "I had a page bring wine."

"Thank you," Nicola murmured. "You may go now."

The maidservant bowed again, then waddled to the door, and closed it behind her.

Nicola went to the table and picked up the ewer. "Wine, milord?"

Fawkes nodded. The room smelled of the bewitching scent that was Nicola. For so many years merely thinking of her had evoked this fragrance. Now he was surrounded by it. His wits seemed to leave him, wafted away on the exotic essence. As he watched her pour the wine, he struggled not to become enraptured all over again. He wanted to feel those graceful white hands on him. Experience that silky ebony hair brushing against his skin. He wanted, oh, he wanted…

He fought back the fierce urges of his body. Before he gave into them, he had to know what kind of woman he was dealing with. He'd told himself that questioning Nicola could wait until the morrow. But he needed answers now. Before things went further between them and he was completely lost.

Nicola handed him a cup of wine. He took a swallow, imagining her on her wedding night with Mortimer. Arrogant, smirking, brutal Mortimer. For years he'd seen her as Mortimer's helpless victim. Now he questioned whether that was true. At this point, it wasn't even clear she'd been afraid of Mortimer. He might have misread the situation from the very beginning. Which meant his dream, the burning goal that had driven him through all the horror and suffering of the last four years, was based on an illusion.

"What do you think of the wine, milord?"

He turned to see her watching him, her silvery gaze as cool and inscrutable as ever. "The wine is excellent. As was the meal, and everything else I've experienced since we arrived. You are a gifted chatelaine."

"I was trained from birth for this."

Did she seek to remind him she had been born in a castle, while he came into life in a simple village cottage? Or, were her words merely a polite response? Somehow he had to cross the icy river of tact and decorum and learn the truth of her relationship to Mortimer. As well as her feelings and expectations for this new marriage.

He put down his cup and approached her. "Lady, I must know. Are you pleased to have wed me?"

She didn't hesitate. "Of course, milord."

The words told him nothing. Her composed and elegant countenance told him less. And standing this close to her, he could again feel himself slipping under her spell. His cock leapt up, rigid and aching, like an eager, obedient hound. It took all his will to stop himself from taking her in his arms.

But thankfully, his brain still functioned. He returned to where he'd left his wine and took another swallow, hoping it would unfreeze his thoughts and allow him to converse in a rational manner.

He fidgeted with the cup. "I'm pleased you're content to marry me. It's an awkward circumstance. You have no say in this, and are transferred from one man to another like a dumb beast sold at the fair." He dared to meet her gaze again. "I would have given you a choice, but I have a duty to my men, and to your knights and villeins. These are precarious times. The people of Valmar and Mordeaux are better off with a strong lord who asserts his right by wedding the woman who holds the ancient writ to the properties."

It sounded as if he was apologizing. If he kept on babbling, she would think him weak and a fool. If she did not already think that. She was so cool and composed. He'd never known anyone, man or woman, so damnably hard to read.

He took another swallow of wine. Clearly, he was over his head. He knew how to fight and kill. How to seize power, but not how to keep it. Somehow how he must learn to strategize, and to take control with words rather than weapons.

"Milord?"

He looked up to see Nicola watching him, as elegant and unknowable as a jewel-eyed cat.

"Other than me, did Mortimer have other enemies?"

She frowned. "Milord?"

"As soon as I arrived, Mortimer immediately led a force out to meet me. How did he know there was a threat to his hold on Mordeaux?"

"I don't know." Her expression was innocent, but he sensed a subtle tension in her body.

He pressed on. "He was well-prepared to do battle. Someone must have alerted him an enemy force was on the way."

She said nothing, merely looked at him. If only he could read her thoughts. If only he'd had a chance to take her measure before they been so inextricably bound together.

"Do you think that's what happened?"

"I don't know, milord."

This was hopeless. He had no way of determining if she told the truth. The heightened alertness in her expression could mean anything. It was entirely reasonable of her to regard her new husband with wariness. The source of her tension might not be guilt, but fear of displeasing him.

****

If only he'd get on with it! Nicola took another sip of wine, taking care to keep her hand steady. It felt as if Fawkes was interrogating her. She worried she would give the wrong answer and make him angry. This business about Mortimer riding out to meet him—how she was to know how Mortimer got his information from the outside world? He must have had contacts in London, men who overheard something regarding Fawkes and his plans and sent a message to Mortimer. What did any of this have to do with her?

It must be the rumors. She knew there were those at Valmar who whispered ugly things about her. That she was a sorceress who'd cast an evil spell on Mortimer. That she'd been slowly poisoning him.

She watched Fawkes pour more wine. As he drank it down, she felt a twinge of warning. Having endured one drunken husband, she didn't want another. Although it seemed unlikely Fawkes made a habit of over imbibing. A drunkard would never have won such acclaim on the battlefield nor attracted a whole troupe of war-hardened knights to his cause. Fawkes was probably drinking because he was nervous. Not that he had any reason to be nervous. He had all the power.

That thought increased her sense of foreboding. Mortimer had been cruel and brutal, but she'd managed to find a way to deal with him. By taking advantage of his craven, fearful nature, she'd been able to regain some control over her life.

But this man... Fawkes was not someone who would be easy to manipulate. He clearly possessed great force of will and was used to being in control. If he were like most men, he would expect her to be obedient and agreeable in all things. How was she to manage that?

The tower room seemed much too small. It was like being caged with a wild creature.

He left the table and approached her. Nicola fought the urge to draw back. He seemed to sense her apprehension, for his fierce expression softened. "I don't want you to fear me, Nicola. Unlike some men, I don't believe in striking women. Or children. Or anyone smaller and weaker than myself. If I were ever to feel the need the discipline you, I would choose other, more civilized means."

Discipline her? What did that mean? His words sounded reasonable and reassuring, but there was an edge of warning there. She must find some way to convince him she wasn't his enemy. She must make it clear she would never deal with him as she had with Mortimer.

Body rigid, her heart pounding wildly, she said, "Milord, you must understand. Mortimer was a brute. There were many times I feared for my life at his hands. Whatever you may have heard of me..." Her hands trembled as she gestured and this time she was glad he saw. "I did what I had to do to survive." *And for Simon to survive.*

His expression softened. His dark eyes again flared with violent emotion. "You forget. I knew Mortimer. He tried more than once to kill me. I have no sympathy for him. None at all."

She let out her breath. Perhaps now they could begin

again, and he would stop playing this game of cat and mouse with her. She nodded. "I'm very grateful you understand. I'd worried you might have heard tales of me, stories meant to portray me as wicked and manipulative."

He watched her intently. "Aye, I have heard tales. 'Tis good you saw fit to reassure me. Perhaps now, perhaps we can..." He let his words trail off and the atmosphere between them shifted. His dark eyes no longer seemed stern and implacable, but smoldered with frank sexual desire. The tension between them changed, erupting with blazing arousal.

Fire started in her loins and spread outward, making her skin ache for his touch. She tilted her head, awaiting his kiss.

He hesitated, as if even now he feared to take this final step and give into what his body obviously desired. Observing his forbearance, she thought for the dozenth time of how different he was from Mortimer. Mortimer had been a slave to his emotions. This man sought control at all times.

But at last he brought his lips to hers. The blaze took them both.

****

An explosion. Like the walls of Acre crashing down as the final missile from the trebuchet shattered the ruined tower. Every nerve and muscle alive. His skin pulsing with desire. She was naught but skin and hair and flesh, and yet she was magic. A triumphant dazzling dream come to life.

He sucked life from her lips. Drowned in her scent. The sheer pleasure of holding her overwhelmed him. He could not think, only feel. And obey his body's command. The imperative to be joined with her.

But her gown thwarted him. He clawed at it, trying to get it off. The fabric was silky and fine but naught but scratchy homespun compared to the soft skin that lay beneath. Damnable laces! How the devil…

"Stop, milord!" She slipped from his grasp, breathing hard, her gray eyes incandescent. "If you wish me to be naked, give me a moment."

He sought to relax a bit as he watched her delicate fingers struggle with the laces under her arms. Not a task for one. At least not the one wearing the gown. "Milord." She gazed at him in helpless frustration. "I can't do it."

He nodded and again moved close, forcing himself to patiently untie the lacings and loosen them so the gown was no longer bound tightly to her body. She turned so he could do the same on the other side. As he undid the second set of lacing, he considered there might be benefits to slowing down. Having waited for this coupling for so long, he shouldn't rush, but savor each exquisite moment.

With his help, she pulled the gown over her head. Her nearly transparent shift only enhanced the splendor of her body. Her hair swirled around her like a cloak of midnight silk. *Blessed Jesu! How was he to control himself?* He stepped away, holding himself rigid as he waited for her to finish undressing.

She hung her gown on the clothing pole, then took off the jeweled circlet and carried it to the wooden coffer on the far side of the bed. Returning to where he stood, her eyes met his. With one fluid motion, she pulled her shift over her head and dropped it to the floor.

He inhaled sharply. A dazzling vision stood before him, all silken curves and glowing ivory skin. She was perfection; he wanted to devour her.

She fixed him with her gem-bright gaze. "Should you not undress also?"

He nodded and jerked his tunic over his head. Then sat on the bed to remove his boots. His hands trembled as he untied his chausses. He pulled them down, then his braies. Naked, he stood and faced her. Her gaze moved over him, etching him with fire. This was no meek maid he had wed. This was a woman.

****

She could not believe she was doing this. Standing naked before this fierce implacable warrior and perusing his body with such aplomb. A few moments before she had feared him. Now she felt only desire. The change had come when she realized the power she had over him. After Mortimer, who regarded her with distaste, it was a revelation to be naked with Fawkes. He looked at her as if she was an angel tumbled down from the heavens.

Her response to him was no less intense. From the moment he kissed her, it had all come back. His smell. Dark and male. Animal warmth and sex. She remembered the passion shimmering between them that afternoon. The way he had made her limp and weak with desire. Until she had arched her back and moaned like a cat in heat. She remembered the feel of him inside her. Impossible pressure, almost pain, then full-out ecstasy. The memory made her realize how much she wanted this man, yearned for him. She felt as if he possessed her.

For long moments, they stared at each other. Then he moved near. He was practically quivering with taut, pent-up energy, like an animal ready to spring. He grasped her around the waist and pulled her against him, then brought his mouth to hers.

They plunged off the precipice into a sea of fire. Except this fire did not scald them but produced exquisite pleasure. They kissed as if breathing life into the other. Gasping and breathless. Inhaling scent and taste. He broke off the kiss with a groan and pulled her closer. His hands and mouth were everywhere. She writhed and moaned as he stroked her body and nuzzled her neck. Now she was the one who trembled as the aching need overcame her.

His hands on her buttocks. The feel of his shaft against her belly. Huge and alive. "Oh, please." She touched his phallus to make certain he understood. He let out a sound, half groan, half growl. Then he picked her up and carried her to the bed and laid her down. She took hold of his arms and pulled him on top of her.

He kissed with her slow deliberation. Her desire built until she felt she would go mad. Finally, he touched between her legs. She moaned and arched her hips. "Please," she whispered. His tormenting hand moved away. He guided himself into position and pushed into her.

Impossible fullness. She was relieved he didn't move, but waited, his body taut as a bowstring. Her own body adjusted, melting around him. He pushed deeper and began to thrust. With each stroke, she was impaled, shredded and shattered. Excruciating pleasure. Mind-numbing satisfaction. He carried her soaring into the heavens, like a great horse with wings. She floated there as the pressure built inside her again. Flashed away into the heavens. And then again.

Somewhere in the haze, she heard his harsh cry and felt his body spasm.

They returned to earth slowly. Sweat-soaked limbs.

Damp, fevered skin. Blood surging in their veins. Hearts hammering. Transcendent, magical passion returned to heavy flesh. She sensed him drawing back into himself as his mighty sword withered. He slipped out of her, then rolled onto his back and lay beside her. Again they were two separate people, and the uneasiness between them returned as swiftly as it had left.

She was reluctant to open her eyes lest the faint memories of ecstasy that danced across her inner vision fade completely. He'd bedded her, as law and tradition demanded. But had it changed anything between them? He couldn't deny that their lovemaking had been exceptional, their bodies perfectly matched.

She finally opened her eyes and glanced at her new husband. Her languorous contentment ebbed away. Fawkes didn't look like a man who'd experienced great passion and pleasure. There was a faint crease between his eyes, the hint of a frown. He appeared unmoved by the splendor of their lovemaking.

She'd always heard men were thus, that for them coupling was only a physical act. An itch to be scratched. An ache to be soothed. They didn't need to feel anything for their bed partner to enjoy sex. She was no more to Fawkes than the mare was to the stallion that covered it.

Disappointment settled on her like a weight. For a few moments she'd thought she might have a tiny bit of power in this marriage. That she might—as Old Emma had advised—use her feminine wiles to bend Fawkes to her will and make him care for her. Clearly, there was no hope of that. Although Fawkes might find her desirable, her ability to affect him was limited to what happened between them in bed. She was as powerless as she'd been with Mortimer. Perhaps more so, for Mortimer had been weak, and like most bullies, deep-down, a coward. This man was not like that, not at all.

She exhaled softly. He probably imagined she sighed in repletion and contentment. In fact, she sighed to think the truce between them was over, and now they returned to their familiar roles of conqueror and conquered.

****

I cannot do this. If I lay beside her all night I will lose any objectivity or control I yet possess.

Nicola's allure surrounded him. Her scent, mingling with the musk of his passion. A miasma of remembered ecstasy that robbed him of reason and will. Their lovemaking had surpassed all his expectations and left him stunned. Vulnerable, almost helpless. He could not afford to risk himself that way. Not when he knew so little of Nicola's mind and motivations.

Fawkes forced himself to get up from the bed and seek out his clothing. He heard her take a sharp breath as she realized what he was doing. Her obvious regret was like a knife blade in his chest. If he chose to stay, they could make love again. He could take it slower this time, now that the edge was off their lust. He could explore her beautiful body at his leisure.

Nay, he could not. If he spent any more time with her, he would become as weak and powerless as Mortimer had been at the end.

Although he had little worry Nicola would poison *his* wine. She had no need to do so. Nicola herself was the potion that addled his wits and confused his judgment. Somehow he must avoid being alone in her company, at least until he knew more about who she really was. He'd fallen in love with a phantom, a dream. Now he must discover the reality of Nicola of Valmar. Was she the calculating viper Mortimer claimed? Or the abused and tormented lady he'd vowed to rescue?

He sat on the stool to put on his boots. In all likelihood she was something between devil and angel. But Reynard was right; he dare not risk everything he'd fought so hard for on a woman whose true character he still didn't know.

He rose from the stool, trying to think what he should say to her. How to explain his abandonment of her on their wedding night.

"I…" He gestured to the beautifully carved wooden bed. "I'm unused to such comforts. I fear I won't sleep even a candle-hour if I stay. I bid you goodnight, lady." He inclined his head, and not waiting for her reply, strode from the room.

Chapter Seven

He sought the battlements, hoping the fresh air would clear his head and help him think. Reaching the top, he gazed out into the darkened valley. How was he to keep his distance from Nicola? He must sleep somewhere, but he didn't want the whole castle to know he spurned his wife's bed. Since Nicola was no longer a virgin, there was no bloodied sheet to show on the morrow, and he could not truly prove he'd bedded her. If he spent his nights elsewhere, the rumors would start. He must come up with a plan to avoid Nicola's bed and yet conceal what he was doing from the entire castle. It seemed an impossible task.

A voice behind him made him jerk around. "De Cressy? Is that you?"

Fawkes turned to see the castellan. "FitzSaer."

"Yea, milord. What are you doing up here? That is, I didn't mean imply you should not be here, but that—"

"I'm thinking." Fawkes spoke sharply. "Tell me, Sir Adam, how long have you served at Valmar?"

"Near four years. I hired on with Mortimer after most of his men went off on Crusade with the king."

FitzSaer had been there since soon after Fawkes left. It was reasonable he would feel some loyalty to Mortimer. He would have to tread carefully. "And what did you think of Mortimer?"

The man hesitated. "He had his faults, of course. I

never did come to terms with his taste for boys, but that doesn't mean he deserved what happened to him."

"You mean his death at my hands?"

"Not that. You killed him in fair combat and everyone says he was the one who issued the challenge. I'm speaking of before you arrived, how he came to such a sorry state. I might not have cared much for the man in some ways, but he was my lord. To see him rot away and become a pathetic shell of a knight…" He shook his head. "If I were you, I would be wary of Lady Nicola. She is no natural woman."

"What do you mean?"

"I'm not saying she uses witchcraft, although she does keep company with Glennyth the healer, who's said to dabble in sorcery. But she did something to Mortimer, fed him poison or something that disordered his wits and made him less than a man. And then there is the matter of the babe. It may be rumor, but the whole thing unfolded so oddly—"

"Babe, what babe?" The blood in Fawkes's veins turned to ice water.

"Three summers ago she gave birth to a babe. Mortimer said it was stillborn, but I have heard otherwise. They say she strangled the babe in its cradle in order to foil Mortimer's ambitions. She never appeared to mourn it. The child—I heard it was a boy—is buried by the chapel, but there is no stone or effigy to mark its passing."

"Take me there," Fawkes said.

"Now, my lord?"

"Yea, now."

A short while later Fawkes found himself staring down at a grave in the small cemetery behind the chapel, a little rounded mound of grass unadorned by marker or memento.

FitzSaer cleared his throat. "What are you thinking, milord? Do you worry if you get Lady Nicola with child, she might kill it? I don't think she would. I think she got rid of this one because she hated Mortimer so much. It was her chance to rob him of what he wanted most. Losing his heir was part of the reason he lost his wits. That was when he changed, guzzled his wine and sat in a corner of the hall staring at nothing."

A dozen wrenching, awful thoughts filled Fawkes mind: *Did the babe look like me? He probably had black hair, and all babes had blue eyes. Had he even opened them? Drawn a breath? My babe. And she had killed it. How could she do such a thing? What kind of woman is she?*

"Sorry to roil the waters between you and your new wife," Fitz Saer interrupted in sympathetic tones. "But I thought it best that you know."

Fawkes nodded jerkily. Best that he know his new wife was a murderess. That she had killed their child.

"To be fair to Lady Nicola, I suppose Mortimer must have done things to make her hate him so much," the castellan continued. "I heard a tale he sent a man to rape her and get her with child because he could not. I guess something like that would harden a woman, make her capable of killing a babe that was so begotten. But still, to kill a child she'd just given birth to, it boggles the imagination to think any woman capable of that."

Fawkes drew a deep breath. If he heard any more, he'd go mad. "Leave me." He spoke as calmly as he could manage. "I have some thinking to do."

****

Nicola stared up at the peaked ceiling of the tower room. After their lovemaking, Fawkes should have been sated and eager to sleep. Instead, he'd been restless and uneasy. The act that should have brought them closer had somehow deepened the chasm between them.

She got out of bed and retrieved her shift, then went to the window and threw open the shutters. She thought of Old Emma's warning about letting in bad vapors, but leaned into the window embrasure and breathed in deeply anyway. Bad vapors were the least of her worries. She'd been wed less than a day and already this marriage had turned out to be as nerve-wracking and challenging as her first one. Nay, more so. Mortimer might have been a cruel, depraved fiend, but at least he was predictable. Fawkes de Cressy remained a complete puzzle.

At the feast he'd appeared wary, then fond, then back to wary and distant. They'd come up to her chamber, where he asked strange probing questions, then seized her and made love to her with astounding passion. Now he'd left, and gave her a ridiculous excuse for doing so. Cold and hot. Hot and then cold.

There must be some reason he didn't want to share her bed. Did he fear the fire that rose between them, threatening to incinerate them both? She did. The touch of this man had the power to turn her wits to porridge.

Sighing, she returned to the bed. She doubted she would sleep, but she must try. At least her body felt soothed and satisfied, content for the first time in years. If only her thoughts didn't spin so wildly. At least for once she wasn't agonizing about her son. This night she struggled to come to grips with the strange ferocious knight who was Simon's father.

****

Fawkes climbed the stairs to Nicola's chamber. He'd endured a long, sleepless night on a pallet in an empty bedchamber. Now his stomach churned with distress and his steps were leaden. But he could wait no longer to confront Nicola. *Furious thoughts roiled through his mind:* She did not have to give the child life and then kill it. If she didn't want the babe, she could have gone to a wise woman for a potion to make her lose it before it quickened. *Women knew of such things, even if the Church and most men abhorred the practice.*

Of course, if she'd done that, her revenge against Mortimer would not have been so complete, so satisfying. Fawkes fought the urge to retch. Could it really be true, that the woman he'd idolized had murdered his son?

Reaching the landing, he took a deep breath and knocked on the door. Nicola bid him enter. She sat on a stool while the elderly maidservant brushed her hair. At least she was dressed, attired in a simple blue gown. If he'd had to confront her while she was clad in her shift, he would not have been able to think of anything besides her glorious body. As it was, the sight of her sleek ebony tresses falling over her shoulders sparked tantalizing memories of her silky hair gliding over his skin.

Somehow he had to force himself to look beyond Nicola's beauty and take stock of her character. She always appeared cool and composed, but he knew she was capable of great passion. She'd proven that only a few hours before, in bed with him. Did that intensity extend to hate as well as desire? Had her loathing for Mortimer been so profound she was willing to do anything to thwart him?

The image of the tiny grave by the chapel flashed into his mind. He told himself he could not condemn her yet. He must give her a chance to explain. Allow her to tell him her version of what had happened.

Fawkes motioned to the servant. "Leave us." The woman placed the brush on the table that still held the wine ewer and cups from the previous night. Then she waddled past him, her eyes focused straight ahead.

As soon as she was gone, he turned back to Nicola. "I have some questions to ask you." He moved nearer, wanting to intimidate her, to make her afraid. "Your castellan told me that some three years ago, you gave birth to a babe."

Something changed in her face. Her pupils turned to deep black pools surrounded by silver rims.

"FitzSaer said the babe died. Clearly that is true, for I see no sign of it." He gave an exaggerated look around the room, as if she might have a cradle hidden under the bed or behind the clothing pole.

Still, she did not speak, and he realized he would have to ask the question directly if he wished her to respond. "How did…the babe die?"

He almost said "my son." But he didn't know for certain that the child was his. It was another question he must ask her.

For a second she looked stricken. Then the cool mask slid back into place. "The babe was born dead. The cord was wrapped around his neck. The midwife said he strangled in the womb."

He refused to soften his gaze. Somehow he had to break through her formidable reserve. "If I bring the midwife here and ask her how the babe died, will she tell me the same?"

Something flickered behind her opalescent eyes. He detected wariness, perhaps even a hint of fear. But when she spoke, her voice was calm and clear. "Of course. Go to the village and ask her."

"And the child," he pressed. "Was it mine, or some other man's?"

Her gaze didn't waver. "It was yours. I felt it quicken ere Mortimer returned from London."

"What did it…he look like?"

She rose from the stool, clearly agitated now. "The babe was good-sized. I carried him a full nine months. If not for the cord, he would have thrived."

"What color was his hair?" He could tell she didn't like these questions. Her unease made him fear the worst.

"His hair was dark. What else would you expect of a child begat of the two of us?"

"What did you name him?"

Again, that hesitation, as if she were deciding how to answer. "Simon. I named him Simon."

Simon. Not the name he would have chosen, but then he'd had little choice in any of this.

"Was he blessed by a priest before he was buried?"

"Of course."

In this, at least, he hoped she told the truth. But she still looked like a bird poised for flight.

"There are rumors you killed the child." He could barely say the words. "Is it true?"

She turned away. He could sense her mind working as she struggled over her answer. The breath seemed to leave his body. *Why does she not deny it immediately?*

She looked back at him, her stance defiant. "I saw an opportunity to torment Mortimer and I took it. I pointed at the dead child in the cradle and taunted him. I told him he would never have an heir of my body. I don't know what he made of my words, how he twisted them. He was a cruel man. Although I was yet weak and bleeding from my travail, he beat me brutally. I nearly died that day, as well as the babe."

Her response increased his loathing of Mortimer, yet did not satisfy him. She had not denied she killed the child. And all along, she seemed to be choosing her words with care.

He felt as if he would burst with frustration. There was no point in questioning this woman. He would not get the truth from her, at least not like this. Stalking to the door, he left her.

****

Nicola winced at Fawkes's footfalls echoing down the stairs. She wanted to rush after him and tell him clearly that she had not killed the child. But if she said more, she feared she would slip and reveal the truth. That the babe she'd given birth to hadn't died but was living at Mordeaux Castle. Then she would have to somehow make Fawkes believe Simon was his son. But why should he believe her tale? It sounded half-mad even to her.

Her thoughts traveled back to those nerve-wracking days. Only a fortnight before the babe was due, Glennyth had arrived in the middle of the night carrying a bundle. Nicola still remembered the horror she'd felt when the wise woman peeled away the blanket to reveal a tiny blue infant, the birth cord encircling its neck. Stillborn, Glennyth said. The mother had died a few hours later.

But what was a tragedy for one village family was the greatest good luck for them. The babe's father had been too sick with grief to take note of what Glennyth did with his dead son. Now, all they needed was for Nicola's babe to arrive. Then they could spirit it away and bury the dead infant in its place.

Nicola paced to the window, grimacing at the remembered pain. 'Twas no easy matter to make a babe be born before it was ready. When Glennyth gave her the potion, she'd warned if the contractions were too intense, Nicola could die. But the midwife offered no alternative. They could not wait until the babe decided to come on its own.

It had seemed as if a beast was inside her belly, devouring her from the inside, and she'd been certain she would perish. So certain she'd made Glennyth promise that if she died, the midwife would still carry out their plan. She meant to cheat Mortimer of his hoped-for heir, even if it was from her deathbed.

Nicola closed her eyes as she thought about the moment when her travail was over and she heard the babe cry. The way Simon had nestled on her breast with such heart-rending sweetness. She'd almost lost courage then, as she realized what she would be giving up. But then she thought about Mortimer and his terrible temper. And the possibility that he would change his mind and lash out at the son who was not his.

That fear had kept her determination strong and allowed her to go through with the plan. And everything had gone perfectly. Sweet little Simon had made not a peep after his first birth throes. She'd tearfully kissed his tiny face. Glennyth had put him in her herb basket, covered him and carried him out of the castle.

Then came the aftermath with Mortimer. She would never forget how his already florid face had turned a violent red when he saw the still, pathetic form in the cradle. Despite his obvious fury, she hadn't been able to stop herself from taunting him, warning him that he would never have what he wished of her.

She remembered the hatred in his eyes and how terrified she had been he meant to kill her. Perhaps he would have if she hadn't swooned from the pain. When she regained awareness, he was gone. That was when she wept with despair. Aye, she had triumphed. Aye, her son was safe. But some other woman would have the joy of raising him, not her. Her swollen breasts would never suckle him. She would not see his first step, nor hear the first word he spoke. Simon. Her darling Simon. And to save his life, she had no choice but to give him up.

Tears blurring her eyes, Nicola closed the shutters. For the past three years her life had been fraught with difficult choices, secrets that threatened to break her. Now Fawkes had come, bringing with him more turmoil. If only she could trust him. But how could she trust a man who seemed so angry and suspicious? From the moment he'd arrived, she'd sensed he was on edge. He should have been delighted to take control of Valmar without doing battle. Instead, he'd appeared dissatisfied, restless and wary.

And there were the tales they told of him, the ruthless knight who'd killed a hundred men. How could she trust Simon's life to such a cold, hardened man? A man who seemed so eager to believe the worst of her? Who clearly thought her capable of killing her own baby?

She shuddered, then went to the door and called down for Old Emma.

The maidservant puffed up the stairs. "What did milord want?" she asked, after catching her breath.

Nicola returned to her place on the stool. "He asked about the child I bore three years ago. He asked if

I'd killed it."

"Jesu save us!" Old Emma screeched. "He didn't?"

"Aye, he did." Nicola exhaled an anguished breath. "We knew there would be rumors. I always feared someone would discover Simon was alive. But I truly didn't consider how the other babe's death would be perceived. Apparently there those at Valmar who think the worst of me, and they have seized upon this means to poison the new lord's mind."

"You denied it, of course. Didn't you?"

"I was so shocked and distressed, I didn't know what to say at first. Then all I could think of was that I must make certain he didn't find out that Simon was alive. I told him the babe was born dead. But nay, I don't think I ever actually said I didn't kill it."

"By the saints, why not? What didn't you deny doing such a terrible thing?"

Nicola took an agonized breath and closed her eyes. Old Emma often said she was her own worst enemy. Once again, she'd proven the maidservant right. "I was so shocked. So angry. To think that there are people at Valmar who think me a heartless murderer. Mortimer was the monster, not I! I can't help resenting Fawkes for listening to such terrible gossip. Ever since he arrived, he's behaved strangely. He acts as if I am his enemy and deals with me as he would an adversary. He doesn't trust me and always seems on his guard when he's around me."

Old Emma snorted. "That must have made the bedding interesting."

"Interesting. Aye, it was that."

"By which you mean awkward? Unpleasant? What?"

She wasn't certain this was something she wanted to share with Old Emma. But she had no other confidant at the castle and she clearly needed help in dealing with her new husband. She'd muddled things terribly so far.

"Whatever is between Fawkes and me in other ways, our bodies are well-matched. We have no difficulties in that regard."

"Hmmm." A glimmer of a smile played on Old Emma's lips. "Then all is not lost. If the man lusts for you, you have far more power than it appears."

"That might be true. If I had some notion how to use that power. But I told you, I have no skills in seduction or cosseting a man."

"Perhaps you could learn."

"From whom? You're the only woman I dare discuss such matters with, and I don't believe you've had much experience in these things."

Old Emma gave her familiar cackling laugh. "Oh, I have experience. But it was long ago. And with village boys rather than lordly knights. Yet, even at that, I think I could give you a few pointers, if you would listen. Or." She shrugged. "There is another way. You could tell him about Simon."

"And how would that help? He's been told the babe died, and I have said the same. If I change my story now, why should he believe me? Even if I brought Simon here and presented him to Fawkes as his son, I can't change the fact that Simon looks nothing like Fawkes. Altering my story now will only make me look even more deceitful. Lie upon lie, and which one should he believe?" Nicola shook her head firmly.

"Mayhaps you are right." Old Emma pointed to the

stool. Nicola took her place and the servant resumed plaiting her hair.

"That leaves only his desire for you," Old Emma said after a time. "Somehow we must find a way to make use of it."

"I'm not certain even of *that*." Nicola stiffened. "Fawkes did his duty last night, but he left immediately afterwards. Then when he returned, he showed no fondness or warmth but instead questioned me in his cold, suspicious way. He may lust for me, but his wariness makes him fight the attraction. For all we know, he may avoid me from now on."

"Then we must find reasons for you to be alone with him."

"I can't imagine what those reasons might be."

"'Twould be perfectly reasonable for you to seek him out to ask questions regarding the running of the castle and business matters regarding the demesne."

"Mortimer never concerned himself with such things."

"But Fawkes is not Mortimer. That is clear to everyone."

Nay, Fawkes was not Mortimer. Mortimer had never aroused her desire. Or made her feel breathless with yearning whenever she was in his company.

Having finished braiding Nicola's hair, Old Emma stepped back. "You've never worn a veil or wimple around the castle, and I see no reason for you to start doing so now. Even braided, your hair will remind Fawkes of how you looked on your wedding night and how your hair felt against his skin."

Nicola turned and gave Old Emma a look. Old Emma let out a cackle. "I came to the castle to serve your mother when I was very young. But not so young that I hadn't learned a thing or two about men."

Nicola stared at the servant's deeply lined face and tried to imagine her as a comely maiden flirting with a village boy. For a moment, she saw Old Emma's dark eyes sparking with mischief and her full mouth quirked in a teasing smile.

Chapter Eight

Fawkes left the castle and walked across the bailey yard. Nicola was hiding something, he was sure of it. Was it guilt over the babe? Or something else?

The more time he spent with her, the more of a puzzle she became. Was she a ruthless and calculating woman who had coldly betrayed him to Mortimer? A cold-blooded monster that had killed her own babe for vengeance? Or had she been driven mad by Mortimer's torture and abuse, until her mind was so deranged that she didn't truly understand what she was doing when she took the life of a tiny, helpless infant?

Or, was she innocent of it all?

He shook his head, wishing he could stop thinking about these things. But somehow he had to discover the truth about the woman he had wed. Even now she might be plotting against him, scheming to rid herself of another unwanted husband.

But the passion they experienced together in bed was so intense, so powerful. Why would any woman reject that? Unless *any* man could satisfy her. She might have lain with other men in the years he'd been away. Mortimer had no reason to care who his wife slept with. If Nicola was careful and her maidservant loyal, it would have been easy for her to take a lover…or several.

He halted, fists clenched and breathing hard. He'd chosen to remain celibate the last four years, but he had no right to expect Nicola to have done the same. They'd made no promises to each other. She'd probably believed he was dead, and why would she not? By all logic, he shouldn't have survived, let alone prospered and improved his circumstances to the point he could return to Valmar and make her his wife.

Slowly, he swallowed his rage. He was being unfair and unreasonable. Letting terrible rumors poison his thoughts. He would not condemn Nicola because of gossip. He must find out the truth.

He went to knights' barracks. Entering, he immediately encountered Engelard. "Where's Reynard?"

"Not up yet." Engelard smirked suggestively. "You might try the stables."

Fawkes went to the stables and stalked past the stalls, redolent with the odors of horse and freshly cut hay. "Reynard, you lustful whoreson! Where are you?"

"Fawkes?" a voice responded. "Is that you? What the devil are you doing out of bed already? I thought you would be—"

"Never mind that!" Fawkes bellowed. "I have need of you. Get down here."

There was whispering and the sound of Reynard dressing. A ladder creaked and Reynard climbed from the hayloft. "Why aren't you with Lady Nicola? You can't tell me you've slaked four years of lust that quickly."

He grabbed Reynard's arm. "I'll thank you not to announce my business to the entire keep. Come with me and I'll tell you what's come to pass."

They went out into the bailey. Reynard jerked his head toward the castle. "Well? How did it go?"

"As soon as we were alone, I asked if she had warned Mortimer. She claimed innocence. Said she had no idea how he knew I was on my way to Mordeaux."

"That is good."

Fawkes shook his head. "There is more. I left her chamber soon after the consummation. I needed to clear my head."

Reynard raised his brows but said nothing.

"I went up on the battlements, where I encountered the castellan, Adam FitzSaer. He told me a horrifying tale. It seems some three years ago, Nicola bore a child."

Reynard's eyes widened. "Yours?"

"She confirmed it. But that is where her story and FitzSaer's diverge. She says the babe was dead at birth. FitzSaer says she strangled the infant herself to thwart Mortimer."

"By the saints! You think it's true?"

"I don't know what to think. I can't imagine Nicola killing her own child. Yet, I have been to the grave, and it is barren and deserted, as if she doesn't mourn the infant. And when I questioned her about the matter, she acted as if she was hiding something."

"So, where do you go from here?"

"I'm going to talk to the midwife."

"What will that tell you? If Nicola's story is a lie, I'm sure the midwife has been well-paid to keep her lady's secret."

"Then I will find a way to convince the woman to tell me the truth. I'm the new lord. She will need my blessing if she wishes to continue to serve as the area's wise woman."

"When will you speak to her?"

"Now. I don't want to give Nicola a chance to send a message of warning to her. And I want you to come with me."

Reynard smiled wryly. "Why me? I'm not the most intimidating fellow, at least not with women."

"It seems best to take some sort of escort, and you're the only person I trust enough to involve in this."

They made their way to the armory to get their weapons. As they were strapping on their swordbelts, Reynard asked, "Do you think we need to take our helmets?"

"Jesu, I hope not! We're only going to the village. Even if the villeins are against me, I can't believe they've had time to plot my downfall."

"That's a relief. Since it's not yet terce and already the weather is sweltering."

"Compared to the hellish inferno of the Levantine coast, the English summer seems very pleasant."

They made their way to the gate. As they started through the portcullis, the knight on duty, Sir Roger, asked where they were headed.

"To the village." Seeing the man's perplexed expression, Fawkes added, "I want to look things over."

"Very good, de Cress—I mean, milord."

Reynard chuckled as they started down the trackway. "It's going to take some time for the men to get used to thinking of you as a lord."

"I'm struggling to get used to the idea myself. Indeed, there are times when a sense of disbelief comes over me and I feel like this must all be a dream. Even a year ago I could never have imagined I would hold a demesne like Valmar." Fawkes gestured. "Look at this valley, the wheat and millet fields, the rich grazing meadows, the plump, sleek cattle. Whatever else you might say about Mortimer, his neglect doesn't seem to have hurt the property."

"If the land and people are still prosperous it's more likely to be Lady Nicola's doing than Mortimer's. Everyone says she's the one who's been managing things. I talked to the reeve last night and he told me she even holds manor court in the village."

Fawkes gaped at him.

Reynard shrugged. "You must look at it from their viewpoint. The demesne may change hands based on the whim of the king, or whichever man has the strength to hold it, but Nicola is their lady always. She grew up here and they know her."

They continued on the trackway to the village, which consisted of several dozen thatched houses. Many had vegetable plots or a shed behind for housing livestock. At the first house they came to, an older woman, her hair covered with a linen cloth, and her face flushed from the heat, was seated on a stool outside her house churning butter.

Fawkes nodded to her as he approached. "Good morrow. Can you tell me where I can find the midwife?"

The woman looked perplexed at first, then she said, "You mean Glennyth the healer?"

"Yea, I do."

The woman pointed. "She lives at the edge of the forest, beyond the common."

"Thank you," Fawkes responded.

They continued through the hamlet. This time of day the men were in the fields, so they mostly saw women seeing to their chores and children playing. The children stopped their play to stare at them, while the women inclined their heads respectfully.

"It would seem they already know you are the new lord," Reynard mused.

"I wonder what they think of me. Do they see me as a usurper? Or are they pleased I've rid them of Mortimer?"

"Most likely they are waiting to find out what kind of lord you will be."

"I didn't consider how awkward this was going to look. By nightfall everyone in the village, and likely the castle, will know I've been to talk to the midwife. I wonder what the gossips will make of that?"

"Since this woman is apparently not only a midwife but a wise woman, I'm sure you can come up with some reason you might seek out someone skilled in the healing arts. Perhaps you could say you were wounded in your battle with Mortimer. A slight wound, but one that needs tending."

"If that were the case, I would have sent for the healer and had her come to me."

"Or, we could say you seek a love potion to help you win the heart of your new bride." Reynard chortled.

Fawkes stopped walking and glowered at him. "If I didn't think it would give the villagers the wrong impression, I would throttle you right now."

Reynard smirked. "Since laying hands on me would cause tongues to wag, you'd best let it pass."

They started walking again and soon reached the common pasture where several black and white cows grazed. Beyond, at the edge of the forest, was a neat daub and wattle dwelling with a newly thatched roof. Behind the cottage, a woman in a linen headwrap tended the garden. Seeing them, she put down her hoe and waited for them to approach.

"By the saints," Reynard muttered, as they got closer. "I expected a weathered crone, not a beauty like this."

Fawkes's thoughts echoed Reynard's. The young midwife's tanned skin was smooth and unblemished, her hazel eyes striking. The simple rust-colored kirtle clung to her body, revealing generous curves and strong, well-formed muscles.

Fawkes motioned to Reynard. "Wait here. I'd like to speak to her alone."

He approached the woman. She didn't bow or make any obsequies, but watched him with casual aloofness.

"I'm Fawkes de Cressy, the new lord of Valmar. I understand you serve as midwife and healer to the people of the castle, as well as the village folk."

The woman's regarded him with narrowed hazel eyes. "That is true. How may I serve you?" Despite the courteous words, her expression was calm, almost disdainful.

Fawkes moved closer and lowered his voice. "Three years ago, Lady Nicola gave birth to a babe. There are those who say it was born dead. Others that it was strangled before it could draw a breath."

The healer's calm expression didn't waver. "People say many things. Have you asked the child's mother what transpired?"

"I have. But I want to know what *you* say."

"The child was dead at birth. The cause was the cord wrapped around its neck. There was no injury to your wife's womb, if that is why you ask." The healer raised an ironic brow. "With a lusty knight like you in her bed, I'm sure she'll be carrying another babe soon."

Was she mocking him? He almost thought so. Her greenish-gold eyes gazed at him condescendingly.

He tried again. "I've heard other stories. That Nicola gave Walter Mortimer a potion that weakened him and caused his wits to grow befuddled and his will to fail. If that is true, then surely the potion came from you."

"Again I remind you, people say many things."

This woman was so smug, so confident. Did she not realize the power he held over her? "Being a healer is a precarious position. Should some of your potions or treatments fail, you might fall out of favor. Or the charms you sell could be perceived as blasphemous, crimes against God and the Church. I'm sure you've heard tales where a healer has been accused of such things and driven from the area. Or worse. A wise woman needs the support of her lord, if she is to prosper."

Glennyth spread her hands, palms up. "What would you have me do, milord, to earn your favor? Have you a wound you wish me to tend? Some malady you want me to treat?"

Fawkes took another step closer, meeting Glennyth's bold gaze. "All I ask from you is the truth. That is all I require."

Her pointed chin came up another notch, and her cat eyes flared with green-gold light. "And I have given it. I will so swear on any oath you wish."

It was hopeless. She would not budge and he dare not engage in further threats unless he meant to act on them. "Good day, Dame Glennyth," he said curtly, and walked away.

He rejoined Reynard, who said, "I see it didn't go well."

Fawkes clenched his jaw. "She told the same story as

Nicola, then she jibed at me being a strong, lusty knight who would soon father more children. I felt like she was laughing at me."

"You couldn't intimidate her?"

"Not a bit. She's worse than Nicola. I felt like a mouse batted between a cat's paws."

Reynard scrutinized Glennyth, who had gone back to her hoeing. "She does have a bit of the feline about her. I vow she can stalk and play with me anytime."

"You're interested in *her*?"

Reynard grinned. "There are women that a man knows he won't have to teach a thing. Women from whom he might even learn something new himself."

"I wish you every pleasure of her. For myself, I prefer women who are a little less smug and sure of themselves."

"Like the Lady Nicola."

Fawkes gave a snort of exasperation.

"Where to now?"

"We might as well go back to the castle."

"Or you could introduce yourself to some of the villagers. That might make your visit to Glennyth seem less a matter for gossip."

"I don't care if they gossip. I need to get back to the castle. There are a dozen things I must see to. I will come back later with the reeve and he can present me properly to the villagers as their new lord."

"And what about Nicola? What will you do regarding her?"

Fawkes shook his head. "Her effect on me is so potent. I feel like I should distance myself from her, at least for now. But if I don't share her bed, the gossip will be worse than ever."

"You could take Mortimer's private chamber as your own. It would not be unreasonable for you to do so. Unless you're distressed by the rumors of what went on there."

Fawkes slowed. "What do you mean, what went on there?"

"Lady Nicola isn't the only one people tell gruesome tales about. While all knew Mortimer didn't like women, only last night did I learn his true preference for bed partners; it seems he favored boys, the younger the better."

"Children?"

"One page was no more than six years. Little Edwin is the one mentioned most. His death shocked many at Valmar. It seems he fell off the high castle wall."

"Fell?"

"Or jumped. There are those who say he met his end by his own hand. But the matter is only spoken of in whispers. No one wanted to see a child refused burial in the churchyard."

"Sweet Jesu! Mortimer was even more depraved than we thought!"

"He was a monster, that is true."

A monster. And Nicola had been wed to him for four years. Given this tale, it was easy to see why she might feel justified in anything she did to defy her husband. Did that include killing her babe to deprive Mortimer of his wished-for heir?

Fawkes spoke wearily, "Given how truly despicable Mortimer was, you would think everyone at Valmar would take Lady Nicola's side and raise her up as a paragon of virtue. Unless some of the things said about her are true. Perhaps people had reason to condemn her as well as Mortimer."

"But do they condemn her? FitzSaer told you the story of Nicola killing the babe. What we need to find out is what everyone else thinks."

"How are we to discover that? They aren't likely to speak openly to me."

"But they might to *me*," Reynard motioned back to the stables. "It was Gillian, the maid up in the hayloft, who told me the sad tale of little Edwin. Perhaps I should ask her opinion of Lady Nicola."

Fawkes made a sound of disgust. "Being a woman, she's probably sympathetic to Nicola's plight, wed to a loathsome man like Mortimer. She might well lie to protect her lady."

"Or, she might be jealous of Nicola and eager to spread gossip besmirching her. That's why we must seek out the opinions of several people in the household, of different ranks and sexes. That's the only way we'll gain a sense of Lady Nicola's true nature."

"But doing that will take time. Not to mention someone is bound to go to Nicola and tell her what we're about. Then she'll know I don't trust her."

Reynard guffawed. "Believe me, Fawkes, she already knows you think the worst of her. By now news of your visit to the village wise woman has already reached her ears."

Fawkes clenched his jaw. Damn it all. Reynard was right. What if it turned out that the rumors were false and Nicola was innocent of everything? Then his treatment of her was unforgivable. What sort of man berated a woman with questions regarding her dead child? Maybe he should forget the stupid rumors and assume all was well. And yet… There was *something*, some lie or secret Nicola was holding back. All his instincts told him that. What was it?

The high stone walls of Valmar Castle loomed ahead. Gazing at them, Fawkes wondered gloomily if he would ever find true satisfaction in the prize he'd won, or if doubts about Nicola would continue to poison his dream.

Chapter Nine

Nicola woke early, after a long and restless night. She'd lain awake for hours hoping Fawkes would come. Of course, once she'd learned he'd been to see Glennyth, she should have known better than to expect him. He thought she was lying and had immediately sought out confirmation of her story. By now, the whole castle and the village were probably buzzing with the news that the new lord had done his duty by his new wife, but naught else. He might despise her and think her a child-murderer, but he could have at least tried to keep up appearances.

Of course, there was no reason for him to care about such matters. His rejection of her did not affect his reputation, only hers.

She climbed slowly from the bed. Was this what her life would be like from now on? Would she have to sit beside Fawkes in the hall for the evening meal and exchange polite, meaningless conversation, then go to her bed alone? Was he sleeping in the lord's chamber in the tower opposite? Or some unused guestroom elsewhere in the castle? Had he slept alone, or found an agreeable serving maid to warm his bed?

Perhaps Old Emma knew. She seemed to keep abreast of the latest castle gossip. Nicola put on her plain blue work gown and covered her braided hair with a linen cloth. Then she sought out the small alcove on the lower level where the servant had moved her pallet in anticipation of Fawkes sharing Nicola's bedchamber.

Old Emma sat up. "Milady, what is? Surely it's not morning yet."

"Aye, it is." Nicola sank down on the end of the pallet. "I spent another night alone. Do you know where Fawkes is sleeping?"

Old Emma got up stiffly. "He sleeps in a chamber in the north tower. It's mainly used for storage, but there's a small pallet there. Similar to mine."

"He said he was unused to creature comforts," Nicola mused. "Still, it seems odd he doesn't use the lord's chamber with its big bed and the solar so close by."

"I presume he chose the place he did because he thought he would not be found there."

"A futile plan. Tell me also, have you heard if he sleeps alone?"

"He does. Apparently several of the maids offered their services, but he turned them all down. Indeed, I heard a tale from one of his men that Fawkes had a reputation for being celibate long before he arrived here. When the other men visited whores and such, Fawkes never went along."

"It would seem he tries to be discreet. Although it's a waste of time here at Valmar, where gossiping is a fine art. I had two people tell me yesterday that Fawkes went to see Glennyth. Clearly, he doesn't believe anything I say and sought out confirmation of my account."

Old Emma nodded. "He's also having his red-haired captain ask everyone in the castle what they think of you."

"I'm certain he will find plenty of people who will speak ill of me." Nicola could not keep the bitterness from her voice.

"Oh, not so many." Old Emma patted her shoulder. "A few men, like that FitzSaer bastard, who dislike the idea of a woman having a position of authority. And of course, the young maids who are envious of you and your handsome new husband."

"Aye, Fawkes is fine to look upon. But if that is all I am to have of him from now on, I would almost rather he was ugly."

"Don't be so discouraged, milady. De Cressy will come around. He's not an unreasonable man. Nor is he blind. I'm sure having to look at you and keep his distance is causing him plenty of frustration."

"Then why doesn't he give me a chance? Why does he insist on acting as if I am some fiend he must avoid at all costs?"

"He's being careful, I think. Fearing to make a misstep and lose what he's fought so hard for. You must admit, to someone coming from the outside, what happened to Mortimer is rather disturbing. Enough to make any man wary."

"I've told you a dozen times, I only gave Mortimer that elixir a few times. If he struggled with impotence later on, then it must have been his own guilty conscience getting the better of him."

"'Twas not the elixir. 'Twas the curse you laid on him."

Nicola gave a humorless laugh. "Aye, the curse. The one I made up in the moment. The claim that I would make his balls wither and his shaft go soft. Words, that's all it was. I had no power to do such a thing."

"But he didn't know that, and so all you had to do was make it appear to work a few times, and it became real to him."

"Well, now I am paying for it, aren't I? I have a virile young husband who has no interest in sharing my bed."

"You should speak to Glennyth. Mayhaps ask her for a love potion." Old Emma snorted.

Nicola ignored the jest. "I would like to talk to her, to know what she and Fawkes spoke of. But there will be gossip aplenty if I go see her now."

"Can it be any worse than what is already being bantered about?"

Nicola nodded. "You're right. I should go. Now, before all the castle is stirring."

"I'm on my way to break my fast. Do you want me to get you anything, milady?"

"What I yearn for is not something you can find in the kitchen."

"Don't give up hope. You've not been wed to the man even a sennight."

Leaving Old Emma, Nicola moved rapidly through the still-quiet castle. Outside in the yard she passed two groggy kitchen boys fetching wood to start the day's cooking and a scullery maid carrying a pail of water from the well.

She continued to the gate, halting when she saw the portcullis was down. Although the gate was closed at night, by this time of day it would normally be raised. Soon workers from the village would begin to arrive, along with fresh produce.

She called up to the guard. "Open the gate, please. I have an errand in the village."

A man poked his head out of the tower, his features indistinct in the dim light. "Who are you and what is your errand?"

"I'm Lady Nicola. And I do not believe I need state my business to you."

She heard hushed, intense whispers, followed by the creak of the portcullis being raised. After passing through the gate, she turned and called up. "I would advise you to leave the gate open. There's always free movement between the village and the castle during the daytime."

"No offense, milady, but that is for Lord Fawkes to decide."

As she made her way down the trackway, the world seemed to brighten moment by moment. Colors crept out of the darkness, grew sharper and more vivid. Halfway down the hill, she paused to enjoy the splendor of dawn's arrival. The mist along the river glowed pink and golden, floating over the valley like some fairy magic. The sun rose as a coppery ball of fire over the blue-green countryside.

She indulged herself a few seconds before continuing on. The village folk rose earlier than those who dwelled in the castle. Men who toiled in the fields depended on the light, and at the first sign of it, they set about their tasks.

The mist had still not burned off as she neared the hamlet. She heard a dog bark and a rooster crow, but could not see either. She skirted the village and sought out the thatched cottage beyond the common. At the doorway, she groped for the rope hanging from the eaves. Finding it, she rang the bell on the end. Glennyth was often summoned in the dark of night, so she'd arranged the bell as a signal that she was needed.

"Enter," Glennyth called.

Nicola opened the door and slipped inside.

Immediately a miasma of scents assaulted her; herbs, some sweet, some pungent, filled the dwelling. They hung from the rafters, covered every inch of the walls and overflowed from baskets on the dirt floor. Nicola wondered how anyone could grow used to such a smothering atmosphere of scents. Of course, it was probably more pleasant than the reek of dung, garbage and cooking smells that permeated most village houses.

Glennyth knelt by the fire, grinding some greenish paste in bowl. She looked at Nicola questioningly. "Lady, what do you here?"

"I heard Fawkes has been to see you."

Glennyth's mouth quirked slightly. "You mean your new husband?"

"Aye."

Glennyth sat back and regarded Nicola shrewdly. "He did come here. Asking me questions about the babe that died."

"What did you tell him?"

"The truth, of course."

Nicola exhaled sharply. Her heart seemed to stop. "Why would you do such a thing?"

"Don't be alarmed. I merely answered his questions. He asked how the babe died and I told him it was born dead, strangled by the birthing cord."

Nicola sank on the stool near the fire. "Oh, thank the saints. I thought you meant you'd told him about Simon."

"And if I had, would that be such a calamity? Simon is de Cressy's son."

"That has no bearing on the matter. Fawkes has already heard the babe was born dead, and I have confirmed it. If I suddenly change my story and produce a living child, a child who looks nothing like him, he'll never believe he's the father. I should have told him when he first asked me. Then there might have been a chance he would accept Simon."

"Why didn't you?"

"When he brought up the matter, we scarce knew each other, except in bed. And the way he questioned me, the harshness of his tone, I felt like he already believed the worst of me. The man has been cold and wary from the very moment he walked into the castle yard and claimed Valmar."

Not true, a niggling voice reminded her. She remembered Fawkes's sweet, boyish manner as he gave her the ring at the wedding feast. But surely that had been another man. That shy, seemingly adoring knight clearly wasn't the real Fawkes de Cressy.

"The man I wed is nothing like the one who fathered Simon. The horror and violence of warfare have changed him. He is hard and bitter now, and suspicious of everyone. I might have trusted Simon's life to the Fawkes of the past. But I can't risk my darling son's life to the cold, suspicious stranger his father has become."

Glennyth nodded thoughtfully. "De Cressy does seem angry and dissatisfied. But perhaps he acts that way because he fears being found weak. He's seized control of Valmar, but he doesn't feel worthy of what he's won. He fears to make a misstep and look foolish and unfit to be a lord."

"He *is not* fit!" Nicola stood, overcome by her resentment. "I can already tell he knows next to nothing about running a castle or overseeing a demesne. All he knows is warfare. How to win a territory in battle, but not how to rule it. He's not as arrogant as Mortimer was. And he certainly isn't as lazy and stupid. But at least Mortimer came from a noble background and knew what was expected of him, even if he failed to do it. As far as I can tell, Fawkes is the son of some hired knight and is far over his head in this thing, yet too proud to admit it. And so, he is suspicious and wary of everyone and willing to listen to any foul gossip he hears."

"I am glad we agree in this. You pretend you don't understand this man you have wed, but I think you understand him very well. He needs the very thing you can give him. You can teach him how to be lord. You can show him how to rule Valmar."

Nicola exhaled in disgust. "You think he will listen to me? He thinks I'm some evil creature who killed her own child!"

"I doubt he really believes that. Give him time. Go about your duties as chatelaine. Show him what needs to be done. He's obviously sharp-witted and shrewd. Otherwise he'd never have risen so high. Eventually he will see you for what you are and forget the foolish rumors. And then when you have won his trust, you can tell him about Simon, and all will be well."

"But what about…"

"About what?"

Another spasm of anguish twisted through Nicola. She didn't want to speak of these things with Glennyth. But the healer seemed a more likely source of advice than Old Emma, despite the servant's claims.

She turned away and spoke quietly. "There is fire between Fawkes and me. There was the first time, and nothing has changed. When we lay together on our wedding night, 'twas like a pot of oil poured on a blazing hearth. And yet, he left soon after, claiming he couldn't sleep in such a fine bed. The last two nights he didn't even bother coming to my bedchamber. I fear he will avoid me from now on, having done his duty."

"And you don't wish him to avoid your bed, is that it?"

Nicola grimaced. Women weren't supposed to be prey to such base desires. At least not noblewomen.

"I could give you a love charm."

"Do such things really work?"

"I sell dozens. If they didn't work, why would people continue ask for them?"

Nicola shook her head. "Given the rumors about me, I shouldn't risk doing something like that. I fear Fawkes already believes I dabble in sorcery."

"Then you will have to rely on the tools you already possess."

"Which are?"

"Your beauty. His memories of what you've already shared. The fact that he is a man, a young, virile man."

"In the meantime, while I wait, I wonder if you could make me a sleeping draught."

Glennyth lit a candle from the hearthfire and carried it into the back portion of her house, which served as her stillroom. Nicola followed the wise woman. She'd always been fascinated by Glennyth. The wise woman knew dozens of herbs and how to mix them, plus the way they should be swallowed, applied to the skin, brewed in a decoction, or otherwise ingested.

Glennyth set down the candle and cleaned off the wooden table, leaving one bowl for mixing. She went to the row of pottery jars on the shelves on the wall and selected several. She placed a fingerful of several kinds of dried herbs into the bowl, then crushed them with a stone pestle.

"What's in the sleeping draught?" Nicola asked.

"I don't give away my secrets, at least not until the time comes for me to pass them on."

"And who will you pass them on to?" Nicola fingered one of the jars on a shelf built into the wall. The strange markings inscribed on the sides meant nothing to her, although she could read and write Latin.

"Maybe I will have a daughter someday."

"But you've vowed never to wed."

"It doesn't require a husband to get with child, nor to raise one either."

Nicola thought of Simon, being raised at Mordeaux. Traveling there to see him would now be more difficult. She'd have to find some excuse, some pretext that would make a journey there believable.

Nicola sighed again, and Glennyth gave her a canny look. "Don't fret. It will give you wrinkles."

****

"What do we do today?" Reynard asked, as he and Fawkes broke their fast in the great hall.

"First, I want to explore the whole castle, inside and out. Assess any areas where there might be weakness." Fawkes took another swallow of bread spread with fresh cheese. "Then I intend to go through all the storerooms and see what sort of supplies we have in case of a siege."

"Is that really necessary? Do you think we'll have to defend the castle this summer?"

"How can I know? I have the writ from Richard. But the longer he's imprisoned, the more likely John and his supporters will try to seize power. I must be prepared for anything."

"I imagine this is also a way to keep busy and not think about Nicola."

Fawkes shot Reynard a warning look and motioned with his head to the serving girl pouring their ale. When she'd moved away, he said, "To assess supplies, I need to spend time with the steward. I hope from him I can gain a better assessment of my wife's character."

"What would you like me to do while you are so occupied?"

"Meet with FitzSaer and try to get the measure of the man. I need to know whether he truly accepts me as his lord. I can't help wondering if the tale he told me about Nicola and the babe was a ploy to set me against her."

"Why would he do that?"

"To cause trouble. He likely resents me for taking away much of his power and position as castellan. Mortimer apparently gave him free rein of the place. I'm not going to do that." Fawkes reached for another chunk of bread. "I also need your help in ascertaining the loyalties of the other Mortimer knights. Some may feel as FitzSaer does, that they've lost their position or been pushed aside by my men. If you can learn who those individuals are, maybe I can find a way to appease them and smooth their ruffled feathers."

"I find it interesting that you are so careful in your strategy in dealing with the Valmar knights, yet charge ahead blindly with Lady Nicola."

"What do you mean?"

"I mean, have you ever thought of trying to woo her, to reassure her that you're not the kind of man Mortimer was and let her know she has nothing to fear from you."

"I did that! I told her I would never strike her or abuse her physically, and that if I felt the need to punish her, I would not do so with my fists."

Reynard answered, his voice dripping irony: "How

very reassured she must be. She knows that if you ever feel the need to punish her, you'll be the very paragon of lenience."

"'Twas not like *that*! I was speaking rhetorically. I wanted her to know she doesn't have to fear I'll abuse her as Mortimer did."

Reynard shook his head. "It seems to me that if anything, you have convinced her that in some ways you are exactly like Mortimer. You act as if she is your property, a dog you must discipline, or a horse you're training for the harness. Even dealing with a page, I don't think your tone would be so harsh. Why bring up the matter of punishment at all? What do you fear she will do?"

"Betray me, of course. She's my wife now. Even if she's seen fit to take lovers in the past, she needs to know I won't tolerate it."

"Blessed Jesu, save us! Now you accuse her of adultery along with murdering her own child! 'Tis a wonder she sees fit to have anything to do with you!"

Fawkes glared furiously at Reynard. At the same time, he had the sinking feeling that his friend was right. Curse Reynard! Dealing with people came so easily to him. For Fawkes, it was more challenging. "But what if these rumors of her are true? What if—"

"What if they're not? Then you will have destroyed any hope of happiness the two of you might have had."

"But I must know the truth. If I've married a deceitful, ruthless woman, I must be aware so I can protect myself." He shot Reynard a resentful glare. "You were the one who issued dire warnings about her on my wedding night."

"I know. But I think now I reacted in haste. I was so

startled when I heard the tale, I didn't think it through. The fact is, even if she betrayed you to Mortimer, that doesn't mean Nicola wishes you ill now. Why would she? She clearly despised Mortimer and is relieved to be free of him. Perhaps if you gave her a chance, you might find she is pleased to have you as her husband."

"But what if it's true she killed my son?"

"Then you must get beyond that. Accept that Mortimer's abuse made her half-crazed. People do things under duress they regret terribly later. Besides, you can make other sons with her."

Could he? Could he ever bear to lie with Nicola if he found out she had killed an innocent babe?

Reynard stood. "I'm off to assess things with the Mortimer knights. I have better hopes for the outcome of my plan than I do for your strategy with Nicola."

Fawkes finished his meal in glum silence and went out into bailey to set out on his survey of the castle. By late morning he had walked the perimeter of the castle and thoroughly inspected the exterior. But he still needed to find out if there were any secret ways out of the castle. FitzSaer would probably know, but he was reluctant to talk to the man. Sooner or later he would have to spend time with the castellan, but he didn't want to do it today. Instead, he would find the steward and ask for his help in assessing the castle's foodstores.

At the gate, Fawkes asked if anyone had seen the steward. Someone suggested he might be in the kitchen and Fawkes headed there. As he drew near he smelled baking bread. Even though he'd already eaten, the rich, fragrant scent aroused his hunger and took him back to his days as a squire. He would wait outside the kitchen hoping to catch the eye of one of the maids who fancied him, so he could cajole a half a loaf of the heavenly manchet bread. Now that he was lord, he could go in and demand a dozen loaves if he wished. The thought soothed his mood.

He didn't find the steward, Warin, in the kitchen, although he did get a fresh loaf. As he munched on the soft, steaming bread, he decided to search for the man in the hall.

A young maidservant was cleaning off the trestle tables. She looked up and smiled at him. "Milord, how may I serve you?"

"I'm looking for the steward. Do you know where he might be?"

"He went off with milady a while ago. I expect they're in the solar. That's usually where she meets with him."

Fawkes felt a flash of jealousy, but told himself he was being foolish. The steward was scrawny and gray-haired, and old enough to be Nicola's father.

He nodded his thanks to the maidservant and sought the stairs to the west tower. Despite his examination of the rest of the castle, he'd never been to the solar. In general, it was considered women's domain.

He reached the sunlit room and paused in the doorway. The opulent chamber oozed comfort, beauty and wealth. Tall windows of greenish glass on one end let in warmth and light. The rest of the space was draped and padded and carpeted with a variety of plush materials. Sheepskin rugs with bright braided edges covered the floor. Expensive Flemish tapestries overlaid every inch of wall space. Velvet-cushioned chairs and a carved wooden table stood by the hearth. Nearby, a tall iron pricket held glossy beeswax candles. A bronze brazier shaped to look like a fire-breathing dragon was pushed back against a row of chests and coffers.

Nicola sat by the window with some sewing in her lap. The steward stood facing her. Fawkes heard the word "seed grain" and then "peas." He cleared his throat to announce his presence.

She started as she saw him, then her expression changed to the queenly mask that so intimidated him. The steward gave a nervous smile and clutched his bony hands together. "Lord de Cressy, how may I serve you?"

Fawkes started toward them, halting as he remembered his mud-caked boots. For a moment, he considered walking defiantly across the luxurious floor coverings, leaving a muddy trail in his wake. Then reason overtook him. The carpets he would be despoiling now belonged to him.

He bent to remove his boots and padded across the floor.

"Milady and I were discussing the food stores," the steward said. "I estimate we have two months worth of salted meat remaining and plenty of peas and beans from last year. But our grain supply is very low. This is always a lean time, until we get the harvest in."

"How long until harvest?" Fawkes went to the window and peered out. The glass was wavy and flawed in places. Since the solar was built on the inside of the ramparts, the view wasn't much. But in the winter these windows would allow in sunlight without also letting in the cold, and this room would be a cozy, glowing haven from the chilly gloom of the rest of the castle.

"Along the river, they've already begun harvesting," the steward answered. "I'm not certain when they will start with the outlying fields. Over by Wilford, they're always a week or so later."

"Wilford?" Fawkes turned. "Is it another village? Part of Mortimer's…my lands?"

"Aye, milord. It's smaller than Valmar, and the harvest not so rich. But their sheep clip is excellent."

Although he tried to focus on the steward's words, Fawkes was acutely aware of Nicola seated a few feet away. He turned to examine the rest of the room. On a table next to a black and white cowhide-covered chair was a chessboard, with the ivory and onyx pieces set up for a game. He immediately wondered if Nicola played. She had the face for it, giving nothing away.

He turned back to the steward. "I'm trying to assess how long we could withstand a siege."

Warin stiffened. "A siege, milord? Do you expect attack?"

"There's no immediate danger, but it's important to be prepared. What about water? Is there more than the one well, in case attackers find a way to poison the main one?"

"Nay. Only one well, but we have a cistern to collect rainwater and barrels for storage."

"What if it doesn't rain?"

Fawkes could see Warin becoming defensive. The steward threw a helpless glance at Nicola, before turning his rheumy blue eyes back to Fawkes. "Milord, I know what supplies are needed to keep Valmar fed and how to prepare for a bad harvest, although it seldom happens. But I have no experience setting aside stores to survive a siege."

Fawkes attempted to soften his voice, although he was losing patience. Warin had likely served Nicola's father, Ruald Luvencote, and Old King Henry would never have allowed Luvencote to control two fine castles like Valmar and Mordeaux if the man knew nothing of warfare. "Why don't you show me what supplies we have on hand right now."

"Of course, milord." Warin glanced at Nicola. She nodded and rose from her chair.

Fawkes stiffened. He had no desire for Nicola to come with them. After Reynard's scolding, he wanted to avoid her. He couldn't get over the gnawing sense that Reynard was right. "Milady, there's no need for you to trouble yourself over this matter."

"But Lady Nicola keeps the keys." Warin pointed to the half-dozen keys hanging from Nicola's belt. "And when it comes to foodstores, she's a better judge of what the cook will need."

Nicola clearly resented his attempt to evaluate the foodstores without her. Her gray eyes seemed even cooler and more distant than usual.

He inclined his head to her. "Very well. Please proceed."

She moved past him in a swish of skirts, trailing the delectable perfume that never failed to affect him. He was glad he had the excuse of putting his boots back on to give him a few seconds to recover his composure.

At the wedding banquet he had complimented her on her role as chatelaine of the castle. He had meant it as flattery, not realizing she truly was in charge. But that was likely the normal role of a noble lady, as any well-born knight would know. Once again, he'd been caught out by his base beginnings.

****

"Most of the perishable foodstores are kept in the souterrain below the kitchen," Nicola explained as they walked out into the yard, Warin trailing behind. "The kitchen itself was built a distance away from the keep. I know it seems inconvenient, but my grandfather once saw a kitchen fire spread through a manor house and destroy everything. He was determined that would never happen at Valmar."

"But the keep is built of stone and mortar. Would that not stop a fire?" Fawkes asked.

"Most likely. But by the time the keep was rebuilt in stone, I'm sure my father was concerned with other matters than moving the kitchen."

All these questions, she thought irritably. Didn't he realize that foodstores and the running of the castle were properly a woman's domain?

Hopefully his interest in foodstores and supplies was only in regard to defense of the castle. Although even that troubled her. Why did he have such an urgent need to make certain the castle was ready for a siege? Did he expect Valmar to be attacked?

She thought uncomfortably of her conversation with Father FitzAlan. If her hints to him bore fruit now it would be disastrous.

She turned to Fawkes. "Why are you so concerned about Valmar's defenses? You've scarce been here three days. I would think there would be more pressing matters than assessing the castle supplies. If you have some reason to believe we might be attacked, you must tell me. I might be able to aid you in planning for our defense."

Fawkes's dark eyes focused on her with unnerving intensity. "And how would you propose to do that, milady?"

Nicola felt her jaw tighten. *He thinks because I'm woman, I know nothing of warfare and defending a castle.* She had to glance away to hide her bitterness. "I grew up at Valmar. I know the property as well as anyone. I was also privy to many of my father's strategy sessions. I even went to London with him for Richard's coronation. There I was exposed to many conversations between him and other barons, and many of their discussions were of warfare."

She would not mention her father had taken her to London primarily to dangle her and her dowry before the unmarried lords as a rich prize they might win if they agreed to support Richard.

"Is that where you first encountered Mortimer?" Fawkes asked. "In London?"

"Nay. But apparently he heard of the wealth of my father's lands and when my father died, Mortimer asked Richard for the honor of Valmar and Mordeaux. Marrying me was an afterthought, as you well know."

By sounding so sour and embittered, she confirmed what Fawkes already thought of her. She must try not to make her disgust for Mortimer so obvious. As suspicious as Fawkes was, he probably saw her words as further proof she hated Mortimer enough to kill the babe meant to be his heir.

As they went out in the yard and headed toward the kitchen, she grew despondent. It didn't seem fair she had the misfortune of marrying not one man who loathed her, but two. And it was much worse this time. Mortimer she could despise unreservedly. But this man... God help her, as much as Fawkes sometimes infuriated her, her desire for him continually overrode her resentment.

"We'll need a torch," she said as they neared the steps leading to the root cellar.

Warin turned to leave. "I'll fetch one."

"Nay, I'll do it." As Fawkes strode off, Nicola could not help perusing his slim-hipped, long-legged form. He reminded her of Gimlyn, the gray-and-white tomcat who prowled the upper portions of the castle, hunting for mice. Both cat and man moved with a lithe agility that belied their size and physical power. She sometimes held Gimlyn in her lap and petted his soft fur. What would it be like to do that with Fawkes? To stroke his glossy hair and caress his rough, whisker-darkened jaw?

She recalled their wedding night. His impressive torso looming over her, his wide shoulders like angel's wings, his heavily muscled chest shadowed with coarse black hair. His flat sleek belly—

"What do you think of the new lord, milady?" Warin's croaky voice shattered her reverie.

She turned to the steward. "He seems to know what he's about when it comes to castle defenses. With him commanding the garrison, and all the experienced knights he's brought with him, we're likely as safe as it's possible to be in these turbulent times."

Warin nodded. "I'm certain that's true. Although having all those knights to feed will put a strain our foodstores, at least until the harvest is in and the grain milled. And I imagine there will be stresses of a different sort as well. I doubt all of Mortimer's men are pleased to have a new man giving them orders. Some will fear being shunted aside or having their status reduced. Sir Adam in particular." Warin stroked his sparsely stubbled jaw. "It's perfectly reasonable for de Cressy to put one of his own men in charge. But what is he going to do with Adam FitzSaer? He could send him to Mordeaux, I suppose."

"I had not thought of any of this. I appreciate your keen assessment of the situation." His concerns added a new worry to her already overwhelming burden. She would be pleased to be rid of FitzSaer, but if he was sent to Mordeaux, he might cause trouble there. She did not want him anywhere near to Simon.

Fawkes returned with the torch and led the way down the stairs. When they reached the bottom, he moved aside so Nicola could get the key from her belt and open the door. Once it was open, he led the way in. Nicola and Warin followed.

Fawkes shone the torch on the many baskets, barrels and piles of vegetables. "This room holds the dried vegetables and root vegetables," Nicola said. "We still have a supply of peas and beans, but the nuts are mostly gone. For seasoning, there are a few dried herbs and crab apples left. The other apples are only good for cider this time of year. And we have few leeks and onions remaining, but we can supplement them with wild garlic. The next chamber holds the oats and sacks of flour. The unmilled grain is stored in the granary. There is little left this time of year, other than what is kept back for seed."

"This is all fine and well." Fawkes sounded impatient. "But what I need to know is, with present foodstuffs, how long could we hold out if we were attacked?"

Nicola motioned for Fawkes to shine the torch in the second chamber, so she could count the flour sacks. She thought a moment, and then said, "Perhaps a month, if we are very careful. And it means pottage and bread every day. Although we do have plenty of cheese. We made several batches a week ago, so the buttery is full. We also have plentiful eggs, at least as long as we have grain to feed the hens. But there is no dried meat or fish left this time of year. And if we were completely cut off from the village, that would mean no milk. If we were truly trapped inside the castle, we wouldn't have access to fish from the river. Or any game or game birds."

"A month." Fawkes shook his head. "The siege of Acre went on for almost two years. Although when Saladin attacked, they were able to get supplies in for a time."

"I've never heard of a siege in England lasting for more than a few months," Nicola said.

"You're probably right." Fawkes started back up the stairs. "But it doesn't hurt to be prepared for the worst."

The worst, that is all this man thinks about, he's so grim and hardened. Even she, who had suffered through the wretched years with Mortimer, even she refused to dwell under a cloud of gloom every moment. What horrors had Fawkes endured that even after winning two fine castles and all the wealth attached, he continued to have such a dismal outlook on life?

By the saints, if he would only give her a chance, she might be able to help him overcome the darkness that haunted him. She imagined him resting his head on her breast while she stroked his thick silky hair and spoke to him soothingly. Nay, that was what one did with a child, not a grown man. It was her longing for Simon that made her have these foolish thoughts.

"Is there anything else, milord?" she asked when they reached the yard. To Warin she said, "Can you think of anything?"

"Not in regard to the castle stores, milady. But certainly Lord de Cressy should meet with the reeve to discuss the crops and livestock."

Fawkes nodded. "I plan to tour the whole demesne. But this is sufficient for now."

Warin nodded back agreeably. "Milady, Lord de Cressy, I need to see about getting more hay from the village. With the addition of the mounts of your men, we now have over twice as many horses to feed."

"While you're doing that, consider how much hay and other fodder we would need to store to make it through a month-long siege," Fawkes said.

When Fawkes turned back to face her, Nicola said, "I also have tasks that I need to see to."

Fawkes nodded, his eyes as dark as obsidian. "Then you should see to them. Although I'm certain I will think of things I need to ask you later."

"Such as what…milord?" She tried not to sound snippy, but she was losing patience.

"About the castle, and all that goes into the running of things. Unlike you, I was not trained for this."

"You would not be. These are not matters men concern themselves with. At least not knights."

"Even so, I would like to know as much as possible about Valmar."

"So you can defend it?"

"Aye, and so I can rule it wisely. I want Valmar, Mordeaux and the adjoining manors to prosper."

"So do I, milord."

"I like to think we have the same goals."

Speaking with this man was like traversing a marsh. She felt at any moment she might make a misstep and sink deep into the muck. She nodded. "I'm certain we do, milord."

Four years ago, when she'd first seen Fawkes's face, she'd thought him almost too handsome, too pretty. Now, with the scar across his cheek and a few faint lines marring his tanned skin, he was the very image of masculine beauty.

Which was part of why he was so aggravating. No matter how high-handed and insulting his behavior was, she still found him irresistible. If he asked her to go to the stables and take a tumble with him in the hay, she would not hesitate. But he would never ask such a thing. Indeed, it appeared he would not deign to touch her. Clearly, his plan was to torture her for all the horrible things he thought she'd done.

Fawkes broke off eye contact and turned away. "Good day, milady." He strode off. Her insides squeezed with a longing so fierce she could scarce breathe.

Chapter Ten

If he did not get away from that woman, he would go mad. She was too beguiling. Too beautiful. No matter how he sought to distract himself by focusing on practical matters, his body never forgot her nearness.

Fawkes doused the torch in the water trough by the stables and left it inside the stable door. The pent-up tension made him feel as if he would explode. In addition to what Nicola did to him, he wasn't used to the tedious life of a lord. Meetings, tallies, account books—God's bones, he wasn't cut out for this! He wasn't a clerk; he was a warrior!

Nay. He was a lord now, which meant he must learn about such things. But he refused to deal with them every moment of the day. Men like Warin did that.

He paused and looked up at the sky. As blue as a robin's egg, with nary a cloud. A fine day and he was wasting it poking around in root cellars and storage chambers. He longed to be out riding. Tomorrow he would do so. He would take a tour of his properties. But that didn't help him today. He felt trapped and confined. Part of it was the awareness that Nicola was so close, and yet so untouchable. Another reason for his restlessness was the way his new responsibilities weighed on him. He could almost feel the massive castle walls pressing down on him, reminding him of the burdens of his new life. Somehow he had to find an escape, at least for a time.

He strode to the stairs leading to the castle's eastern ramparts and climbed them with brisk, rapid steps. As he neared the top, he felt a twinge of apprehension. He had no desire to encounter FitzSaer. But surely this time of day there would be no reason for the castellan to be up on the tower wall.

Reaching the top, he walked the parapet, surveying the area around the castle on all sides. On the side away from the village and the river, he saw sheep grazing, their fleeces creamy white against the green pasture. Nearer the castle was the practice ground, rutted with pathways worn into the grass by men and horses. He squinted, noting the quintain pole listed to one side and the archery targets were losing their stuffing. It didn't appear Mortimer's knights had spent much time practicing their battle skills. That would have to change. If a knight didn't drill continually, he lost his edge.

That thought spurred another. He left the wall and returned to the castle yard, heading for the workshop near the armory. He hoped Old Thomas was still the castle carpenter. The man could make or repair almost anything. He didn't recall seeing Old Thomas at the wedding or the banquet afterwards, but then he'd been so preoccupied with Nicola he'd scarce paid attention to anyone else.

His jaw clenched at his foolishness. As the new lord, he should have made it a point to meet with all of Valmar's craftsmen and skilled laborers as soon as he could. They were as important to the security of the castle as the garrison.

As he'd hoped, Old Thomas was at his workbench. The man's fair hair was almost all silver now and his shoulders slightly stooped, but he still looked fit and capable. "Old Thomas," he called.

"Fawkes. Or should I say milord?" The carpenter stood and greeted him.

"Fawkes will do. It makes me feel like a worthless dolt to have everyone call me milord all the time."

Old Thomas smiled, showing that his teeth were still good. "What can I do for you...Fawkes?"

"I was looking over the practice field and noted that the practice targets and quintain need some attention. Mortimer doesn't seem to have cared if his men kept up their skills."

"I will see to it. Indeed, I'm pleased to have work more interesting than building barrels and repairing tools."

"Good. I'll get a couple of the squires to bring you the targets. As for the quintain, I think the arm needs to be replaced. It's listing a bit, so we may need to reinforce the base." Fawkes turned to go. He had another thought. "Are there other things Mortimer ignored that you think should be repaired?"

"Not that I can think of. You might look over the armory and the stables. Lady Nicola saw to it that most of the other aspects of the castle were well maintained. She is a fine chatelaine, mil—Fawkes."

"So it would seem." He clenched his jaw.

"She's been supervising the castle for years. After her mother died, her father didn't want to concern himself with what he considered woman's business. Lady Nicola and Warin have managed things since then. I suspect Lady Luvencote knew her husband would not remarry if something happened to her, so she made certain her daughter knew how to run the place in her stead."

Fawkes nodded to the carpenter. "I will do as you

suggest and look over the armory and stables and the other aspects of the castle that are a man's domain."

"Very good...Fawkes."

Fawkes immediately headed to the armory. There he encountered Reynard talking to a grizzled knight.

"Fawkes," Reynard began. "This is Philip de Dreux. He served Mortimer, and before him, Mortimer's father."

Philip dipped his head courteously, but his deep-set eyes were wary. "Milord."

Fawkes's first thought was to tell the man to call him Fawkes, as he had Old Thomas. Then he thought better of it. He needed all the authority he could muster when it came to dealing with Mortimer's sworn knights. Instead he said, "I'm pleased to come here and find such a fit, well-disciplined garrison."

The man quirked an eyebrow skeptically at the term *well-disciplined*. "If you find us to be competent, it has naught to do with Mortimer. He let FitzSaer give the orders and see to any training that was done."

"And *was* there any training? The practice field seems all but abandoned."

"A few of us older knights drilled the squires in the basics of fighting, but it was mostly here in the castle yard. Not much was done while mounted. And no archery training. I suppose Mortimer thought we could rely on the villagers, who have the skill from hunting."

"I'm having the targets replaced," Fawkes said. "And the quintain repaired. If the men's riding skills are rusty, we must remedy that immediately. Have you some authority over the younger men? Or is it FitzSaer they look up to?"

Philip gave him that look again, as if the question was ridiculous. "FitzSaer? Nay, he believes himself above mingling with us mere fighting men."

"But he is the castellan," Reynard said. "He's the one who would give orders in the event the castle was attacked."

"Orders, aye, he's good at that." Philip's mouth twitched in scorn.

"Then it should be you who tells the men they will have their first lesson in mounted warfare in a candle-hour," Fawkes said. "Tell them to assemble in at the practice area behind the castle."

"Do you want them to be mounted?" Philip asked.

"Not for this first session. This one will be a demonstration only."

"They will be there," Philip said.

Fawkes left the armory. Reynard followed. As they walked to the stables, Reynard asked. "What does that mean—a demonstration?"

"You and I will joust and show the men how it's done."

"What about FitzSaer?"

"What about him?"

"If you set up this demonstration without consulting him, he may feel slighted. He's still officially the castellan here. At least until you replace him."

"Which is something I need to do quickly. It's bad enough that he tried to poison my mind regarding Nicola. Now I find out he's nearly as lazy and worthless as Mortimer was. I intend relieve him of his command as soon as I can manage it."

"And then what? If he stays here at Valmar, he might cause trouble."

"I'll send him to Mordeaux."

"But Gilbert de Vescy is castellan there, and from

what I saw when we were there, he's a good one. It seems unfair to relieve him of his post and have FitzSaer take his place."

"I'm not going make FitzSaer castellan of Mordeaux. I'm simply sending him there to get him out of my sight."

"Is that wise? He strikes me as the vindictive sort."

"What can he do? He has no claim to authority other than what Mortimer gave him, and Mortimer is dead."

"It seems unwise to make an enemy of him."

Fawkes halted and glared at his captain. "You agree I should remove him, but when I say I intend to, you bring up all sorts of objections. Must you always seek to make my life difficult?"

Reynard shrugged. "I'm merely anticipating problems and thinking ahead."

Fawkes started walking again. "Three days ago, my circumstances seemed like a dream come true. Now everything is so complicated and frustrating."

Reynard gave him a poke in the arm. "You'll sort everything out in time. If you could come to some agreement with Nicola, I vow your life would look much rosier. You might even see your circumstances for what they are. Not a dream perhaps, but great good fortune nonetheless."

"Speaking of which, have you learned anything regarding Nicola?"

"Most of the castle folk all but think she walks on water."

Fawkes nodded. "Old Thomas the carpenter is the same. The castle folk might be so loyal they wouldn't change their opinion of her no matter what she did. Even if they knew she killed the babe, they might think it was justified. Especially if they knew how the babe was begat. Which is another question I'd like an answer to. Do you think the castle folk know that Mortimer sent me to Nicola to get her with child?"

"I'm certain most people suspect Mortimer didn't impregnate his wife, given his preference for bed partners. But I doubt they know Mortimer sent you to her bed. Other than Nicola's elderly maidservant, that is. And the midwife."

"The cursed midwife. She knew who I was before we even talked of the matter."

"Ah, the cursed midwife." Reynard smiled.

Fawkes looked at Reynard sharply. "If I were you, I would get Glennyth the Healer out of your mind. She's far too shrewd and cunning."

"Exactly why she entices me. I'm so successful with the wenches that it's no longer a challenge. I'm pleased to meet one who it will take some effort."

"You always were an arrogant prick," Fawkes muttered.

Reynard laughed.

****

What was that terrible racket? Nicola rushed out of the weaving shed and looked around, trying to decide where the noise was coming from. Shouts and whistles echoed in the distance, and the castle yard was near deserted.

She hurried to the gate and shouted up to the guard in the tower. "What is it? Are we being attacked?"

"It's Lord Fawkes and his captain putting on a display."

"Where?"

"On the practice field."

Nicola hurried across the bailey and climbed the stairs to the ramparts. She made her way around the wall to the rear of the castle and looked out. On the worn, rutted practice field, two knights garbed in full armor rode toward each other carrying heavy lances. Along the edge of the field, several dozen men were lined up, watching.

Nicola held her breath as the two horses raced forward. Before they met, the men's lances collided. It made a thunderous sound, but neither man was unhorsed. They pulled in their mounts and circled around for another go at each other.

"Are they mad?" Nicola muttered to herself.

She focused on the knight on the chestnut charger, who was clearly Fawkes. His horse's hooves dug into the ground, scattering clots of earth and grass. Beneath the glossy brown coat, the animal's muscles bunched and stretched in sleek rhythm. Fawkes's mail glinted in the sunlight and his lance thrust forward like a streak of light. Horse and man and weapon moved in perfect deadly harmony, Nicola felt a surge of exhilaration.

Her elation turned to apprehension as the two knights neared each other. A moment before they met, Fawkes leaned in hard and his lance struck Reynard's lance from the side. Reynard's weapon flew from his hand and he tumbled from his horse.

Fawkes circled around, as if he meant to charge. Reynard scrambled to his feet and drew his sword. Nicola watched disbelieving as Fawkes raced his mount directly at Reynard. At the last moment he turned and the lance pierced empty air instead of solid flesh.

Nicola let out a gasp of relief. She hadn't really believed Fawkes would run down his own man. But he'd come so close. What an incredible display of skill and strength and lightning quick reflexes. It took her breath away.

Fawkes circled around to where Reynard stood. He dismounted and a squire rushed up to take the reins of his lathered destrier. Both men pulled off their helmets and cradled them under their arms as they walked toward the line of spectators. The men milled around, cheering. Fawkes raised his hand and silenced them, then spoke.

Nicola couldn't hear what he was saying, but from his gestures he appeared to be explaining details of the jousting match. Nicola watched him, her chest tight with longing. He cut such a striking figure, with his raven-black hair and tall, broad-shouldered physique. Her husband was a heroic figure, a knight among knights. The awareness tormented her. Would he ever return to her bed? Or now, having done his duty, would he seek satisfaction elsewhere, in order to scorn and punish her?

****

"My lord." FitzSaer approached as Fawkes entered the gate. "That was an awesome display. I've never seen the like."

Fawkes gave the castellan a curt nod. Once they were out of his earshot, he said to Reynard, "Now he seeks to flatter me. Only days ago he was whispering dark tales about my wife."

Despite his bitter words, Fawkes had to admit his mood had lifted substantially. It had felt good to challenge himself, to test his strength and skill against another man's. He was soaked with sweat and his muscles throbbed with a pleasant sort of soreness. Best of all, much of the unbearable tension had left him. But he could hardly risk his neck and Reynard's like this every day. He would have to find some other sort of release for his frustrations.

As they moved through the bailey, he found himself looking around for Nicola. The next moment he cursed himself. As hard as he tried to banish her from his thoughts, she was always there. To Reynard he said, "Let's get this blasted armor off."

They went to the armory and helped each other remove their long mail shirts, then hung them on pegs on the wall, along with their shields and gauntlets. Fawkes pulled open the padded gambeson he wore under his mail and flapped it to cool himself.

"Tomorrow I'm going to take a tour of my properties. Visit Mordeaux and Rosebrook and then this place called Wilford."

"Maybe visiting Mordeaux will help you decide how to handle FitzSaer."

"Perhaps it will. Now if I could only find a means of dealing with my wife." Fawkes let out a sigh. "At least this trip will temporarily free me from having to see her maddeningly beautiful face every time I turn around."

Chapter Eleven

The next morning Nicola was headed toward the kitchen to talk to Agelwulf about the evening meal, when she saw Fawkes and several other knights mounted up and on the verge of leaving the castle. "Fawkes!" she called.

Fawkes turned his horse.

Resisting the urge to run, she approached. "Where are you going…milord?"

"I'm going to tour the properties of the demesne I haven't seen yet. I also plan to stop at Mordeaux."

"When will you be back?"

"We'll likely spend the night at Mordeaux and return tomorrow."

Nicola felt a pang of longing. If only she could think of some reason to go with him. It had been weeks since she'd seen Simon.

She could see Fawkes was growing impatient. Unable to think of anything else, she said, "Will you be back for the evening meal tomorrow?"

"I will."

He watched her, his onyx eyes unreadable. She took a deep breath. "Fare thee well, milord."

He nodded curtly, then turned his horse and continued out the gate. Six mounted knights followed him.

Nicola watched him go, feeling resentful. Fawkes

could go to Mordeaux any time he wished, while she had to make elaborate plans ahead of time. And what was he doing at Mordeaux? How would it affect Simon? Somehow she would have to find out.

****

"Jesu, you are a rich man, Fawkes," Reynard said, as they rode through the countryside of golden grain fields bordered with strips of brilliant green pastureland. "I had no idea the demesne was so vast, your holdings so fertile."

"Grain in the field is not flour in the storehouse," Fawkes reminded him. "Until the harvest is actually reaped, I cannot count on it."

"But it's not merely the thick stands of barley, millet, and wheat. I'm thinking of the orchards down by the river, so heavy with apples that you can almost hear the trees groaning with the weight. And the hay fields everywhere, promising excellent forage for livestock over the winter. Nearly every family seems to have chickens and a goat or cow, and that bunch of pigs we saw rooting in the forest will make for plentiful bacon and ham this winter."

Fawkes had to admit he'd been astounded by the plenty all around them. On their visit to Wilford they'd seen two mills—one for grinding grain and one for fulling cloth, as well as an alehouse, a chapel and a cluster of neatly kept houses. The sunburned, buxom goodwives of Wilford had welcomed them with fresh-brewed ale and hot bread spread with creamy butter and golden honey. The children of the village looked well fed and healthy, and their livestock was also in fine condition. Then they'd gone to Mordeaux and found the area around it to be equally prosperous, and the castle in excellent order.

"Aye, I can have no complaints about how my holdings have been managed," Fawkes said. "I'd feared with Mortimer in control, the demesne might be neglected. But the area has obviously prospered."

He inhaled deeply, enjoying the fresh scent of new-mown hay. On either side of the trackway, huge haystacks rose above the stubbled fields where crows and magpies were busy picking insects from among the gleanings. Overhead, a goshawk circled, searching for mice or voles in the newly disturbed landscape. From behind him, Osbert the reeve called, "Milord, do we go back through the village? It would be pleasant to sit in Maude's ale yard and rest for a time."

Fawkes turned to look at the thick-bodied reeve. The man's face was bright red and he was sweating profusely.

"You haven't made an official visit to the village yet." Reynard said.

Fawkes nodded. "This seems as good a time as any."

They approached Valmar by way of the river. The smooth surface of the millpond glittered in the bright sunlight like polished steel, and as they neared the mill, a man came out to greet them. He had lank ruddy hair and whiskers, a pointed nose and currant-black eyes. "Milord, I'm Ethelbert, the miller." He glanced up at the cloudless blue sky. "It's very hot, sir. You must be thirsty. Can I have my wife fetch you a drink of buttermilk?"

"We are headed to Maude's ale yard. But thank you, Ethelbert, for the offer," Osbert called from his mule. Now that they were in his home territory, the reeve seemed to sit up straighter and not droop so much in the heat.

The miller gave the reeve a peevish look and then

stepped forward to stand at Fawkes's stirrup. "Are you going to hold manor court soon, milord? Lady Nicola always held it in conjunction with the Lammas celebration."

Manor court? Another responsibility he had not considered. "I'll consider doing so." Fawkes urged the destrier away from the miller.

As they left the river behind, Fawkes guided his horse near to Osbert's mule. "Did my wife really hold manor court?"

"Indeed, she did," the reeve answered.

"And the people accepted her judgments?"

"Since her mother died ten years ago, Lady Nicola has been mistress of Valmar. Besides, there was no one else to see to things. Mortimer was piss-eyed with drink most of the time and never troubled himself with anything happening in the village."

His wife had done it all: managing the castle, holding manor court, overseeing a vast and prosperous demesne. Nicola seemed to be a part of the very heart of Valmar and the countryside surrounding it. It was unnerving. If he ever opposed her, he suspected almost everyone would side with her.

They reached the village. At the first dwelling a young woman with yellow braids flapped her apron to shoo a gaggle of geese away from a flush-faced toddler playing in the dirt. Seeing Fawkes and his escort, she picked up the toddler. The boy shrieked and squirmed as they passed, but the woman smiled at them.

"That Avisa. Her husband's the smith," Osbert said. "He has his shop down by the river."

Nearby, another woman sat cross-legged in front of her hut, shelling peas. She paused and wiped her brow, then hastily dumped her apron full of peas into a bowl and stood to greet them. "Welcome, milord," she said, fussing awkwardly with the strands of dark gold hair creeping from under her sweat-stained linen coif.

Fawkes nodded to her.

"And that's Hawise, widowed these past five years," Osbert said, when they had moved out of earshot. "Her husband died from an ax wound that putrefied."

"Ax wound?" Fawkes asked.

The reeve shook his head. "Not in battle. I think he was chopping wood and the ax handle slipped and struck him in the foot."

They continued on, the reeve introducing people and telling Fawkes a little about them. Finally they reached the aleyard and were seated at a table in the shade of a huge oak. Fawkes raised his brimming pewter cup and took a swallow of the rich, yeasty ale. He smacked his lips in satisfaction. Nowhere else but England did they brew this beverage to such perfection.

"Manor court is traditionally held at the Lammas celebration, which is only a few days away," Osbert said. "Of course, there are other festivities you will be expected to take part in, milord."

"Such as?" Fawkes asked.

"Nothing too onerous, I assure you." Osbert stood. "In fact, I need to speak to some of the villagers regarding the celebration. Are you content to stay here for a short while, milord?"

Fawkes nodded.

"After what we've seen the last two days, you should be content," Reynard said after Osbert had left them. "Yet I sense there are things worrying you."

"I'm still trying to get used to my new

circumstances. Nothing is the way I expected. I came to Valmar thinking to rescue this helpless damsel, imprisoned and abused by her cruel husband. Instead, I discover Lady Nicola does not need rescuing. That she has somehow managed to reduce Mortimer to a worthless tosspot, and, at the same time maintain a rich and profitable estate. Furthermore, from what you say, except for a few sour-minded servants who would find fault with any mistress, Nicola appears to be well-liked and respected by almost everyone at the castle."

"These are all excellent things, are they not?"

"As long as Nicola and my objectives are the same, then, yea, it is excellent. But if Nicola ever decides to undermine or defy me, I dread what would happen. Other than my men, I believe almost everyone here would take her side."

"Then it's clear you must learn to work with Nicola."

"But it makes me uneasy to think she has so much power. I'm already in thrall to her beauty and allure. Now I must accept I am the weaker partner in our marriage in every other way as well."

"Is that why you still refuse to share her bed?"

"She has such a potent effect on me. Until I know for certain I can trust her, I'm loath to risk entangling myself even more."

They stayed a while longer, then rode back to the castle. As they dismounted Nicola appeared. "Milord, if I might speak with you."

Fawkes instantly tensed. "Is something wrong? Did something happen while I was gone?"

"Nay. Nothing is amiss. Can you come to the solar?"

"Why not speak to me here?"

Nicola glanced around the crowded yard. "I would like a bit of privacy, milord."

"Very well. Let me wash off the traveling dust and I'll meet you there."

"Thank you," she said.

"I wonder what that is all about," Reynard said after she left.

"I'm half afraid to find out."

"Perhaps she means to seduce you."

Fawkes shot his friend an incredulous look. Although he supposed the idea was not impossible. Perhaps Nicola could not forget the incredible pleasure they'd experienced on their wedding night any more than he could.

The thought tantalized him as he washed at the cistern. He'd vowed not to bed Nicola until he was more certain of her. But if they were alone and she gave any hint of wanting him, he wouldn't be able to resist. An image filled his mind, of himself and Nicola, naked and entwined on the thick sheepskin rug on the solar floor.

He shook his head to banish the bedeviling thought. There were a dozen boring, tedious reasons Nicola might want to speak to him. It could have to do with food supplies or a problem with one of the servants. He should not assume anything.

He entered the castle and started up the staircase to the solar.

****

Nicola took a tiny stitch in the tunic she was making for Simon and tried to control the trembling of her hands. She worried she was making a mistake. Sir Guy had said it might only be a rumor that Fawkes meant to make FitzSaer the castellan of Mordeaux. She should probably not say anything until she knew for certain what Fawkes intended. But now it was too late; Fawkes was most likely already on his way.

She fought the urge to get up and pace. If she appeared anxious, he would immediately suspect some sinister reason for her mood. By the saints, dealing with this man wore on her. Every conversation was like a walk across a thawing pond. At any moment she expected the ice to give way and pitch her into freezing water. Closing her eyes, she took a deep breath to calm herself.

"Nicola."

She started at the sound of his voice, and opened her eyes to see Fawkes standing in the doorway of the solar. "Come in." Her voice came out breathy and strained. "Sit down." At least sitting he would seem less intimidating. Although perhaps not. His lanky body seemed too large for the chair. His dark hawk eyes were now level with hers. They bored into her, as if he would look into her soul.

"I asked you here because… It's about Adam FitzSaer. I heard you were sending him to Mordeaux." She met his gaze, waiting breathlessly. He said nothing. Forced to continue, she said, "I wouldn't presume to advise you in such matters, but it seems to me that—"

"But you do presume. You're doing so now."

She lowered her gaze and stared at the half-finished garment on her lap. She'd purchased the beautiful and expensive blue wool fabric because the color exactly matched Simon's eyes. The thought of him gave her courage.

Once again, she met Fawkes's gaze. "'Tis true these matters aren't my responsibility. But I've been here the last four years while you have not. I think I'm a better judge of FitzSaer's abilities than you are."

****

A muscle twitched in Fawkes's jaw. "I suppose since you command everyone else at Valmar, you think you can tell me what to do as well."

"Of course I don't think that! I'm only saying I have knowledge of FitzSaer that you may not be privy to!"

"I see. And what exactly has FitzSaer done to win your loyalty?" Why was Nicola defending FitzSaer? The man had done everything he could to ruin her reputation.

Nicola lowered her gaze, and he could sense she was thinking hard. She obviously hadn't put much thought into her argument for keeping FitzSaer on. Did she really think she had so much power over him that she had only to suggest something and he would listen? Once that might have been true, but he refused to be that weak and foolish now.

She finally looked up at him, her gray eyes flashing silver. "Surely you can see Valmar is thriving because of FitzSaer. Mortimer did little more than drink and take up space in the hall. It was FitzSaer who actually saw to the defense and running of the castle."

Fawkes gave a snort of disgust. "If Valmar is prosperous, it's because of *you,* not FitzSaer. As for the security of the castle—can you think of an instance when Valmar was ever under threat? Not counting when I arrived here, of course."

"Nay. But that's because Valmar has a reputation as a formidable fortress that would not be easy to attack."

"A reputation that was built by your father and well in place when FitzSaer arrived. I stand by my assessment of the man. He's made no effort to see that the garrison knights keep up their skills. He's done nothing to prepare

Valmar for a siege, should it come. All he's done is maintain what your father already put in place."

She opened her mouth to respond, then closed it again. He sat back, wondering what she would say next. Everything he said was true, and she knew it. Which meant Nicola had some ulterior motive for not wanting FitzSaer sent away. Was it possible they were lovers? He could not see it. FitzSaer clearly disliked Nicola. But if it wasn't that, then *what* was the connection between them?

"If you want to be rid of Sir Adam, it is certainly within your rights to do so. But if he is such a poor castellan, why inflict him on Mordeaux? You know as well as I that if an enemy were to seize control of Mordeaux Castle, they would have the perfect base from which to attack Valmar. The current castellan at Mordeaux, Gilbert de Vescy, was raised to that position by my father. Although I haven't been to Mordeaux recently, I've heard nothing to suggest De Vescy's competence has declined. So what is the point of replacing a good commander with a mediocre one? Or, do you mean to bring De Vescy here?"

She looked as if the idea of having De Vescy come to Valmar displeased her. Why? What was he missing? "I'll make you a bargain, Nicola. I won't interfere in the running of the household, if you will cease meddling in issues regarding the defense of the castle. We should both keep to the areas in which we have expertise."

Her expression remained troubled, but her words were placating. "Of course, milord. I'm sorry to have questioned your decision. I'm certain you're trying to do what is best for all involved. But I do ask that if you make changes like this, you give me some warning."

"Why do you need warning? What difference does it

make to you who is castellan here, or at Mordeaux?"

"I care not what you do with FitzSaer. But Gilbert de Vescy...his wife is a childhood friend of mine. I don't want to see her life disrupted. Or that of her children either."

So this was what was bothering her. Why hadn't she mentioned this childhood friendship when she first brought up the matter? Did she see him as such a fiend she believed he would not consider her feelings when making his plans?

The thought made him resentful, but then he realized she likely had good reasons for her doubts. In many of their interactions, he'd been indifferent to her feelings. He'd coldly interrogated her on their wedding night and even mentioned disciplining her. No wonder she didn't trust him enough to ask him for things outright, but constantly matched wits with him.

His anger softened, and he began to regret he'd spoken so sharply. As he was trying to think of a way to make it up to her, he noticed the blue fabric in her lap. It looked like she was sewing a child's garment.

"Who's that for? The small tunic in your lap?"

She stiffened. A simple question, and yet it immediately put her on alert.

"It's for Hilary de Vescy's son."

The fabric looked costly. Not the sort of thing usually made into a child's garment. Perhaps it was a scrap left over from one of her gowns. But why use it to make a child's tunic? Why not gift the fabric to Lady Hilary?

"How old is the boy?"

Again, she hesitated. He could not credit it. Why did the discussion of her friend's child alarm her?

"Near four years, I think."

He stared at her, disbelieving. If there was one thing he knew about women, it was that they paid attention to details, especially those involving children. If this was her friend's child, she undoubtedly knew the very month of his birth. Once again, her response seemed false. She had to be concealing something from him.

This was why he didn't trust her. Because she continually lied to him. Even about the most trivial details!

Or were they trivial? Her concern about De Vescy losing his place. Her worries for his wife, Hilary, her good friend. And now the lie about Hilary's son. There was a mystery here, one he definitely needed to investigate further.

But not now. Right now he needed to be away from this woman. He couldn't think clearly in her presence. Nay, in her presence he didn't *want* to think. He wanted to give into his desire and yield to his longing for her. The attraction was marrow deep. If he let down his guard for a second, he would be undone.

He asked sharply, "Will there be anything else?"

She gazed up at him, and for a moment her beautiful eyes looked distraught. Then the cool mask slid back into place. When she spoke, her voice was brisk and emotionless. "Nay, milord."

He tore his gaze away from her. But as he rose and crossed the room, the carpet beneath his feet blurred and he once again imagined the two of them sprawled there, naked as they made love with wild abandon.

"Good day, madam." He strode rapidly from the chamber.

****

Nicola let out a sigh. Talking with Fawkes had been a waste of time. Although for a moment she'd sensed his attitude toward her softening. Then he'd noticed the tunic.

What a cunning, wary man Fawkes was, questioning and scrutinizing every detail. Clearly she should have kept the tunic well out of sight and embroidered an altar cloth or something safe. But she'd never imagined Fawkes would pay any attention to what she was sewing. Damn his hawk eyes!

And damn him for being so handsome and compellingly masculine. It was hard to match wits with him when the distraction of his hard male body and the memories it evoked scrambled her thoughts and make her say foolish things.

She glanced at the garment on her lap. "Simon, my dear one, what am I ever going to do about your father?" Would there ever come a time when she was sure enough of Fawkes to tell him the truth? And how would she ever convince him it *was* the truth? There were so many lies between them, she could scarce keep track.

Sniffing back her tears, she regained control. For Simon's sake, she must be strong. And careful. Ever so careful. Fawkes was unpredictable, dangerously so. She never knew what he might do. Even now, after that brutally tense conversation, she had no idea of his plans. Whether he would heed her request or ignore it.

She needed to warn Gilbert and Hilary what might happen. And come up with a plan in case Fawkes decided to bring them to Valmar. She'd slipped up badly when she told him Simon was the name of the baby who died. If he discovered Hilary had a son of the same name, he would be suspicious.

Simon. She was desperate to see him. But how could she, with Fawkes watching her every move? She should have gone yesterday, while Fawkes was away from the castle. It was unlikely he would leave again for awhile. Especially with the Lammas celebration coming up.

Of course! The Lammas celebration. Fawkes would be busy all day. First with manor court and then the celebration in the village. If she left at first light, she would have time to travel to Mordeaux, spend time with Simon, and get back before all the festivities were finished.

She let out a sigh of relief.

Chapter Twelve

Fawkes sat at a table under the trees holding manor court. He tried not to yawn as Ethelbert the miller complained interminably about the villagers who failed to pay him the proper amount for grinding their grain. Between complaints, the man tugged at his ginger-colored beard and glanced around, his dark gaze darting here and there.

A shrewd, avaricious man, Fawkes thought absently. No doubt he cheated the villagers when he could, and their slowness in paying was their way of getting back at him. "...and Godwit promised me two hams and a dozen cabbages," the miller whined. "I refuse to grind any more of his corn unless he pays me what he owes."

Fawkes put up his hand. "'Tis not the season for salt pork, and the cabbages aren't ripe yet. Why can't he pay you with honey or eggs or some other foodstuff?"

"'Twas ham and cabbage we agreed upon," the miller said, stubbornly.

Fawkes struck the table with his fist. "This court is not the place for these petty disputes. Settle this between the two of you."

The miller gave him a sulky look and moved off. Fawkes turned to Osbert, sitting beside him. "Did Lady Nicola really involve herself with this sort of nonsense?"

"She would hear him out, then suggest some

compromise. Same as you did."

"Jesu, she has more patience than me."

"Most women are patient. They are always waiting, for men to order their lives, for their babes to be born, for their husbands to come back from war." Osbert shrugged.

"Lady Nicola does not strike me as having the placid nature you describe," Fawkes growled. It was on the tip of his tongue to ask the steward if Nicola frequently visited the village, but he restrained himself. He didn't want the man to think he wasn't able to keep track of his wife.

Fawkes perused the next petitioner. The fellow was lean as a sapling and had squinty blue eyes and a flushed face. "I've come to make a complaint, my lord. That witch Glennyth has cursed me. She's caused my manhood to shrivel up. I can barely make water, let alone swive my wife. You've got to do something about her. She's an evil, meddlesome creature. I'm not the first man she's struck down, milord."

"I'm afraid there have been complaints about her before," Osbert confided in Fawkes's ear. "Several villagers have suggested she doesn't always use her knowledge of herbs and simples for benign purposes. There has been talk of people who've crossed her falling sick or even dying." He nodded gravely.

Fawkes motioned to the villein. "How do you know it was Glennyth who did this to you?"

"I came home one day to find her and my wife whispering together. Before she left, Glennyth gave me the evil eye. It was soon after that I discovered I could no longer…do what a man needs to do."

"What do mean by the *evil eye*?" Fawkes asked.

"Did she say something to you? Chant a spell?"

"Nay." The man looked down at the ground and shuffled his feet. "She has a way of looking at you, as if you were a loathsome sort of bug and she is about to squish you. All I'm asking for is justice. I think you should banish her from the village."

Fawkes realized he would have to pronounce some judgment, or the fellow would never leave. "I'll speak to the woman, Glennyth," he said.

The man nodded, although he looked dissatisfied. "Beware that she doesn't do something to you, milord," he finished sourly.

Other complaints and disputes followed, all insignificant matters. Fawkes had the sense the villagers simply wanted to see what sort of man he was. More than once he told the individuals involved they must find ways to work out things themselves. He wouldn't concern himself with every missing pig or every cow that trampled a vegetable patch.

At last, the line of petitioners ended. Fawkes rose stiffly. "I vow, that is thirsty work."

"Indeed, it is." Osbert grinned at him. "Why don't we go to Maude's ale yard? At least until it's time for the people to bring you gifts and for the corn queen to arrive."

"Gifts? Corn queen?" Fawkes looked at the reeve in surprise.

"The gifts are nothing much, merely small tokens to show they honor you as lord. As for the corn queen, every year a maid is chosen to represent the fertility of the harvest. In the old days, in the Saxon tradition, all the men of the village would couple with her in the newly harvested field. Then they would ritually kill her, chop her body into pieces and plow it into the ground to ensure the next year's harvest. Of course, we don't do that now."

"Jesu!" Fawkes exclaimed. "Those old Saxons were savages!"

"Not really," Osbert said, defensively. "It was all done with reverence, and it was considered an honor for the maid chosen."

Fawkes realized suddenly that Osbert was at least half Saxon, as were most of the people of Valmar. He'd best watch his tongue.

They entered the ale yard. Fawkes took a seat on the bench beside Reynard, and watched as Maude the alewife poured him a foaming tankard. "Are there any rituals involving the corn queen these days?" he asked, after taking a hearty swallow.

"Indeed there are." Reynard spoke before Osbert could respond. "The maid is decked in flowers and necklaces of braided wheat grass. Then she is given to the lord of the castle for his pleasure." A sly grin curved Reynard's mouth.

Fawkes set down the tankard with a thud and turned to Osbert. "He's jesting, isn't he?"

"No, milord." Osbert shook his head. "Although we haven't observed the tradition for several years, the people wish to revive it."

"But why?" Fawkes asked. "This year's harvest seems bountiful enough. Why do they think it's necessary to bring back what is obviously an old pagan rite?"

"You're not a man who makes his living from the earth, milord." Osbert gestured with broad, blunt-fingered hands. "Nature is fickle. One year the harvest is bountiful. The next, it fails. It doesn't hurt to remember the old ways, to propitiate the old gods."

"When will this...ceremony take place?"

"Oh, later in the day." Osbert gave a careless wave. "There's plenty of time for you to eat and drink your fill."

Fawkes exchanged a glance with Reynard and took another swallow of ale. By the Cross, this was all he needed, to be forced to take another virgin to bed, and once again have no choice in the matter! He well remembered what had happened the last time he was in these circumstances. A quick tumble, he'd thought, an easy means of winning the goodwill of his employer. Hah! That one incident, lasting little more than a candle hour, had been his downfall. He'd fallen in love with Nicola, and his life had not been the same since. But how was he to refuse this time? He didn't want to offend the villagers.

And where *was* Nicola? Taking another deep draught, he glanced around. The village women, after fussing over the food table, had retired beneath one of the oaks with their sewing and spinning, to gossip and relax. The men congregated in another area to drink ale and discuss the weather and the crops, subjects of endless fascination to men who toiled in the earth. The village children were occupied in exuberant play. The older ones had devised a game using a stuffed pig's bladder and sticks. One group batted the bladder toward the other group, which then sought to bat it back out of their territory.

The young men had gone down to the river to swim, and predictably enough, the maids had followed to watch. Fawkes imagined the young bucks showing off for their giggling, wide-eyed audience, entertaining them with fancy dives and daring acts, then making them shriek and run by splashing water at them. He well remembered those carefree days. No more, he thought resentfully. Now his life consisted of responsibility and duty, and a bewitching wife who was fast driving him to lunacy.

He looked around for Reynard and saw him beneath a tree, talking to Glennyth. Her stance was bold and the provocative expression on her face said that this was no maid to be cozened, but a grown woman who knew exactly what she wanted and was determined to get it. Perhaps this time Reynard had taken on more than he bargained for. Fawkes certainly hoped so.

His thoughts had again turned to Nicola when a woman came and asked him if he would judge the handiwork competition among the women of the village. Lady Nicola had always judged it, she said, but since she wasn't there, they wished for him to do it. She led him to a table on which were arranged a dizzying array of braided belts, embroidery, colorful pieces of woven fabrics and other sorts of needle and weaving work. As he examined the things, all he could think of was Nicola.

He chose those pieces that appeared the most pleasing to the eye. To his dismay, the women who had made the things immediately insisted he accept them as gifts. He called for Osbert to gather up everything, then started to walk off, intending to find Reynard and ask him what he made of Nicola's absence. Edith, the smith's wife, stopped him. "Milord," she said, sweetly, "the food is ready. We would like you to be the first to dine upon our humble fare."

He was led to a table groaning with food. There

were pickled eggs, fresh cheeses, griddle cakes seasoned with herbs, lampreys cooked in butter, dumplings in gravy, meat pasties, honey cakes with hazelnuts, spiced pasties and apple and blackberry tarts. As the women who had cooked all this bounty watched, he filled a wooden platter with food.

He tried to sample everything, lest he offend any of the women who prepared the repast. But he didn't care for sweets, so he ignored the tarts. He was told he must have a blackberry one as it was traditional fare for Lammas. Another woman suggested a sort of seedcake. All the women giggled, and Edith, blushing, told him that the poppy and caraway seed topping was supposed to be an aphrodisiac.

Fawkes decided he might as well take one. He would need all the help he could get for the coming ritual. Finally he stepped back from the table. "Please, if you have any mercy, you won't force me to eat anything else. I vow I'll feel like the stuffed pig's bladder the children are kicking about."

The women laughed gaily.

He went back to the table beneath the oak and ate what he could. It was all delicious, better than the food at the banquets he had attended when he served King Richard. When he couldn't eat another bite, he made his excuses and went to the midden heap behind the ale yard to relieve himself. All he could think about was Nicola. Where was she?

As he started back to the ale yard, he decided the villagers be damned, he was going to find her. Then he saw the miller and the smith coming toward him and knew he was trapped. "Milord, it's time," the smith said, grinning. "You and the corn queen will eat the first loaf and then go off together."

"Don't look so sour," the miller added. "You've not seen the corn queen yet. She's a ripe, juicy piece. Myself, I'd give my right ball for the chance to swive her."

When the girl was brought to him, Fawkes had to agree she was a beauty. Her hair was the pale hue of fresh butter. Her eyes, cornflower-blue. Her slim figure was arrayed in masses of flowers, with a chaplet of woven wheat encircling her head like a crown. But for all her fresh, blushing beauty, she did not move him.

He took his place beside her near the center of the common, and as the villagers and a few of his knights gathered around, he broke the steaming-hot loaf and took a bite, then offered some to the girl. It was maislin bread, dark, rich and chewy, unlike the refined wheat bread served at the castle. As he ate, the people cheered before stepping forward to take their own shares of bread.

The girl took his hand. "Come."

The corn queen led him to one of the finer houses near the river. He followed, trying to think how he could gracefully refuse to bed her. They entered the dwelling. Inside, the hard-packed floor had been swept clean, the walls whitewashed, all the foodstuffs and cooking things arranged neatly near the hearth. There was a plank table, a bench and two stools in the main room. As he glanced around the dim interior, thinking he should find a lamp or candle, she grabbed his hand and tried to pull him toward the ladder that led to the loft.

"Wait," he said. She was obviously nervous. Her hand felt clammy and cold in his, and the pulse in her throat was rapid. "We must talk first."

She shook her head. "They expect this." She pulled

on his hand again. When he resisted, she cried out, "Please! Let us finish the thing!"

Her words flung him back into the past, back to another virgin who waited for him to deflower her, another woman who urged him to hurry, that the thing might be finished quickly. But that woman had spoken like a queen ordering a servant. This woman sounded hysterical.

He removed her clutching fingers from his hand. "What's your name? Tell me."

"Alwen, my name's Alwen," she gasped. "Oh, please. Come to bed! Do it now!"

"Nay, I will not." He grasped her by the shoulder and shook her gently. "I don't want to do this either. I'm a Christian; I don't believe in these old pagan ways. Besides, I don't want to get a bastard on you."

All at once, she began to weep. At first, he could not tell if it was relief or disappointment. Then she began to babble. He was so kind, she said, to spare her. She had a sweetheart already and she feared he would not feel the same way about her, knowing another man had had her. Besides, she sobbed, she was not a maid anyway. Johnny had taken her down by the river and he had done it to her. It had hurt, but he promised it would get better. Was that true? Would it feel better next time?

Fawkes stared down at this lovely woman-girl, her tear-filled eyes wide and rapt as she waited for his reassurance, and almost groaned aloud. He felt like the most cynical, hardened man in creation. He wanted to tell her that her Johnny was probably a crude, stupid lout who didn't deserve her. That he would never give her any pleasure, but grunt and groan and sweat over her and get her with a babe every year until her looks were ruined. And then, once she was not so fair, he would leer after that year's corn queen and say crude things like the miller had.

Instead, he said, "Yea, it will get better."

She gave a little sigh and hugged him. He gently pushed her away. "Now, go throw your crown and your garlands upstairs on one of the pallets. I'll find a way out the back for you, and after a while I'll go out the front and make a show of adjusting my clothing and grinning like a man well-satisfied."

She hugged him again, then climbed the ladder with the agile grace of a child. Fawkes stood in the empty room and caught his breath. He was aroused. Who would not be with that exquisite young woman pressing close? But he did not regret his decision. That his own life had turned out sourly did not mean he had to crush the youthful hopes of others. Let them find out for themselves how unsatisfying love really was.

****

"Oh, Simon, you've grown so much!" Nicola felt tears prick her eyelids as she held out her arms. So quickly the time was passing. Her son was not a baby anymore.

Simon hugged her back, his bright blue eyes round and curious.

"Do you remember me?" she asked.

He nodded. "You bring sweets."

Harsh pain shafted through her. That she must buy her son's love with confections. "That's true, my darling. I bring you sweets. This time I have brought you some blackberry tarts. Do you like tarts?"

Simon nodded. She offered him the basket the Valmar cook had prepared. He took out a pastry and concentrated on eating it. Nicola looked up and met Hilary's gaze. A few years older than Nicola, Hilary had soft hazel eyes, reddish-blonde hair and a mild manner.

"He's growing so fast," Nicola choked out.

"That he is." Hilary smiled. "He talks more and more every day. Quite a chatterbox he's become."

Simon finished cramming the tart into his mouth and swallowed. He turned to Hilary. "Mama? Joanie like tarts." He nodded wisely.

"Of course, love, go fetch her," Hilary responded. "Hurry now."

As Simon rushed from the solar, little legs churning, Nicola let out a sob.

"I'm sorry," Hilary whispered. "He began calling me Mama a while ago, and I had not the heart to correct him."

Nicola nodded. "I wouldn't want him to think he doesn't have a mother." Her heart was breaking. She knew this day would come. If only she did not have to hide the truth from everyone, even her son.

"I do love him like my own." Hilary's fine-boned face suffused with tenderness. "And he is as much an angel as he looks. Most children of his age are willful and selfish, fighting over toys and such. But he is, as you see, ever generous and sunny-natured. I wish my own Joanie were half so easy to manage. I vow, she is a little tyrant. And with Simon a year younger, he gets the worst of it. I have to keep an eye on them, to see she does not bully him too much." Hilary paused in her cheerful rambling and looked at Nicola. "Now that Mortimer is dead, can't you finally tell the truth about Simon?"

Nicola stiffened. She shook her head. "I must keep his identity a secret a while longer."

"I met Lord de Cressy when he was here. He didn't seem either unkind or unreasonable. I can't think he would do anything to hurt a child, even if the child stood in the way of a son of his own inheriting in the future."

Nicola nodded. So far she'd observed nothing in Fawkes' character to suggest he would be a danger to Simon. The real trouble was between her and Fawkes. If she wanted him to not merely tolerate Simon, but accept the child as his son, she must somehow mend things between them. But how was she to do that when he would not give her a chance?

"'Tis a complicated matter. Suffice to say that my husband doesn't trust me. Until he does, I dare not trust him with Simon's future."

Simon came scampering back into the room, followed by Joanie, who had reddish blonde braids and a stubborn set to her small jaw. The two children proceeded to the basket of tarts and gleefully began stuffing themselves, purple berry juice running down their small faces and smearing their chubby fingers.

"But look at him," Hilary murmured, wistfully. "Who could behold Simon's angelic countenance and wish him ill? I don't understand, milady."

Nor do I. It had all turned out so differently than she'd anticipated. Who was to guess that the unknown squire Mortimer had sent to her bed would turn her whole life upside down? And now, four years later, he was still wreaking havoc on her peace of mind.

****

Fawkes waited a while after Alwen had left the house, then ventured out. He'd expected catcalls and rude jests, but in fact, most of the villagers were too busy to notice him. The storm he'd anticipated earlier was well on its way. The sky had become a dark mass of roiling clouds and the air felt damp and unsettled. Sudden gusts tore at the villagers' clothes as they struggled to put away the food and cover the tables and benches.

He been told that under normal circumstances there would be more drinking and merriment, and later on a bonfire would be lit and people would dance and carouse around it late into the night. But a thunderstorm might well ruin that plan. No matter what happened, Fawkes decided he was finished with the Lammas festivities. He was going back to the castle and find Nicola. Her absence in the village had gnawed at him all day.

As the first raindrops splattered cold against his face, he looked around for his knights. They all seem to have vanished. He finally spied Oliver hurrying away from the area where they'd picketed the horses. He had a wineskin in one hand and his gambeson hung open.

"Oliver!" Fawkes shouted against the fierce wind. "I'm returning to the castle."

"What the devil for?" Oliver retorted. "The storm's almost here. Why don't you find a warm, sheltered place and stay cozy until it passes?" He raised the wineskin and winked. "That's what I'm doing."

Fawkes shook his head. "I want to go back. Do you know where Reynard is?"

Oliver jerked his head toward the healer's cottage. "What do you think?"

Fawkes swore. By now, Reynard and the wise woman were probably well into their second bout of lovemaking. He headed for the horses. The rain was coming down in earnest, soaking his heavy tunic. One of the squires, Robbie, was searching out supplies from his saddle pack. The squire straightened. "Milord, I was just getting some things for Engelard."

"Where is he?" Fawkes asked.

"The shed behind the tanner's." The youth grinned. "With all three of the tanner's daughters."

He had half a mind to drag Engelard out of the shed and order him to accompany him to the castle. Then Robbie said, "By the way, Engelard said to tell you he saw Lady Nicola ride out of the castle this morning at first light. He thought you'd want to know."

Fawkes stood stunned for a moment, then strode after the squire and pulled him around. "Get Engelard!" he gritted out. "Get him now!"

His thoughts churned wildly. She'd ridden out, but hadn't come to the village. Where was she? Who was she with?

A dozen times he'd considered that she might have a lover. A dozen times he dismissed the thought. But where else could she be?

Engelard came running toward him, his clothing in considerable disarray. "I'm here, milord. What is it?"

"Lady Nicola," Fawkes said. "You saw her leave the castle?"

"I assumed she was going to the village. It didn't dawn on me until we were here a while that she wasn't around, and by then..." His voice trailed off uneasily.

"By then you were too busy futtering the tanner's daughters—all three of them!" Fawkes's voice rose in a bellow.

"I'm sorry, milord," Engelard said. "But you didn't tell us to watch Lady Nicola." As the knight regarded him uneasily, Fawkes realized what Engelard was thinking—that Nicola was cuckolding him. It was beyond awkward; it was humiliating.

Fawkes struggled to sound calm, to behave as if he was simply concerned for Nicola's welfare. "In the future, I don't want my wife riding out alone. It isn't safe. Who knows what could happen to her? She might have been set upon by brigands, anything."

"I thought she was going to the village," Engelard said. "I assumed she would be safe here."

Fawkes nodded. "Of course she would. But since she isn't here, I must look for her." He started for his horse.

"Milord?" Engelard called. "Do you want me to come?"

If there was any chance he might find Nicola with another man, he certainly didn't want the whole world to know. "That won't be necessary."

Engelard hurried off, obviously eager to be out of the rain, and away from Fawkes and his problems.

Fawkes went to his destrier, Scimitar. He'd said he was going to look for Nicola, but where the devil should he start? He could search every house in the village, sword drawn, looking for his wife. What a fool he would look like then. Besides, for all he knew, the two lovers had parted and Nicola had already returned to the castle.

There was a flash of lightning, then the low rumble of thunder. The destrier nickered uneasily. The other horses also seemed restless. Fawkes glanced up at the slate-gray sky and the advancing darkness in the west. This storm was no little squall, to pass by quickly. It would be foolish to try to ride to the castle in this. His tunic was soaked. He grabbed his saddle pack and raced toward the nearest dwelling.

As he neared it, he realized with dismay that it was

the healer's cottage. He rushed past the cottage and headed for the shed behind. He yanked open the rain-swollen door and pushed inside.

The shed was dark and close and humid, but unoccupied by either man or beast. He felt his way around and found bundles of raw wool, a small table and a heap of straw, probably for use as bedding. He put down his saddle pack, then stripped off his sodden tunic and dried himself with the hay.

Outside, the storm had worsened. There was a low rumble of thunder and the wind shrieked. He thought of the horses and wished he had managed to get them to shelter. Guilt gnawed at him. Scimitar hated storms. He swore, realizing he had no choice but to go out again.

Then he thought of Reynard, snug and comfortable in the healer's bed, and decided if he had to suffer, then his captain should also.

He retrieved his saddle pack, intent on having some wine to warm his blood before he fetched Reynard. They should be able to get the horses to the cover of the oaks that sheltered the ale yard.

Chapter Thirteen

Nicola shivered in her light summer mantle as the raindrops pelted down. If only she'd worn her fur-lined cloak. But the sky had been clear and blue when she set off that morning. Even when she left Mordeaux, the weather hadn't seemed threatening. Although she might have been too caught up in her regret at leaving Simon to notice. Now she was stuck out in the storm.

She rode on, bending low over the horse's withers, feeling the rain seep through the mantle and chill her skin. Not much farther now. The village was a blur of buildings huddled beneath the stormy sky, which glowed with an odd, sickly light. A jagged bolt of lightning flashed to her right, followed by a boom of thunder. The mare shied, forcing Nicola to cling to the saddle pommel. The castle was too far; she'd never make it. Glennyth. If she could reach the healer's cottage, she could wait out the storm there.

Nicola dug her heels into the mare's sides, urging her on. The wind tore the mantle from her head and whipped her hair around her face. At last she neared the thatched dwelling. She slid off the rain-slicked horse, grabbed the reins and staggered to the storage shed behind the house. If she could get the mare inside, she wouldn't be spooked by the storm and run away. When it cleared, she would be able to ride to the castle.

She fought the heavy door, struggling to pull it open

in the wind. Behind her, the mare whinnied. "Easy girl. We're almost there."

At last the door gave. It swung outward, nearly knocking Nicola over. She started to pull the horse into the shed, but a figure blocked the doorway. She froze at the sight of her husband. His black hair was plastered to his head, and his upper body was bare. He stared at her, his dark eyes wild in the strange light. "You," he rasped.

The intense look on his face made her want to get back on the mare and ride away, but he grabbed her by the arm. The wet reins slipped out of her hand and she careened into the shed, landing in a pile of straw. He pulled the door shut behind them and everything disappeared into darkness.

His breathing was harsh, almost labored. If she hadn't seen him, she would have thought he was ill. But she suspected it was not breathlessness that made him sound like a man with a lung wound, but powerful emotion. What was he going to do to her? Had he discovered she'd gone to Mordeaux? Did he still think she plotted against him?

When he grabbed her cloak, she nearly fell. His arms went around her and his mouth met hers. She struggled for breath, then tilted her head back to return the kiss.

Lips hot against her chilled skin. She could taste the warm sweetness of his breath, tinged with wine. Her fingers stroked his bare shoulders, feeling the smooth heat of his skin. His scent blended with the odors of wool, hay and damp that filled the shed. His mouth devoured her. She parted her lips, wanting more, the liquid fire of his mouth. He gave her his tongue briefly, a lush, satisfying taste of fulfillment, then his mouth left hers.

He fumbled with the brooch fastening her cloak. Nicola felt breathless with excitement and anticipation. *Please. Love me. Fill me. Make me yours.*

He finally got her cloak unfastened and flung it down. Then he pressed her even more tightly against his body. She could feel his jutting erection. He stroked her neck with his warm fingers, pushing the wet strands of her hair away from her jaw and neck. His lips made a shimmering foray of the sensitive skin there and teased her earlobe.

Waves of rapturous pleasure made her knees go weak. He held her up, clutching her buttocks with both hands, lifting her so the juncture of her thighs met the swollen heat of his shaft. A piercing ache shot through her, making her moan. He tried pulling at the neck of her gown, but was thwarted by the tightly woven linen. Finally he gave up and kissed her. His hard, demanding lips urged her to yield, to surrender. She kissed him back feverously.

He drew away to struggle with his own clothing. Then he reached for her, pulling at her skirts, working them upward. She helped him as he tore off her loincloth. His hard fingers fondled her wet aroused flesh. She gasped, leaning into him. A few provocative strokes. Then he was lifting her, his hands on her bottom. She grabbed his shoulders and held on.

He set her down on some sort of table. Her legs dangled over the edge as he raised her skirts to her waist. Then his fingers were on her wet center, stroking. One callused fingertip probed the entrance of her slippery sheath. Then, with a suddenness that robbed her of breath, he removed his hand and thrust into her violently.

Nothing could have prepared her for this. Not even the memory of their first coupling. Unbearable fullness, hot and alive flesh wrenching hers apart. He seemed twice the size she remembered. Closing her eyes, she took deep, even breaths.

Still, he didn't move. He was panting, his hands beneath her bottom, clutching desperately. "God," he breathed.

They were locked together, frozen. The pressure was unbearable. She wriggled, trying to ease it. He let out a deep, husky groan, the sound echoing through her. She sought to shift her thighs farther apart, to assuage the throbbing ache. Then she tilted her head up and moved her hands from his shoulders to his face. She stroked his cheek, feeling the prickle of his whiskers growing in from when he'd shaved that morning. His mouth felt smooth and soft.

She moved her hand lower, exploring. As if by knowing his body intimately, she could come to fathom what went beyond his cool, onyx eyes. His shoulders were hard and wide. His chest was silky smooth at his neck, then rough with tufts of coarse hair. His thick chest muscles tightened as she trailed her hands down to where his chest hair became a thin line.

His skin shuddered beneath her fingertips and his breathing quickened. She savored the hard, taut strength of his belly. Then, slowly, breathlessly, she brought her hand to where they were joined. So strange to have this part of him deep inside her. But it wasn't an invasion, but a joining. As if his flesh was the key that opened her. Not merely her body, but something deeper. Her being, her essence.

Her body was so eager for his. Wet, swimming with

moisture. The smell of her own arousal mingled with his sexual musk. She touched herself again, feeling the slippery opening of her sheath stretched around him. Deep inside, her womb convulsed, throbbing. Her nipples grew harder still. Her mouth watered with expectation.

When she encircled the root of his shaft with her fingers, he groaned and began to move. Her body tightened around him. He plunged into her, his hands gripping her buttocks, spreading her, opening her for his assault.

Her back arched, she thrust her hips forward, enduring the tempest of sensation. Ripples inside her became waves, great roaring torrents of pleasure. Yearning finally satisfied. Ecstasy. The table shook. The shed shook. The world shook. She clutched at him, seeking his solid strength in the storm of sensation. He thrust into her with one last wild lunge and his body stiffened. He gave a cry like the bellow of a stag before going still.

It had been like no coupling she'd ever heard of. So frenzied and violent. As if both of them had been powerless against the forces compelling them. What did it mean? Their bodies had reached a truce, a glorious, magical truce. But were they any closer to solving the rest of the conflicts between them?

****

Was he still alive? Fawkes wondered. Or had he died and gone to heaven? Nicola's lithe body in his arms. His whole being relaxed and deeply satisfied. If there was a paradise, how could it be better than this?

But there were prickling reminders of the corporeal world. He was still wearing his boots and hose, and his damp braies were bunched around his ankles. Nicola squirmed as if uncomfortable and he felt a tickle of cool moisture against his groin.

He released her and his mind slowly began to function again. He heard the rain on the roof and remembered taking shelter in the shed. The shock of seeing Nicola in the doorway. Her oval face stark white against the sleek blackness of her wet hair and the vivid crimson of her cloak. Those unforgettable eyes, as gray and pearlescent as the stormy sky.

He had not planned to do this. Some madness had come over him, and nothing had mattered but that he should possess her. He felt as if he were under some sort of spell, as if nothing was real in this place. The past, the future, neither seemed important. There was only the two of them.

At the thought, desire again built inside him. He wanted to see her, to behold the remarkable beauty that haunted his dreams.

He drew up his braies and fastened them, then went to his saddle pack and searched for his flint stone and the bundle of pitch-dipped rushes he always carried. The rushlight caught, then sputtered out. He swore and tried again. A small glow in the darkness. He looked around for a place to put the light. Somewhere secure so it would not fall into the straw and incinerate them both. He finally found a small knothole in the wall and secured the rushlight. He lit another and stuck it in the dirt floor.

She was still sitting on the table, although she had pulled down her skirts. Her braids were half undone, her eyes dazed. He walked over to her, wanting her naked, wanting to see it all. He began with her hair, starting at her temples, raking his fingers through the tangled strands, dragging out the braids and the ribbons that secured them. She sat utterly still as he smoothed her hair so it lay like a dark cloak around her shoulders.

He played with one strand, rubbing it between his fingers. How many times had he dreamed of her hair against his skin? A cool, soft river flowing over his chest. Slippery coils stroking his body. A web of silk entangling their nakedness. Unbearable, tickling rapture as the long strands brushed against him.

He exhaled deeply, then found the lacing on her gown and undid it.

****

Nicola knew a deep satisfaction as she realized he wanted her again. The wild, raw ride he'd taken her on wasn't enough. His desire thrilled her. They might not have more than this intense, breathless interlude. Soon they would return to the castle and the wall of deception and mistrust would loom between them once again.

She let him unlace her gown, sitting passive and still. She wanted him to do whatever he wished. For him to bend her body to his will and make her desire things she could never have imagined.

As Fawkes struggled with the laces, Nicola watched him, thinking how beautiful he was. His hair damp and loose around his face, framing his well-made masculine features. Relaxation had muted the sternness of his jaw, and made his mouth appear soft and sensual. For once, his fierce hawk eyes did not hunt her.

And his body. The intriguing contours of his chest—rounded muscles, dark nipples, black curling hair. The flat plane of his belly with the tantalizing arrow of hair leading downward. Down to that miraculous piece of masculine flesh.

She thought of touching him there. Mayhaps even kissing him. Then a sound outside made them both stiffen and glance at the door.

"I don't care whose horse it is, get it out of my garden!" A woman's angry shriek. The near inaudible voice of a man answering.

She met Fawkes's gaze, feeling dismay. For a time they had been held in a spell of enchantment. As if there was no one else in the world but the two of them. Now the spell was broken.

****

Fawkes felt a bitter resentment. How dare his responsibilities intrude just when he began to realize his dream? But the world out there was real, while this one…

He had no idea what the last few moments meant. A kind of madness had overtaken him, and he'd cared about nothing but his furious desire, that white-hot lust born of years of longing. Now he could not help wondering what Nicola thought of it, if she'd enjoyed what he had done to her.

The voices outside intruded again. Nicola started lacing up her gown. He sought out his tunic. Once Nicola had arranged her clothing, she shook out her mantle, smoothing the blood-red fabric. Watching her, Fawkes felt an aching regret for the magical world of sex and sensation they had shared. It was over now. Reluctantly he extinguished the rushlights. Then he pushed the door open and went out.

He blinked in the sudden brightness. The storm was over and the sky was clearing. The world was transformed to jewel-like green, glistening with wetness. He went around to the other side of the shed and saw

Nicola's white palfrey grazing in a garden a few houses away. A village woman and a knight were trying to grab the horse's trailing reins, but every time they got near, the animal shied away. Fawkes ran to help.

The garden was a slippery morass of mud. The mare maneuvered easily, but the three of them struggled to find sure footing. Fawkes almost fell twice, barely escaping landing in the black ooze. Finally, between the three of them, they were able to corner the beast. Fawkes grabbed the reins on one side, while the knight got hold of the horse's bridle on the other. As he murmured soothing words to the mare, Fawkes realized the fair-haired knight helping him was Engelard.

"Isn't this Lady Nicola's horse?" Engelard asked. "Did you ever find her?"

Fawkes nodded to both questions. Engelard would have to think what he liked.

Fawkes led the horse to the shed. He wondered how much the animal had eaten while running free. Probably enough cabbage and other succulent vegetables to give it terrible colic. "Stupid beast," he told the mare. "If you suffer from a bellyache and bloat, it's no more than you deserve."

Then he considered that his own situation was not much different. While the storm raged, he'd indulged himself in the erotic madness Nicola aroused. He wondered what price he would pay for his rash behavior.

Nicola came out of the shed looking delectable. Her already formidable beauty was heightened by her flushed glow, the unmistakable look of a woman well-tumbled. She'd given up on her braids and wore her hair loose.

Fawkes wanted to smooth it away from her face, then kiss her and hold her in his arms. But she seemed so distant and remote. "I found your horse," he said. "Can you ride?" She nodded. He led the palfrey over to her. "I'll help you up."

The horse greeted her and suddenly became docile. Fawkes dared let go of the reins so he could grasp Nicola by the waist and lift her. The fragility of her body in his arms aroused a pang of guilt. She was such a fine-boned, delicate woman. And he had ridden her like a stallion.

He settled her on the mare and handed her the reins, then looked up. Was she sore? Another arrow of guilt afflicted him. He wanted to take her down from the horse and carry her all the way to the castle.

Someone called his name, He grimaced. "I'll see you at the castle. Godspeed." He slapped the horse on the rump and watched her ride away. The graceful white horse, Nicola, in her crimson mantle, her long hair black as midnight, streaming over her shoulders. A fantasy from his dreams.

But the fantasy was over, gone with the storm. The world was returned to normal. His body felt replete, deliciously satiated. But he still did not know where his wife had been, or what she'd been doing. Nor did he have any idea if he could trust her.

He returned to the shed to fetch his saddle pack, then went around to the cottage entrance. Seeing a bell on a rope, he grabbed it and rang it loudly. When there was no response, he shouted through the wooden door, "Reynard, you lustful prick, get out here."

He shifted impatiently as he waited. He was about to go inside and drag Reynard out, when the door opened and Reynard appeared, followed by Glennyth. They were both decently dressed, and their relaxed manner suggested they had sated themselves some time ago and were lingering in the afterglow of their pleasure.

Reynard bowed low over the wise woman's hand and kissed her capable tanned fingers. She smiled, looking amused and indulgent. "Mistress Glennyth, I bid you good day. It has been a pleasure."

She nodded, her face smug with feline contentment.

"She seems an odd sort for you," Fawkes remarked when they were a few paces away.

"I found her to be a delightful change from giggling maids and frowsy kitchen wenches. You know I've always fancied experienced women."

"And is she?"

"Deliciously so. She has her own sort of magic, more subtle than the eastern dancing girl in Jaffa, but potent nonetheless." Reynard gave a satisfied sigh.

Fawkes thought of his liaison with Nicola. There had been more than a little magic in it. Dark, dangerous magic.

"What of you?" Reynard asked. "Did you find the corn maid to your liking?"

"What? Oh, the corn maid. She started babbling about her sweetheart and how he'd done her down by the river. After that, I didn't have the heart for it."

"You know if the crops fail next year, it'll be your fault."

Fawkes snorted. "If the fertility of their fields depends on the potency of the man who rules them, it seems to me the people of Valmar should have starved years ago. You know Mortimer didn't plow the belly of any corn maid in his time."

"Maybe he had some other man do it for him," Reynard jibed. "Speaking of which, did you ever find Lady Nicola?"

They'd reached their horses, which amazingly, had not broken free of their hobbles and run off. Fawkes went to Scimitar and busied himself with tying his saddle pack onto the destrier. Reynard followed. "Well?"

Fawkes turned, thinking of exactly how he had found Nicola, wet and wild-eyed from the storm. Of dragging her into the shed and what he had done to her. He took a breath and said, "Yea, I found her."

"And…"

"I still don't know where she was all day."

"Did you ask?"

"Nay. We were… It didn't seem appropriate at the time."

"Well, you should ask her. It seems to me that most of the difficulties between you and Nicola could be settled by talking."

Fawkes clenched his jaw. That was all well and good for Reynard to say. Words came easily to him. Not to mention he wasn't easily intimidated by a woman. Perhaps that was it, the reason he had so much difficulty with Nicola. A part of him still felt like a squire seeking the favor of his lady. As much as he told himself he was now Nicola's equal, and indeed, by law her master, he could not make himself act as if it was true.

Except when it came to sex. Then he had no difficulty forcing her to submit to him. In carnal matters, he had no doubt of who was in control. Somehow he must learn to take charge in other matters besides those of the bedchamber.

They were almost to the castle now. He glanced up at the tower that housed Nicola's bedchamber. He would do it. He would go to her and demand to know where she had been all day.

Chapter Fourteen

When she got back to the castle, Nicola decided the first thing she needed was a bath.

She had some squires drag a wooden bathing tub up to her bedchamber and fill it with hot, almost-scalding water. Old Emma brought towels and a bowl of soap. After tossing a handful of herbs into the tub, the servant asked, "Do you want me to bathe ye?"

Nicola shook her head. She wanted to be alone, to deal with the thoughts and feelings swirling in her brain.

Old Emma helped her undress and left. Nicola sank down into the steaming water, sighing as the blissful heat soothed her. The muscles in her thighs were tense and sore from riding all day as well as from lovemaking. Was she a fool to call it that? Did the sizzling fire between her and Fawkes have anything to do with love?

She had no doubt there was a bond between them. But she wasn't certain it was connected with love, or even affection. A melancholy mood assaulted her. Fawkes had taken her to paradise, but it seemed unlikely anything would change between them. And if she was honest with herself, what she wanted was for Fawkes to care for her. To feel genuine affection. To *love* her.

At first her feelings for him were related to desire. But gradually she'd learned what sort of man he was. He was tough but fair, and willing to listen and learn, even from his underlings. When she and Warin showed him the castle's foodstores and assessed supplies, he'd paid attention and been respectful of their knowledge. He seemed determined to be a good lord, to see to the defense of Valmar and look after the people who lived there. He even seemed to appreciate the effort she put into being a good chatelaine.

She respected Fawkes, and was pleased to earn his admiration. But she wanted more. She wanted him to love her. Perhaps over time it would happen. Perhaps the deep connection their bodies shared would lead to a deeper bond between them. But it still seemed she had a long way to go toward winning Fawkes's wary, suspicious heart.

She stood to soap her body. After rinsing, she climbed out and dried herself, then went to the coffer and searched among the jars and vials stored there until she found a container of rose oil. She poured some into her hand and smoothed it over her skin. She recalled Glennyth grumbling about how many roses it took to make this small jar. After picking dozens of blossoms at the height of their lushness, the wise woman had crushed the petals and distilled them in oil.

Nicola recalled Glennyth teasing her about wanting a love potion. She'd dismissed the idea at the time. She was too worried about Simon and hiding the truth from Fawkes. But now the idea tantalized her. Although she was dubious of such things, most of the medicines and salves and decoctions that Glennyth made were effective. Even the elixir she'd devised to turn Mortimer impotent had worked. If Glennyth could make one man impotent, then perhaps she could also make another man fall in love.

Nicola slipped a shift over her head. She was still

toying with the idea of visiting the wise woman when there was a knock on the door.

"Nicola. I need to speak to you."

Fawkes! There was no time to get dressed. And what would be the point? He already knew her body intimately. She took a deep breath and called, "Come in."

****

As soon as he opened the door, Fawkes realized he should have sent someone to fetch Nicola and had her meet him elsewhere. This place, with its memories of making love to her in that bed, was hardly the right setting for the conversation he wished to have. Worse yet, Nicola was wearing nothing but a shift, and he was acutely aware of what lay beneath the nearly transparent fabric. As if he wasn't distracted enough, the room was filled with that beguiling scent he associated with Nicola. The fragrance entwined itself around his senses and ensnared his wits until he could scarce remember why he came.

He took a deep breath and forced himself to recall his purpose. "I need to know where you went today. You weren't at the celebration in the village. Or here at the castle. Where were you?" He stared at her face, trying to gauge the truth of her response.

"I went to Mordeaux."

"Mordeaux?" He had not expected this. "By the saints, what were you doing at Mordeaux?"

"I went to visit Hilary de Vescy. I told you we are friends."

"But why today?"

"I knew you would be occupied all day with the Lammas Celebration. Holding manor court. Talking with the villagers. Accepting their gifts. And of course, the ritual."

The ritual. The damned corn queen. Of course. Nicola would not want to be part of that. What wife would? Fawkes felt himself flushing. She probably thought he'd bedded the girl. "I didn't follow through with the ritual. I pretended to, but I couldn't go through it. She seemed so young. So naïve and innocent."

Nicola nodded. Was that relief in her expression? Did she care enough that she didn't want him to bed other women?

The thought pleased him, but he pushed aside his sense of satisfaction. He must remember why he'd come. His goal was to get beyond Nicola's beauty and calm, cool competence and discover whom she really was.

"What did you do at Mordeaux?" he asked.

"As I said, I visited with Hilary."

"It seems like a long ride to make to visit with a friend. You could not have spent much more than a candle hour or two in her company."

"I have no female companion here at Valmar, other than Old Emma. I can hardly speak openly with the young women who work in the kitchen or the weaving shed, or the village wives. And even though Glennyth and I are comfortable with each other, our lives are very different. Only Lady Hilary shares my interests and concerns in running a castle household."

Her response was utterly reasonable. And yet... There was something she was hiding. "Did you take Hilary's son his new tunic?"

She started and her eyes went wide. Then looked away. "It's not finished yet. I haven't had the time to do so."

"It looked near finished to me. I'm surprised you didn't wait until you were satisfied the tunic was done before making this trip. Now you will have to make another journey there to take it to the boy. What did you say his name was?"

This time her alarm was unmistakable. "Alexander. His name is Alexander."

She was lying. Every instinct told him so. Why would she lie about the child's name? Unless the child was more to her than simply the son of a friend. Was it possible Nicola had given birth to a *second* child?

But that was ludicrous. Someone as slender and delicate as Nicola could never have concealed a pregnancy, not in the final months. It must be something else. Perhaps this *Alexander* was close in age to what the babe who died would be and so she lavished her affections on him as a way for mourning for the child she lost. But if that was true, then why did she not tell him that?

Familiar frustration gnawed at him. No matter how he tried, he could not break through Nicola's formidable reserve. Instead, every time he spoke to her, it fueled the aching doubt in his gut. Winning Valmar and Nicola had been too easy. He couldn't help worrying that something was going to happen to snatch it all away from him. Something connected to Nicola.

She gazed at him expectantly. "My lord, will there be anything else? Almost everyone went to the village for the Lammas Feast, so there will be no formal meal this evening. If you're hungry, you can ask for something in the kitchen."

"And you? You didn't partake at the feast. Aren't you hungry?"

Nicola shook her head, but something in her expression made him sense she was reluctant for him to leave. He longed to stay, even if he did nothing more than sleep beside her. But his emotions were too much in turmoil.

"Very well. I'll leave you then." He must get away now, while he was still able to do so.

****

"Aren't you coming in?" Reynard asked, as he and Fawkes walked to the knights' barracks after eating some bread and cheese in the hall. "We could share a jack of wine and you could join in the dicing."

Fawkes shook his head. "I think I'll go to bed."

"With your wife?"

Fawkes didn't answer.

Oliver walked by and punched Reynard in the arm. "What are you doing here, Reynard? Why aren't you in the hayloft with some wench?"

"Believe it or not, I'm sleeping alone tonight."

"Surely you jest!" Oliver clutched his chest in mock horror. "Can it really be true that the randy fox has satisfied his ferocious lust?"

Henry de Brionne leaned out the doorway. "The fox has at last been bitten by the love bug. And right glad of it, I am. Now there might actually be some wenches left for the rest of us!"

Henry and Oliver erupted with guffaws. Fawkes looked at Reynard, expecting him to deny his interest in Glennyth. To his surprise, Reynard said nothing.

A thought came to Fawkes. "While you're spending time with the wise woman, you might give a thought to my circumstances."

"What do you mean?"

"I'm certain Glennyth knows what truly happened to the babe Nicola gave birth to. When she is sated and relaxed from lovemaking you could ask her about it. She might be truthful."

"You think she was lying when you questioned her?"

"Not lying, nay. But choosing her words with care. There's something she's holding back, I'm certain of it. If I could unravel the truth, perhaps all would be well between Nicola and me."

Reynard stopped walking and faced Fawkes. For once, his green eyes were deadly serious. "What if you don't like what I learn from Glennyth? What if it's true Nicola killed your son? Will you be able to forgive her? Even knowing she was driven to it by Mortimer's abuse?"

"I don't know." Could he really love a woman who could do something so cruel and unnatural? "I can't bear *not* knowing. If the truth is something terrible, I must find it out now. Before I become even more entangled with Nicola and more settled in with my life here as lord of Valmar."

"What are you saying? That if you discover Nicola killed your child, you would set her aside? Even knowing that doing so will probably cause you to lose Valmar and Mordeaux? Are you truly willing to give up all that you've won?" Reynard shook his head. "Think of all the people who would suffer if you gave up your claim. Not only the men who have followed you, but the people of Valmar. For the first time in years, they finally have a competent lord."

Put that way, it did make Fawkes feel petty and foolish. There were likely a great many men in England who were married to women they neither loved nor respected. He doubted they let it affect their lives in any substantial way.

"I see I've given you something to think about," Reynard said. "I regret adding to your worries. But as your friend and companion, I have to point out these things."

"So, you think I should let the matter go? Accept Nicola's tale as the truth?"

"You used to be a strong, decisive leader, Fawkes. One who could not be shaken from his path nor deterred from reaching his goals. Now you're like a maid, clutching your hands together and worrying, should I or shouldn't I?" As he spoke, Reynard pantomimed what his words evoked.

Fawkes glared at him. "Friend or no, if you don't cease mocking me, you'll have to back up your words with your sword!"

Reynard grinned and punched him in the arm. "You're always such a grim, serious bastard. And arrogant too. Do you think you're above being made fun of? We all deserved to be called out for our foolishness. I'm no different. Here's your chance to call me an utter dolt for getting involved with a woman whose entire cottage is jammed with herbs that could kill me, emasculate me or render me a simpleton."

"You're a fool, Reynard," Fawkes growled.

"There." Reynard poked his shoulder again. "You feel better now, don't you? Stop being so serious all the time, Fawkes. Enjoy what you have and don't think so much about what might have happened before you arrived here. If you had discovered she was truly plotting against you, or that she had a lover, I wouldn't tell you to forget and forgive. But this babe, an infant long dead and buried..." Reynard shook his head. "Babes die all the time, for dozens of reasons. Or no reason at all. Frankly, instead of mourning this one, I think you should concentrate on begetting another."

"Mayhaps you're right. Thank you for helping me see reason."

"You're welcome," Reynard said, grinning. "Now hurry off to your wife. Before you think of another foolish excuse to avoid her."

Fawkes returned to the keep and took the stairs to the tower two at time. He felt lighter and more carefree than he had in a fortnight. Reaching the landing, he knocked on the door. When there was no answer, he tried again. "Nicola. It's Fawkes."

He opened the door and gazed around at the empty room. She'd probably gone to the kitchen to fetch some food. Surely she would be back soon.

He sat on the stool to wait, then caught sight of a leather bag on the bed. He picked it up and examined it. This must be the one he'd seen tied to Nicola's saddle.

He hesitated for a few moments, then undid the drawstring, opened the bag and took out a small child's tunic. It must be one little Alexander had outgrown. She'd probably brought it back to pass it on to some other child. He stroked the soft, finely woven cloth. Reynard had urged him to forget the matter of the babe. But how was he to do that when there were going to be these constant reminders?

He turned as the door opened. Nicola stepped in the room. She looked at him and then the child's garment in his hand. The blood seemed to leave her face.

He had a perfect right to inspect his wife's things,

but he still felt wrong-footed and embarrassed for doing so. But he was not so flustered that he failed to notice her reaction. The expression on her face could only be described as one of dread. He told himself not to think about the reason she was afraid. Having come here to start over with her, he could not let a little scrap of cloth deter him.

He put the tunic back in the bag and set it on the floor. Then he met her gaze. "I came looking for you. I wanted to say that I am sorry."

****

Sorry? He was sorry? For what? For snooping in her things? And what did he make of Simon's shirt? Had he guessed the truth? Nay, that was impossible.

A frown creased his forehead. "Nicola, since I arrived here I haven't dealt with you in a way that was considerate, or even reasonable. I want you to understand why. Before I killed him, Mortimer taunted me. He said you warned him I was coming; he implied you didn't want me to prevail." He took a deep breath. "I've heard other rumors as well. That you had put some sort of curse on Mortimer, and caused him to lose his wits and his will. That you dosed him with some potion that robbed him of his manhood. And then, of course, there is the matter of the child you bore…our son." His voice wavered. Then he continued, his tone once again steady. "FitzSaer told me you had killed the babe. He took me to the grave. When I saw that there was no marker or sign of remembrance there, I thought…I thought his words must be true."

He turned back to the window, as if even now, he could still not quite overcome his doubts, and he didn't want her to know. Then he faced her again.

"We got off to a bad start in our marriage. I want us to begin again. Do you think that's possible?"

If he wanted to start over, with everything open and honest between them, then this was the perfect moment to tell him about Simon. But if she told him now, he would know she had lied to him many times. That might arouse his doubts all over again.

Rapid footsteps sounded on the stairs, then a banging on the door. "Milady! Do you know where Lord Fawkes is? There's a fire in the village and we need his knights to help put it out!"

Fawkes strode to the door and opened it to reveal a flushed and breathless page. "Where's the fire? What happened?"

The page, Thomas, froze for a moment, as if startled to find Fawkes there. Then he blurted out, "It's the healer's house. It's ablaze."

"Is Glennyth all right? Did she get out?" Fawkes demanded of the page.

"I don't know. I wasn't there. One of the villagers came to the castle and told me to fetch you."

Fawkes pushed past the page and raced down the stairs.

Thomas looked at Nicola, eyes wide. "What should I do now?"

"Go through the castle and tell everyone to fetch a bucket or pan anything that will hold water and hurry down to the river."

Thomas nodded and was gone. Nicola wished she knew how bad the fire was. If Glennyth's cottage were truly ablaze, it would take a huge amount of water to put it out. But if part of the structure was not yet burning, they could soak sheepskins and hides in water and use them to smother the flames or at least keep them from spreading. But Glennyth's house was full of dried herbs, perfect fuel for a fire. By the time they got the sheepskins to the river and then to the house, it would probably be too late.

And the healer—had she gotten out? Was she injured? Even if she was safe, it was likely some of those fighting the fire would end up getting burned. She'd better fetch healing ointment and some bandages. As Nicola started down the stairs to get the things, she had the awful thought that after this fire, her small stash of medicines might be all that was left at Valmar.

By the time she reached the village, a line of people extended from the river, rapidly passing containers from one to the next. She ran past them to the common and across it to Glennyth's cottage. Half of it was a blackened ruin. The other half smoked and steamed but was no longer aflame. She looked around frantically for Glennyth and saw her nearby, staring gloomily at the wreck of her home. Next to Glennyth was Reynard. They were both disheveled and streaked with soot, Reynard even more so than Glennyth.

Nicola rushed to them. "Are you both well?"

"I am," said Glennyth. "But Reynard's hands and face are burned."

Reynard's clothing and hair were also singed. Nicola shot a questioning glance at the healer.

"He went into the fire to fetch Tom." She nodded to the bundle in her arms—Glennyth's cat.

"I wasn't home when the fire broke out," Glennyth said. "Thankfully, I came back and discovered it before the flames had spread too far. But Tom was sleeping in the loft, and I was afraid he hadn't gotten out. I was in a panic. When Reynard arrived, he soaked himself in the river and then went in after Tom."

Nicola looked back at Reynard. There were reddened patches on both cheeks and his chin, but his face didn't look too bad. "Your hands. Let me see."

Wincing, Reynard held put out his hands and showed the raw-looking flesh on the backs of them.

Nicola turned to Glennyth. "I brought some all-heal ointment." She dug in her basket and retrieved the pottery jar.

Glennyth nodded. "That will help. I'm glad you had some on hand. All of mine is likely gone." She gazed bleakly at the smoking cottage. "'Twill take me a year or more to replace my supplies. That is, if I decide to remain at Valmar."

"What do you mean?" Reynard sounded alarmed. "Where would you go?"

Glennyth gave him a bitter look. "Mayhap I'll go to some village that appreciates a wise woman rather than seeking to burn her out."

"You think the fire was set deliberately?" Nicola was horrified.

Glennyth turned to her. "How else could it have started? All was well when I left."

Nicola felt a chill. Because of her role as wise woman, Glennyth knew many secrets about the people in the village. Secrets that might make someone see her as a threat. There were also people who resented Glennyth. Men who thought women should not have so much authority, and women who were jealous.

"We must find out who did this," Nicola said. "They must be held accountable, and pay to rebuild your home and replace your belongings that were destroyed or damaged."

"How will you find that person and prove they are responsible?" Glennyth snapped.

"I will find a way. I vow this act will not go unpunished." They all turned to see Fawkes standing on the pathway to the common. His eyes were dark with anger and his jaw tight.

He motioned to the smoking cottage. "I will have my knights continue to douse the fire, to make certain it is truly out. The rest of you should go back to the castle."

"This is my home," Glennyth said. "I don't want to leave it."

"You can't sleep here," Fawkes said bluntly. "Besides, if someone seeks to do you harm, you'll be safer at the castle."

Reynard took a step toward Glennyth. "I'll make sure of that."

"Where will I sleep?" Glennyth regarded him skeptically. "With you in the knights' quarters?" Her caustic tone made it clear how appalled she was by the idea.

"There's a bedchamber in the lord's tower," Nicola said. "No one is using it."

"I couldn't sleep there." Glennyth was clearly aghast. "Many people at the castle already resent me. If you put me in such a fine bedchamber, that will cause me more trouble."

"We'll say that Reynard's wounds need tending, and you're staying there to take care of him," Nicola said. "Burns are always at risk of putrefying. Everyone knows that."

"Burns?" Fawkes stared at Reynard. "I didn't know anyone was injured."

Nicola spoke up: "Reynard saved Tom from the fire."

"Tom? You mean, Thomas, the page? But I just saw him." Fawkes frowned.

"Nay, *Tom*, Glennyth's cat." Nicola pointed to the bundle in Glennyth's arms. "He was sleeping in the loft when the fire broke out. Reynard rescued him."

"How noble of him." Fawkes glowered at Reynard, although his mouth twitched, giving away his amusement. "You went into a burning building to rescue a cat."

Reynard made a sheepish gesture.

"Tom isn't merely a cat. He's my family," Glennyth grumbled.

"Well, what's done is done." Fawkes turned to Glennyth. "As Nicola said, you will stay with Reynard and tend his wounds. If he suffers ill from this, you will owe me a debt." He nodded to Nicola. "Take them to the castle and get them settled. I will deal with things here."

****

After they left, Fawkes made certain the fire was out, then ordered the knights who'd been fetching water to return to castle. The villagers who were helping also left, either back to their own homes, or to clear away what remained from the Lammas celebration. Due to the fire, festivities had been cut short. No one was in the mood for music and dancing now. Fawkes wondered how the villagers would react to being cheated out of an evening of revelry. Would they blame Glennyth?

Fawkes approached the ruins of the cottage. If the hearthfire had caused the blaze, the damage should be greatest in that area. Instead, the portion of the dwelling that had burned most fiercely was the side facing the forest. The only way that made sense was if the fire had started there. Had someone crept up to that side of the cottage, doused the wood with oil and set it alight? The wood would burn slowly at first, but eventually the fire would reach the herbs inside the cottage and turn into a fierce blaze.

Fawkes frowned at the smoking building. He would have to speak to Glennyth. She implied there were several people who resented and disliked her. Like Eadulf, who blamed Glennyth for the loss of his potency, and who had accused her publicly of putting an evil spell on him.

Fawkes walked back to the castle, his mind swirling with thoughts. He was worried about Reynard's wounds and troubled by the cause of the fire. And then there was Nicola. Before Thomas arrived with news of the fire, Nicola had seemed on the verge of telling him something. Somehow he had to get things between them back to where they had been before the page's arrival.

At the castle, he headed for the lord's tower. He encountered Nicola on the stairs. "Glennyth gave Reynard some poppy juice to help him sleep," she said. "It might be better if you don't disturb them."

"Poppy juice? Where did she get poppy juice? I thought all her herbs and potions were destroyed in the fire."

"I gave her the juice. I have my own store of medicine. Some of it is from Glennyth, and some from the peddler who visits now and again."

"I'm glad to know you have some healing potions stored away. That means everything wasn't destroyed in the fire."

Nicola motioned. "I wish to speak to you about the

fire, but I don't want anyone to hear." She led the way to her bedchamber. When the door was shut, she turned to him. "We must find out who set the fire."

"I agree."

"We can't let this pass. I think whoever caused the fire meant to do more than destroy Glennyth's livelihood. I think they meant to kill her."

"She's that much hated?"

"It could be a way to strike at me."

"You? Why would setting the fire and killing Glennyth be an attack on you?"

"Because Glennyth is my friend. And because she was involved in things I'm blamed for: Mortimer's decline and the tales I used witchcraft to destroy him."

Fawkes nodded thoughtfully. "For that matter, I suppose it's possible the fire was set as a means of discrediting me as the new lord."

Her eyes widened. "I had not thought of that."

"Do you think I have enemies here who might do such a thing? Are there people in the village who don't accept my right to rule Valmar?"

"I don't know. I wish I did." She sighed. "It's all so upsetting."

At this moment, he could do naught about the fire and who caused it. But he must let her know he meant to protect her. He drew near. "Don't worry, Nicola. I will keep you safe."

****

A tremor went through Nicola. No one other than her father had ever promised such a thing. Could she trust Fawkes to honor his words? And why did he promise her this? Was it because he truly cared for her? Or did he see her as the key to possessing Valmar, and valuable for that reason?

At this moment, she found she didn't care. She let him pull her into his arms. He was so big and solid and strong. It was a comfort to have him close. To feel his muscular arms around her. As she rested her head against his broad chest, she felt the tension in her body drain away. It was a relief to feel like she didn't have to do everything herself. To realize she had someone to help her deal with this matter of the fire.

It was like being a little girl again, safe and secure in her father's arms, where nothing could harm her. And yet it wasn't quite like that. Even as she relaxed against Fawkes, she felt flickers of arousal. This wasn't her father holding her, but her lover.

She thought about their first encounter and how her anger and resentment had slowly melted away as he explored her body with tender, almost reverent caresses. He had seemed so young then. She had been young, too. Although that day was only four years in the past, it seemed a lifetime ago. They were much different people now. He a hardened knight instead of a boyish squire. And she no longer a pampered, spoiled girl, but a wife and mother.

Life had tested them and made them stronger. But it had also made them wary. Both of them feared letting down their guard and risking true intimacy. And yet, he was taking the first step in holding her like this. Not like a lover, but as someone to lean on, someone to trust. If he was willing to risk himself at this moment, she must take a risk as well.

She turned in his arms, so her breasts were pressed against his chest. A moment later she was rewarded by the unmistakable feel of his shaft prodding her belly. In an instant they were back to the incendiary passion that burned between them from the beginning.

She raised her face and kissed him. As the familiar fire flared, she felt him holding back. This time he was letting her set the pace and take control. Exhilarated, she nibbled at his lips with teasing, tantalizing kisses and then kissed along his hard, stubbled jaw. Down to the hollow of his throat, tasting the salt of his skin and his warm, earthy scent. She went back to kissing his mouth. Daringly, she used her tongue to coax his lips open and explored the silken cavern within, savoring the textures of teeth and tongue and lips.

His tongue joined hers in a sensual dance that shimmered pleasure down her body. It was intense and satisfying, yet she wanted more. She stepped back so she could touch his face. Her fingers brushed along his jaw where she had kissed him, the stubble of his beard raking against her fingertips. His body was so different from hers. Scratchy where she was smooth. Hard where she was soft. And yet his lips were soft, and his hair as silky and fine as hers. She played with the thick wavy tresses for a few moments before stroking the hard column of his neck. As she kneaded the muscles there, he sighed.

She moved her hand lower and met the rough wool of his tunic. He removed her hand from his chest and pulled the tunic over his head to reveal a sleek, tanned chest. His body was so beautiful. Smooth glossy skin. Muscles rippling with power. She met his gaze and smiled. He gazed back her, unsmiling, his dark eyes fierce.

She used a finger to trace the dark areole of one of his nipples. As it peaked, a sweet arrow of delight pierced her. His body was a mirror of her own, yet wonderfully unlike in so many ways. She fondled his other nipple, then made lazy circles on his chest, exploring the padded contours. When she wearied of that, she moved her hand down to his navel and the line of coarse hair there.

His body went rigid, as if he could not bear to have her touch him so close to his groin. She felt no sympathy. He had done the same to her more than once, arousing her to fever pitch.

After a few seconds, he grabbed her hand. "If you continue doing that, I fear I will lose control."

She shot him a defiant look. "Would that be so awful?"

"But you…you must be sore from this afternoon."

"Aye. But that doesn't mean I can't get pleasure from touching you."

"I don't think I can endure it."

She gazed at him steadily. "I didn't say I wouldn't give you satisfaction. There is more than one way for you to find release."

Her words seemed to make him even more uncomfortable. He frowned at her. "But that's not how it's done. 'Tis the man's part to pleasure the woman."

She raised her eyebrows at him. "And *this* woman's pleasure comes from touching you." When he still frowned, she added, "I think you fear the loss of control. Always you must be in charge, the stallion covering the mare. Have you never had a woman arouse and tantalize you?"

"Of course. But in the end I always…" He gestured vaguely, as if he did not want to use some crude term to describe the act.

She regarded him steadily. "Perhaps it is time for

you to be the one who is fondled and teased."

He hesitated a few heartbeats, then said, "Perhaps it is."

Despite his assent, she could tell he was uneasy. Clearly, he disliked not being in control. He couldn't imagine what it was like to be a woman. Few females ever had control over their bodies, or their lives. They were ruled by first their fathers and then their husbands. Of all the women Nicola knew, Glennyth was the only one who had any measure of true independence. Perhaps that's why someone had sought to burn her out.

The memory of the smoking, ruined cottage aroused Nicola's bitterness and anger. But, nay, she would not dwell on what had happened to the wise woman. Instead, she would concentrate on the man in front of her.

Young, powerful and virile Fawkes. At this moment, he was hers, and she meant to take advantage of the fact. She reached for the waist of his chausses. After loosening the drawstring, she pulled them down, exposing his ruddy, up-thrust shaft. She took it in both hands, reveling in the feel of soft skin and hard flesh. It felt so marvelously warm and alive. She used one finger to touch the tip, stroking tenderly.

He made a sound as if he was in agony. She ignored him. Had he not tormented her in similar fashion—his fingers playing with the most excruciatingly sensitive parts of her body? She slid her hand down the smooth length of his shaft, then back to the tip. She repeated the motion while looking at his face. His eyes were closed, his features taut. She returned her gaze to his groin and gave his sleek, lovely rod of flesh several more provocative, lingering caresses, then reached for the silken sacks beneath.

She took the soft, fleshy orbs in her hand, manipulating them tenderly. He gasped, choking on a groan. How vulnerable this part of him was. How intriguing. Loose skin enclosing plum-sized spheres. The source of his seed, the slippery liquid he put inside her. She thought of how it felt, the hot fluid pulsing as he reached his peak. Did she wish for him to do that to her now?

It was impossible to touch him like this without thinking of what his body did to hers. His shaft inside her, filling her, making her wet. Thrusting into her, battering against her womb. Riding her, taking her on a journey to the stars. Thinking of it, she had to take a deep breath herself. The faint ache between her legs had become a fierce throb. He was right. She was sore. But at this moment, it didn't matter. As always, her body sought his.

She returned her attention to his shaft. After a few lingering caresses, Fawkes's breath came short and fast. She finally took pity on him, and drew her hand away. But this didn't bring him ease. Instead, he opened his eyes and gazed at her with a look of desperation.

"You wish me to stop?" she asked.

He frowned and didn't answer. Perhaps he didn't know what he wanted. Or, perhaps he did but was honoring her wish to fondle and pleasure him.

She glanced again at his rigid shaft, boldly jutting upwards. A thought came to her. Perhaps there was a way to soothe both her desire for his body and her yearning for control.

She gestured. "Lie on the bed."

His eyebrows shot up, but he did as she asked. Although first he sat on the side of the bed and removed his boots and braies and chausses. When he was naked, he got on the bed and lay on his back. His shaft thrust up like a beacon.

Nicola loosened the lacing on her gown, hands trembling. She wanted him so badly. The flesh between her legs was taut and aching, and near dripping with wetness.

Once the laces were undone, she pulled the gown over her head and slipped free of her loincloth. Then she went to the bed and climbed onto it. She knelt next to him, trying to decide what to do next. Should she fondle him some more? Or straddle him and push herself down onto his thick, lovely shaft?

How wanton she would appear if she did that. Not to mention he would see her private parts as she spread her legs to straddle him. The idea gave her a strange thrill and she moved into position.

As she straddled him, his hands came up to grasp her hips. Within seconds, he had scooted down on the bed so his face was between her thighs. She was too startled to protest as gripped her thighs and spread her legs wider. Then he raised his head so her cleft was only inches from his mouth. Nicola felt a stab of embarrassment. But her body seemed to have a mind of its own, for she found herself leaning forward and allowing him to put his lips on her most intimate, secret place.

She gasped as he nuzzled her there and then began to lick and suck. Quivers of ecstasy darted through her body and she could hardly hold still. When he stuck his tongue inside her, she found herself whimpering. Even though she was on top, she was no longer in control. He was dominating her with his mouth, making her as helpless as ever. As always, it was her body that betrayed her, revealing her desire and need for him. She wanted him so much. Inside her, filling her deep. And she wanted it now.

She pulled from his grasp and slid down until she was poised over his thick, jutting shaft. Taking hold of it, she lowered herself until the plump tip pressed against her wet, tender opening. Wriggling into position, she slowly lowered herself, gasping as each inch of his solid flesh slid inside. Despite how wet she was, it was still a slow and agonizingly intense process. Inch by inch his shaft impaled her. Inch by inch her body yielded.

When he was fully inside, she sought to relax and catch her breath, to adjust to the almost unbearable pressure. She felt split apart, pierced by his massive spear. Then he bucked upwards, sending rays of pleasure shimmering through her and more wetness seeping from inside her with each thrust of his hips.

She gave in, realizing her plan to be in control was hopeless. No matter how she sought to take charge of their lovemaking, he always managed to thwart her. He had all the weapons, dominating her with his size and strength, and now with this fleshly lance that penetrated her defenses utterly.

Once again, she was defeated. Conquered. Overpowered. Her body yielded like a castle wall shattered by a missile from a trebuchet. As her defenses crumbled completely away, she had no choice but to surrender.

As she did so, the shattering pleasure sent her flying to the heavens.

Afterwards, when she was limp and mindless with completion, he grabbed her hips and reversed positions.

Now he was on top and in total control as he drove his shaft into her.

Incredibly, her spent, satiated body responded; the fire of arousal blazed through her once more.

On and on he rode her down a fiery magical trail to paradise. As they reached the thrilling heights, she realized they were no longer two separate people, but one being, one soul. They began their descent and she clutched his arms and pulled him down onto her. His breast heaved and his skin was slick. His heart beat against hers, and utter contentment filled her. There was no battle between them now. They had sought out and shared the incredible ecstasy together.

****

Ahh, what this woman did to him. Fawkes lay sprawled next to Nicola. Each time he made love to her was better than the last. As his knowledge of her body increased, so did his pleasure. And each time he felt the distance between them narrowing. As he came to understand her body, and its effect on his, he felt closer and closer to her. She was no longer the distant, unapproachable goddess he had once imagined her to be, but simply a woman. He yearned for that woman as passionately as ever. But now it was her essence he sought—her soul—as much as her body. He loved Nicola, not as an ideal or a dream, but as a woman.

The idea both exhilarated him and terrified him. When she was a fantasy, he might have been able to go on if his dream was shattered. But now that he loved her as a flesh and blood woman, he wasn't certain he could survive without her.

She shifted and he realized she must be uncomfortable. He moved so he was no longer lying halfway on her. She wriggled beneath his arm and laid her head on his chest. He exhaled a long sigh. This is exactly what he wanted. This sense of peace and perfect repletion. Somehow holding her like this made him feel that all was well in the world.

Of course it wasn't. A dozen troubling problems faced them. But now they faced them together, which made it so much less wearying.

He gave into the languorous contentment. Eyes closed, he inhaled her warm, sweet, delicate scent. The perfume of soft rain and sunshine on the grass. Of summer and childhood.

The thought made him half-smile. Then his thoughts blurred and he thought no more.

Chapter Fifteen

Nicola woke to a tapping at the door. Daylight oozed through the window. She gently removed Fawkes's arm that was draped over her and slipped out of bed. After pulling the shift over her head, she went to the door.

"I'm going back to the cottage," Glennyth said.

"Why?"

"Many reasons. I want to see what I can salvage. I feel trapped and closed in here at the castle. And then there's Tom. He can't roam free the way he's used to doing. There are other cats here and I don't want there to be a fight."

Nicola realized Gimlyn might not be pleased to have another male cat in his territory.

"I'm taking your basket." Glennyth held it up. "I left the medicines that were in it in the solar."

"How is Reynard?"

"He's quite sore. I think perhaps he's regretting his noble gesture. He needs to avoid using his hands, so they will heal. I'm worried the smoke has also injured his lungs. He seems short of breath."

That wouldn't please Fawkes. Although what did it matter if Reynard did nothing for a few days?

Fawkes called, "Who is it?"

Nicola turned. "Glennyth. She's going back to her cottage to see what can be saved from the fire."

Fawkes appeared beside Nicola, still fastening his chausses. "You must be careful," he told the wise woman. "Whoever set the fire might be lurking around, waiting for you."

"I don't think whoever did this is bold enough to confront me," Glennyth said. "The way they tried to burn me out seems like the work of a coward."

"I think Glennyth is right," Nicola said. "She's not in danger now that it's clear she's under our protection."

"Unless part of their reason for attacking Glennyth was to undermine my authority," Fawkes said.

"Or mine," Nicola retorted. "They might have meant to strike at me."

"That's true," Glennyth said. "The person who did this might resent both of us, women who have too much power. But no matter their motivation, I'm certain this person is not bold enough to attack me in broad daylight."

"You're likely right. Go then. But don't stay away too long. You must see to Reynard until he is healed."

"Of course I will," Glennyth replied, hazel eyes flashing. "I'm well aware I owe him a debt."

Fawkes bristled at the woman's tone, and Nicola realized what she'd been doing wrong. If someone appeared to defy him, Fawkes grew angry. She must stop being so defensive and resentful. As Old Emma had once told her, she had all the weapons she needed to prevail in this battle between her and Fawkes. But she must stop thinking of it as battle. Fawkes was not her adversary. They had the same goals. They simply differed in how to reach those goals.

The thought eased some of her tension and when Glennyth left and Fawkes turned to her with a gleam in his eyes, she responded eagerly as he took her in his arms.

"I'm certain you are sore. But if I promise to be very gentle, do you think we might go back to bed and…" He nibbled on her neck. Nicola shivered and gave in to the magical fire that burned between them.

****

Once again Fawkes sat in the lord's chair in the sun-dappled common pasture. But this time the reeve didn't stand beside him, but Gerard of Malmsbury. The lean, dark-haired knight had been one of Mortimer's knights. But as soon as Fawkes's arrived he'd seemed eager to switch his allegiances. So far Fawkes had found him solid and stable, and less likely to indulge in the questionable behavior some of own knights had displayed. Now Gerard stood sentinel as people from the village came to speak to Fawkes and explain their whereabouts during the fire. Some came willingly. Others were grudging and suspicious.

To those who seemed less than eager, Fawkes reassured them he was questioning everyone. This appeared to ease the mood of some, while others remained tight-lipped and resentful. Fawkes was puzzled. It was one of the women who clarified the reason for her sullen mood. "All this trouble for that haughty bitch." She jerked her head in the direction of the ruined cottage. "If my house burns down, are you going to do this?"

"Yea, if I think the fire was set deliberately." Fawkes held the woman's gaze until she looked away. "'Tis clear you resent Glennyth. Has she never aided you? Given you medicine or advice on some ill or another?"

Orva, one of the villein's wives, stiffened and her scowl deepened. "Of course I've had medicines and advice from her. But I've paid for all of it. How do you think she came to have such a fine dwelling? She doesn't offer her services for free. At least not to *my* family. There are those she is willing to do anything for, even though they have no means to pay her."

"Perhaps that's the point," Fawkes said. "She asks for payment from you because you have the means, but gives away her services to those who can't afford them. It seems fair to me. Glennyth must have some means of survival, so she sells her skill at healing. 'Tis no different than the miller charging you to grind your grain."

"But she is a woman." Orva's eyes flashed with animosity and her weathered features grew tight. "'Tis not fitting for her to live that like, with no man to keep her."

Fawkes had thought the village men might resent Glennyth. He had not imagined women would feel that way. This woman was clearly not fond of Glennyth. There might be others. Wives who felt that if they were subject to the authority of their husband, then other women should endure the same fate.

Orva was looking at him, expecting him to agree. He did not. Although he'd clashed with Glennyth in the beginning, now he admired her. She was strong and independent, but also fair and compassionate. Those qualities were commendable in anyone, man or woman.

But it would be foolish to share such thoughts with the bristling matron before him. Defending Glennyth would only anger Orva. And despite her comment about being under her husband's authority, he suspected Orva was actually the one who made most of the decisions in her household.

He nodded to Orva. "Thank you for you speaking with me. I'll take your words under advisement."

The woman's frown eased, but didn't go away altogether. Straightening, she said, "Are you certain you have no more questions for me?"

"What do you think I should ask you, Goodwife Orva?"

"Why, who set the fire, of course!"

He was taken aback. "You know who set the fire?"

Orva nodded, eyes glinting like a contented cat. "Eadulf. You know how much he hates Glennyth. When you turned down his plea for compensation, he decided to get even in his own way."

"Do you have proof of this?"

"Proof?"

"Yea. Did you see him near the cottage before it caught fire?"

Orva's scowl was back. "The cottage is hidden among the trees. Anyone could have crept through the woods and done this."

"And you think Eadulf had the greatest reason to do so?"

"I'm certain it was him."

"Thank you." Again, Fawkes inclined his head politely, hoping Orva would take the hint that she was dismissed. She frowned at him a few moments longer, then gave a curt bow and walked off.

"Do you think she's right?" Gerard leaned near.

"I don't know," Fawkes answered. "It's possible, I suppose. But it wouldn't be very clever of Eadulf to try to burn out the wise woman so soon after petitioning me to punish her. And Eadulf strikes me as clever. Clever and cunning."

Gerard nodded and went to fetch the next villager.

It was Alwen, the corn maid. She smiled as she approached, then drew near and murmured, "Thank you again for yesterday."

"'Twas naught," Fawkes answered, embarrassed. He didn't want Gerard to get the wrong idea.

He leaned back so Alwen's pretty face wasn't so close. She took the hint and straightened. "Do you know why you're here?"

"The fire at Glennyth's cottage."

"Do you know anything about it?"

The young woman cocked her head. "I know you're questioning all the villagers. But I wonder if you're looking in the right place. It could have been someone from the castle."

"That's true." He waited for her to say more.

"'Twas Glennyth's cottage that burned, but that doesn't necessarily mean she's the one who was meant to suffer." Alwen's blue eyes focused intently on his, as if she could convey her meaning that way.

Fawkes grew impatient. "Go on."

"Glennyth is friends with Lady Nicola, your wife."

"My wife. What about her?"

"She often seeks out the wise woman. She did so when she was married to Lord Mortimer as well."

Fawkes wanted to shake Alwen. Why could she not simply say what she meant? "I've heard the tales that she poisoned or drugged her first husband," he said, curtly. "What does that have to do with any of this?"

Alwen met his gaze, then glanced away. "Lady Nicola has been to see the healer since you became the new lord."

Fawkes stared at Alwen. "What are you suggesting? Surely you don't think Lady Nicola is drugging me."

A fleeting smile. "Not exactly. Not as she did Mortimer."

Fawkes couldn't help himself. "What the devil are you trying to say? Tell me!"

Alwen flinched, and Fawkes forced himself to sit back. He didn't want the young woman to think he would strike her.

"Tell me," he repeated, more softly. "I swear no ill will come to you for speaking the truth."

Alwen held onto the skirt of her kirtle and twisted it in her hands. After giving him a quick nod, she said, "I didn't mean to eavesdrop. I went to the wise woman seeking a...something for myself. When I drew near the cottage, I heard them talking, Glennyth and Lady Nicola. I didn't catch all that was said, but I did hear the words, *love potion*."

It was all Fawkes could do to keep from laughing. If there was anything Nicola did not need to seek out, it was a love potion.

Alwen bit her lips. "They say that's how Lady Nicola keeps you faithful to her. That's why you didn't futter me yesterday but merely pretended to do so."

Fawkes could not restrain himself. He laughed. "Lady Nicola doesn't need to give me a love potion to keep me from straying from her bed. She's a beautiful, desirable woman, and we've not yet been wed a month."

Alwen nodded. "Of course. I did not mean otherwise."

"And yet you assumed I would dishonor my marriage vows."

Alwen gave him a helpless look. "I don't know what

I thought. I'm merely going by what I was told."

"By whom?"

She bit her lips again. "I can't say."

Fawkes considered threatening to punish Alwen if she didn't tell him, but found he had no heart for it. This was petty stuff, the kind of jealousy-fueled gossip that always made him wary of getting involved with women. He was glad Nicola wasn't like that, always comparing her lot to that of other women.

Unless Alwen was speaking about a man. Fawkes had a sudden uneasy thought. He'd told FitzSaer yesterday that his services as castellan were no longer required and that he should gather his things and go to Mordeaux if he wished to remain employed in Fawkes's mensie. What if, before he left, FitzSaer struck back by setting fire to Glennyth's house?

But that made no sense. Why would FitzSaer take his vengeance on Glennyth? Unless he thought Nicola was behind his dismissal and sought to get back at her through Glennyth. Still, that seemed a stretch.

"Does this person you speak of live at the castle?" Fawkes asked.

Alwen nodded.

"And is it a man or woman?"

"I cannot say."

Fawkes studied her a moment. "I thank you for coming to me with this information, Alwen. I will take it under advisement."

She smiled uncertainly, bowed, and left. Fawkes watched her go, thinking it was a good thing Alwen was so fine to look at. Otherwise he would be heartily annoyed with her for wasting his time.

He said as much to Gerard as they waited for the

next villager. "I'm not certain there's any point continuing. It seems like everyone has an idea who could have set the fire, but no one saw anything or can provide any proof."

"Are we going back to the castle then?"

"If we halt the interrogations now, those who've already been questioned may feel as if they were singled out. And those we haven't questioned may think I'm discounting any information they have. Nay, as tedious it is, I think we must proceed."

****

Nicola stopped by the kitchen. The scullery maids were shelling peas, and there was no sign of the pot boys. Nicola approached Agelwulf, who was butchering a hare. Two other skinned and gutted carcasses lay on the table. "One of the squires, Robbie, has been setting snares in the forest," the cook said.

"We're having rabbit stew for supper?"

"Aye."

"Speaking of the forest, have you heard anything regarding the fire in the village?" Nicola asked.

"Not a word. But then this lot..." Agelwulf gestured toward the skullery maids. "They probably think themselves above anything that happens in the village. Since they dwell at the castle these days."

Nicola nodded. To be chosen to work at the castle rather than laboring in the fields was considered a great opportunity. "Well, keep your ears open. Fawkes is questioning all the villagers, but Glennyth did mention that there are people here at the castle who might bear her ill will."

"I will do so," Agelwulf said. "Although I don't understand why anyone would want to harm a wise woman. Glennyth is always generous in aiding those in need of her services. We're fortunate to have her to tend to our injuries and ills. I keep a supply of salve from her here in the kitchen to use for treating burns. I also get cooking herbs from her. Since Rorik the peddler hasn't been here since spring, I've had to rely on the wild garlic Glennyth gathers for flavoring. Even my supply of salt is running low. In fact, I was going to ask if you could send someone to Mordeaux to see if they had any to spare."

"I will go myself," Nicola said. Fetching salt would give her an excuse to return to Mordeaux and see Simon. Her heart squeezed with happiness at the thought. But then she thought of Fawkes. He might think it strange if she went to Mordeaux again so soon. Nay, it would be better to send one of the squires. There would be other opportunities to see Simon. Indeed, if things continued to progress between her and Fawkes, she might finally be able tell him about Simon. How wonderful that would be, for them to all live together as a family.

To Agelwulf, she said, "I'll send Robbie. He deserves a reward for his efforts to stock the castle larder. Where do you think he is?"

"He goes off to the forest a lot. Or he could be with the other squires in the barracks."

Nicola left the kitchen. She was halfway to the barracks when she realized this errand to Mordeaux might be useful for other things besides fetching salt. Hilary kept a good supply of herbs and decoctions, more so than Nicola. Now that Glennyth's stores had been destroyed, it might be a good idea to see if there was anything in Hilary's supply that Glennyth thought they should have at Valmar.

She headed to the castle. Glennyth was in the solar,

kneeling on the floor examining piles of herbs spread out on the cowhide rug. She looked morose. "So many of the herbs I gathered this summer were destroyed, and some of the plants won't be in season until next spring. I'm especially worried what I'll do without any angelica or foxglove."

"I have an idea how you can replenish some of your stores. I was going to send a squire to Mordeaux to get some salt. Perhaps he could also fetch some healing herbs from Hilary who has a small store."

"'Tis a relief to think Hilary might have some of what I need. But you can hardly send a squire to fetch herbs. Especially since I don't know exactly what herbs Hilary has. I must go myself. That is, if Fawkes will let me leave Reynard on his own." Glennyth motioned with her head toward the bedchamber, where Nicola presumed Reynard was resting.

"If you go, you'll have to ride there. It would take you near all day to walk."

Glennyth shot her an alarmed look. "I've never ridden a horse. I don't think I could do it. At least, not without days of practice."

"I wouldn't expect you to ride alone. You could ride pillion with one of the knights."

Glennyth still looked uncomfortable with the idea. "I suppose I could do that. If Fawkes allows it."

"Maybe we won't tell him." Nicola liked the idea of sending Glennyth to Mordeaux. Glennyth could talk openly with Hilary and find out how Simon was faring. It wasn't as good as going herself, but certainly better than sending Robbie.

Glennyth raised her brows. "Another secret from your husband?"

"I wouldn't keep it secret. I would tell him after you left." She motioned toward the bedchamber. "How do you think Reynard will fare if you're not here to tend him for a day or two?"

"He'll do well enough. His burns are healing, which was the main concern. As for his injured lungs, there is naught I can do to aid in their healing. He will either get well or he won't."

"That's what I thought." Nicola met Glennyth's gaze. "So will you do it, even if you are uneasy riding a horse?"

"I will do it. I'm eager to find out what stores Hilary has. And I should probably get used to riding a horse anyway. There are times when being able to reach a patient quickly is crucial."

"I'll go arrange a knight to take you."

"I'll put these things away. And say farewell to Reynard."

"You might wish to save your farewell until it's time to leave. I don't want Reynard to try and stop you. Or for him to seek out Fawkes so that he does."

"Reynard has no control over what I do. But I will heed your advice."

Nicola started to leave. Then she turned back. "Pack some things to stay the night. 'Tis nearly sext. By the time you get there and talk to Hilary, 'twill be too late to ride back."

"I'll put these things away and get ready."

Nicola left the solar feeling a nagging twinge of guilt. She told herself she wasn't exactly deceiving her husband, merely delaying telling him what she'd done until there was no time for him to undo it.

She sought out Sir Godfrey, who had been in the

castle garrison for years, and would not question whether she had the right to give him orders. She told him to prepare his mount and meet Glennyth outside the castle on the trackway. Then she hurried back to the solar to help Glennyth get ready. In less than a candle-hour the wise woman was on her to Mordeaux.

With that task out of the way, Nicola went to the weaving shed. Most of the latest wool clip had been spun into thread and it was time begin dyeing. Leaving the weaving shed she started toward Old Thomas's shop. Two of the vats for dying were leaking and needed to be repaired. On the way there, Will the squire rushed up. His freckled face was flushed with excitement. "A group of mummers and musicians are at the gate. Can we invite them in?"

"Of course. Is it the same troupe that came last summer?"

"I think so. Their wagons look familiar, although I don't recognize their leader. Should I go to the kitchen and tell them we have visitors?"

"I will do that. Although, on second thought…" Abruptly Nicola realized it wasn't really her place to invite the traveling troupe to perform. Fawkes was lord of the castle now; it should be his decision. She felt a sudden stab of resentment. She'd managed well enough these past years, dealing with things like this on her own. Surely he would not care if she invited the entertainers to perform.

"Aye. Go to the kitchen and alert Agelwulf."

Will ran off, and Nicola started down the trackway to the village. The performers and their wanes were in the field below the castle. Their leader came forward to greet her. He had glossy black hair in long curls and wore a crimson tunic with gold braid.

"Lady Mortimer." He bowed low. "I'm pleased to meet you. I've heard much of your grace and beauty. I'm Alan de Ronay, jongleur. I've performed all over the realm, including for Lady Eleanor, the queen mother herself."

Nicola was rather taken aback by the man's fine speech and elegant manners. She managed to say, "I'm no longer Lady Mortimer. I'm wed to Fawkes de Cressy now."

"De Cressy? I haven't heard of him."

"He's recently back from Crusade with King Richard."

"What happened to Lord Mortimer?"

"He's dead. He was killed in combat with de Cressy."

"How long ago was this?"

"A little more than a month past." Nicola was puzzled by the man's questions. Traveling players usually took little interest in local politics. They should be discussing the fee for the troupe's performance, not these matters.

"That may complicate things," de Ronay said.

"I may have a new husband, but he is an honorable man and if he agrees to have you perform, you will be well-paid for your performance."

"That's not what I am concerned about." The jongleur drew near and lowered his voice. "Do you recall speaking to Father FitzAlan about the circumstances here at Valmar?"

Despite the heat of the day, Nicola's body turned cold. "I do recall that conversation. But it took place months and months ago. Things are entirely different now."

"That may be, but the prince's plans haven't changed."

She thought of Father FitzAlan's words: *When Prince John has decided on a course of action, he will send a message.* "Nay." She shook her head vigorously. "This is a mistake. Mortimer was a drunken fool. That's partly why Fawkes was able to defeat him easily. But Fawkes is an altogether different sort of man. He's a skilled warrior, and he leads a troupe of experienced knights. If Prince John sends someone to attack Valmar now, I vow they'll meet with fierce resistance."

"The plan isn't to attack Valmar, but Mordeaux. Once it falls, it will provide a base of operations for the assault on Valmar."

Nay! Not Mordeaux! Nicola was on the edge of hysteria. She sought to calm herself and reason with this man. "Is the Prince prepared for a long siege? Because that's what he can expect. My father built both Mordeaux and Valmar to withstand a powerful assault. It would take months and months for an enemy army to take either castle."

De Ronay shrugged. "I know nothing of warfare. I'm merely delivering the message. As a courtesy to you, the woman who set these events in motion."

"And I'm telling you, you must go back to John's court and explain the changes that have taken place here. You must convince him to alter his plans."

"I'm not in John's employ. I'm a jongleur. I don't involve myself in politics. I can't afford to take sides in this conflict between the king and his brother."

"But you *are* involved or you would not be carrying this message. You must take this one back for me."

Nicola reached out and grasped de Ronay's arm. "Please! I'm begging you!"

Chapter Sixteen

As Fawkes and Gerard approached the castle, Gerard pointed to several dozen wagons near the gate. "It looks like a troupe of entertainers have arrived."

"Probably the same bunch that came through last summer," added Geoffrey, the other Mortimer knight who'd accompanied them. "If it's the same group, I can tell you, the tumblers are very skilled. I would very much like to see them again." He gave Fawkes a hopeful look.

"I suppose it would be a welcome distraction after the fire," Fawkes answered.

As they drew nearer, Fawkes saw Nicola talking to one of the performers, a dark-haired man in a gaudy red tunic. At first he assumed she was arranging the fee to be paid or other details. Then he saw how close the two were standing and that Nicola was holding the man's arm. Jealousy shot through him and he glanced at Gerard and Geoffrey, wondering if either of them had noticed. But they were both watching two comely young women unloading one of the wanes.

Fawkes looked away and continued to walk toward the castle. He wished he could as easily distance himself from the thoughts swirling in his brain: *When the dark-haired performer came last summer, had Nicola dallied with him? And if she had, what was it to him? He'd had no claim upon her then. But if she'd been unfaithful, even to worthless, despicable Mortimer, didn't it show a lack of honor and loyalty? Especially if she'd cuckolded Mortimer with a man like that, a flamboyant coxcomb who likely bedded a different woman at every castle and village he visited.*

By the time he reached the castle, Fawkes was furious. So furious he had to keep away from Nicola. He started toward the barracks, then abruptly realized Reynard wouldn't be there. If his captain had followed Glennyth's orders, he was resting in the lord's tower.

He found him there, seated in the solar with a large book in his lap. Fawkes stared at his captain in astonishment. "You can read?"

Reynard looked up. "Of course I can't read. Who would have taught me? And when? But I can still admire a book. Look at this. How beautifully the letters are formed. On some of the pages there are pictures. 'Tis truly a work of art."

Fawkes went to the bed and leaned over Reynard's shoulder. He traced the elegant curve of a large letter at the top of the page. "They must have used gold ink. You're right 'Tis beautiful. And that letter, it's an S. I know that much."

"There must be a dozen books in the chest in the bedchamber."

"They must have belonged to Nicola's father."

"Probably. But I found one of them in a basket with some thread, cloth, and the like. I'd be willing to wager Nicola has been reading that one."

Fawkes nodded. "When she went over the accounts with the reeve, 'twas clear she can read and write. But something like this...this is the sort of thing that's read for pure enjoyment."

His wife was not only beautiful and highly

competent, she was exceedingly well educated. More so than most men.

"And there's another thing I found," Reynard said. "In the basket were several half-finished garments. Children's garments."

"I know about that. She said she sews for the son of Lady Hilary, who is wed to Gilbert de Vescy, the castellan at Mordeaux."

"But de Vescy also has a daughter. I remember her because of her reddish hair. As one who's endured such unfortunate coloring all my life, I take special notice of children who are similarly afflicted." Reynard grinned ruefully.

"What of it? Why are you mentioning these things?"

"Doesn't it seem odd that Nicola sews garments for one child and not the other?"

"Perhaps she has a special fondness for the boy for some reason."

"Aye. Perhaps because he is near the age her child would be if he had not died at birth."

Fawkes felt his chest squeeze. As foolish it was, he could not help mourning his dead son.

"I thought you should know," Reynard continued. "Because it does seem to give lie to the tale that she killed the child. If she strangled the babe, why would she go to all the trouble to sew for another child of similar age?"

"Perhaps she feels guilty and sews these garments as a sort of penance."

Reynard's green eyes fixed on Fawkes. "I thought things were better between you, and you'd decided she wasn't capable of doing such a thing."

"Things were better."

"*Were?*"

Fawkes felt a muscle twitch in his jaw. "I just saw her talking to some fop of an entertainer. Her hand was on his arm and they were standing very close."

"An entertainer? What do you mean?"

"A troupe of traveling performers has arrived. Geoffrey says they've been here before. He mentioned how skilled the tumblers were. I presume Nicola has asked them to stay and perform. They're outside the castle right now, unloading their wains."

"And you think Nicola knows this man from previous visits, and that they…"

Fawkes raised a hand. "Don't say it. 'Twill make my blood boil and I won't be fit company for anyone."

"But if she did have a…liaison with this man, what of it? She wasn't wed to you at the time. Indeed, she didn't even know you were alive, let alone that you would return."

"I know it's irrational and foolish, but I can't help it." His hands were clenched into fists. He unclenched them and took a deep breath. Reynard was right; he was acting like a lackwit.

"I think you're losing your temper over nothing. That Nicola was behaving familiarly with the man in clear view of everyone makes it unlikely there is anything scandalous or improper between them. Perhaps the troupe has been coming here for years and she's simply pleased to see him."

Everything Reynard said made perfect sense. And yet, there was something about the way Nicola clutched the man's arm. All his instincts told Fawkes there was something between her and this man beyond fondness or friendship.

"I will do as you suggest and try to forget what I saw. Because if it wasn't for my concern over this man, things have been very good between Nicola and me the last few days."

"Concentrate on that then. I can't imagine an elegant and refined lady like Nicola—who can read and write and run a castle to perfection—that she would have any interest in a tumbler or knife thrower."

Fawkes nodded. He'd done the right thing in seeking out Reynard. For all his jesting, Reynard had an excellent understanding of human nature. He could scarce think of a time when Reynard steered him wrong. "I presume that since you've been out of bed and snooping around the solar, you must be feeling better?"

"My chest still hurts, but Glennyth said that will take time to ease. And I'm very fortunate the burns are on the back of my hands, and don't interfere with my use of them. At any rate, she thought I was doing well enough that she's left me on my own."

"Left you? What do you mean?"

"She's gone to Mordeaux. Apparently de Vescy's wife has a supply of herbs and Glennyth hoped to replenish her own stores with some of hers."

"I'm pleased to think Glennyth believes you're well enough to be on your own. But I'd rather she hadn't gone off like that. I was clear I expected her to stay and see to you."

"I'm well enough, and growing tired of being an invalid. I wish I could have gone with you to question the villagers. Did you find out anything useful?"

"Nay. The whole day was a tedious waste. My questions yielded nothing."

"No one saw anything suspicious?"

"Several people made suggestions as to who could have set the fire, but no one would say anything that could prove it. "

"Who do they think did it?"

"The miller mostly. And then there was Edith, whose husband died last winter. She's bitter that Glennyth couldn't save him. And young Alwen, the corn queen, hinted it was someone who lived here at the castle, but she wouldn't give me a name." Fawkes let out a sigh. "We may never know who set the fire, which is both infuriating and concerning. It means there is someone living in the village or the castle that is capable of murder. Worse yet, they may try again."

"You think Glennyth is still in danger?"

"I doubt the person who set the fire would strike again so soon."

"At least she is out of the way for now. She should be safe on this journey to Mordeaux."

"Is she walking there? 'Tis quite a distance."

"Nay. She's riding pillion with some knight."

"And that doesn't bother you?" Fawkes asked.

Reynard shrugged.

"I wish I could trust Nicola. Sometimes I get close. But then she does something to make me doubt her all over again. Like seeing her holding on to the arm of a traveling player." Fawkes made a disgusted face.

"Give her a chance to explain. I suspect it's nothing like what you think."

"I hope not." Fawkes started to leave, and then stopped at the doorway. "Do you feel well enough to come to the hall for the evening meal?"

"I'm certain I can make it there. I wouldn't want to miss the performers."

"Ah, the performers," Fawkes muttered as he left Reynard and started down the stairs. He enjoyed tumblers and mummers as much as anyone, but he resented this bunch. Why did they have to come now, and ruin the fragile trust he had been building with Nicola? But Reynard was right. He must talk to her and get her explanation for her behavior before he became too angry.

He found Nicola in the kitchen talking to Agelwulf. She seemed to tense when she saw him, and there was a hint of wariness in her eyes. Once again, her manner suggested deceit. He forced himself to set aside his instinctive response. "Nicola, can I speak to you?"

She followed him outside the kitchen. He halted by a water barrel and tried to decide how to approach the matter. "I noticed you talking to one of the performers—that dark-haired fellow. Is he the head of the troupe? Is he the one I should see about payment for their performance this evening?"

"I…that's already arranged, milord. You needn't concern yourself with those details."

"You paid him *before* they performed?"

"Nay. But we have agreed on the terms."

"Is that what you were talking to him about when I arrived at the castle?"

"I'm certain it was." She gave him a fleeting smile.

"This mummer, or tumbler, or juggler, or whatever he is, does he come regularly to Valmar?"

"The troupe has been here before, but not de Ronay. This is his first visit here."

A lie? If so, it would be easy enough to find out. "So you don't know this man, this de Ronay?"

"Nay, milord."

There she was, back to calling him *milord*. It seemed

to make a mockery of the intimacy they'd shared.

Fawkes cleared his throat. "I find that strange since I saw you with your hand on his arm having an intense conversation with him."

"We were discussing payment, as I told you. And I...I asked him for a favor."

"What favor is that?"

"I asked him to sing a special song for Agelwulf, the cook, for arranging a fine meal on such short notice."

Fawkes stared at her. He felt certain she was lying. "There's also this matter of Glennyth going off to Mordeaux. She should have asked my permission before leaving. And you should have spoken to me before arranging for one of *my* knights to take her."

Nicola gestured vaguely. "You were off in the village. I didn't think you'd mind, since Reynard is improving. Glennyth is very concerned about the loss of her medicinal herbs this late in the season. If Hilary can provide some of the plants destroyed in the fire, 'twill benefit everyone."

Fawkes said nothing, but stared at her for long moments. Then he turned and walked away.

****

Nicola's stomach twisted with anxiety as she watched him go. Once again she lied to him. Or, not lying exactly, but not telling the full truth either. She had no doubt he would soon forget this business of Glennyth going to Mordeaux. But this situation with Prince John, that was far more troubling. For a few brief days, she had felt hopeful and relaxed. Now she was back to being poised on a knife's edge.

Maybe she should give up and tell Fawkes the whole wretched tale. But if she did that, she would have proven him right—that she *was* scheming and manipulative. She didn't want to risk having to start over again in winning his trust. Better to try untangling this mess on her own. She would write a letter to Prince John and explain how unwise it would be to launch an attack on Mordeaux, or Valmar either.

For a while Nicola was too busy to worry. It was not easy pulling together a festive meal with so little notice. Especially since once word of their arrival had spread, many of the villagers had come to watch the performers, near doubling the crowd in the hall.

But somehow they managed to get everyone fed. Then the trestle tables were moved to the sides of the hall and everyone waited for the performers.

Two young women appeared, dressed in costumes of bright rose and saffron. They wore short snug tunics on their upper bodies, along with braies that gathered at the waist and ankles, covering their legs. A short filmy skirt preserved a bit of their modesty, but as they began to perform graceful cartwheels and flip head over heels, the shape of their legs and hips was clearly visible. They had dark hair and eyes and looked as if they might be sisters. They both had pulled back their hair in a single tight braid that whipped around wildly as they performed.

A man joined them. He wasn't much bigger than the women, but his muscles bulged beneath his snug costume, which was dyed the brilliant hues of scarlet and apricot. He walked halfway across the hall on his hands, and then executed a series of flips high into the air. Gasps and exclamations erupted from the crowd

The man did several more amazing flips. Then he joined hands with the two women and the three of them performed flips and cartwheels in unison. The acrobats finished and bowed. Another man appeared, in vivid green and saffron. The two men balanced the women on their shoulders and performed several more amazing feats.

Nicola glanced briefly at Fawkes. Having seen the entertainers before, she knew that after the tumblers finished, the mummers would appear and perform a raucous, silly skit portraying a man and a woman taking a pig to market. As the husband and wife fought, near beating each other black and blue, the *pig* would escape and end up sitting on the lap of the one of the prettiest maids in the hall.

Nicola had never understood the hilarity of watching people strike each other and shout insults, but she knew by the end of the performance most of those gathered in the hall would be so overcome with mirth they would be wiping tears from their eyes. If Fawkes was like his fellow knights, he would be amused enough by the skit that he would take little note of her absence.

When the acrobats began their finale—forming a tower with their bodies—Nicola stood and mouthed the word *garderobe*. Fawkes frowned at her, but said nothing.

Nicola found de Ronay at the back of the hall and bid him follow her outside. She halted near the cistern. "Two things I must tell you. If my husband seeks you out, you must explain to him that earlier today when we speaking outside the castle, we were discussing your fee and that I asked you to perform a special song for Agelwulf, the cook, who supervised the preparation of the fine repast this evening. Then, of course, you must sing something in Agelwulf's honor when you perform.

Do you understand?"

De Ronay nodded.

"Second, I know you said that it is too late to change the prince's plans, but I must try. I'm going to write a message for you to carry to court explaining my concerns."

"A message? Aye, I'm willing to carry a message. Give it to me ere we leave on the morrow."

"How soon will you be able to take it to London?"

"The troupe has several more stops planned before we head back to court."

That might be too late, Nicola thought in panic. "Do you have to remain with the troupe? Could you not leave now and go to London?"

De Ronay's dark eyes glittered. "I could. For a price."

"How much?"

"Ten silver marks."

Nicola gasped. "That's a fortune!"

De Ronay shrugged. "I must be compensated for my share of what the troupe will earn over the next fortnight. And I'll need a horse."

"I can provide you with a horse." Nicola wondered how she would ever explain this to Fawkes.

"We're agreed then?" the jongleur asked. "Ten marks?"

Nicola made her voice hard. "Five."

De Ronay stared at her a moment. Then he grinned. "Very well, milady. And now I must get back to the hall. I perform next." He bowed.

****

"You hedge-witted varlet!" the woman screeched. "With the money from the pig, we must buy a new cauldron. My old one has so many holes you could use it for a fishing weir!"

The man thrust his shoulders back and his chin forward, glaring at the woman. "We'll buy a plow!" he bellowed. He took a swipe at her, nearly knocking her off the table that served as their stage. "Take that, you sow-faced, swag-bellied old wench!"

Next to the two, the *pig*, that was really a man in a tan costume, complete with real pig's ears and a curly tail, waggled his rear end and farted loudly.

Loud guffaws of laughter sounded. Fawkes took no part in the hilarity. All he could think of was Nicola, and the fact that she had been gone longer than it took to go to the garderobe. He was on the verge of getting up to look for her when she entered the hall and sat next to him. Although he gave her a long, searching look, her expression remained cool and collected.

The mummers finished their performance and the jongleur appeared. He took a seat on a stool, strummed his lute, and began to sing. Fawkes had to admit the man was talented. His voice was rich and deep and filled the hushed hall as he sang.

After a long, sad ballad, the jongleur performed several lighter, more playful songs. The mood in the hall changed from somber to boisterous. As people stomped their feet and sang along, Fawkes lost interest and again focused his attention on his wife. Should he ask where she'd been so long? There seemed no point. She likely wouldn't tell the truth anyway.

It was so frustrating. She'd had to be devious and cunning to survive being married to Mortimer, but her circumstances were completely different now. Didn't she realize he would never hurt her? That he wanted nothing more than to protect her and keep her safe? Couldn't she trust him to do that?

The jongleur finished the bawdy ditty and began another ballad. Fawkes focused on the singer. Perhaps instead of questioning Nicola, he should speak to de Ronay. But the man seemed so sly and slimy. With his glossy dark hair falling in curls around his shoulders and his ostentatious clothing, de Ronay was the sort of man who sought the favor of women over men, undoubtedly because he had a better chance of manipulating them.

Fawkes regarded the jongleur's bright red samite tunic, with its lavish gold embroidery, with distaste. Some woman had clearly slaved for hours making the garment. Some woman de Ronay had left behind when he moved on to the next castle or town. It must be very easy for him. Right now it appeared every woman in the hall was watching him with adoration and awe, even the kitchen wenches and Old Emma, who leaned heavily on a walking stick.

Fawkes struggled to tamp down his disgust. He turned to look at Nicola. At least she didn't appear to be mooning over de Ronay. Indeed, she didn't seem to be paying any attention to his performance. Her expression was distant. When she caught him looking at her, she gave him a nervous, distracted smile. "He's very good, isn't he?"

"I suppose so. If you like that sort of thing."

"You don't like music, milord?"

Fawkes's irritation burst its banks. "I've told you not to call me, *milord*. I'm your husband, not your liege."

"Of course."

Although she didn't add the dreaded title this time, Fawkes heard her saying it in her head. How was he to ever make her feel comfortable with him? Would she always remain so wary and distant? He wanted so much for her to trust him, and to feel that he could trust *her*. But every time they seemed to be growing close, something happened.

Fawkes scanned the hall for the tumblers and the mummers but didn't see them. They'd probably gone back to their wagons to rest and relax. This might be a good time to question them.

He rose from the table and made his way through the crowded hall. Once in the bailey, he quickened his pace. As he passed through the gate, he nodded to the guard in the gate tower.

Outside the castle, the performers were gathered around their tents. They had food that appeared to have been specially cooked for them, roast fowl and berry tarts, along with cheese and bread. He approached the two female tumblers, who were seated on a blanket on the grass. They both got to their feet, their movements as effortless and graceful as their performance had been. They looked very young, barely into womanhood. Their fresh beauty reminded him of Alwen.

He nodded to them. "I enjoyed your performance. You're very skilled and lovely to watch."

"Thank you, milord," answered the one who looked a bit older. They dipped their heads in deference.

"I understand you've performed at Valmar before."

"Aye," the older one answered. "We have been here the past two summers, close to St. John's Day."

"All of you? Including the jongleur?" Fawkes gestured in the direction of the castle.

The younger woman spoke: "Alan de Ronay joined us this spring. We're fortunate to have him as part of our troupe. He's performed for the royal household in London."

"And where do you travel to from here?"

"We're on our way to Shrewsbury, milord."

He suddenly realized that young as they were, these women might not have any idea what de Ronay was up to. "I'll let you get back to your meal."

The two young women bowed to him and then resumed their seats. Fawkes headed to the castle. When he arrived, de Ronay had finished his performance and a number of women had gathered around him. There was no sign of Nicola, but Fawkes did see Reynard. He went over to him. "Did you see where Nicola went?"

"She said she was going to get the money to pay the performers."

Fawkes nodded in distraction. Everything Nicola had said and done this day made sense. But he couldn't get over the sense she was lying about something.

"What's amiss now, Fawkes?" Reynard asked.

Fawkes didn't answer. He should be relieved that Nicola wasn't with de Ronay. Although the jongleur had plenty of attention. Observing the bevy of women surrounding him, Fawkes muttered a curse.

****

Down in the storage cellar, Nicola carefully blew on the piece of parchment, trying to dry the ink so she could roll up the missive and give it to de Ronay. She wished the jongleur could leave tonight. But it would seem odd if he left before the rest of the performers.

She shook the parchment again, then carefully rolled it up and secured it with a piece of yarn and slipped it in a basket. After covering the missive with dried-up apples from last season, she grabbed the candle and started up the stairs. Out in the bailey, she looked for Fawkes. Seeing no sign of him, she crossed the yard, hurried through the gate and down the trackway to the performers' camp.

She sought out the two female tumblers. They were seated on a blanket with the Valmar knights Guy and Oliver. The squire Will sat on the grass nearby. The five appeared to be sharing a jack of wine.

She drew near, smiling. "It appears you are enjoying this fine evening."

"Aye, milady." Guy rose quickly to his feet, followed by the other two men.

She motioned to the young women, "I wonder if one of you could show me which wagon belongs to the jongleur.

"None of them do," the younger of the women replied.

"Well, who does he travel with? Where does he keep his things?"

"He rides with Roald," the woman answered. "Come, I'll show you."

The woman took Nicola to a large wagon. The cargo area contained several bags and chests. "Do you know which of these belong to Alan?"

"I think this chest is his."

Nicola nodded, but she needed to be sure. She leaned over the wagon and opened the chest. Observing the elaborate men's clothing inside, Nicola felt confident the chest belonged to the jongleur. She took the missive out of her basket and laid it on top of the clothing, then shut the lid. "Thank you," she told the woman.

Nicola returned to the castle and went looking for de Ronay. When she didn't find him in the hall, she asked the serving girls cleaning up if they had seen him. They told her he had left with Maida. Nicola was surprised. Maida seemed so young and innocent. But perhaps that was how de Ronay liked them.

Nicola felt a flare of distaste. De Ronay was the sort of man who charmed and seduced women and then left them alone and heartbroken and likely sometimes pregnant.

She began her search in the stables. When she first called out for him, there was no answer, even though she heard rustling noises in the hayloft. Changing strategy, she called Maida's name, and was rewarded when a soft female voice responded, "Milady?"

Nicola made her voice hard. "De Ronay, are you there?"

More rustling. De Ronay leaned over the edge. "Milady?" he asked in a cool, sardonic tone.

"Please come down here. I must speak with you."

More rustling and tense whispering. The jongleur appeared, wearing braes and chausses but no tunic. Nicola glanced at his bare chest and decided it was easy to tell de Ronay was not a knight. His lean, tanned body was as smooth and unmarred as a woman's. "I left the missive you will carry to London in your storage coffer in the wagon," she said, quietly.

"What about my payment?"

"I could hardly leave it with the missive. It would not be safe."

"But when will you pay me? If you wish me to leave at first light, you should give it to me now."

"Very well. Come with me. But put some clothes on first."

De Ronay climbed back in the loft. Nicola looked

around the stables, feeling a vague sense of unease. She hoped Maida hadn't been able to hear their conversation.

A few moments later, de Ronay climbed down the ladder. This time he was fully dressed.

"Come," Nicola said. Near the entrance of the stables, she hesitated, wondering if she should peek out and see if anyone was around to see them.

Even as she had the thought, a dark shape loomed in the doorway. "Nicola? What are you doing here?"

Chapter Seventeen

Nicola froze like a cornered coney. De Ronay was behind her. Long seconds passed as terrible thoughts went through Fawkes's mind. *Truly? You would dally with a jongleur in the stables? What sort of slut—*

"My apologies to your wife, milord. I'm afraid she found me with one of the serving maids." De Ronay's tone was apologetic, but his words were smooth and practiced. "I didn't realize the girl was so young."

"He was with Maida," Nicola said.

Relief crashed through Fawkes. The next moment his outrage returned. *Cradle-robbing bastard! The girl couldn't be more than thirteen summers!* Fawkes felt the urge to grab the jongleur, throw him to the ground and pound his face to mush.

But he could not. It was an old belief, but deeply ingrained. Musicians and entertainers were special and must be protected. He could no more batter and beat de Ronay than he could a priest who angered him. Besides, it would not be a fair contest. He could easily kill de Ronay with one calculated blow.

"Get out of my sight, de Ronay. If I see you within the castle walls, or hear tell you have been with any female under my protection, I'll cut your pretty face to ribbons. Do you understand?"

"Aye, milord." The jongleur bowed and walked off, the lack of haste in his movements suggesting he had experienced many similar threats and survived them all.

"Thank you." Nicola exhaled in apparent relief. "I don't mind him dallying with the women, but when I learned he was with Maida, I thought about how I would feel if it were my younger sister."

Fawkes nodded. His relief was so intense it made him almost dizzy. When he'd gone looking for Nicola and learned she'd asked about de Ronay and been seen going into the stables, his jealousy had flamed out of control. Convinced she was alone with the jongleur, he'd wanted to kill both of them. Thankfully, he'd been wrong. "Have you checked to see if Maida is well?" he asked.

"I thought I'd give her a moment to make herself presentable."

"It got so far as that?"

"I'm afraid so."

Fawkes felt a renewal of his outrage, as the image of Maida's pert freckled nose and strawberry blonde curls filled his mind. The girl was too young to know what she was doing. "After you've seen to the girl, please meet me outside."

He left the stables. As he waited for Nicola, he sought to calm himself. He still wanted to throttle de Ronay. At least the man would be gone on the morrow. That was something to be grateful for. With luck, Nicola had intervened before things went so far that Maida ended up with child. He wondered how Nicola had found out what was going on. He hadn't seen her in the hall when de Ronay was flirting with the group of women. Indeed, he still didn't know where she'd been that last few minutes.

He told himself to let it go, but somehow he

couldn't. Nicola had behaved oddly ever since the entertainers arrived. He kept going back to seeing her holding de Ronay's arm. It had seemed like a gesture of familiarity. Now, looking back, he wondered if she'd grabbed the jongleur's arm in distress. But why? What had he done to upset her?

A few moments later, Nicola came out of the stables with her arm around Maida. "I'm going to take her to the weaving shed. It may take a few moments to get her settled."

He didn't really want to stand around by the stables. "I'll wait for you in the hall. Be as quick as you can. There are things I need to speak to you about."

Nicola nodded in response.

****

"You need to know that some men are like that," Nicola told Maida as they approached the rear of the weaving shed, where the castle's unmarried female servants slept. "They'll say all sorts of things to get you into bed."

"I don't care if he didn't mean any of it!" Maida pulled away from Nicola. "This was my chance to lie with a man who is handsome and charming. To have a *man* rather than some stupid boy, or that old dullard my father arranged for me to wed!"

"You're betrothed? To whom?"

Maida's comely face twisted with scorn. "To Old Edwin. He must be thirty-five summers or more!"

Oh, aye. The man's practically in his grave, Nicola thought irritably. Foolish Maida didn't know how fortunate she was. Thirty-five was hardly old. She suspected the real reason Maida scorned Edwin was because he was a stolid, rather boring man. Yet he was also kind and generous. Maida could do much worse. Even so, Nicola couldn't help asking, "Is there someone else you prefer? Some young man you have a fondness for?"

Maida shrugged. "I would fancy any man who could take me away from this place."

"And you think the jongleur would?"

"He said as much."

"That is most certainly a lie." Maida gave her a sullen look. Nicola had the horrible thought that de Ronay might be lying to her as well. How would she know if he delivered the message or not? Again she focused on Maida, "Why do you want to leave Valmar?"

"I have no future here. The best I can hope to be is the wife of a farmer. It's either that or a landless knight."

"You must understand, Maida, the world the jongleur sings about isn't real. It's made up. A pretty tale. I know for a certainty he has no intention of taking you with him when he leaves, no matter what he promised you. You must find a way to be content with your lot in life, as we all must."

Maida nodded, but there was resentful look in her eyes and a mutinous set to her jaw. As Nicola left she couldn't help wondering what had happened to make this young woman so dissatisfied and restless. But she didn't have time to worry about Maida. She must get the money for de Ronay, or all their futures would be in peril.

She crossed the yard. Avoiding the main entrance to the castle, she slipped in on the side. Her heart raced as she hurried to the tower stairs. If Fawkes saw her, her plan would be ruined.

She took the stairs as rapidly as she dared. In her bedchamber, she threw open the chest and dug beneath the clothing until she found the money pouch. She counted out the silver and then tried to decide what to carry it in. The silk wimple she wore for mass was hanging from the clothing pole. She snatched it up, wrapped the coins in it and tied the ends into a tight knot. After shoving everything else back in the chest and shutting the lid, she headed for the stairs.

Nicola made it out of the castle without incident. Near the gate, she slowed, not wanting to attract the guard's attention. Only as she reached the entertainers' camp did the anxiety squeezing her chest begin to ease.

Seeing no sign of de Ronay, she went to the wagon where he kept his things. Nicola opened his storage chest. The missive lay on top as before. She put the coins underneath it, then shut the chest and walked away. She had to get back to the castle.

On the way, she encountered one of the male tumblers. "Have you seen de Ronay?" she asked.

The man smirked at her. "Last I heard, he was meeting someone in the village."

De Ronay was unbelievable. The jongleur had barely left Maida before setting up another assignation. Or perhaps he'd arranged both of the trysts earlier and planned to bed both women one after another. The sick feeling in her belly intensified. How could she trust a man who was so deceitful?

When she went through the gate, Fawkes was waiting. She squared her shoulders and prepared to face him. One more time she would lie. Then, God willing, she would be done with deceiving him.

****

"I don't understand." Fawkes said as he and Nicola walked back to the castle. "What good does it do to talk to the man now? I ordered de Ronay to leave. Surely you knew I didn't want anyone at Valmar to have anything more to do with him—including you." Fawkes sought to control his temper.

"I wanted to give him a piece of my mind. I can't believe the lies he told poor Maida. That he meant to take her with him when he left tomorrow. As if he would make her his leman, or some such thing. And all the while he was planning to bed another woman as soon as he was done with her."

"Truly? He arranged to meet someone else?"

"Aye. He's with that woman now."

"Who is it?"

"I don't know."

Fawkes shook his head, feeling the rage build up inside him. "I'm going to find him and give him a piece of *my* mind." He started off.

Nicola was instantly beside him. She grabbed his arm. "Fawkes, you can't! You know bards are protected. Well, he's not a bard exactly, but close."

"I'm not going to kill him. Or even hurt him very much. I'm going to put him in the souterrain and let him rot!"

"Nay, Fawkes! You can't do that!"

He turned to look at her. Her face was pale and her gray eyes wild. For the thousandth time he wondered what was truly going on in her mind. "Why? Why can't I imprison him?"

"Because…because as long as he is here, especially if he is your prisoner… What reason will you give people for what you're doing? Even if he's besmirched Maida's honor, and that of some other woman, that still doesn't give you cause to imprison him. You could demand he pay a fine perhaps. But I doubt he has much coin."

She took a long breath. "Wouldn't it be better to get de Ronay away from here? At least for now? If we find he's left a bastard in Maida's or some other woman's belly, then you can seek justice. But I suspect he's clever enough to avoid getting them pregnant. Otherwise he wouldn't have survived this long."

"You think I should let him go. Walk away. Even after what he's done to Maida?"

"Aye. Because if we keep him here, Maida will never move on with her life. She needs to wed the man her father has betrothed her to. Or find some other man who pleases her more. As long as de Ronay is here, she'll cling to her silly fancy that he might take her with him someday. She'll never be content."

Fawkes had little hope Maida would ever be content anyway. But Nicola did have a point. He wanted de Ronay out of his sight and far, far away from Valmar.

"Very well. I'll let the matter drop. As long as the sly bastard leaves in the morning."

Nicola nodded, looking very relieved. "'Twill be better this way. I promise you."

All her arguments were sound. He could not fault her reasoning. Still, he could not overcome the sense she was protecting de Ronay for some reason.

He shrugged to ease the tension. It had been a long day. Although he wasn't physically fatigued, his mind was weary. There were times the responsibilities of being a lord were downright onerous. But there were benefits to his position. He glanced at Nicola and then took her hand. "Let's go up to the bedchamber. You've done a great deal this day. You deserve to rest."

She smiled at him. "I would like that. Although first

I have another errand I must finish."

"What is it? Why cannot it not wait until the morrow?"

"I need to tell Agelwulf to prepare some food for the performers to take with them. I promised I would do so, and I think they've earned it."

"Aye," Fawkes said, grudgingly. "All except that foul scoundrel de Ronay."

"I won't be long." She touched his arm. "I promise."

He nodded, wondering if it would always be like this. If he would have to share his wife with every other person in the castle, as well as visitors.

****

Nicola started toward the kitchen, then looked back across the bailey to make certain Fawkes entered the castle. When he did so, she turned and headed to the stables, circling around to the back where Theobald had his sleeping quarters. The ostler was seated on bench mending a harness by the light of a horn lantern. He got up as soon as he saw her. He smiled warmly, the skin around his rheumy blue eyes crinkling. "'Twas fine entertainment, wasn't it, milady?"

Nicola smiled back at him. "I'm pleased you enjoyed it."

"The jongleur was especially excellent, wasn't he?"

"Aye. Indeed, that is the reason I am here. The jongleur has had a message from Prince John asking him to return to court. We must lend him a horse, so he can make the journey quickly. I'm not certain when he will be able to return the animal. Is there a mount we can spare indefinitely?"

Theobald thought a moment. "Arrow would do. He's a young gelding, tolerably well-trained, but spirited. Is this man a skilled rider, do you think?"

"I don't know. I hope so. 'Tis a long journey."

Theobald nodded. "Then he will need a strong mount. Aye, Arrow is the one for it. Although I don't know how I'll explain the matter to young Geoffrey. He's been training the beast all summer."

"Leave that to me. I'll think of some way to make it up to him. The important thing is that we do what we can to get de Ronay to London."

"Of course, milady. Mayhaps they've had news of King Richard. Mayhaps he's been freed and is coming back to England at last."

"We can hope so. At any rate, please have Arrow mounted and ready in the morning. I presume the jongleur will ride out quite early."

"Of course, milady." Theobald inclined his head.

Nicola let out a sigh as she crossed the bailey. If de Ronay was dallying with a woman tonight, who knew when he would actually decide to leave? She would have to rouse early and make certain of him.

She sighed again. After this day, all she wanted to do was sleep. Nay, that was not true. What she wanted was for Fawkes to make love to her. Or at least for him to hold her close so she could listen to the steady beating of his heart.

How dear Fawkes had become to her. She'd always felt affection for him, her first lover, who'd taken her maidenhead with such exquisite care. But since he'd returned, her affection had grown into something else. She yearned to be with him, to please him and make him happy. It was as if he'd become a part of her, and without him she would be bereft and empty. Her feelings for him were almost as intense as what she felt for her son.

A terrifying thought. She'd always been willing to do anything for her son. Take any risk, give up everything, even her own life. Now she'd begun to feel that way about Fawkes. And he was a grown man, a warrior. How was she to keep him safe? She could not. Especially if some greedy baron allied with Prince John attacked Valmar or Mordeaux.

But she'd done all she could to prevent that. Now it was in God's hands. She should go the chapel and pray. But Fawkes was waiting for her, and she didn't want to make him wait any longer.

Her longing for him almost made her ache. She thought of the scent of him, tangy and male. The warm strength of his chest. The feel of his firm skin. The shape of his jaw and the gleam in his dark eyes when he looked at her. A shiver coursed down her body. Not from cold or dread, but desire. She quickened her pace.

****

Where was she? If she didn't come soon, he would fall asleep. The bed was soft and the breeze wafting through the tower window lulled him even closer to slumber. The balmy air carried the peaceful scent of new-mown hay and the sweetness of the late summer roses in the castle garden.

As pleasant as these odors were, they were nothing compared to the heady, intoxicating scent of Nicola's skin. Breathing in that fragrance always scattered his wits. Even when Nicola's behavior was maddening, he was in thrall to her. Was it love, this bone-deep yearning? This longing that turned him as helpless and foolish as a moonstruck boy?

He still had doubts. Still felt certain she kept secrets from him. Yet, it didn't seem to matter. Even as he told himself he couldn't trust her, her hold on his heart remained as fierce as ever.

The sound of dainty footsteps on the stairs. At last. A few heartbeats later and she was in the room with him. His lovely dream come to life. He sat up in bed and said, "I've been waiting a long time." The next moment he cursed himself. He sounded a peevish child. Nothing mattered but that she was here with him now.

"I'm sorry I made you wait. Agelwulf and I were discussing what food to send with the entertainers that would keep well in the heat."

Nicola undressed. Fawkes watched, glad he had left the night candle burning. All day she'd worn her plain blue work gown. She probably hadn't had time to change. At least with her simple attire the lacing was in front rather than under her arms. He sat back and watched as she undid the laces and pulled the gown over her head.

She hung the garment on the clothing pole, then removed her linen shift and did the same with it. He threw aside the light coverlet as she approached the bed. She climbed in next to him. He leaned over and pulled her on top of him. When she raised herself, he gently touched her face. "Lie still."

She settled her head on his chest and he exhaled deeply. There was something so satisfying in holding her close like this. Even though his body urged him to join with her, another part of him preferred this tender intimacy. Their hearts beating close. Their breathing in soft rhythm. The heat of their bodies mingling. As if they were one being rather than two.

He savored each moment. The soft breeze wafting through the windows. The captivating scent of her, both enticing and soothing. The silky feel of her body molded to his. The tickle of her hair against his chest.

She sighed faintly and he wondered if she was impatient to make love. She must feel his cock hard against her hip and wonder when they would couple. Or how they would do it. Whether he would roll her on her back and enter her immediately. Driving deep, making her cry out. Or if he would start slowly and leisurely. Gently caressing her. Exploring her delicious, pliant flesh. He might use his mouth, licking and sucking. Teasing her with his tongue and lips until she trembled with arousal. So many delightful choices. And they had the whole night ahead of them. Time to do it a half dozen different ways.

And yet, that was not what he wanted. What he yearned for most was not to satisfy his body's craving, but his soul. He wanted to be close to Nicola, to join with her in some deep profound way. He stroked her hair, smoothing it away from her face. Her beautiful face. So elegant, remote and mysterious. Would he ever really know her? Would he always wonder about her secrets? If she remained forever an enigmatic puzzle, would he be able to live with that? Perhaps her elusiveness was even part of her allure. She was the lady of Valmar, and in some ways he would always feel as if she was above him. As if, instead of expecting her to do his bidding, he was the one who should grovel at her feet and seek to please her.

Yet there was one thing between them where he had been confident from the very beginning. Even when he'd been a raw squire and she the mistress of the household, he'd believed that in the bedchamber, he must be the master, the one who took control. He'd never doubted he knew how to make her moan and sigh, to pleasure her and to give her what she needed. His big cock inside her, filling her, satisfying her, carrying her away to rapturous release.

The thought robbed his body of its tenuous control. He could no longer ignore the building tension in his groin, the hard ache of lust. His breathing quickened and his body came alive. His desire was too fierce to tamp down. Yet he would not take her heedlessly. At least in this he could find out what she was thinking.

He rolled on top of her, so they were face-to-face. "What is your desire, Nicola? How would you have me love you?"

She touched his face. Her voice was husky, "I want you to be bold. To love me with no restraint. I would forget this day and the last few days. Fill my senses and make me think of you, only you."

Her words fired his lust even higher. He bent his head to kiss her and the irresistible passion exploded between them.

****

She woke to darkness. The night candle had gone out, perhaps extinguished by the breeze from the unshuttered window. If only she didn't have to get up and make certain de Ronay left. If only she could stay here in bed, content and protected in Fawkes's arms. He made her feel safe. Cherished. Loved.

She wished she could see him. Peruse his handsome face, soft and relaxed in sleep. His arm was draped over her waist, as if he kept watch over her, guarding against all threats. Surely this man who was so protective of her would never harm her child. Even if Fawkes didn't believe Simon was his son, it wouldn't matter. Simon would be safe. And he would be with her. Fawkes would not refuse her if she asked him to bring Simon to Valmar.

Aye, she would tell him. Today. Once de Ronay was

gone, and she'd done all she could to avert the disaster she'd set in motion last winter. It was time to stop hiding things from Fawkes, to trust him. The thought brought her a sense of relief. Her eyelids drooped, her limbs slackened and she knew no more.

She woke as the first gray light of dawn seeped through the window. Fawkes's arm was draped over her. She eased from his embrace and got out of bed. After putting on her shift, she grabbed her other clothing and her shoes. She left the room as quietly as she could and padded down the stairs. Near the privy, she encountered Old Emma. "You're awake early."

"Aye. 'Tis the curse of old age. I can't sleep at night, yet yearn to nap all day." The servant yawned. "And what of you? Here you are, prowling around in your shift like a serving maid leaving her lover's bed."

"I have to make certain of something."

"Does it involve the jongleur? 'Twas gossip in the hall that you sought him out not once, but twice."

Nicola drew in her breath sharply. *She could do nothing but the whole castle knew every detail.* "Who spoke of it?"

"'Twas Alys. You know her, always one to gossip. Especially if it has to do with you. I think she has a *tendre* for Fawkes. When he first came and the two of you were at odds, I know she sought him out and tried to get him to bed her."

A flash of jealousy pierced her. "He didn't do it, did he?"

"I think not. Otherwise Alys wouldn't be so peevish and spiteful in the way she speaks of you."

"Aye. My mission does involve the jongleur, and it's nothing like what people think." Nicola considered telling

Old Emma the whole tale, then realized she did not have time. "Can you help me dress and tidy my hair? I must hurry."

"Of course, milady."

Old Emma helped her into the gown and laced up the front. Then she had Nicola sit on the stool in the alcove while she smoothed her tangled hair and worked it into two plaits.

Old Emma stepped back. "That's the best I can do without fetching your brush. I don't like this, lady. Sneaking out of the castle like this. What if Fawkes wakes and asks about you?"

"Tell him…tell him I had to see to something in the kitchen and that I will be back very soon."

Old Emma shook her head and made grumbling sounds as Nicola hurried off.

Chapter Eighteen

Theobald met her at the entrance to the stables. "Arrow is chomping at the bit, but the jongleur has not come yet."

Nicola gave the ostler a tight smile. "I'll see what's keeping him."

Her heart raced as she hurried to the gate. Did the fool jongleur not realize the matter was urgent? She'd done all that he'd asked. Paid him well. Surely he would not fail her.

She passed through the gate and her anxiety grew tenfold. There was no sign of the entertainers. They'd packed up and left, leaving only a trampled mess of grass. Now her only hope was that de Ronay was still in bed with some woman in the village. But she could hardly go to every house and ask for him.

She felt completely defeated. Then she had a sudden thought. She quickly climbed the gate tower. Sir Guy was there, his dark eyes bloodshot.

"How long have you been on watch?" she asked.

"Since before dawn," Guy stifled a yawn.

"Did you see the performers leave?"

Guy seemed to perk up. "I did. 'Twas not long after Henry woke me to take his place as guard."

Nicola took a breath, dreading the answer. "Was the jongleur with them?"

"He was. Indeed, he was the one who seemed most

anxious to be off.'

"You talked to him?"

"Nay, but I…" Guy gave her a guilty look. "I talked to Glyda, the tumbler, the older one. To say goodbye to her. She told me the jongleur insisted they leave at first light."

"Mother of God." Nicola exhaled in disgust. "That bastard."

"What is it? What's wrong?" Guy straightened, instantly alert.

"Nothing is wrong. Not yet anyway." All those lies. All her careful scheming. And the slimy toad of a jongleur had tricked her.

"Lady?"

She returned her attention to Sir Guy. "'Tis nothing, I asked the jongleur to speak to me before he left. He was…supposed to do something for me. It appears he could not be bothered."

"Is there anything *I* can do, lady?"

She gave Guy a weary smile. "Nay. I'm afraid not." She turned and made her way down the stairs and walked numbly across the bailey. After a few steps, she switched direction and started for the stables.

****

As soon as he woke, Fawkes felt a twinge of alarm. Where was Nicola? He'd dreamed of waking up with her next to him, but the bed was empty.

Nothing to worry about. She'd probably gone to the privy.

He lay there thinking she would return any moment. Finally, he decided she must be seeing to things around the castle. There were always a dozen tasks she looked after every morning. But surely she could neglect them one day and relax in bed beside him for a time.

He shouldn't complain, since he benefited from all she did. Not all castle households were so well maintained. With good, plentiful food available twice a day. Clean rushes and well-scrubbed tables in the hall. A sense of order and comfort everywhere he looked. Those things didn't simply happen. It was due to Nicola that everyone at Valmar lived so comfortably.

During times of peace, a knight's life was one of relative leisure. Other than tending to his weapons and training, there wasn't much to do. But for a noblewoman, peace or war, winter or summer, there were always a dozen tasks at hand. And after everything else was done, there was always needlework.

He recalled the child's garment Nicola had been working on in the solar. And the other one he'd found in her satchel after her visit to Mordeaux. It was not surprising she might sew for her friend Hilary's son. But he did wonder why she had brought the outgrown garment back to Valmar. Why not leave it there to pass on to some other child to use? Unless she kept it hoping someday *they* would have a son together.

And God willing, they would. He would do his duty and make certain of it! The thought brought a smile to his lips. A moment later, his light mood faded. There were things he should be seeing to himself, such as finding out who had burned Glennyth's cottage. Stirred from his languorous mood, he got up and began to dress.

He must discover who was responsible for the fire and punish them. The people of Valmar could not think he would tolerate such a cruel act. Glennyth was a good healer. If she had perished, all of Valmar would have suffered. And because of the fire, Reynard was injured.

Reynard. He would talk to Reynard. Together they would come up with some means of catching this would-be murderer.

He made his way to the lord's tower, but when he reached it, there was no sign of Reynard. Fawkes stood a moment in the solar, admiring how the light came through the greenish glass windows. Without a doubt, this was the most pleasant room in the castle. Although it was hot this time of year. In the other tower rooms, open windows provided a breeze that cooled things down.

He went down to the hall. Reynard was there, breaking his fast. He scrutinized his friend as he greeted him. "You look more like yourself today. Although with your coloring, that only means you aren't as white as a corpse."

"You needn't be so scornful, Fawkes. Glennyth fancies my fair, freckled skin."

Fawkes gave Reynard an incredulous look. Then he sat down across from Reynard and reached for the loaf of bread and the knife. He cut himself a piece and buttered it. "But you are better, aren't you?"

"I am better," Reynard answered. "Coming down to the hall doesn't tire me as much as it did yesterday."

"With luck, you'll continue to improve. Any sign of Glennyth yet?"

"Nay. But it's early. If they started back this morning I wouldn't expect them to arrive for a while."

Fawkes, mouth full of bread and butter, nodded. When he could speak again he asked, "By the way, have you seen Nicola?"

"Nay."

That seemed strange. Nicola was always around the hall in the morning. He finished his bread, then brushed the crumbs off his hands and rose from the bench. "I'll go look for her."

He checked the kitchen first. Then the buttery and the weaving shed. No one had seen Nicola.

Puzzled, he went to the gate. Although he could not imagine why, it seemed clear Nicola had left the castle. A disturbing thought came to him. The performers were leaving this morning. Was it possible she'd gone to see the jongleur one last time?

He climbed the gatetower. Sir Guy immediately straightened.

"Have you seen Lady Nicola?" Fawkes's heart pounded as he waited for the answer.

"Aye. She rode out a while ago."

"Did she say where she was going?"

"Nay. But I can't help wondering if she went after the performers. She was asking about the jongleur, if he'd left with them. She seemed distraught when she discovered he had. She'd said she'd asked him to do something for her and he hadn't done it."

Fawkes clenched his hands into fists, fighting the panic and fury building inside him. *It could not be what it sounded like. She would not betray him. Not with that wretched fop. Not with any man. There was some other explanation. There had to be.*

"Milord?"

"I… Which way did she ride?"

"North."

The performers were on their way to Shrewsbury, which was to the north. Fawkes nodded curtly and left the watchtower.

He strode to the stables, intent on ordering the first squire he saw to saddle up his horse. But by the time he reached the building, the intense rush of emotion had faded. It was ridiculous to believe there was anything going on between Nicola and de Ronay. She'd caught the man with two different women. There was no way she thought so poorly of herself that she would dally with such a faithless scoundrel.

He halted. If he pursued her, the whole castle would think she had cuckolded him. Nay, better to go about nonchalantly as if he thought nothing of his wife going off riding in the early morn.

****

The pathway narrowed. The horse jerked at the reins and sidestepped, causing Nicola to curse. Her frustration was with herself as much as her mount. She should have waited until the ostler had saddled Mist rather than riding off on this half-trained animal. She also should have taken the main pathway, instead of the route through the forest. But this way was quicker, and when she set out she'd been convinced she must warn Gilbert about the impending attack. Now she realized waiting a few minutes for another horse would not have mattered. Besides, she should have told Fawkes what was happening. She'd be forced to tell him everything anyway.

She grimaced. Fawkes would be very angry. Not only because of her foolishness in conspiring with Father FitzAlan, but also because she hadn't told him about it right away. If he'd known the situation when he first came to Valmar, they might have been able to send some sort of envoy to London, making it clear that Mortimer was dead and Fawkes had taken his place. That alone might have been enough to deter John from scheming to seize Valmar and Mordeaux. Now the only thing they could do was prepare for the arrival of the enemy force.

The horse balked again, jerking Nicola sideways. She needed to calm herself. Her distress was affecting the horse. If she weren't careful, she'd end up getting thrown. She sought to focus on the pathway and ignore her troubling thoughts.

There was a rider coming from the opposite direction. For a few seconds she was uneasy, then she realized it was Robbie. Since he'd grown up at Valmar, he would know about this shortcut to Mordeaux.

They reined their horses. Robbie gazed at her in surprise and puzzlement. "What are you doing here, lady?"

"I'm going to Mordeaux. I must speak to Sir Gilbert about an important matter."

"He's not there."

"What do you mean he's not there?"

Robbie shrugged. "Apparently, he rode off to visit one of the holdings and never came back."

Nicola went rigid. "When was this? When did he leave?"

"Two days ago. In his absence, Adam FitzSaer has taken charge."

"FitzSaer! But what about Sir Gavin? In the past, he was in charge when Gilbert was away."

"I don't know, milady. I didn't speak to him."

"Is Lady Hilary concerned her husband hasn't returned?"

"Aye. She wanted to send out men to look for him. FitzSaer said he would if Gilbert is not back soon."

"But no one has gone to look for him *yet*?"

"Nay."

Nicola wondered if FitzSaer was in on the prince's plot. Was it possible he'd done something to Sir Gilbert to get him out of the way?

She had to know what was happening at Mordeaux. But if FitzSaer was involved in Gilbert's disappearance, then confronting FitzSaer could be very dangerous. She also had to get word back to Valmar, so Fawkes would know what was happening. She nodded to Robbie. "Continue on to Valmar. When you get there, immediately find Fawkes and tell him what you've told me about Sir Gilbert and FitzSaer." Should she also have him warn Fawkes about the prince's plot? That seemed too complicated a message to pass on through young Robbie. And she wanted to be there to explain herself when Fawkes found out what she'd done.

"And you, lady? What are you going to do?"

"I'm going to try to find out what is happening at Mordeaux. I won't stay long. Tell Fawkes I will return to Valmar very soon."

Robbie nodded.

They maneuvered past each other and Nicola continued on the narrow trail. When Fawkes had sent FitzSaer to Mordeaux, she'd worried the knight would cause trouble. But she'd never considered he'd do something like this. The more she thought about it, the more convinced she was that FitzSaer was somehow involved with Gilbert's disappearance. It was also very possible FitzSaer was involved in the impending attack on Mordeaux.

Although how could he know about that? Even she hadn't known of the prince's plans until de Ronay told her. Still, if there was a chance FitzSaer was involved, for her to go to Mordeaux by herself might be dangerous. If FitzSaer took her prisoner, he would possess a powerful bargaining tool.

By the time she reached the edge of the trees and

Mordeaux Castle loomed ahead, she'd made up her mind. Instead of proceeding on to the castle, she turned the horse and headed for the houses down near the river. The first one she came to belonged to an old woman named Ethelinda, who grew vegetables for the castle kitchen. This time of year she was at the keep almost every day.

She found Ethelinda in her garden, harvesting beans. She looked up. "Where's the horse you usually ride?" Ethelinda motioned to the gelding. "That one looks bad-tempered. You'd best keep him away from my garden."

"I will." Nicola tightened her grip on the reins. "Have you been to the castle today, Ethelinda?"

"Aye. Right after sun-up."

"Was…did anything seem amiss?"

"The gate was down, if that is what you mean. And I guess everything is all topsy-turvy since Sir Gilbert left."

"Have you heard any more about where he went or why he went there?"

"Not a thing."

"And what about Adam FitzSaer? How did he take charge? Why him and not someone else from the garrison?"

"Don't know, lady."

"Have there been any visitors to the castle recently?"

"The entertainers were here two days ago. Word is that FitzSaer turned them away."

Nicola's breath caught. "FitzSaer spoke to them? *Not* Sir Gilbert?"

"Nay. He was already gone."

Nicola's anxiety turned to fury. What a lying sneak de Ronay had turned out to be! Not only had he taken her money and broken his agreement with her, he'd come to Mordeaux first and likely shared the news of the enemy army's arrival with FitzSaer. Which meant FitzSaer might already be planning to surrender the castle to the prince's allies, with the idea he would be rewarded in some way.

She dare not go to Mordeaux now. Instead, she must make haste to Valmar and tell Fawkes everything she knew.

To Ethelinda she said, "I must go. Thank you for the information."

****

"Fawkes!"

He turned to see Robbie coming toward him.

"What is it?"

The young squire was out of breath. "I've just come back from Mordeaux. Lady Nicola told me to tell you that Sir Gilbert has disappeared. He rode out two days ago and never came back. Adam FitzSaer has taken control."

"FitzSaer? What the devil! What gives him the authority to do such a thing?"

"I don't know. Lady Nicola seemed alarmed as well."

"You say you saw her and she told you this? Where did you see her? And where is she now?"

"I met her as I was coming back from taking Glennyth to Mordeaux. She bid me rush back and tell you about Sir Gilbert and FitzSaer."

"Did she say what she was doing?"

"She was on her way to Mordeaux. I suggested she ride back with me. She declined, saying she must find out what was happening there."

So, she hadn't followed after the jongleur after all. Fawkes was relieved to think he had not pursued the entertainers and made a fool of himself. But what was it at Mordeaux that drew Nicola so intensely?

Nay, he could not think about that. He must focus on

271

the real issues. His castellan had disappeared and a man he didn't trust was in charge of Mordeaux.

Fawkes dismissed Robbie and walked back to the keep and up to the solar. He explained to Reynard what Robbie had told him, then said, "This business with Sir Gilbert being missing is alarming. Especially since FitzSaer is the one who's taken charge."

"Why would FitzSaer be in charge?" Reynard asked. "At Mordeaux, he has no more authority than any other knight."

"Which likely infuriates him. That's probably why he's taken this opportunity to seize control. And the thing is, who would stop him? When I sent him off to Mordeaux, I didn't really give any explanation for doing so to anyone there but Gilbert. With him gone, who's to know how sly and untrustworthy FitzSaer is?"

"Glennyth knows. But she may not be able to convince anyone at Mordeaux. I wish she hadn't gone there. I feel as uneasy as you do about all of this." Reynard looked down at his still-bandaged hands. "If it wasn't so far, I'd go with you to fetch her."

"I'll take an escort." Fawkes said. "I've underestimated FitzSaer so far. I won't do so again."

****

By the time she rode into Valmar Castle, both Nicola and her horse were sweaty and fatigued. Alexander hurried down from the gate tower to help Nicola dismount. As soon as he drew near, she asked, "Where's Fawkes?"

"He went to Mordeaux."

"Alone?"

"He took a handful of knights."

What if he encountered the army sent by Prince John? They'd be hopelessly outnumbered.

"Lady Nicola."

She turned to see Reynard. Except this wasn't the cheerful, easygoing man she remembered. Reynard's green eyes were wary and accusing. "Fawkes was distraught when he discovered you'd left this morning. I know you are used to doing whatever you wish, but you're married now, and 'tis inconsiderate to worry him."

"I know. I'm sorry. But I'm more worried about Fawkes going to Mordeaux. He might be in danger." How was she to explain? The only way was to tell Reynard everything. She dreaded revealing to Fawkes's captain her foolish attempt to play politics. He would think she was a lackwit. Looking back, her actions did seem very ill-advised. She'd let her fear and hatred of Mortimer cloud her reason, and foolishly offered her dowry, and herself, to some unknown ally of Prince John's. Her hatred of Mortimer had gotten the better of her judgment. Now she must now deal with the consequences.

Nicola took a deep breath. "I will tell you why I rode off this morning. And the rest of it."

Reynard's green eyes widened. "What is it? What's wrong? Has something happened at Mordeaux? Is Glennyth in danger?"

"I don't think she is. At least not yet."

"Not yet?" Reynard took a step toward her. The jovial knight had vanished. In his place was wild-eyed stranger. She didn't really want to face Reynard alone, but the bailey was hardly the place for this conversation. "'Tis a lengthy tale. I think we should go to the solar."

Reynard gave her a hard look and started off. Nicola followed, her stomach tight with foreboding. After this, Reynard might despise her. She could hardly blame him. It was her fault Mordeaux and Valmar were threatened. Her fault there might be a battle in which people she cared about could die. Even now, she worried for Fawkes. He'd taken a handful of knights to Mordeaux. How would he and his men fare against an army?

As she climbed the tower stairs, she was consumed with regret. Why couldn't she have trusted Fawkes? Why had she been unable to see him for what he was? A man who was reasonable and fair. Fawkes would have been angry with her, but he would not have let that anger rule him. And now, because of her stupid lies, his life might be in danger. When she thought of him riding off to Mordeaux with only a small escort, her insides twisted with warning. Maybe they should send more knights after Fawkes. But for that to happen, Reynard would have to give the order. And he would not do that unless he understood what was at stake.

They reached the solar. Reynard, who was clearly winded from climbing the stairs, sat down. Nicola remained standing. She felt too restless and unsettled to sit.

She began by telling Reynard of her conversation with Father FitzAlan the winter before. Then she explained what de Ronay had told her, and how she tried to get a message to Prince John to stop the plan. But de Ronay had taken her money and gone off with the other entertainers. Now she feared FitzSaer was somehow involved in the prince's plot. It was possible he had seized control of Mordeaux with the intent of handing it over to the enemy army.

She stopped pacing and halted in front of Reynard. "If I'm right about FitzSaer's intent, Fawkes might be in danger."

Reynard's eyes flashed with fury. "If you had told Fawkes the truth in the beginning, there would be nothing to worry about. All of this mess could have been avoided."

"Except the part involving Gilbert and FitzSaer," she said, defensively. "I told Fawkes not to send FitzSaer to Mordeaux."

"That's still your fault. Fawkes wanted rid of FitzSaer because he was spreading lies about you. And having just learned of your scheming and manipulation, I'm not sure everything FitzSaer said *was* a lie."

Nicola wanted to scream with frustration. Men were all alike. None of them understood what it was like to be utterly powerless and unable to choose your own destiny. Neither Reynard nor Fawkes would ever understand the choices she'd made.

But she couldn't think about that. The important thing was what she did from now onward. "I've made mistakes, I admit it. But dwelling on them helps nothing. We need to concentrate on the present, and deal with what has happened, no matter whose fault it is." She wished Glennyth was here. The wise woman would be able to defuse Reynard's anger and help him see things logically.

Reynard crossed his arms over his chest. "What do you think we should do?"

"First, we must get Fawkes back here. Once he knows everything, he can decide on a course of action."

"Why are you worried for Fawkes? What other secrets are you holding back?"

"Nothing. As I just told you, the attack on Mordeaux could come at any time. I don't want Fawkes to face an enemy army when he's unprepared."

"Other than the word of this jongleur, do you have any reason to think John has sent a force to seize Mordeaux?"

"Nay. But de Ronay was very clear. He said John

planned to attack, and the attack would come soon."

"But how can we believe a man like that? He seemed so sly and devious."

"He has no reason to make up this tale. Nay, I'm certain an attack will come despite my attempts to prevent it. The truth is, even if de Ronay *had* taken my message to Prince John, it probably wouldn't have made any difference. The enemy is likely on their way here already."

She sat in her sewing chair, feeling as if a great weight was crushing her chest. Her decisions might have endangered everything and everyone she cared about.

Reynard was silent. Finally, he said, "I can't decide whether to send more knights after Fawkes, or wait and see what happens." He raised his gaze to hers. "Do you think the people of Mordeaux will support FitzSaer? Will they follow his orders?"

"Perhaps. For a time. Since Sir Gilbert is missing and FitzSaer has taken charge. But I also don't believe they would take FitzSaer's side against Fawkes."

"Then I think we should wait for Fawkes to return."

She didn't want to wait. All her instincts told her to get on a horse and go after Fawkes. She looked up to see Reynard watching her.

"I can guess what you're thinking. Don't you dare even consider it. If you run off and anything happens, Fawkes will move heaven and earth to rescue you. I don't intend to see him risk his life over you again."

There was reason in his harsh warning. If she went to Mordeaux and FitzSaer took her hostage, he would have a powerful advantage over Fawkes.

Nicola got to her feet. "I won't leave Valmar before Fawkes returns, I promise."

****

As he rode toward Mordeaux, Fawkes's fury at FitzSaer gradually faded, replaced by a creeping unease. He'd been too comfortable with Gilbert de Vescy, the calm, competent castellan. It had never occurred to him to replace the man with one of his own. Nor had he seen fit to leave more than a couple of his knights at Mordeaux. He'd been so intent on seizing the main prize, Valmar, he had not taken the right steps to protect his hold on the other castle. Now he was paying for his lack of foresight.

Mordeaux Castle came into view. Protected on the one side by the river and a deep sloping hill on the other three sides, it was not without its defenses. Fawkes squinted; the portcullis was down. He would have to ride up and demand entrance, and hope they would let him into the castle. If they would not, there was nothing he could do. Other than go back to Valmar and get more knights and build siege engines.

He led his men toward the portcullis and then halted. Would the guards at the gate be loyal to him or to FitzSaer? "It's me. Fawkes de Cressy. Open the gate."

There was murmuring in the tower above. Then someone called down, "A moment."

Fawkes studied the complex pattern of the iron portcullis. A moment later, footsteps echoed down the stairs from the gate tower along with whispered conversation. After what seemed like an eternity, a face appeared in the opening of the gate tower. "Under what authority do you claim overlordship of this castle?"

Fawkes was furious now. They were clearly stalling. "I have a writ from King Richard, as everyone at Mordeaux knows. If you do not open the gate instantly, I vow I will see you all punished."

"What is their plan?" Engelard asked in a low voice.

"Do they really mean to turn us away?"

"They're stalling, for some reason," Fawkes answered. "Although I can't imagine what it is."

The face appeared again. "Do you have the writ with you?"

"Of course, I don't have the writ with me!" Fawkes shouted. "I have visited here twice in the last month and been welcomed into the castle without any trouble. Why are you refusing me now? Who's in charge—who would deny entrance to me, your rightful lord? It's FitzSaer, isn't it? Well, bring him here. Let me speak to him."

More whispering. Then, "My lord FitzSaer bids me tell you that he can't come to the gate right now. Perhaps if you returned later, he could accommodate you."

"The bastard's stalling," Engelard said. "Why? What does he hope to gain?"

"Perhaps FitzSaer is having trouble exerting his authority," Fawkes said. "Some of the knights may still hold out hope that Sir Gilbert will come back."

"But Sir Gilbert is under your command," Oliver put in. "It doesn't matter whether he's here or not. These men ultimately answer to you."

Fawkes nodded. He wished Nicola were with them. If she were, they would not refuse them entrance. According to Robbie, Nicola had been headed here when he left her. In fact, she might already be inside the castle.

An awful thought came to him. Perhaps Nicola was behind this defiance of his order. Perhaps she had told the men not to let him enter. He shouted up to the guard: "The Lady Nicola. Is she inside the castle?"

The face appeared again. "Nay. Lady Nicola is not here."

Was it the truth? Or a lie? FitzSaer might be holding

her hostage. But if that was the case, why wasn't FitzSaer gloating? He was the kind of man who wouldn't be able to stop himself from giving Fawkes the gleeful news himself. If Nicola was working with him, or she was his hostage, FitzSaer would make certain Fawkes knew of it.

Where the devil was FitzSaer? He wasn't the sort of man to hide in the background. If he were in control of Mordeaux, he would want everyone to know it.

Gerard brought his horse up beside Fawkes's. "What do we do?"

"We can hardly besiege the castle on our own. And if they won't let us in, there's no point remaining here."

Fawkes turned his horse, his body taut with frustration and confusion. Nothing made sense. Not Sir Gilbert's disappearance. Nor the behavior of the guards in refusing him entrance. He should have brought Robbie. The squire had been here only hours ago, inside the castle. He might have been able to convince the guards to let them in now.

Fawkes turned to look back at the castle. There was a hissing sound. Something struck him in the shoulder, knocking him from his horse. The world swirled around him and then dissolved into blackness.

Chapter Nineteen

"My lady! Come quickly!"

Nicola rose from the prie-deux. She'd finally found some peace praying in the chapel. But her sense of reprieve vanished like smoke in the wind as she hurried to follow the page. When she reached the yard, Gerard, Engelard and some other knights were gathered there, but not Fawkes. The expressions on the men's faces alarmed her. She turned. A still form was draped over Fawkes's horse Scimitar.

There was a rushing noise in her ears. The world turned gray and distant. Gerard hurried over and grabbed her arm. "Don't worry, lady. He's alive."

"What…what happened?"

"A crossbow bolt. Went clean through his mail. But the good news is their aim was off. The bolt hit high, near his shoulder. "

She still felt stunned. Finally, she choked out, "Where did it happen?"

"Right outside of Mordeaux. They wouldn't let us in, so we started to leave. We'd only gone a short distance when Fawkes turned to look back at the castle. That's when he was struck. I'm certain they were aiming for his heart."

Nicola closed her eyes, feeling sick with regret. If only she'd been able to convince Reynard to send someone after Fawkes. She drew near to Fawkes. He was as still as death. "Why is he insensible? Did he faint from the pain?"

"He might have hit his head. Or it could be because we gave him two full jacks of wine. Oliver thought we should get the bolt out right away. But when we tried to remove it, we realized if we did it wrong, he might never use his arm properly again. We decided to bring him back here and let the healer remove it."

"But Glennyth is gone," Nicola said.

Gerard's eyes went wide. "You're right. I'd forgotten Robbie took her to Mordeaux."

Nicola nodded numbly. "We'll have to do the best we can without her."

"Lady, what can we do to help?" Engelard asked.

All four knights watched her, depending on her to save Fawkes. She was trained in basic medicines and tending wounds. But she'd never treated anything as serious as this. But she had no choice. Fawkes's life was in her hands. She must not fail him.

"Get him down," she said.

With Engelard on one side and Gerard on the other, the two knights got Fawkes off the horse. They tried to stand him up but he slumped over. The men staggered under the dead weight until they found their footing. Fawkes sagged between the two of them. His face was ashen, his eyes closed.

"Where should we take him?" Engelard asked.

Nicola stared at the broken end of the bolt protruding from Fawkes's shoulder and the blood staining his chain-mail shirt. *Two inches lower and he would have died instantly.* She pushed the thought from her mind and concentrated on Engelard's question. If they tried to carry him up the twisting stairway to her bedchamber, they might jar the bolt and drive it in deeper. "Bring him into the hall."

Nicola ordered a page to get bandages and another to fetch mead. Oliver she sent to the kitchen to get a bowl of vinegar and a small, sharp knife. Alexander went after blankets. By the time she reached the hall, Gerard and Engelard already had Fawkes stretched out on one of the trestle tables.

Reynard stood gaping at Fawkes in horror. "Who did this?"

"Someone at Mordeaux. They were on the castle wall. We couldn't see them," Engelard answered.

"Good God," Reynard breathed. "We need Glynneth."

"But she's not here and this can't wait," Nicola said. "We must get the bolt out soon, and clean the wound."

"We?"

Nicola had never seen Reynard look so pale. "I know you don't trust me, but you have no choice. My mother taught me basic healing skills. They will have to suffice."

Reynard pulled himself together. "To get the bolt out, you'll need proper tools. I'll fetch some tongs from the smith." He started off.

"Bring the smith with you," Nicola called. "We may need his strength to hold Fawkes down."

Poor Fawkes. Removing the bolt would cause him terrible pain. But she had no choice. Better to cause him pain than let him die.

She kept that thought in mind as she went to the lord's tower to get blankets and poppy juice. Vial in hand, she raced back to the hall. The three knights and the smith were waiting. They stepped back to let her near. Seeing how waxen and still Fawkes looked, her panic returned.

Then she took a deep, steadying breath. She must not think about what Fawkes meant to her, or the pain she was causing him. All her focus must be on getting the bolt out.

The page had left the cup of mead on a nearby table. Nicola looked at it, then at the vial of poppy juice. If Fawkes had a head injury, giving him poppy juice could be dangerous. She leaned over and spoke his name. When he didn't respond, she bent nearer. "Fawkes, can you hear me?"

He opened his eyes and gazed at her, his dark eyes glazed with pain. "Nicola," he whispered.

She was relieved he was aware enough to speak. But then she thought about the pain he would face. "I'm going to give you some poppy juice,"

He gave a faint nod.

"We have to get the quarrel out."

He nodded again.

She lifted his head with one hand and held the cup to his lips with the other. He swallowed, grimacing. Even the cloying sweetness of the mead wasn't enough to mask the bitterness of the poppy. When he'd finished, he lay back on the table again. Telling herself that it would take some time before the poppy took effect, she gave in to impulse and stroked his brow. He gazed up at her. "Nicola," he said in a ravaged whisper.

She choked back a sob. She must not let him see how terrified she was. "Hush now. Don't waste your breath talking."

"But I…"

She pressed her fingers to his lips. "Save your strength. Lie back. Let yourself drift away. "

He closed his eyes. She turned to the waiting men. "While we wait for the poppy to take effect, we need to cut his mail and gambeson away from the wound."

"I brought something for that." Ellis, the burly smith, moved in with a scissor-like tool. Nicola looked away as he wielded it to cut through the chain-mail links. When she looked back, he was trying to remove Fawkes's gambeson, which was stuck to the wound. Fearing he would cause Fawkes more pain than was necessary, she said, "Let me do that."

She ordered a nearby maidservant to fetch her sewing scissors from the solar. By the time the maidservant returned, Fawkes's breathing had slowed, showing the poppy was working. Nicola used scissors to painstakingly cut away the blood-soaked gambeson. The fabric had stuck to the wound in places, and Fawkes groaned as she pulled it away. She fought to keep her hands steady. If that small movement caused pain, he would be in agony as she cut out the bolt. But she could delay no longer. She turned to the waiting knights. "Hold him."

Engelard and Gerard went to either side of the table and grasped Fawkes's arms. Oliver and Reynard restrained Fawkes's lower body. Nicola washed the knife blade in the bowl of vinegar and moved next to Engelard. With the knife poised over Fawkes's shoulder, she said a silent prayer. Then she began her terrible task.

She made small cuts around the bolt. With each one, the tension in her stomach increased. She tried to pull out the bolt, but could get no purchase. To the smith, she said, "Do you have some tool that might work to pull it out?"

Ellis tried to remove the bolt using a pincer-like implement. "I'm not sure you've loosened the arrow enough,"

Once again, Nicola used the knife to cut around the bolt, digging deeper this time. Fawkes moaned and muttered as the knights held him. Sweat formed under Nicola's arms and between her breasts. She told herself she must not think of Fawkes's body as flesh, but like an ell of cloth. Samite or silk—some fine, delicate material. She must cut swift and true and precise, so it would not ravel and go to waste.

She rinsed her hands in the bowl of vinegar and slipped her fingers into the wound to search for the arrow tip. At last she found it. It was blessedly small. But she must free it completely, or it would do more damage as Ellis pulled it out.

When she'd finished cutting, she stepped back. "Now," she said.

Ellis grasped the arrow bolt with his tongs and pulled. Fawkes's body arched and he let out an anguished cry as the bolt came out. Blood oozed from Fawkes's shoulder. Nicola grabbed some bandages and held them against the wound. Blood soaked the cloth. "More bandages. Nay, forget them. Give me a blanket!"

Oliver quickly brought a blanket and she secured it over the seeping bandage. When the top remained dry, she let out a sigh of relief. "Thank God."

She continued the pressure for a while longer, then eased up on it and stepped back. The bolt was out. Now what should she do? She must try to wash the wound out with vinegar as she'd been taught. But after that, should she try to stitch it closed, or let it drain? Glennyth would know which method would make the wound less likely to putrefy. She did not.

Reynard seemed to be thinking the same thing. "Now what do we do?"

She met his gaze, seeing her own fear mirrored in his eyes. "We need Glennyth."

"We must send someone to fetch her back." Reynard said.

Oliver stepped up. "I'll go."

"You weren't allowed in when you were with Fawkes. I doubt anything has changed." Nicola pointed out. "Nay, we must send someone who will not be seen as a threat, who will be allowed to enter the castle. FitzSaer meant to kill Fawkes. He will be wary of anyone arriving from Valmar."

Reynard nodded glumly, and Nicola felt panic seize her belly. What if they could not get Glennyth back in time? "I'll try to think of a plan. In the meantime, we must get Fawkes into bed."

****

Pain. Terrible pain. Fawkes tried to cry out, but could not. It felt as if someone was poking hot needles into his shoulder all the way to the bone. He'd tried to fight them, but they held him down.

Beside the pain, his wits were muddled. He wasn't certain where he was. Although it felt as if he was being tortured, the few times he'd managed to open his eyes, he thought he'd seen Nicola. How could that be? Unless she'd also been captured by the enemy.

The horrifying thought made him force his eyes open. He saw Nicola leaning over him. Dread choked him. He could endure torture, but fine, delicate Nicola would never survive. Somehow they must escape.

"We have to get out of here," he whispered. "Now, while they've left us alone!"

"Shhh. 'Tis all right. Lie back. All is well."

She stroked his face as if soothing a child. Didn't she understand? Didn't she realize what the Saracens would do to her? "I can't lie back," he muttered through clenched teeth. "We have to get out of here."

"Fawkes, you must lie still. I haven't stitched your wound yet. I wasn't sure if I should."

He stared at her a moment, trying to focus. Slowly, he realized they were in Nicola's bedchamber. Not a Saracen prison. Relief washed through him. He wasn't being tortured; the pain was from a wound. He reached up and felt the bandages swaddling his shoulder. How had he been injured? He couldn't remember.

She held a cup to his lips. "Drink."

He expected water but the heavy taste of wine filled his mouth. Bitter wine.

"It will help with the pain," she murmured.

Only half-willingly, he drank. In moments, all his questions, his words, vanished.

****

Nicola pushed the stool closer to the bed and sank down. The crossbow quarrel was out, and Fawkes was not only alive but able to speak. The wound was deep and ragged-edged. If it weren't stitched, it would never heal properly. On the other hand, if she sewed it up and it festered, the putrefaction would kill him. *I need you, Glennyth! I need you now.*

Nicola felt Fawkes's forehead. It seemed very warm. Not uncommon for someone who had been wounded. But if his fever rose, that meant he was in danger.

She went to the window and opened the shutters. It had rained overnight. As the sweet, clean air filled her lungs, she felt better. She reminded herself she didn't have to face this alone. She was surrounded by people who cared about Fawkes, and who would do whatever she asked of them. If she ordered the whole garrison to march on Mordeaux and attack, they would obey.

But attacking Mordeaux wasn't the answer. Now was not the time to confront FitzSaer. Instead, they must outsmart him. That thought triggered another, and all at once she had a plan. Mordeaux had a hidden entrance, one that FitzSaer would not know about. Nicola recalled following behind her father and his newly appointed castellan as he showed the man the underground passageway. But that had been years ago. Could she still find the opening? She thought so, although she would have to search awhile.

A sense of purpose flooded her, filling her with renewed energy. She could do this: find the secret entrance, get into the castle and get Glennyth out safely.

She approached the bed, her stomach knotted with worry. Fawkes reminded her of a wounded wild creature, a magnificent stag brought down in a hunt. She caressed his face, following the line of his jaw, now roughened with whiskers. An aching love suffused her. He was so dear to her, as dear as Simon. It was terrifying to realize how much she loved him. She would do nearly anything to keep him safe. It was difficult to protect her son, but how did she protect this man? A knight. A warrior. If only she could harden her heart against him. Tell herself nothing mattered but Simon. But she could not do that. She loved Fawkes.

She touched his mouth and he stirred, sighing softly. Tears pricked her eyes. If only she could change the past. If she'd known Fawkes was alive and meant to return and save her from Mortimer, she'd never have risked everything in a desperate attempt to rid herself of her husband. Now her foolhardy act might have doomed them all.

She swiped at her tears and sniffed. It was impossible

to change the past. She must move forward. And every moment she wasted at Fawkes's bedside meant a moment longer before she could get Glennyth here to treat him.

She went to the storage chest in the corner to fetch some old clothing. As she dressed, she wondered whom she could get to care for Fawkes while she was gone. Old Emma was the only person she trusted. Was she up to it? Going up and down the stairs was difficult for her. But she could always get a page to fetch things for her.

She finished dressing, then went to the bed and bent to kiss Fawkes's cheek. He stirred and reached up with his good arm to grasp her hair and try to pull her close. "Nicola," he murmured.

"I must leave, my love." She gently disengaged his hand from her hair and laced his fingers in her own. "But I will be back soon, I promise."

He mumbled something else, seeming dazed and half aware.

Again, she kissed him on the cheek. He seemed even warmer now. Sick with worry, she gently disengaged her hand from his and turned from the bed. What if something happened to him while she was gone? What if she never saw him alive again? She pushed the thought from her mind and left the room without glancing back.

On the lower level she found Old Emma. Nicola told her about her plan to fetch Glennyth as well as the need to watch over Fawkes.

"I can do it," Old Emma asserted. "I may be old, but I've nursed a lot of people through illnesses in my day. Including both your father and mother."

"If you need help, ask any of the pages. And I'm certain you can get Reynard to aid you."

"I can manage." Old Emma got to her feet. "I'd best

go up and see to him. Is he awake?"

"He's still mostly insensible. I'm not sure if it's due to the bump on his head, the poppy juice, or the fever, but he isn't fully aware."

"Mayhaps he'll think I'm you and pull me into bed with him." Old Emma chortled.

"We can only hope his wits are not that confused," Nicola retorted dryly.

Leaving the servant to make her slow progress up the tower stairs, Nicola hurried to the kitchen, where she grabbed a fresh loaf, buttered it and headed to the hall. She found Reynard there, along with the knights who'd rescued Fawkes and others. Between hasty bites of bread, she told them of her plan.

Reynard regarded her skeptically. "Yesterday you told me it was too risky for you to go to Mordeaux, for fear FitzSaer might imprison you. Now you mean to go there alone."

"He can only imprison me if knows I'm there. If I sneak in through the hidden passageway and am very careful, I should be able to get Glennyth and myself out the same way without anyone being the wiser."

"It sounds foolhardy," Reynard said. "At the very least, you must take an escort. You can't travel all that way alone."

"Stealth is what matters now," Nicola argued. "I vow, I will fare better by myself."

"What about sending someone else?" Oliver asked in a tentative voice. "Why couldn't I, or another knight, accomplish what you mean to do?"

"No one else knows where this secret entrance is located. Even I will struggle to find it. It was well-hidden when I was a child. By now the weeds and brush will have grown up and obscured it even more. Besides, none of you are familiar with the layout of Mordeaux. It will be much easier for me to find Glennyth than it would for anyone else."

"Fawkes would never allow you to do this," Reynard said.

"Nay, he would not. But at the moment he's in no position to exert his authority. And if you want to do something to help him while I'm gone, you can help Old Emma. She's watching over Fawkes until I get back."

"Of course I'll look after him," Reynard said.

Nicola hurriedly finished her bread, then went to get a basket to carry supplies.

Chapter Twenty

Nicola rode down the forest trail, scanning the thick stands of oak trees on either side. She needed to find some place to leave her horse. Although this route to Mordeaux wasn't much used, she didn't want anyone finding Mist.

Seeing an opening in the trees, she dismounted and led Mist off the trail. She secured the horse's reins to an ash tree in a sheltered glade. Then she untied her basket from the saddle and adjusted her head covering. If anyone saw her now, with luck they would think she was a village woman taking produce to the castle. She gave Mist a quick pat goodbye and started off.

Although she worried about getting lost, there was enough sunlight shining through the trees to give her a sense of direction. It also helped that she'd spent a fair amount of time in these woods as a child and recognized distinctive trees here and there. Although it was yet summer, there were already signs of the coming fall. A stand of elderberries. Late flowers like asters and loosestrife.

Nicola finally reached the place where the forest met the river and followed the pathway along it. When she passed the castle, she left the river path and made her way to the rear of the keep. As she'd expected, the area was overgrown with willow and alder. It was also very marshy. Either it had rained recently or the nearby stream had changed course and now ran closer to the castle.

After a short search, she found the entrance. The slab of stone was covered with dried mud and the iron ring that served as a handle was badly rusted. Now, she had a new worry, that the passageway would be flooded and impassable.

She cleaned the ring with the hem of her coarse-woven gown and gave it a swift hard tug, but the slab of stone didn't budge. She tried again, pulling with all her strength. The trapdoor still refused to move. Frustrated, she lifted her skirt and withdrew her dagger from the sheath securing it to her thigh. She poked the dagger around the edges of the stone to loosen it. This time when she pulled the ring, she felt movement. Again she used the dagger to clear around the edges. She pulled and the stone came loose, pitching her backwards into the damp grass.

She got up and bent to peer into the dark passageway, cursing herself for forgetting to bring a torch. After lowering herself into the opening, she pulled her basket in after her. The passageway had seemed roomy when she was a child; now it was scarcely big enough for her to stand up in. But at least it wasn't full of water.

She bent and entered the tunnel. The cold of the stone walls immediately seeped into her bones, and she fought to suppress her dread at the thought of the spiders, rats and other vermin lurking around her. Balancing the basket on her arm, she reached out for the clammy walls on either side and inched forward.

The tunnel seemed to go on forever. Her neck and shoulders ached from being bent over. She considered crawling, but having felt things brushing against her ankles, she'd rejected the idea. Why in heaven's name had she thought this fun as a child? Of course, she'd been much smaller then and had a candle to light the way. She'd also been certain of what lay at the end. Now she worried the opening might be sealed.

A short while later, her head banged into a solid surface. She winced and drew back. This was the end of the tunnel. The trapdoor must be directly above her. She felt for it, grimacing as falling dust and debris struck her face. Finding the trapdoor, she pushed upwards. Nothing happened. Remembering her experience at the other end, she retrieved her dagger and worked at the edges of the trapdoor. After resheathing her dagger, she shoved with all her strength.

More debris fell, coating her face and shoulders, but the trap door shifted. She tried again and was able to move the door and the object holding it down clear of the opening. She used the steps cut in the wall to scramble up and drag herself into the chamber above.

Nicola sat on the dank stone floor to catch her breath, inhaling the scent of apples and the earthy odor of root vegetables. She was inside Mordeaux Castle. Now all she had to do was find Glennyth.

****

Wild, blurry dreams, the pain in his shoulder a constant. What woke Fawkes was thirst. This time it was worse than ever. "Water," he whispered.

Someone supported his head and held a cup to his lips. It was wine, rather than water, but he drank it anyway. When his most urgent thirst was quenched, he opened his eyes, expecting to see Old Emma. A pair of hazel eyes stared back at him, disorienting him.

"It me. Alys."

It took a moment to connect the name to the tawny-haired serving girl. "Wh-what are you doing here?"

Alys's hazel eyes narrowed. "I'm looking after you."

He raised his head, trying to see if there was anyone else in the room. "Where's Old Emma?"

For a moment the young woman looked unsettled. Then she spoke soothingly. "Old Emma is resting. It tires her out to climb the stairs."

Fawkes struggled for more of the pieces missing from his memory. "Where's Nicola? I thought she was going to fetch the healer."

"She's not yet back from Mordeaux."

"Mordeaux? Why did she go to Mordeaux?"

"The healer is there. Or at least that was Nicola's excuse for going there. 'Tis more likely she went there to be with her son."

Her son? Fawkes shook his head, as if that would dislodge the cobwebs of confusion. "What are you talking about?"

Alys smiled smugly. "I forgot you didn't know. Lady Nicola had a son with Mortimer. A fine, fair-haired boy."

"The baby died."

Alys shook her head. "That was some other babe. Her son has been living at Mordeaux all this time."

He must be dreaming. Yet when he clutched at the bedcovers, they seemed real enough. And the woman looking down on him appeared to be flesh and blood. But what she was telling him, it could not be true. "I don't believe you."

"Why else do you think Nicola goes to Mordeaux? Why else is she so secretive?"

Fawkes felt like he was falling. Things he'd believed solid and secure seemed to be breaking off and scattering into an endless dark abyss. "But why would she lie about it? And for all this time?"

Alys shrugged. "I think she feared Mortimer's wits

were so addled he might harm the child in a drunken rage."

"Nay. I meant, why did she keep the child a secret from *me*?"

"Who knows why Lady Nicola does anything? She's a queer one, as my ma would say. Perhaps she thought you would not accept another man's son."

He focused his gaze on Alys and tried to figure out if she was telling the truth. Her hazel eyes seemed guileless, and yet there was something in her expression. A hint of satisfaction. Of triumph.

"Who else knows about the child? Who else at Valmar can confirm this tale?"

"Why...I... 'Tis not common knowledge, if that's what you mean. I doubt any of the knights knew of the boy. 'Tis a matter whispered among the women."

Alys was right. This was a something women would know about. But the only woman he'd questioned in the matter was Glennyth, and since she was Nicola's friend and confidant, she'd had every reason to lie. And now both women were at Mordeaux. Leaving him here, with his injury. "How long ago did Nicola leave?

"'Twas yesterday. I thought she would hurry back. I'm surprised it's taking so long. Something must have happened. Perhaps her son is ill and she felt Glennyth was needed there. So easy for a child to die. And you're a grown man. A strong, robust warrior."

Were her words meant to soothe him? Or torment him with the awareness that Nicola, or any woman, would undoubtedly make her son her first priority?

Now it all made perfect sense. Nicola traveled regularly to Mordeaux and sewed children's clothing. The tunic in her satchel was likely one the boy had outgrown.

He'd guessed it would fit a child of three or four years. The age his son would be if they had conceived one.

Alys seemed to think the boy was Mortimer's. But he could not believe Mortimer had managed to overcome his aversion to Nicola long enough to lie with her and beget a child. It was more likely Mortimer had been so desperate for an heir that he'd tried a second time to secure one. Perhaps some other man had fathered Nicola's son. Was that man still around? Perhaps living at Mordeaux?

The thought made him feel sick. If that was true, then Nicola had no reason to return with Glennyth. Indeed, it would be much more convenient for Nicola if he died of his wounds.

Even so, he remained convinced that Nicola loved him. Or at the very least was fond of him. She'd seemed so upset that he was injured.

Although her anxiety might stem from something else. Perhaps she'd had news her child was ill, and that was the reason she'd rushed off in such a hurry, leaving him in the dubious care of Old Emma, and now Alys.

Old Emma. Nicola's servant must know the truth about the child. It would be impossible for Nicola to hide something like that from the woman who was with her every day. Somehow he would make the old crone tell him what she knew.

"Fetch Old Emma for me," he told Alys, who was now sitting on the stool by the bed.

The young woman grimaced. "I would if I could, my lord. But you see, she fell on the stairway and hurt herself. I'm afraid she's not able to climb the tower stairs. Not for several days."

"Then have some of the knights bring her! I want to speak to her, and I won't be denied!"

A mixture of emotions crossed Alys's face: Anger. Irritation. Calculation. "Of course, milord. I'll do it anon. But would you not like another drink first? I don't know how long it will take to find some knights to carry that fat old thing up here. I'm sure you're still thirsty, milord. With your fever and all."

He wanted another drink. But not wine. Every time he drank some, he fell asleep. He wanted to stay awake and find out the truth once and for all. "Fetch Old Emma. And while you are at it, have her bring me some water."

"Of course, milord."

Perhaps it was his imagination, or his weakened state, but he swore there was something scornful and gloating about Alys's tone. As she closed the door, he had the disturbing thought that if she never came back he'd have to crawl down the stairs and fetch help himself.

****

Nicola moved gingerly, fearful of tripping over the baskets and barrels filling the storeroom. She bumped into a pile of cabbages and nearly fell. At last she encountered the earthen wall and was able to follow it around until she reached the smooth surface of the door.

Once out, she made her way up the stairs, trying to remember the layout of this side of the castle. A moment later, she smelled baking bread and the odors of cooking food. She followed the smell until she was near the kitchen. Then she veered the other way, toward the stairway leading to the solar and the private chambers of the castle. With luck, Glennyth would be with Hilary. Joy filled Nicola at the thought of seeing Simon. She would give him a hug, but that was all. She had to get Glennyth back to Valmar as quickly as possible.

But as she climbed the stairs to the castellan's

chambers, she felt something was wrong. She paused to listen, expecting to hear the sounds of children playing. There was nothing. Perhaps Hilary had taken the children out in the bailey. That was certainly possible, but still…

She moved up the stairs, her foreboding growing each moment. At the top, she peered cautiously into the solar. What she saw hit her like a blow to the belly. There were no toys strewn around the hearth. No sign of Hilary's sewing materials. Except for the furniture and the tapestries on the walls, the solar was empty.

Where were they? What has FitzSaer done to them? Panic engulfed her, making it hard to breathe. She'd feared FitzSaer had imprisoned Gilbert, or even killed him; she'd never dreamed he would do anything to Hilary and the children. And where was Glennyth?

She forced herself to take deep breaths. FitzSaer might be cunning and ruthless; he wasn't completely depraved. He might have killed Gilbert but he was unlikely to harm a woman and two small children. *At least she hoped that was true.*

She moved cautiously through the solar into the bedchamber. Men's clothing was scattered on the floor. A cup and ewer sat on the table with a dried pool of wine where the ewer had slopped over. The night candle had guttered and never been replaced. The windows were shuttered and whole chamber smelled stuffy. FitzSaer had clearly taken the room for his own.

Anger energized Nicola. She would find Hilary, the children, and Glennyth and take them back to Valmar. Then she would make FitzSaer pay for what he'd done!

But she needed help from someone inside the castle. She didn't know the cook very well. But the brisk, bustling woman was fond of Simon and Joanie. For their sake,

Morwenna would surely help her.

Nicola crept back down the stairs, aware that at any moment she might come face-to-face with FitzSaer and have all her plans destroyed. But she made it to the kitchen without encountering so much as a servant. Everyone stopped what they were doing and stared at her.

"Lady!" Morwenna exclaimed. "What are you doing here?"

Nicola moved past the gaping kitchen wenches to reach the cook, a solid, dark-haired woman of middle-age. "I'm looking for the healer, Glennyth." Nicola kept her voice low. "I'm also hoping you know what has happened to Gilbert and Hilary and the children."

The cook's mouth set in a grim line. "Bad business, that. Sir Gilbert vanished three days ago. Rode out alone and never came back. Then, just yesterday I waited for Lady Hilary to come and discuss the evening meal. But she never did. I sent one of the pages to look for her. When he returned he told me Hilary and the children were gone. This was late morning, so they must have left, or been taken, sometime in the middle of the night. I did hear a commotion around then. Horses in the bailey, that sort of thing. But I dismissed it as nothing to worry over and went back to sleep."

"Glennyth, the wise woman, have you seen her at Mordeaux?"

Morwenna shook her head. "I don't pay much attention to who's coming and going. I assume if there are visitors, Lady Hilary will tell me, so we can make more food."

"Have there been any visitors recently?"

"There were a couple of knights here a few days before Sir Gilbert disappeared. Well-born men. Good manners."

"How long did they stay?"

"One night only. Then they were gone."

John's spies, most likely. Nicola wondered what they had told Gilbert. It didn't matter. What was important was what they had told FitzSaer. Perhaps they'd informed him of the attack to come and convinced him to aid them in the plan to take over Mordeaux. Their visit might have sparked FitzSaer's scheme to seize control. Or had he been plotting even before that? Perhaps since Fawkes sent him to Mordeaux?

She could not take time to untangle it now. All her efforts must focus on finding Glennyth and making certain Hilary and the children are safe. A cold hand of terror clutched her throat at the thought of Simon being in danger. She forced away the paralyzing dread. FitzSaer must have imprisoned the women and children somewhere. But where?

She thought of her father's little used dungeon. Like the secret entrance, it dated from a time when her father's hold on his lands had been much more precarious. As a child, he'd warned her not to play near the opening of the oubliette lest she fall in and be injured.

Caught up in her thoughts, she jumped when Morwenna grasped her arm. "If there is anything I can do, lady, let me know. I'm fond of Lady Hilary. And the children, of course. It troubles me to think they might be in danger."

"Thank you. For now, there's nothing I would ask of you. But later, after I find them, we may need supplies."

Morwenna nodded. "I'll gather some things together."

Nicola left the kitchen. The oubliette was on the other side of the castle. To reach it, she would have to pass through the hall or circle around the outside of the castle through the bailey. Either way, she risked encountering people whose loyalties were unknown. Deciding the hall was safer she pulled up her hood, and set off.

Nicola passed through the hall without anyone taking note of her. Reaching the passageway on the other side, she turned to see if she'd been followed. Distracted, she ran straight into a small page carrying a bucket. The bucket spilled and the boy gave an angry cry. "Watch where you're going, you stupid wench!"

The next moment, his eyes went wide and he gasped, "Lady!" He gestured. "Your clothing...I didn't know you."

She smiled. "It's all right, Johnny. I'm here to visit Lady Hilary and the children. Do you know where they are?"

Johnny shook his head. "I thought they were in the tower."

"They're not. Indeed, it doesn't look as if they've been there for several days. All their things are gone." The boy gaped at her. She continued, "Something is strange here, and I'm trying to discover what has happened. Please tell no one you saw me."

The boy nodded.

"Now, go about your business." She motioned to the nearly empty bucket he carried. "I'm sorry about the water."

Again the boy nodded.

She gave him an encouraging smile. "Don't worry. All will be well."

After Johnny left, she let out an anguished breath. Hilary and the children had been taken from the tower in secret. That could not be good.

Nicola followed the little-used corridor to the narrow stairs leading down to oubliette opening. At the bottom, it was very dark, and once again, she was without a light. She got down on her hands and knees and searched for the metal grate covering the underground cell.

She found the grate and leaned near to it. Hearing nothing, she brought her face close again and called, "Hilary, are you there?"

Rustling noises made her heart leap into her throat. Then a man's voice answered. "Who is it? Who's there?"

Although the voice sounded hoarse and raw, her mind immediately registered it as belonging to Gilbert de Vescy.

Chapter Twenty-One

Fawkes opened his eyes and looked blearily around the bedchamber. It seemed as if hours had passed since Alys left. Where was she? Damn her! He hated being so helpless. He eyed the ewer on the table. Nicola usually kept some wine there. Although wine wasn't what he needed right now, he was desperate for anything to drink.

Using his good arm, he edged himself to the side of the bed. He gritted his teeth against the pain and sat up. When the worst of the pain and dizziness passed, he stood and staggered to the table. Bracing himself against it, he grabbed the ewer, unstoppered it and drank.

The first few swallows were so bitter he almost spit them out. But then he decided he didn't care. At least it was liquid. He gulped down the rest and immediately regretted it. In seconds the wine seemed go to his head. He grabbed for the table, but his legs failed him and he sank to the floor. For a few moments he lay there. Then he gritted his teeth and tried to stand. He couldn't.

He told himself he would lie there until he felt a little stronger and then get up. There was no point waiting for Alys or Old Emma. This time he was going to head for the door and make his way downstairs.

****

He was so hot. So thirsty. Fawkes struggled to open his eyes. Gradually the familiar images of the tower room came into view. He was lying on the floor. The bed was near, but so far away. To crawl over and climb onto it seemed an insurmountable task.

But he needed water. His thirst was unbearable. And he was so hot, burning with fever. That must be why his thoughts were so fuzzy and confused. He'd had some sort of dream about Alys, about her telling him that Nicola's babe hadn't died but was living at Mordeaux. It had to be a dream. Otherwise it made no sense. Clearly his wits were addled by the fever. But why didn't anyone come? Old Emma? Reynard? Why had they left him here, lying on the floor, in pain, feverish and desperate for water? Had the castle been attacked? Were they dealing with some other crisis and too intent on it to see to him?

He could feel his strength fading; he feared slipping into delirium. Gritting his teeth, he tried to sit. The pain in his shoulder was unbearable. Spinning, swirling darkness surrounded him.

"Fawkes! Fawkes!"

Someone was calling him. Then they were shaking him. The movement aroused agony on his wounded side. He followed the pain back through the darkness into harsh, dizzying light.

Now they were carrying him. The feel of the soft bed beneath him. He breathed deeply, fighting through the pain.

"Fawkes, can you hear me?"

Reynard. At last.

He mumbled his friend's name and was rewarded by a deep sigh of relief. "Blessed Jesu, you had me worried. I thought you'd hit your head and that's why you wouldn't wake up. But by the saints, why did you get out of bed?"

"So thirsty. No one would come." Reynard must know he'd been left alone for hours, if not days.

"What about Alys? Why didn't you tell her what you needed?"

Alys. So he hadn't dreamed her being there. Did that mean the rest of it was true? Some tale about Nicola's dead baby being alive? That part must be a dream.

He sought to focus his thoughts. "I need water."

"Get it, Oliver. And hurry." Reynard put his hand on Fawkes's forehead. "I'm sorry, Fawkes. Alys offered to look after you, and I thought she would do better than that old crone Emma. Besides, Old Emma is Nicola's servant, and I'm not certain how much your wife cares for you. But it seems Alys is the one who is untrustworthy. And now you're fevered. God's teeth! I wish Glennyth was here."

"Where is she?" Fawkes asked, groggily.

"She went to Mordeaux. Remember? Nicola has gone to fetch her back."

But Nicola wasn't coming back. Alys had said so. Nicola was staying at Mordeaux with her son. "How long has Nicola been gone?"

Reynard was moving restlessly around the room. He didn't answer.

"Reynard?"

"Too long. She said she would enter the castle by some secret way. But something must have happened."

"What do you mean? What could have happened?"

Reynard approached the bed. "Don't worry about Nicola. She's like Glennyth's cat, Tom. She'll land on her feet. Do not doubt it."

Such bitterness. 'Twas not like easygoing, cheerful Reynard. He must know about the babe. Perhaps Alys had told him as well. If only he could think more clearly. Maybe water would help. Once he'd drunk his fill, his thoughts would run smoother and the world would make sense again.

****

"Gilbert!" Nicola exclaimed. "Thank goodness."

"Lady Nicola?" Gilbert responded in shocked tones. "What are you doing here? How did you find me? Has de Cressy retaken the castle?"

Nicola leaned nearer to the grate. "Fawkes has been injured and the castle is still under FitzSaer's control. I came here to get Glennyth, but I've seen no sign of her. Nor of Hilary and the children."

"What? Has FitzSaer done something to my family? The puling little bastard! You've got to get me out of here! We have to find them!"

"I know. I'm thinking. Where can I get a rope?"

"I believe there's one up there, near the opening. They use it to lower food and water down to me."

Nicola searched and found a rope with a basket tied to it. She removed the basket and took the rope back to the opening, wondering what she could fasten it to, so Gilbert could climb up. Close to the oubliette opening was a bracket on the wall meant for a torch. It was never intended to bear the weight of a man, but with luck it would hold for a short time.

She tied one end of the rope to the bracket and lowered the other into the cell. Gilbert grunted and groaned as he climbed the rope, and Nicola held her breath that the bracket would hold. At last he got near enough to the top to grab the side of the opening and with Nicola's help, scramble up.

He sprawled next to her for a moment, panting. "Have you any water?"

"A small jar." She retrieved it from her basket and he drank it down.

"Now what do we do?"

"We must find Hilary and the children. With luck Glennyth will be with them."

"Glennyth? You mean the healer at Valmar?"

"Aye. She came to Mordeaux to get some healing herbs from Hilary, since most of her supply was burned in a fire."

"Why are you so desperate for a healer?"

"Fawkes is wounded." She explained how he'd been hurt. Even speaking of it made her throat choke with helpless horror.

"How bad?"

"The quarrel struck him in the shoulder. I had to cut deep into his flesh to remove it."

Gilbert exhaled deeply. "I would never have believed FitzSaer capable of such cool-headed scheming. To imprison me and then try to kill Fawkes, it speaks of someone very cunning and ruthless."

"It's possible other people are behind this and he's simply following orders."

"Who?"

"There isn't time to explain. We must act quickly. First, we must get you out of the castle. Then I want you to find my horse in the forest and ride to Valmar and tell them what's going on."

"You expect me to leave you here?"

"I have to discover what's happened to Hilary and the children. And to Glennyth." She must find the healer. Fawkes's life depended on it.

"Lady, it doesn't seem right. I should be the one who searches for my family."

"If FitzSaer finds you, he'll kill you. Me, he won't. I'm too important to John's plans."

"John?"

"The prince. Richard's brother."

"He's behind this?" Gilbert was clearly aghast.

"I'm afraid so. As I said, it's a long tale and now is not the time for telling it. Come. We'll go back the way I came, through the hall."

"How will I get out? The man at the gate might be allied with FitzSaer."

"I know of another exit. Come."

****

Nicola waited impatiently in the stables for the young squire to saddle and bridle a horse. After searching the granary and the stables, she'd given up on finding Hilary and the children at Mordeaux. The only other place she could think to look was Rosebrook, a nearby manor. If only she was able to get out of the castle. The squire who was helping her clearly had no knowledge of FitzSaer's scheme, but the knights at the gate might be different.

She followed the squire as he led the horse out of the stable and took the animal to the mounting block. He was about to help her up when an angry voice called, "Stop her! Don't let her leave!"

FitzSaer raced toward them. The squire froze. Nicola grabbed the reins and scrambled onto the horse's back. She dug her heels into the horse's flanks and the horse shot past FitzSaer toward the gate.

"Stop her!" FitzSaer cried again.

Before she reached the gate, an armed knight appeared in her pathway. She tried to urge the horse past the knight, but the animal shied.

The knight ran up and grabbed the horse's bridle. FitzSaer raced over from the other direction. His eyes raked her, narrowed with malice. Nicola glared back at him. "I'm the lady of Mordeaux, and you will not keep me here against my will." She turned to the man holding the bridle. "FitzSaer has no authority here. I am the wife of your liege lord. I command you to let me go."

"That's where you're wrong," FitzSaer retorted. "Prince John, soon to be King John, has appointed *me* castellan of Mordeaux. He disavows the claim of the usurper, Fawkes de Cressy."

"Fawkes de Cressy has a writ giving him Mordeaux, as well as Valmar. And his writ is from the true king, Richard the Lionheart."

"Ah, but Richard rots in the emperor's prison, so he's hardly in a position to enforce his decrees." FitzSaer voice was full of gloating.

"Fawkes doesn't need the king's support. He will come and take Mordeaux back."

"Aye, he would do that, lady. Except he is badly wounded. One of my men saw him being carried off, draped over his horse like a corpse."

"Wounded, aye. But not so badly he will not heal. And as soon as he does, he'll come and take Mordeaux from you, and see you hanged!"

FitzSaer made a sound of disgust. "Bold words. But completely untrue. I've had word from Valmar that de Cressy is already sickening. He may linger awhile, but he'll die all the same. I have nothing to fear from him."

FitzSaer's words were like a knife in her belly. But she would not let him see her fear. She faced him defiantly. "Your spy is a fool. De Cressy will survive and make you pay for your treachery." She turned her gaze to the knight. "And he'll punish anyone who has helped this man. You can be certain of it."

"Enough!" FitzSaer shouted. "I'm done arguing with

you. I'm sick of your meddling. You've never behaved as a proper lady should. That will all change when you're my wife. And now, you will get down off *my* horse, or I will have Baldwin drag you off!"

"What do you intend to do to me?"

FitzSaer's smile was grim. "Lock you away where you can't get into any more mischief."

Nicola struggled to repress a shudder at the thought of being imprisoned in the oubliette. But there were worse things. If Fawkes died, FitzSaer would try to force her to marry him. She would never relent. Better to die than to once again be wed to a man she loathed.

Taking bitter satisfaction from the thought, she allowed the knight to help her dismount. The two men, one on either side, led her back to the castle and to the oubliette. As they neared the dungeon, Nicola fought panic. She focused on her hatred for FitzSaer. Hanging would be too easy a death for the filthy swine! Perhaps she'd have *him* thrown into the oubliette and leave him to die slowly by starvation.

The rope was still tied to the bracket on the wall. FitzSaer had Baldwin untie it and then fasten it around Nicola's waist. Baldwin moved aside the grate covering the oubliette opening and the two men lowered her into the dark cell.

"Now, untie the rope so we can pull it up," FitzSaer ordered. "Otherwise we won't have any means of lowering you food and water."

"Perhaps I'll starve myself. Once I'm dead, my dowry will pass back to the king. Who knows whom Richard—or even John—will choose to give it to? It won't be you. They'll gift it to someone who has more power and wealth."

FitzSaer laughed. "You won't starve yourself. Otherwise I'll make certain your son comes to a very unpleasant end."

As FitzSaer's words echoed in the cold darkness of her prison, Nicola pressed a hand to her mouth to keep from crying out. *Simon! Dear Simon! Oh, my darling, what have I done!*

Chapter Twenty-Two

Fawkes woke from a fitful sleep to find Reynard sitting by the bed. Old Emma was also there fussing with some of Nicola's things.

Reynard told the servant to fetch Fawkes some broth. Then he rose and moved restlessly around the room.

"What is it?" Fawkes asked after Reynard paced back and forth a few times. "What's wrong?"

Reynard faced the bed. "Before she left for Mordeaux, Nicola told me something very disturbing. Apparently, last winter a priest came to Valmar and hinted that Prince John was looking for allies in his quest to seize power while Richard was imprisoned. Furious, Mortimer told the priest to leave. But Nicola met with the priest. She told him if some ally of John's were to seize Valmar and Mordeaux by force, she would not be displeased. It seems she hated Mortimer so much she had decided to betray him, even if it meant being wed to some other man of John's choosing."

This wasn't what Fawkes was expecting. Yet, it fit what he knew of his wife. He could well imagine Nicola doing such a thing.

Reynard shook his head. "I don't understand why she didn't tell you about this plot long ago. It's hard to believe she cares for you when she failed to warn you what she'd done. She claims she forgot the whole conversation and only started to worry again when the jongleur de Ronay told her the enemy army was on the way."

"So that was what she was up to with de Ronay." Fawkes was relieved there was nothing between Nicola and the jongleur. Even so, what his wife had done could be considered treason.

"Nicola says she paid de Ronay to convince the prince to stop the plot. Instead, de Ronay left for Shrewsbury. FitzSaer now commands Mordeaux. I'm certain his plan was to kill you and wed Nicola. Then he could swear allegiance to Prince John and claim Nicola's dowry." Reynard gave Fawkes a grim look. "The thing is…I'm not certain Nicola isn't involved in this plot as well."

Fawkes stared at his captain. "You think she wants me dead?" He shook his head. "I don't believe that. I remember her tending to my wound. She was frantic with worry."

"I know she appeared convincing at the time. But think of all the other things she's lied about. All the things she's kept from you. So many secrets."

Alys had said something similar. Even so, all his instincts told him Nicola didn't want him dead. No one was that good at pretending. Why would she want to be rid of him so she could marry FitzSaer? She despised the man. Unless… Was it possible FitzSaer was the father of her son? The babe that didn't die but grew up and was now living at Mordeaux?

The thought of it made Fawkes feel sick, a sickness that went beyond the fever and pain wracking his body. The next moment he remembered Reynard didn't know about Nicola's son. He met his captain's gaze. "When I was desperate for water and Alys was taunting me, she told me something strange. She told me Nicola's baby didn't die. That he is alive and living at Mordeaux."

Reynard gave a snort of disgust. "I wouldn't trust anything Alys says. Not after the way she treated you."

"But think about it. The story does explain things: Nicola's trips to Mordeaux and the children's garments she sews." *And the fact that she hasn't come back from Mordeaux.*

"But why would she lie about something like that? Why let everyone think she'd killed her child and then hide the boy away all this time?"

"Maybe FitzSaer is the boy's father."

Reynard shook his head. "As much as I mistrust Nicola and doubt her feelings for you, I can't believe she has any fondness for FitzSaer. And why did she tell me about the conversation with this priest and the whole business with de Ronay? If she'd kept quiet, we would never have known what was happening until it was too late to do anything."

"First, you accuse her of wanting me dead. Now you defend her. Which is it, Reynard?"

Fawkes knew what *he* felt. He could not believe that everything between Nicola and him was a lie. He could not accept that. No one could feign the sort of passion they'd shared.

Unless that's all it was. Passion. Perhaps Nicola desired him in bed and reveled in their lovemaking, but never let it touch her heart. He'd never known a woman to be so cold, but it wasn't impossible. Nicola's experience with Mortimer might have damaged her somehow. Killed her normal womanly feelings. She might be incapable of caring for anyone but her son.

Fawkes closed his eyes. The thought of Nicola *not* loving him made him feel unbearably desolate.

"I don't know what to think," Reynard said. "We

have to find out if this tale about the babe is true. But who can we ask?"

"Old Emma must know."

"But she's been Nicola's maidservant since Nicola was a child. She would give her life to protect her lady."

Fawkes sighed wearily. "I feel like I'm being torn apart. One part of me is utterly convinced Nicola loves me and would never betray me. But she has all these secrets. There are things she's done that make no sense at all. No sense, unless..." Fawkes let his voice trail off. He would not say it. It was impossible Nicola cared nothing for him.

"When Old Emma comes back, we'll ask her," he said. "Nicola may be clever and devious enough to fool us. But plain, solid Old Emma will tell the truth."

Even as they waited for the servant, there was a clatter on the stairs. Gilbert de Vescy rushed into the room. His eyes were wild. "Fawkes! Reynard! I've just escaped from the oubliette at Mordeaux. Adam FitzSaer is the fiend behind all of it!"

They stared at the haggard-looking knight. "Tell us," Fawkes said.

Gilbert took a deep breath. "It started several days ago. I'm not certain exactly how long. Someone knocked me unconscious. When I awoke, I was in the oubliette. I've been there all this time. Until today, when Lady Nicola set me free."

Fawkes exchanged a look with Reynard. "Nicola set you free? Where is she?"

"She stayed at Mordeaux to search for Hilary and the children, and the healer, Glennyth. They've disappeared. Nicola helped me out of the oubliette and showed me a secret tunnel leading out of the keep. I rode here as fast as I could."

"Now Glennyth is missing." Reynard sounded as overwhelmed as Fawkes felt.

Gilbert ran his hand though his disheveled, silver-threaded brown hair. "I'm sorry, my lord. I should never have left Lady Nicola there. But she *ordered* me to leave her. What do we do now? If we send an armed force to Mordeaux, FitzSaer might hurt my family." He took a ravaged breath. "I can't bear being so helpless."

Gilbert had no idea, Fawkes thought grimly. A man could hardly be more helpless than he was now, weak, burning with fever and unable to get out of bed. He wanted nothing so much as to lie back and sleep for hours.

"Perhaps someone could get inside the castle using the secret entrance," Reynard suggested. "Then they could find FitzSaer and kill or imprison him."

"'Twill not be easy," Gilbert said. "FitzSaer is certain to be on guard, now that I've escaped. He may have discovered the passageway and closed it up."

"Where does this passageway lead inside the castle?" Reynard asked.

"It goes to a cellar where they store the winter vegetables."

"We need to find someone who knows the layout of Mordeaux castle," Fawkes said. "Once they get inside, they can find out who supports FitzSaer and who does not."

Gilbert nodded. "I could do it. Except if FitzSaer discovers me, he might do something to my family." His blue eyes darkened with anguish.

Fawkes noted that Gilbert spoke of *his family*. Did that mean Alys was wrong and the little boy wasn't really Nicola's son? Fawkes wanted to ask, but right now there were more pressing issues.

Gilbert narrowed his eyes. "We could get someone who regularly goes to the castle to find out more. I could talk to the villeins who live nearby. Some of the women regularly bring produce to the kitchen. I should have spoken to them before I came here. But I knew I had to come here immediately and tell you what's happening. Now I should go back. Not to get inside the castle, but to find someone who can."

A wave of dizziness passed over Fawkes, and for a moment he worried he might faint. He didn't want Gilbert see how weak he was. He motioned brusquely. "Go. Take a knight or two. Reynard, get them whatever they need."

Reynard told Gilbert he would meet him in the hall. After Gilbert left, Reynard leaned near to the bed. "What's wrong, Fawkes? You don't look well. Is it the fever?"

Eyes closed, he nodded. "It makes me dizzy and muddle-headed."

"Try to rest. I'll organize some men to accompany Gilbert. Then I'll be back."

After Reynard left, Fawkes tried to sleep, but his agonized thoughts kept him from true slumber. Did Nicola care for him? Or was she plotting with FitzSaer to kill him off? And what of the babe? Was that all a cruel tale told by Alys to torment him, or was Nicola's baby alive? And who was the father? Him, or another man?

It was all a jumble. As if one of the glass windows in the solar had been shattered and he was trying to put the pieces back together. It seemed far too difficult to do in his weakened state. And what was the point? His fever was worsening, which meant his wound had turned poisoned and he was probably going to die.

He must have finally dozed. Next thing he knew, Old Emma was wiping his face with a cool wet cloth.

"Are you in pain? Do you want some poppy?"

"No more poppy." Too many important things were happening for him to have his wits confused. "But I could use more water."

"Of course, milord."

Old Emma poured him a cup of water. After he drank it, Fawkes grasped Old Emma's plump hand. "There's something I must ask you. When Alys was supposedly taking care of me, she told me...she told me Nicola's babe didn't die. She said that all this time the boy has been living at Mordeaux."

Old Emma fixed him with a steady gaze. "I wondered when you would find out. Nicola should have told you long ago. I urged her to do so many times."

"You mean it's true?"

"Aye."

"Why didn't she tell me?"

"In the beginning she was too afraid."

Fawkes jerked his hand away from the servant's. "Did she really think me so depraved and cruel she thought I would harm the child?"

Old Emma's dark eyes grew sorrowful. "I'm afraid Mortimer was capable of doing exactly that. That's why she had to hide the child away when he was born. When you came... Well, she didn't really know you, milord. One afternoon she'd spent with you, and then only in bed. Also, there were these tales of you killing the Saracen prisoners, one after another."

"I never killed women or children! I'm not completely without conscience!"

"I know. I know, my lord." Old Emma patted his good arm. "By the time we realized you weren't a monster like Mortimer, Nicola had already lied. Having learned of the tales some of Mortimer's men were telling about her, she was afraid you wouldn't believe her."

"Not believe her? All she had to do was produce the child. I could hardly deny the boy's existence!"

"Nay, not about that. About the fact that the boy is your son."

Fawkes focused on the servant's face. Was this another tale meant to manipulate him? "Of course the boy is my son." His voice was harsh with sarcasm. "That's why Nicola hid him from me for weeks. Because she thought I would be upset to learn I had a strong healthy son. It makes perfect sense!"

"I haven't seen him since he was born, but Nicola says Simon doesn't resemble you in the least. Indeed, she insists anyone looking at him would think he was Mortimer's get."

"She thought I would despise the boy as I did the man and *do* something to him?" He could not keep the resentment from his voice. How could Nicola think him capable of such cruelty?

"Well, not hurt him, nay. But deprive him of his birthright, his rights as her heir."

"That's all Nicola thought about, her child's birthright? That was more important than telling me he was alive? She could not tell me even after we got past the early awkwardness and doubts? Even after we..." He couldn't say it. If he told Old Emma how close he felt to Nicola when they made love, she would think him an utter fool. Only young maids believed in such fancies.

Old Emma made a helpless gesture. "I know, my lord. My lady can be witless sometimes. It's because of Mortimer. The things he did when they were first married were so awful, she never got over it. I know you've heard the tale that she poisoned Mortimer and turned him into a shell of what he once was. But even after he lost his will, she never felt safe. Then you came and killed Mortimer. It should have made everything right. Yet even that didn't allay her fears. So she lied to you. By the time she realized you weren't going to turn into a beast like Mortimer, she couldn't see a way past the lies."

Old Emma's explanation sounded ridiculous. Yet, who was he to say? He'd never experienced the sense of powerlessness Nicola must have felt, at the mercy of a deranged, violent husband. He looked Old Emma directly in the eye. "You say the child is my son? You're certain?"

"Aye, my lord. If Nicola ever lay with anyone else, I would have known of it. I was never far from her bedchamber in those days."

Nicola had a son and the boy was his. He should be elated. But all he could think of was that the child was somewhere inside Mordeaux castle. If they could not find him and get him out before this army arrived, his son might end up a hostage.

Maybe that's what Nicola had planned. Perhaps as Reynard suggested, she was working with FitzSaer, intending to surrender the castle to Prince John. Her plan might be to get rid of him so she could wed someone else. Some wealthy lord, a man of her own rank.

He had to know. So far, Old Emma had been honest with him. Would she tell him the truth about what Nicola felt for him?

The elderly maidservant was fussing with the covers on the bed. He reached out with his good hand and grasped her arm. "There's something else I need to know."

"Of course, my lord."

"How does…how does Nicola feel about me? Is she

pleased to have me for her husband?"

Old Emma made a choked sound. Then she grinned at him. "Pleased? Nay, more like you are the answer to her dreams. She never forgot you from that afternoon you spent in her bed. She's in love with you, milord. Do not doubt it."

Chapter Twenty-Three

Nicola paced back and forth in her prison, cursing FitzSaer. And cursing her father for designing the oubliette so there was no chance a prisoner could escape. Someone would have to rescue her, or she was doomed. If Gilbert managed to get to Valmar, he would send rescue. But how long would that take? In the meantime she had no idea what was happening.

The fury and frustration built inside her until she felt she would explode. So much of her life had been spent like this, waiting for others to decide her fate. She was always at the mercy of someone, usually a man. Being helpless had shaped her life. It had also caused her to make terrible mistakes. Like plotting with the priest and Prince John. And all the lies she'd told Fawkes. She should have trusted him long ago. Then Simon would be at Valmar, instead of missing, and Fawkes likely wouldn't be injured.

All that time she wasted, when she and Fawkes could have been happy together. Now he might die and she would never have a chance to tell him she loved him. Tears filled her eyes and her throat grew tight and aching. So many foolish choices. And because of them, she might have lost everything.

She slumped to the ground, feeling the deep chill of the oubliette floor seep through her gown. An ancient, empty cold that seemed to deaden her body even as her heart froze with despair and grief. She could kneel here until her life force ebbed away. Give up the battle, the endless struggle. She'd failed so miserably at her life. What was the point of continuing?

Then all at once, she saw herself as she would look to FitzSaer if he opened the grate and gazed down at her. He would think he had won. And he *would* win if she died of despair. He might not end up as the lord of Mordeaux and Valmar, but he would have destroyed the lives of so many people. Her life. Fawkes's. Simon's. Gilbert's, Hilary's and Joanie's. Not to mention the knights and servants and villagers who depended on her and on Fawkes.

Nay, she would not be defeated. She was the lady of Valmar. To give up now would be an insult to the memory of her father, and a cruel blow to everyone in the demesne who depended on her.

She got to her feet and stood tall and straight. There was still hope. Hope that she would get free. Hope that Fawkes would survive. She must not panic and make foolish decisions, as she had so many times.

The anguish and despair weighing on her lifted. It was as if telling herself to have hope had freed her and cast away the chains of fear and dread that bound her. She glanced up, wondering if this change in her outlook was a message from God. Even as she did so, she heard footsteps. The grate moved aside and the light of a torch flickered down on her.

"Lady!" A fervent whisper. "I'm sending down the rope. Do you think you can climb up?"

"Morwenna? How did you… Send it down and I will try."

Summoning all her strength, Nicola clawed her way up the rope. When she was half-way up, Morwenna began to pull. As she neared the top, Nicola grabbed the edge of the opening.

"Take my hand," Morwenna said.

Nicola did so. Morwenna seized her other wrist and dragged her up. Years of lifting heavy pots and pans had made the cook very strong.

For a few moments Nicola lay panting next to the opening. "Thank you," she breathed.

"We must hurry." Morwenna helped Nicola stand. "I don't think we should risk taking the torch. Do you think you can find the hidden tunnel without light?"

"I must."

Leaving the torch burning on the wall, they crept up the stairs and through the hall, where a half-dozen knights slept. They hurried to the other side of the castle to the souterrain.

"I could fetch you a candle from the kitchen," Morwenna suggested in a whisper.

"I don't want to take the time. I'll have to manage in the dark."

"How long will it take you to get out?"

"Not long."

"Good. Goddard, the reeve, is waiting behind the castle. He couldn't risk taking a horse from the stables, but he has a mule. 'Tis hardly a fitting mount for a lady, but better than nothing."

"No matter." Nicola choked back a laugh. "I'm certain I look nothing like a lady now anyway." She grasped Morwenna's right hand. "Thank you. I will make certain you both are rewarded for this. Rewarded handsomely."

"For you to get free and sort out this mess, that will be reward enough. I want Gilbert back as castellan. And Hilary and the children in the tower where they belong."

"I'll make certain of it." Nicola gave Morwenna's hand another squeeze. Then she fumbled for the door to the souterrain and entered the pitch-dark chamber. She found the tunnel entrance and drew the covering aside, then climbed down into the passageway. After pulling the covering into place, she began her journey.

Her shoulders ached, both from climbing the rope and being hunched over. To distract herself, she focused on what she must do next. Ride to Rosebrook where there was a good chance FitzSaer had imprisoned the two women and the children. She would free the captives and send Glennyth on the mule to Valmar, while she and Hillary followed on foot, carrying the children.

A deep weariness came over her as she thought of walking miles carrying Simon. And what if she was wrong and they weren't at Rosebrook? She had no other idea of where to look for them.

Once out of the tunnel, she found the mule tied to a thorn bush. It was still dark, but the light of the waxing moon was enough to see her on her way. And for a time she would be able to follow the river.

She mounted the mule and urged the animal forward. It obeyed willingly but moved with a slowness that was maddening.

It was growing light by the time she neared Rosebrook and every inch of her ached. She tied the mule to a tree in the apple orchard behind the manor house and approached the dwelling. Everything seemed quiet, but when she circled around to the front of the house, she saw two knights sprawled out, sleeping by the door. There was no way to get past them. She'd have to get inside by other means.

She leaned against the side of the house,

overwhelmed with fatigue and frustration. Her beloved Simon must be here. And Glennyth, the one person who might be able to save Fawkes's life. Somehow she had to find a way in.

Nicola went to the large window on the side of the house and used her dagger to pry open the shutter. At first the wood refused to give way. Then she sought a different angle and was rewarded when the shutter popped open with a sharp creaking sound. Terrified the guards had heard, she waited, the dagger poised in her hand and her heart thrumming in her chest.

When nothing happened, she returned to her task and finally managed to wrench open the shutters several inches. But she couldn't climb into the high window. She would have to find something to stand on to reach it. In the outbuilding behind the house, she found a wheelbarrow and quickly maneuvered it in place by the window. Nicola climbed into it, drew the shutters farther apart, and eased herself into the opening. She swiveled her hips and dropped to the floor. It took a moment for her eyes to adjust to the dim light. Relief flooded her as she saw Hilary, Joanie, and Simon asleep in the bed.

She moved closer and softly called Hilary's name. Hilary sat up with a gasp. She stared at Nicola, then looked around as if she did not know where she was. "How did you get in here?"

Nicola held a finger to her lips and whispered, "The window."

"And the guards?" Hilary asked, also in a whisper. She cast a fearful glance at the door.

"Sleeping. But they could wake at any moment. We must hurry." Nicola gestured to the window. "You climb out first, and I'll hand the children down to you."

Hilary shook Joanie. The little girl woke up, looked around, and let out a whimper. "'Tis all right, love," Hilary said. "See, Lady Nicola is here."

Joanie stared at Nicola.

"We're playing a game," Hilary said, quietly. "We're going to climb out the window."

"Simon too?"

"Aye. Simon too." Hilary nudged Simon.

The boy woke, saw Nicola and smiled. Unable to help herself, she went to the bed and gathered him into her arms. "Come sweeting. We must hurry." As Hilary went to the window, Nicola asked, "Where's Glennyth?"

"I don't know. She was with us when we were brought here, but I don't know where they took her after that."

A horrible thought came to Nicola. What if they had killed Glennyth? But that made no sense. Why would FitzSaer have his men bring her here to murder her?

Hilary stood by the window as if frozen.

"You can do it," Nicola said.

Hilary nodded, but her eyes were wide with anxiety.

"I'm hungry," Simon said.

"Of course you are. We'll eat soon. But first we're going to play a game. Hilary is going to climb out the window, and then I will hand you out to her." Simon giggled. "The other part of the game is that we must be very quiet so the knights won't know what we're doing." Nicola nodded to Hilary. "Please. There's little time."

Hilary boosted herself up on the windowsill, then turned and slid down to the waiting wheelbarrow. Nicola put Simon on the bed, then picked up Joanie and handed the little girl out the window to her mother. Once Joanie was on the ground, Hilary reached for Simon.

Nicola handed over Simon. "There's a mule in the orchard. The children can ride while you lead it. Don't wait for me. I'm going to look for Glennyth." She indicated the direction of the orchard. "Hurry."

Hilary took Simon and Joanie by the hand. Once they were gone, Nicola climbed out the window. She wondered where to look for Glennyth. Besides the house there was a stable and a buttery.

Nicola searched both buildings before returning to the manor house. The only other place she could think to look was the storage area under the kitchen. But that meant getting inside the house again.

It was fully light now and at any moment the two knights might decide to check on the captives. Although her arms and legs were almost numb with fatigue, Nicola returned to the window and climbed inside. She eased open the door of the bedchamber and peered into the main living area. The coals of a banked-down fire glowed in the hearth, but the room was empty.

Nicola crossed to the door leading to the kitchen. Inside it was pitch dark. She got down on her hands and knees and crawled around on the floor, feeling for the latch to the root cellar. She finally found a metal ring and pulled to open the trapdoor, wincing at the loud creak the hinges made. Leaning down, she whispered, "Glennyth? Glennyth, are you there?"

She waited breathlessly, and then again called the wise woman's name. Still hearing no response, she started to close the trapdoor. She paused at a shuffling sound. Had she disturbed a rat or some other vermin? As she hesitated, there was a low groan. She slid into the opening and down the stairs. At the bottom, she crouched and felt around. She came upon a large basket. It was empty and starting to fall apart, indicating the storage area hadn't been used for some time. She moved further into the room. Another low moan. She made her way toward the sound, cursing as she encountered another basket. A few feet more and she stumbled onto a body. Glennyth. The healer's wrists and ankles had been tied and there was a gag on her mouth.

Nicola tried to untie the gag. When it would not come free, she used her dagger to cut the strip of fabric. As soon as the gag fell loose, Glennyth blurted, "Curse him, that wretched, filthy swine!"

"Shhh. We don't want to alert the guards."

"What do you mean?" Glennyth whispered. "Is there no one else with you? The guards are still here?"

"Aye. That's why we must hurry." Nicola cut the ropes tying Glennyth's wrists and ankles. "Can you walk?"

"I think so."

Nicola helped Glennyth stand, then held her arm until they found the stairs up to the kitchen. Nicola closed the trapdoor, and she and Glennyth tiptoed through the house to the bedchamber. After helping Glennyth out the window, Nicola followed.

Once outside, Nicola debated whether to go to the stables for a horse. At the sound of voices from the front of the house, Glennyth shot Nicola a look of dread. Nicola grabbed her arm and they took off at a run.

They were almost to the orchard when someone shouted behind them. Two knights were chasing them. "Sweet Jesu, we'll never get away!" Nicola cried.

The footfalls of the men grew nearer. One of the men grabbed Glennyth and she went down. Nicola took a few more steps and whirled around. She bent, retrieved the dagger sheathed on her leg, and held it up threateningly.

The man pursuing her halted. He looked at her face and his expression changed to one of shock. "Lady? Lady Nicola?"

Nicola stared at the man. His sloe dark eyes and full mouth seemed familiar.

"What...what are you doing here?" The man took a step back. He looked horrified.

"Will, what is it?" his companion asked. "Why are you staring at her like that?"

"It's Lady Nicola," Will answered. "Also known as Lady Mortimer and now de Cressy. She's your liege lord's wife, you fool!"

The man holding Glennyth gaped at Nicola. "What are you doing here?"

"Freeing Glennyth. I need her to come back with me to Valmar."

The man shook his head. "This woman has been plotting with Sir Gilbert. The two of them have a plan to surrender Mordeaux to Prince John's men and betray the castle."

"That's not true." Glennyth pulled away from her captor. Her hazel eyes flashed. "I haven't even seen Sir Gilbert. By the time I arrived at the castle, he'd disappeared."

Both men stood silent, absorbing this.

"What were you told?" Nicola asked. "About Sir Gilbert and the plot?"

The one named Will answered, "Sir Adam said Gilbert had gone to Chester to meet up with the prince's forces. They plan to march on Mordeaux, claim the castle, and make Gilbert the lord."

"The person behind the plot is FitzSaer, not De Vescy." Nicola said. "*FitzSaer* is the one who's trying to seize control. And he's using you to carry out his plan. Sir Gilbert didn't go to Chester. He was locked in the oubliette. I found him there yesterday and set him free."

Will looked at his companion, dismay written on his face. "That means we brought Lady Hilary and her children here for no good reason."

"And don't forget what you did to me, you ignorant, hen-witted fools!" Glennyth struck the man holding her on the arm. The man stepped back, alarmed.

"We didn't know," Will said. "We had no idea."

Nicola waved dismissively. "All that matters now is getting Glennyth back to Valmar. Lord Fawkes is badly wounded and needs the wise woman's aid."

"Fawkes is wounded?" The other man stepped forward. "How did that happen?"

"A crossbow bolt in his shoulder. It happened when he was at Mordeaux, trying to get them to open the gate. I would wager FitzSaer was behind it." The men looked even more appalled. Nicola faced them sternly, hoping to spur them into action. "Go now and fetch mounts for us. The swiftest horses you have. Lord de Cressy's life depends on it."

As the knights hurried off, Glennyth sank down on the ground. Nicola sat beside her. "Thank you for rescuing me," Glennyth said. "I truly feared I would die here. How did you find us?"

"I searched the castle first. That's how FitzSaer caught up with me and put me in the oubliette."

"He imprisoned you as well?"

Nicola explained the events at the castle.

Glennyth met her gaze with a wry look. "I would not have thought you so brave and resourceful to do all of that, my lady. No offense intended."

"Even a sennight ago I would not have thought myself capable of such things either. But knowing Fawkes's life is at stake made me desperate. Once I discovered Hilary and the children had disappeared, I was frantic to find them as well."

"They're on their way to Valmar?"

Nicola nodded. "They have a mule, the only mount Morwenna could arrange. It will be slow going, but with luck Hilary and the children will reach Valmar before FitzSaer sends someone after them. And if those foolish knights would hurry up and bring us horses, we should be able to get away as well."

Glennyth shook her head. "You forget, Nicola. I don't know how to ride."

"You'll have to ride pillion behind me. It will be slower that way, but still faster than walking."

Will and the other man returned with two horses. "We're only going to need one," Nicola said. "Glennyth can't ride on her own."

"Sarcanet is faster." Will led the chestnut mare over to them. "But she can be skittish. Are you certain you're strong enough to ride all that way, my lady?"

"I have no choice."

Will held the reins as the other man helped Nicola mount and then boosted Glennyth up. Unused to two riders, the mare shifted and shied.

"Whoa, Sarcanet." Nicola spoke softly to the mare and patted the animal's neck. When the mare settled, she told the men, "Go back to the manor house and pretend all is well. We need to keep FitzSaer from discovering his prisoners have escaped for as long as possible." She turned the horse and called out to the men. "Thank you for your aid. I'll make certain Lord de Cressy rewards you for your loyalty." *If he lives.* The terrible fear that he would not gnawed at her.

They hadn't ridden long before they encountered Hilary and the mule. Nicola cursed herself for not bringing the other horse.

Simon riding a mule made her uneasy. But his big grin made her realize he was enjoying himself. Indeed, both children seemed to think they were on a grand adventure.

"What should we do now?" Hilary asked. "Do you each want to take one of the children and I'll follow on foot?"

"Perhaps I should go back and get the other horse," Nicola said. "Riding would be much faster."

Hilary shook her head. "I'm sorry, milady. I never learned to ride."

Nicola nodded. "Glennyth is the same." She wanted very badly to take Simon with her and Glennyth. But even his extra weight would be too much for their horse. She couldn't risk overtaxing the animal and delaying their arrival at Valmar. Fawkes's wound must be treated as soon as possible. She felt as if she was being torn in two, having to decide between Fawkes and her son. Always before, she'd chosen her son.

"Are you all right to continue on with the children?" she asked Hilary. "You can manage this?"

"I think so. If you tell me the way. What of you? You look worn to nothing."

Nicola glanced at Glennyth. "We'll make it." To Hilary she said, "Can you check the saddlebags? I'm hoping they might contain some supplies."

Hilary searched the saddlebags on the mare and came up with a flask but no food.

"What's in it?" Nicola asked.

Hilary pulled out the stopper and sniffed. "Wine."

Nicola motioned for Hilary to hand the flask to Glennyth. Some wine might hearten her a bit.

While Glennyth drank the wine, Nicola gave Hilary directions to Valmar. "You can't risk taking the main road. You'll have to go through the forest. After you cross the river, keep near it until you pass the castle. Then look for the pathway at the edge of the forest. If you have trouble finding the way, ask Ethelinda who lives by the river. You know her, of course."

Hilary nodded.

"Now we must go," Nicola said.

"Wave farewell to Lady Nicola," Hilary told Simon. "You'll see her soon."

"Bye, lady!" Simon called.

"Bye, lady," echoed Joanie.

Nicola shot one last longing look at Simon, and then urged the mare forward.

It was late afternoon when they reached Valmar. Having scarcely slept for a day and a half, Nicola was so weary she could barely stay upright on the horse. Glennyth was not much better.

The guard in the watchtower must have seen them coming and sent someone after Reynard. When they reached the castle yard, he was waiting for them. Reynard reached up to help Glennyth down. "God's teeth, I'm glad to see you. When Gilbert arrived and told us you and Hilary and the children were missing, I didn't know what to think."

Glennyth stood unsteadily. Reynard seized her arm. "What's wrong?"

"I'm not used to riding," Glennyth said. "Not to

mention FitzSaer left me bound and gagged in a cellar for nearly two days."

Reynard made a hissing sound. "I'll kill him, I'll kill the bastard!"

Nicola dismounted. For a moment she also had to struggle to stay upright. Every inch of her body ached. "Glennyth must see to Fawkes immediately," she told Reynard.

Reynard regarded Glennyth dubiously. "Perhaps she should rest first."

"I'm well enough," Glennyth said. "How fares Fawkes?"

Reynard's expression was grim. "His fever has risen and he seems much weaker."

"Then there's no time to waste." Glennyth turned toward the castle.

Reynard joined her. When he saw that Nicola wasn't coming, he demanded sharply. "Why are you standing there? Don't you care what happens to Fawkes?"

"Of course I care. I'll be there soon. First, I must send someone after Hilary and the children."

"Why didn't you bring them with you?"

Nicola felt like she would explode with exasperation. "It was impossible to bring everyone back with one horse and one mule. Now I must find someone who knows the route through the forest from Mordeaux. That's the way they'll be traveling."

"Why didn't you have them take the road?"

"FitzSaer won't be expecting them to go through the forest."

"I wish I'd known this before Gilbert set off for Mordeaux. He and his escort could have taken the forest path and looked out for Hilary and the children."

"Who did you send with Gilbert?"

"Oliver and Alexander. They hope to discover what is really happening in the castle."

"I can tell you what's happening. FitzSaer has spun a story that Gilbert intends to betray Mordeaux to John's army. He's painted Gilbert as the villain when in fact it's FitzSaer who means to surrender the castle."

Reynard cocked his head. "It seems very odd that you know exactly what FitzSaer intends."

"Not so odd when you consider he taunted me with his plans when I was imprisoned in the oubliette."

"You were imprisoned? How did you escape?"

She'd had enough of Reynard. It didn't matter if he believed her or not. She made a shooing gesture. "None of this matters. What's important is getting Glennyth to Fawkes."

Reynard seemed to recover himself. "You're right, of course."

"Certainly she is, you fool." Glennyth took Reynard's arm and led him away.

Nicola hurried to the stables. Sending a cart would be the easiest way to bring Hilary and the children back, but a cart would never manage the narrow forest trackway. She'd have to send mounted knights. Three of them, so each horse would only have to carry two people. But who knew the route through the forest?

Even as she had the thought, she saw Anselm crossing the yard. He'd grown up at Valmar and knew the area well. She motioned for him to approach. "Do you know how to get to Mordeaux by going through the woods?"

"Aye, milady."

"Good. I need you to find two other knights with swift mounts. The three of you must take the path through the forest and look for a woman walking and two children riding a mule. The woman is Sir Gilbert's wife. She is on the way here with her children. I need you to bring them to here as quickly as possible. You can leave the mule behind if it's faster."

"Of course, my lady."

Anselm hurried off. Nicola wished she could go with him. But she must see to Fawkes.

By the time she arrived in the tower room, Glennyth had peeled off Fawkes's bandages to reveal his badly swollen shoulder. Seeing the streaks of red around the wound, Nicola gasped in dismay. "'Tis as I feared. The putrefaction has started."

"Aye. But the poison hasn't yet spread to the rest of his body. We have a chance."

"What will you do?"

Glennyth led Nicola away from the bed. "We must drain as much of poison as we can, then I'll make a poultice to draw out the rest. I've already sent Reynard to have the cook prepare a bucket of hot bran and boiled onions."

"Bran and boiled onions?"

"Aye. It must be applied when it's very hot. 'Twill not be pleasant for Fawkes. Although the fever has already rendered him partially insensible, he'll still feel this. We'd best give him some poppy."

Nicola went the storage chest and took out the vial of poppy juice. She frowned as she shook it. "We gave him quite a bit before I removed the crossbow bolt, but I thought there was more left than this."

Glennyth took the vial. "'Tis enough, I think."

Chapter Twenty-Four

He was trapped under the walls of Acre. It was boiling hot and a great pile of stones pinned him to the ground. His body was burning as if the flesh of his shoulder was on fire. Or perhaps he was in Hell itself, being punished endlessly for his sins. The thought disturbed him so much he cried out.

"'Tis all right." Someone touched his face.

"Nicola?" Fawkes opened his eyes. It was not Nicola leaning over him but Glennyth, the wise woman.

She lifted his head and held a cup to his lips. "Drink this."

He grimaced as he tasted poppy-laced wine. "I would rather have water."

"You'll get water soon enough. For now, we need you to sleep deeply. What I'm about to do will cause you great pain. We must drain the wound."

He wasn't a coward, but he dreaded what was to come. Already he was in agony.

"I'm here, Fawkes." Nicola approached the bed and took his hand.

He clutched her fingers tightly. Seeing her heartened him as nothing else could. "Where have you been? I can't remember. Nay, it doesn't matter. All that matters is that you're here now."

She gave him a rueful smile. "'Tis a long tale. I'll save it until you are better."

Looking at Nicola, seeing the tenderness and worry in her eyes, Fawkes decided Reynard's fear that she wished him dead was ludicrous. The next moment he remembered the babe. *His son.* He longed to hear the words from Nicola's lips. But already the poppy was muddling his mind and rendering him unable to speak.

****

Nicola sat down on the bed next to Fawkes. She held his hand and focused on his face. She would not look at his shoulder, which was an oozing mess of raw-looking flesh, bran, and onions.

Glennyth sat on a stool. She appeared even wearier than Nicola felt. "I've done the best I can. He's young and healthy. His chances are good."

"And his shoulder? Will he be able to ride? Wield a sword?"

"Perhaps not as skillfully as before, but aye, if it heals clean, he should not be a cripple."

"If it doesn't?"

"Mayhap he'll wish he *had* died. Some men feel that way when they lose full use of their body. I don't think Fawkes is one of them. I think he will realize he has much to live for."

Please, God, let him recover. "He still burns with fever."

"That's to be expected. The poultice was burning hot, and he had a fever ere we even began." Glennyth rose. "I'm going to get some rest, and you should also. Mayhaps you should send for Old Emma to keep watch."

"See if you can find her. I don't want to leave him alone."

Glennyth nodded. "Make certain he drinks water when he wakes. Lots of water. It will purge the poison and

340

help him heal."

Nicola stood. "I'm so grateful for what you've done. Especially after the ordeal you've been through."

"You're welcome, lady. I hope he recovers. For your sake and for Valmar's."

As Glennyth reached the door, Reynard entered. "How fares he?"

"It's far too soon to tell," Glennyth answered.

Reynard focused on Nicola. "Did you send someone after Hilary and the children?"

"Aye. Anselm, Gerard and Engelard. Anselm knows the forest pathway."

Reynard nodded, then asked, "Are any of them involved with Alys?"

"Why do you ask?"

Reynard grimaced. "While you were gone, Alys tried to kill Fawkes."

Nicola gaped at him. "Why? How?"

"She left him alone and refused to give him water."

Glennyth made a shocked sound. "She wouldn't give him water?"

Reynard nodded. "She finally admitted her plan was to neglect Fawkes until he died."

"But why?" Nicola asked. "I've always thought she was enamored of Fawkes."

"Perhaps she was. But when she realized he would never care for her, she became angry and resentful. But that's not all of it. I think she's allied with FitzSaer. That's she's involved with someone who is in communication with FitzSaer at Mordeaux."

A cold dread climbed Nicola's spine. She had not considered anyone at Valmar might be part of FitzSaer's plot. "Anselm serves Sir Robert, who was one of

Mortimer's men. And I know he has dallied with Alys. Most of the knights and squires have."

"He may well be in on the plot."

Nicola let out a gasp of dismay. "By the rood! This is disastrous! I asked Anselm to bring Hilary and the children here. What if he takes them to FitzSaer instead? FitzSaer knows he can use Simon to force me to do his will."

"Aye, because Simon is your son." Reynard's voice was harsh with bitterness.

Nicola met Reynard's gaze "How did you find out?"

"Fawkes told me. He learned about his son from Alys."

"I wonder how Alys knew."

"I have no idea." Reynard stepped nearer to Nicola. His eyes were as cold as the green glass in the solar windows. "You should have told him the truth long ago. If you had, none of this would have happened."

"You can't say that," Glennyth said. "Even if Fawkes knew about Simon, he would still have sent FitzSaer away."

"But if he knew about Simon, he wouldn't have been so suspicious of you." Reynard fixed Nicola with a look of contempt. "Then he wouldn't have pursued you to Mordeaux and ended up with a crossbow bolt in his shoulder."

"If Fawkes hadn't gone to Mordeaux then, I'm certain FitzSaer would have lured him there by other means," Glennyth said.

"But it *is* my fault." Nicola shook her head in misery. "If I hadn't plotted with Father FitzAlan to be rid of Mortimer, FitzSaer would never have dared take control of Mordeaux. Knowing an ally of John's was coming, FitzSaer decided to imprison Gilbert and took his place as castellan. The fact is, even as I sought to protect my son, I ended up endangering both him and his father." Nicola looked toward the bed, her heart twisting in her chest. She might yet lose both of them.

Glennyth touched her shoulder. "Don't despair, Nicola. We don't know for certain Anselm is in league with Alys and FitzSaer. There's no reason to believe he won't follow your orders and bring Hilary and children back here. Besides, he's with Gerard and Engelard, and they are both loyal to Fawkes."

"At least we think they are." A cold blade of fear seemed lodged in Nicola's belly. She told herself she must not despair.

Reynard motioned to Fawkes. "How long until we know if he is better?"

"It might take a day or more," Glennyth answered.

"Poor Fawkes," Nicola said. "He's gone through so much already."

Reynard glared at Nicola. "Alys's cruel plan almost worked. Having lost blood when he was wounded and then being fevered, Fawkes might well have succumbed." He turned to Glennyth. "You've done all you can. You need to rest."

Glennyth nodded. She motioned to Nicola. "You will stay with him?"

"Of course."

After Reynard and Glennyth left, Nicola went to the bed and tenderly stroked Fawkes's face. He was so dear to her. She loved him so much. "Come back to me," she whispered. "Come back and I will do whatever I can to make you happy."

****

Fawkes opened his eyes to the sight of the peaked

ceiling of the tower room. Relief flooded him. It had all been a dream. A horrible dream. Of being burned alive and tortured by the Saracens. Although his shoulder still throbbed with pain. He turned his head to look at it, and was confused by what he saw. It appeared someone had poured a bowl of pottage on his wound. Pottage that smelled strongly of onions.

He was still puzzling on this when there was a soft sigh. He turned the other way. Nicola slept on the bed next to him. Her worn russet gown was dirty and wrinkled, and her lovely hair was a rat's nest. For once she did not look like the perfect, elegant lady. But she was still beautiful. She would always be beautiful to him.

Emotion filled in his chest, choking his throat and making his eyes water. If he'd been able to pray in the midst of his terrible dreams, this is what he would have prayed for: To be alive, with Nicola beside him.

Clearly, she was very weary. He was weary also. Even lifting his head fatigued him. The urge to sleep dragged him down. He used the last of his energy to reach out and clasp Nicola's hand in his. Nicola was here beside him. Nothing else mattered.

****

Nicola was awakened by her aching muscles. She stretched to ease them and wrinkled her nose at the smell. Onions and something else. Something foul. She sat up. Fawkes's wound was an ugly mess and he still appeared flushed and feverish. Water. Glennyth had told her to make sure he drank lots of water.

She got up, poured a cup of water, and brought it back to the bed. Touching his good shoulder, she sought to wake him. "Fawkes, you must drink."

He mumbled something. She lifted his head and held

the cup to his lips. To her relief, he drank. When he was finished, he lay back and returned to his fevered dreams. She returned the cup to the table, then went to the window and opened the shutters. It was full dark. If the knights hadn't yet found Hilary and the children, they were likely somewhere in the forest. She imagined how frightened Simon and Joanie would be. Poor Hilary. She must be wondering if she would have been better off staying at Rosebrook.

Nicola was torn between her anxiety for Fawkes and her fears for her son. There was naught she could do for Fawkes at this moment, and it seemed unlikely he would rouse anytime soon. She would fetch Old Emma and have her watch over him for a time.

When she woke the servant, Old Emma stared at her in dismay. "Lady, you're a mess. We must find you a clean gown and fix your hair."

"My appearance is the least of my worries. I want you to sit with Fawkes for a time. If he wakes, give him water. I won't be gone long."

"What's so important that you must leave him?" Old Emma struggled from her pallet and rearranged her gown.

"I sent some knights on an errand, and I have to find out if they've returned."

When they reached the tower room, Old Emma went in ahead of Nicola. She leaned over the bed and felt Fawkes's forehead. "He's still fevered." She tsked in dismay.

"Aye. But with luck, Glennyth's treatment will work and he'll be better soon."

"I've never seen a poultice like that before."

"Boiled bran and onions. It's meant to draw the poison out."

"Your mother used moldy bread."

"What?"

"Aye, moldy bread. Said the mold helped stop the poison."

Why hadn't Old Emma mentioned this when Fawkes was first brought in wounded? Nicola spoke sharply. "I'll ask Glennyth about that treatment. For now, keep watch over him. Give him water if he wakes."

"Lady, before you leave, can we not do something about your appearance. You look like a scullery maid."

"Very well." If there was news, surely someone would come and fetch her.

She let Old Emma help her into a clean gown, brush out her hair and braid it away from her face. Then the servant wet a cloth and cleaned the smudges from Nicola's face.

Old Emma stepped back. "There. You look almost passable as the lady of the keep." Nicola gave the servant a severe look. Old Emma grinned at her.

Nicola gestured to the bed. "If you must fuss, do so over Fawkes. If he stirs, give him water."

"Aye, milady I'll guard him well."

Nicola hurriedly made her way down the stairs, ignoring the hard knot in her stomach. She hated to leave Fawkes; she would return to his side as soon as possible.

She stopped first in the hall. The only person there was Maida, putting out slices of maislin bread for the evening meal. "Have you seen Reynard or Glennyth?"

"Nay, milady."

Nicola left the castle and hurried to the gate. She called up to the guard in the watchtower, "Any news? Has anyone arrived since you've been on duty?"

"Nay, my lady. All is quiet."

She wanted to scream with frustration. Or climb on a horse and race off to search for Hilary and the children herself. But she couldn't do something so foolish. She must be patient, although it was difficult.

She turned to go back to the castle. Behind her the guard called, "Riders. It looks like Gerard and Engelard."

She rushed back to the tower. "No sign of Anselm?"

"Nay, my lady. Just the two of them."

Determined to see for herself, she climbed the stairs to the watchtower. As the guard had said, two riders were approaching. Nicola clutched her hands together and forced herself to take deep breaths. Had her worst fears been realized? Had Anselm come upon Hilary and the children and taken them back to Mordeaux?

As soon as the two men rode through the gate, Nicola rushed down the tower stairs to confront them. "What's happened! Where's Anselm?"

Gerard removed his helmet. "We followed the trackway through the forest but didn't find them. When we left the woods, we saw an army camped outside Mordeaux Castle. So we came back here to report what we'd seen."

"And Anselm?"

"He said he was going to continue on to Rosebrook, thinking maybe Hilary and the children never made it as far as Mordeaux."

Nicola felt almost faint with worry. An enemy army was outside Mordeaux and she had no idea where Hilary and the children were. Had FitzSaer found them and taken them back to Mordeaux? Or were they lost in the woods?

"Lady?" She turned. "Should we come with you and report to Fawkes what we've seen?" Gerard asked.

"Nay, not Fawkes. He's not well enough to deal with this. You should make your report to Reynard. He's likely in the solar."

The knights handed off their mounts and started for the castle. Nicola followed, her body tense with dread. Reynard already blamed her for Fawkes's injury. Now he would have another reason to despise her. She didn't want to face his anger, but she had no choice. It was too late for her to play the helpless lady who cedes her authority to men.

By the time she arrived in the solar, it appeared the knights had told Reynard what they knew. The look Fawkes's captain gave Nicola was cold as stone. "There's no reason for you to be here. We'll do much better without you."

"I know much more about Mordeaux Castle and its defenses than any of you. If Fawkes was awake and able to take part in this discussion, he would want me here."

"But he isn't. Instead he's fighting for his life…and it's your fault."

Gerard let out a gasp.

Nicola struggled to control her anger. "You have no right to speak to me that way. I had no way of knowing FitzSaer would try to kill Fawkes. I endured much hardship and risk to bring Glennyth back here to treat his injury. I care for Fawkes as much as you do. I also care what happens at Mordeaux."

Reynard narrowed his eyes at her. "Is it Mordeaux you care for, or your son who dwells there? That's it, isn't it? That's the real reason you went to Mordeaux. Not to get Glennyth but to make certain nothing happened to your precious son."

Nicola's distress turned to fury. "Today, when I rode back from Mordeaux, it was Glennyth I brought with me. I knew Fawkes needed the healer as soon as possible. For

Fawkes's sake I left my son behind to face an unknown fate."

Engelard cleared his throat. "Beg pardon, lady, but are you saying one of the children with Lady Hilary is your son?"

"'Tis true."

"Although you never saw fit to tell your husband any of this, did you?" Reynard goaded.

Nicola met his gaze stonily. "What matters is how we deal with this army outside of Mordeaux."

There was an uncomfortable silence. Gerard spoke, "I wish we could ask Fawkes what to do. Are you certain he's not well enough to discuss strategy? He wouldn't have to do anything, merely listen and give advice from his bed."

"Only Glennyth can truly say if he is well enough," Nicola said.

"For once I agree with you," Reynard retorted.

Nicola motioned to the two knights. "Go and find Glennyth and bring her here. Tell her we need her opinion."

The two men returned with Glennyth only moments later. She arched a brow. "I understand you wish my opinion on something."

"Have you been to see Fawkes?" Reynard asked.

"He was sleeping. As was Old Emma. I doubt either of them will wake for a while."

"Can you tell if he will recover?" Engelard asked.

Glennyth's voice was crisp. "Some things require patience. This is one of them."

"We have a dilemma," Nicola said. "There's an army at Mordeaux, and we need to decide what to do. Do you think Fawkes is well enough for us to consult him in this matter?"

Glennyth shook her head, frowning. "Knowing what I know of Fawkes, I would advise against it. He needs all his strength to heal. His fever has lessened, but it's still there, which means his body is still fighting the poison in his wound."

"Looks as if I will have to deal this on my own." Reynard fixed Nicola with a glare.

She glared back at him. "This is not all your decision. I have a say in this as well."

"How so, lady?" Gerard appeared genuinely puzzled by her words.

"Valmar and Mordeaux have been ruled by my family for generations. I vow, if Fawkes was lucid and aware, he would listen to me."

"He probably would." Reynard's tone was caustic. "But only because he is besotted with you. I, however, am not."

"That's not the only reason." Nicola spoke boldly. "He knows I've been a good chatelaine at Valmar and I have knowledge of Mordeaux and Valmar no one else does."

"I think Nicola is right," Glennyth said. "You should involve her in the decision. For three years, Mortimer did little but drink himself senseless, while Nicola saw to it that Valmar prospered."

"That was different," Reynard said. "We're talking of matters of warfare. Nicola has no experience in such matters."

"Even so, she knows FitzSaer much better than you do," Glennyth persisted.

"FitzSaer's likely no more than a pawn in this thing," Reynard said. "The man we must deal with is the one who leads the army camped outside Mordeaux."

"I wonder who he is." Nicola glanced toward the window. "'Tis not impossible I've met him, or at least heard of him."

"Is this something we must decide at this moment?" Glennyth asked. "In a day or two, Fawkes may be well enough to take charge."

Engelard stepped forward, clearly unable to hold back. "But by then Mordeaux might well be lost. Then they'll have a base from which to attack us."

"FitzSaer may have surrendered the castle already," Nicola said.

"It's your fault FitzSaer is even at Mordeaux." Reynard said.

Nicola glowered at him. Reynard was like a dog with a bone. He could not stop blaming her for her mistakes.

Glennyth stepped between them. "You both care for Fawkes. For his sake, you put must put aside your ill will. We are all of us weary and hungry. Let us go down to the hall and eat. Then take some rest before making any decisions."

"Your words are wise, Glennyth," Nicola said.

Reynard's expression was grudging. But he would not argue with Glennyth.

They all went down to the hall. While everyone ate, Nicola wrapped some bread and cheese in a cloth. Glennyth raised her eyebrows questioningly.

Nicola said, "I'm going to look in on Fawkes." She hastened up the stairs. Fawkes would not be ready for such hearty fare, but Old Emma was, and she definitely needed it. If Fawkes roused, she would fetch him some broth.

If he roused. The thought made tears prick her eyes. What if he never awoke, but slipped into unconsciousness and died? She would never be able to tell him all the things she yearned to share with him. About Simon, and why she'd hidden him away. And how much she loved Fawkes and had from that first fateful afternoon when he came to her bed.

She forced herself to fight off the crushing despair. Glennyth believed Fawkes would heal. She must take courage from that.

Old Emma was dozing on the stool, snoring loudly. Loud enough that it seemed Fawkes should have awakened. He lay as still as a carved effigy. But his face was flushed and glazed with sweat.

Nicola shook Old Emma's shoulder. The servant let out a snort. "Milady, I'm sorry. I didn't mean to drift off. But as you can see, Fawkes hasn't awakened and there's been no change in his breathing or color."

"Did you give him water?"

"He didn't rouse, and I was loath to disturb him. After mumbling and groaning in his sleep for a time, he finally went quiet. I thought it best to let him rest."

That Fawkes did not rave or thrash around seemed like a sign he was mending. Or it could mean his will to fight was weakening.

"I see you've brought food," Old Emma said. "I doubt he'll be able to eat."

"The food is for us. We must also keep up our strength."

"Very good, lady." Old Emma accepted a chunk of bread spread with cheese.

Nicola sat on the side of the bed and ate as well. Old Emma finished first and got up and poured them each a cup of water from the pitcher on the table.

The food and water revived Nicola. Not only did she

feel less tired, her mood was better. The terrible dread lurking in the pit of her stomach for the last two days eased a bit.

"Now what?" Old Emma asked.

"I need to sleep. I am near dead on my feet."

"Sleep then, lady. I'll keep watch over the two of you."

Nicola felt a surge of affection for the elderly servant. Old Emma could be annoying at times, and bold to the point of insubordination. But there could be no doubt she loved Nicola and would do anything for her.

Nicola washed her hands in the basin and loosened the lacing on her gown. Then she went to the bed and lay down beside Fawkes. Between the mess of the poultice and the smell of sickness, she couldn't detect his usual enticing masculine odor. After the poultice was removed, she would have to bathe him. The thought of washing his smooth-skinned, hard-muscled body soothed her, and she drifted to sleep.

****

It was a lovely dream. He was riding in the forest. Nicola followed on her mare. The trees echoed with the trills of birdsong and the ground was flooded with the hazy violet mist of bluebells. He turned to look at Nicola. The look of loss and despair on her face startled him and made him want to go back to her. But there wasn't room on the pathway to turn his horse. He could only go forward.

When he turned back again, Nicola was far behind. Even from a distance, he could see her expression was heavy with grief. She looked as if she'd been weeping. He tried to call a reassurance, but no sound came from his throat. Desperate, he managed to turn his horse. But when he rode back, all he caught was a glimpse of her crimson cloak and long black hair as she vanished among the trees.

He sought to hurry after her, but the pathway disappeared before his eyes. Faced with an impenetrable mass of forest, he halted. Loss and grief choked his throat. Nicola was gone and he was utterly alone. A moan of despair escaped him.

The forest vanished as he woke. He realized he was in bed in the tower room. Old Emma leaned over him, her dark eyes narrowed in concern. "Sa sa." She stroked his arm. "'Twas a bad dream, is all. You're safe, and there is Nicola beside you."

He turned to look. Nicola appeared deeply asleep. "Is she well?"

"She's very weary. But sleep is all she needs. And you..." The servant scrutinized him. "You look a mite better. While you're awake, you should drink some water. Glennyth insisted."

"I also need to *make water*. Can you fetch Reynard or one of the other knights?"

"No need for that. I'll help you."

The servant brought a tall narrow jar so he would not have to get out of bed. He felt himself flush with embarrassment but allowed her to assist him. Afterwards, he lay back, panting. "Jesu, I'm as weak as a newborn. And what's this stuff on my shoulder? It smells foul."

"'Tis not the poultice that smells, but the poison it's drawing from your flesh. I had my doubts, but I vow Glennyth's scheme is working. We'll see tomorrow. For now you should sleep."

Old Emma brought a blanket to cover both of them. Fawkes took Nicola's hand. She didn't wake, and he soon joined her in slumber.

The next time he roused, it was to the sound of

snoring. Old Emma dozed on the stool by the bed. Nicola was still asleep beside him. She'd scarcely moved since he last woke. He took her hand again, feeling the delicacy of her fine bones, the sharpness of her fingernails. One of her nails was broken and jagged and her fingers were roughened. What had she been doing these last few days?

For a time Reynard had made him think she didn't care for him. But now, lying beside her, remembering what they'd shared, he decided his friend's doubts were nonsense. It was true Nicola wasn't like other women. She was fiercer. Bolder. More independent. She would not have survived if she had not been like that.

He wondered how many days ago he was injured. He couldn't be certain. It felt like he'd been insensible for a sennight, but he doubted it was that long. At least his fever had eased and his head was clearing. He was aware enough to know he was lucky to be alive. His wound could have been mortal, but he'd been given more time. Time to feel the sunshine on his face. To smell the sweet scents of flowers and fresh-cut hay. Taste the tart bite of berries, the hearty richness of roasted meat, the yeasty perfection of a fresh loaf. To enjoy the fruity intoxication of wine and the dark bitter goodness of ale.

All the pleasures of the flesh, including the greatest one of all. The delight of loving a woman. And not just any woman, but Nicola. Beautiful Nicola. He squeezed her hand. She made a soft sound in her sleep and stirred. Reluctantly he let go of her hand, not wanting to wake her. 'Twas clear she needed her rest.

Exquisite Nicola. So fine and delicately made. And yet beneath her seemingly fragile beauty, she had a core of iron. Like the most skillfully crafted damascene steel sword, she could endure great trials and challenges and yet not break. His lady of steel. She might seem as cool as an ice-covered blade, or burn as hot as molten iron in a forge. When he'd met her, she'd seemed remote and distant as the stars. But then in his arms she'd turned as hot as a summer bonfire.

He sighed, wishing he could hold her close. But even if he was willing to risk waking her, he wasn't certain his left arm was capable of such movement. He flexed it and felt the answering shriek of pain. It would be a long while before it healed and it might never be the same. If his left arm ended up useless, how would he wield a sword? Or ride? Would Nicola still love him if he were a cripple who could not defend her or her lands and property?

His sense of reprieve faltered, but the next moment he thrust his fears aside. He had not suffered through all of this to end up a broken, ruined man. Somehow he would find a way to do what needed to be done. He would not waste this second chance he'd been given.

Determination flared in him, but his body still felt weak. Reluctantly, he gave in and closed his eyes. He savored the moment of lying peacefully next to Nicola. For once she wasn't leaving him and riding off to Mordeaux.

Mordeaux. All at once he remembered the babe. Alys had told him Nicola's babe was alive. He had a vague memory of Old Emma telling him the babe was his son. Had that really happened? He had to be certain.

But he would not wake Nicola. Old Emma could tell him what he needed. There was a damp cloth near his head. With his good arm, he lobbed the cloth at Old Emma. She woke with a start.

"Emma," he whispered. "I need you."

"What is it, my lord?"

He motioned for the servant to approach. "I have a memory of Alys telling me that Nicola's babe didn't die. And another of you telling me the boy is my son."

"Both things are true." Old Emma bobbed her head emphatically.

Fawkes let out a sigh of contentment.

Old Emma grinned. "I told Nicola you would feel this way. I told her she was foolish to keep the truth from you."

"I still don't understand why she did so."

"I've told you all I know. But when she awakes you should hear it from her lips." The servant perused him. "I'm thinking you're well enough to eat something. I'll get some broth from the kitchen." Old Emma shuffled from the room.

Fawkes closed his eyes and tried to rest. But the emotions churning through him would not relent. He had a son! They must send someone after the boy as soon as possible. The next moment, he remembered the child was at Mordeaux, and in danger. And here he was, trapped in this room. Old Emma might not be back for a while. Frustration built inside him. Part of him wanted to wake Nicola. But he knew she needed her rest.

He shifted restlessly on the bed. Now that his fever had eased, maybe he could get up and make his way down the stairs. Find someone and get them to fetch Reynard.

Gritting his teeth, he sat up. Dizziness overwhelmed him. He went still, waiting for it to pass. When he felt better, he held his left arm against his chest and shifted to the side of the bed. He lowered his legs to the floor and attempted to stand. His vision went black. When it cleared he lay half on the bed and half off it. With great effort he maneuvered himself back into bed and lay panting from exertion. It was hopeless. He had no choice but to wait until Old Emma returned.

She finally did so. He ordered her to fetch Reynard, but the servant insisted on feeding him some broth first.

When he finished, she went to get Reynard, and after what seemed like a long while, his captain entered. "What's wrong?" Reynard glanced at Nicola, still asleep. "What do you need that Nicola or Old Emma could not fetch for you?"

"Is Gilbert back? Is there any news about his family? Hilary and the two children?"

"Nicola found them, but she was forced to leave them behind so she could bring Glennyth here to treat your wound."

"No one's gone after them?"

"Nicola sent young Anselm and two knights."

"Have they returned yet?"

"Gerard and Engelard did. They brought news. News that complicates everything."

"What do you mean?"

"Glennyth said not to tell you until you were stronger."

"God's bones, Reynard! I'll go mad if I don't find out what's happening."

"We can deal with this, Fawkes. There's no reason to trouble yourself."

"No reason? I find out I have a son and now he is missing and possibly in danger and there is no reason to trouble myself?" He wanted to shake Reynard.

"Nicola says the boy is your son, but I don't know if I believe her."

"Old Emma said he was."

"Old Emma would always back her mistress."

Fawkes glared at Reynard. "Why do you refuse to

believe he's my son? Do you think Mortimer sent another man to her bed?"

"If the boy is yours, why didn't she tell you? I'm sorry, Fawkes. I wish it were true. I wish…"

"You wish what?" Nicola had awakened. She sat up in bed.

Chapter Twenty-Five

Nicola saw Reynard and was immediately on edge. She could not escape the man. He was everywhere, constantly reminding her of her mistakes. He spoke now, his sarcasm as cutting as ever. "Fawkes wants you to explain why you didn't tell him about Simon, *his* son."

What could she say? The truth sounded witless even to herself. But it was all she had. "At first I didn't know you, and 'twas clear you believed the worst of me. And then later…" Her voice softened as she recalled the moments of tender lovemaking they'd shared. "Then I was afraid if you knew I'd lied, it would ruin everything…everything that we shared." She met Fawkes's gaze, willing him to recall the splendor of their lovemaking. They closeness they had shared in bed.

Reynard made a sound of disgust and Nicola's insides squeezed with anguish. It was long moments later before Fawkes spoke. "I want to see him."

She nodded. "I warn you, he looks nothing like you. Anyone would think he was Mortimer's. And yet, that's not possible, as you know."

"I want to see him," Fawkes repeated.

So do I, Nicola thought miserably. *And hold him in my arms and know he is safe.*

"If the boy is missing, it's your fault," Reynard said. "Indeed, all of this is your fault. If Mordeaux falls…" Reynard broke off as he realized he'd said too much.

Fawkes stared at Reynard. "If Mordeaux falls? What do you mean?"

Reynard's expression was grimmer than ever. "Nicola's plotting has finally borne fruit. There's an army outside Mordeaux's walls."

"Glennyth advised us not to tell you, lest we distress you and slow your healing," Nicola gave Reynard a reproving look.

"How big an army?" Fawkes asked. "Who commands them?"

"We know very little." Reynard shot Nicola a baleful look. "For all we know, your wife is a part of it. Perhaps her plan was to have FitzSaer kill you and then cede both castles to this ally of John's. She plotted to rid herself of one husband and succeeded. Why should she not do so again?"

Nicola made a sound of exasperation. "I despised Mortimer! Fawkes I love!" She spoke with passion, and sought to convey her feelings to Fawkes with her expression. Words were far too empty and inadequate to explain what she felt for him. The truth shone through only in those moments when they were alone and their bodies were joined in perfect, magical rhythm.

If they were alone now, she would touch him. Caress his flushed, sweaty face. Press her lips to his, not caring that he stank of sickness, stale bran and onions.

But with Reynard in the room, she could not do it. He would mock any tender gesture she made and find a way to twist it, until the pure love that poured from her heart became something sly and malevolent.

All she could do was plead with her eyes, begging Fawkes to remember what it felt like to be joined with her. Their bodies like two rivers flowing into each other, violent and wild and yet mingling so completely they became one powerful, unstoppable current.

That was what had produced their son. Suddenly, she knew that Fawkes was right. If he saw Simon, he *would* know. He would see beyond Simon's fair angel looks, and remember the passion that created the child and believe that this was his son. Only a child born of their love could have made her do the things she'd done the past four years.

She saw the anguish in his gaze and knew he understood. He'd gained a son and in doing so, lost control over his life. All his previous hopes and dreams were banished now, made shallow and insignificant. All that mattered was ensuring the safety and the future of his son.

Perhaps that's what Reynard had fought so hard against. Not because he feared Nicola's hold on Fawkes's heart, but because he feared Simon's. Reynard's role in Fawkes's life would be changed forever, and he did not like it.

Fawkes turned his attention back to Reynard. "Do we know if FitzSaer has surrendered Mordeaux to this invader? Do we have any idea who leads this enemy army?"

"It seems certain FitzSaer has surrendered the castle," Reynard answered. "I don't think he would dare imprison Sir Gilbert if he didn't feel confident he would have support from one of John's allies."

"And you say Sir Gilbert has not come back yet. It would help greatly if we had his counsel. He knows the garrison at Mordeaux far better than we do."

"He hasn't returned. But you must remember his mission was to seek out his wife and the children. He cares more for what happens to them than he does for the future of Mordeaux."

Fawkes nodded.

"I suppose whether he has found them has great concern for us all. If FitzSaer controls Gilbert's family, then he has a powerful bargaining tool."

Fawkes looked at Nicola. "Does FitzSaer know Simon is your son?"

"I'm afraid so. I don't know how he found out. I can't believe Hilary or Gilbert ever revealed the truth to him."

"Perhaps he found out when he was living here," Fawkes said. "From Alys."

"I had not thought of that," Reynard said. "I'd assumed someone from Valmar was in communication with FitzSaer at Mordeaux, but maybe FitzSaer and Alys plotted this ere he even left."

"That would make sense," Fawkes said. "I was supposed to die when I went to Mordeaux. When I didn't die, Alys came up with this plan to kill me off by drugging me with poppy-laced wine and refusing me water. That's why she offered to take care of me."

"She wouldn't have had a chance to try and kill you if Nicola hadn't left you." Reynard's voice curdled with resentment.

Fawkes made a sharp gesture. "Enough! I will not have my captain and my wife at each other's throats like two hunting hounds fighting over a bitch in heat. Or like Gimlyn and Tom hissing and snarling and puffing up like wildcats as they dispute the territory of the castle."

"You're right," Nicola said. "The dangers facing us are too grave for us not to be united in our purpose."

Reynard nodded, although Nicola sensed he was reluctant. "We didn't mean to burden you with these things, Fawkes, but now you know what we face, what do you think we should do?"

"Part of the key to untangling this coil might be to find out if anyone else at Valmar is involved besides Alys and FitzSaer."

"How we do that?" Reynard asked.

"Perhaps you should question Alys."

"But what about the army at Mordeaux?" Reynard persisted. "How do we deal with that?"

"We must find out what's happening inside Mordeaux castle," Fawkes said. "Do all the garrison knights support FitzSaer? Or, are there some who remain loyal to me?"

"That's what Gilbert is supposed to be finding out." Reynard said.

"It seems we should send a spy to find out what has happened to our spies. But we may need all the knights we can muster to deal with this army camped outside Mordeaux."

"What about this army?" Reynard asked. "Should we not engage with them?"

"If they already control Mordeaux, what's to be gained by attacking now?" Nicola asked. "And if they don't hold Mordeaux, then we need to know the reason. Maybe some of the knights at Mordeaux have turned against FitzSaer. Or FitzSaer himself has discovered he is being used, and is refusing to surrender."

"Used? What do you mean?" Reynard frowned at her.

"Any baron John sends will install their own man as castellan. The only way FitzSaer's plan works is if Fawkes is dead and FitzSaer is wed to me—and in that regard, we have thwarted him."

"That still doesn't answer the question of who to send," Fawkes said. "We need someone unobtrusive. Someone who can gather information without arousing

FitzSaer's suspicions."

"Why does it have to be a knight?" Nicola asked. "Could it not be a squire, or even someone from the village?" The next moment it came to her. "I know who we can send. Temmen, a youth from the village. He has carried messages to Mordeaux for me before. All he has to do is find the cook Morwenna and she will be able to tell him everything that has happened. She keeps abreast of all the castle gossip, and she is firmly on our side. She hates FitzSaer."

"Temmen? But he's little better than a child. Is that not expecting a great deal of him?" Reynard asked. "To walk to Mordeaux and then back?"

"One of the knights can take him most of the way on horseback. They could let him off in the woods near the castle and then wait for him to return."

"Can he be trusted?" Reynard asked.

"Glennyth has used him to run errands herself," Nicola said. "And he's not as young as you might think. I'd guess him to be near twelve winters. His family is all small-statured. I'm sure you recall young Alwen, the corn queen. She's his sister."

"Fetch the boy up here," Fawkes said. "His demeanor will reveal whether he can be trusted. He's young enough it's unlikely he's skilled at deception."

Reynard went to get Temmen. Fawkes lay back and closed his eyes.

"Are you well?" Nicola moved closer to the bed. "I know this must be overwhelming, especially when you're only beginning to recover." She gently touched his wounded shoulder. "Glennyth still needs to remove the poultice and stitch you up."

Fawkes made a sound of assent but didn't open his

eyes. Nicola felt a prick of fear. Fawkes appeared better but he was still in danger. He needed rest. And water. The ewer on the table was empty. She must fetch more.

When she was halfway to the door, Fawkes called, "Come back."

She returned to the bed. They had not been alone since he learned about Simon. If he wanted to shout and curse at her, this would be the perfect time. "What is it?" she asked, her nerves taut.

Fawkes opened his eyes. "Tell me about Simon. You say he doesn't look like me. But what sort of temperament does he have?"

"He's a very sweet-natured child. Hilary is always saying so. While her Joanie can be difficult and demanding, Simon never is. He loves animals. One of the hunting dogs had a litter of puppies and Simon wanted to be with them and play with them every moment of the day. Gilbert let him pick one out for his own, and now the dog sleeps beside his pallet at night."

She wondered what Fawkes would think of this. Most people used dogs for hunting and regarded them as nuisances the rest of the time. For that matter, Fawkes probably didn't relish hearing about his son's gentle nature. Men wanted their sons to be tough and strong, not tender-hearted and sweet.

"Beyond his coloring, what does he look like?" Fawkes asked. "Is he slender? Or stout and strong?"

"He is tall for his age and well-made, which surely comes from you."

"What else?"

"I'm certain many mothers think their child is well-favored in looks. But truly, Simon is as comely as an angel."

"An angel." Fawkes's mouth twisted. "The world is a harsh place. If Simon is to thrive and prosper, he'll have to toughen up. 'Tis clear he's been too much in the company of women. That will have to change, or he will have no future as a knight."

"I don't want him to be a knight!" The words were out before she could stop them.

Fawkes stared at her. "You don't want him to be a knight? That is foolish. If Simon is to claim his birthright, he must be able to fight his enemies and be a strong leader."

She knew he was right. But that did not change how she felt.

Fawkes was silent for a time. Nicola gnawed her lower lip. Perhaps this was part of the reason she hadn't told Fawkes about Simon. Now that he knew he had a son, Fawkes would want to take control over Simon's upbringing. As soon as Simon came to live at Valmar, Fawkes would seek to mold his character and make him into what he thought a man should be, someone capable of ruthlessness and brutality.

All those lies, everything she'd done to protect her son—all of it was a foolish waste. One way or another, she would lose Simon. Even if all was well now, someday he would be a man and she would lose him anyway. The thought of it made her deeply melancholy. She closed her eyes and repressed a sigh.

Fawkes touched her hand. She opened her eyes and was startled by the tenderness in his expression. "I care naught that you lied to me. I know you did it to keep our son safe. Simon was born into a household of treachery and cruelty. I can't blame you for being cautious. For all we know, your deception is all that kept him alive."

"We can only hope my stupid plotting hasn't put him in terrible danger now."

A wry smile touched Fawkes's lips. "Plots are only stupid when they fail. We do the best we can for the ones we love, all of us."

Nicola's throat swelled with emotion. Fawkes was telling her that he forgave her. "You need to eat something. I will take the broth to the kitchen and warm it up."

****

Soon after Nicola left, Reynard arrived with Temmen. Fawkes motioned for the boy to approach the bed. "We have a task for you. Reynard will explain."

Reynard told the boy what had happened at Mordeaux and about the secret passageway. Then he explained what they wanted Temmen find out once he was inside the castle. Temmen seemed over-awed, but listened intently. Observing him, Fawkes felt a twinge of hope. This plan, odd as it was, might work.

They discussed other details, such as where Alexander would be waiting for him, and how long the task might take. By the time Nicola returned, there was little left to explain, other than the exact instructions of how to find the tunnel into the castle. Nicola gave him those details and offered to escort him to the kitchen to get him supplies for the journey.

As soon as Nicola and Temmen had left, Reynard said, "Now we need to talk about what to do about this army."

Fawkes shook his head. "I'm at the end of my strength. Dealing with that will have to wait. Besides, I think we should delay making any decision until Temmen returns."

Reynard did not look pleased, but he nodded curtly. "I'll leave you to rest."

A while later, Fawkes gritted his teeth as Glennyth drew her needle through the raw, mangled flesh of his shoulder. "Jesu, that hurts."

"I did advise you to take more poppy."

"No...more...poppy." Fawkes forced out the words as his eyes watered and his body trembled from the pain, as well as the strain of remaining still.

"Almost done. Nicola did well in getting the crossbow bolt out. The cuts she made are clean and easy to repair."

"She took the bolt out?"

"Aye. Don't you remember?"

"I remember very little between riding away from Mordeaux and waking up here."

"You probably hit your head when you fell from your horse. You're very fortunate it didn't damage your wits."

Fawkes winced again. "Where's Reynard? Why isn't he here? Is he too cowardly to watch?"

"I told him to stay away. It serves no purpose to have him nearby, grumbling, and glowering."

"What does he have to be angry about?"

"You know he blames Nicola for all this. According to him, she started everything when she conspired with one of John's lackeys to bring Mortimer down."

"She was trying to protect her son. That's what any mother would do."

Glennyth sat back and surveyed her work. "Nay. Most women would not meddle in the affairs of men the way she has."

"I'm not pleased about what we face. But I can't truly blame Nicola. I likely would have done something similar, given the circumstances. Nicola's boldness is part of who she is. I can't separate that part of her from everything else I admire."

Glennyth smiled, her hazel eyes glinting. "You mean, what you *love* about her."

Glennyth was right. His feelings for Nicola went far beyond admiration. He looked away while Glennyth tied and cut the thread binding his wound. When she bathed his shoulder in vinegar, he gasped, "Curse it, but that stings!"

"The vinegar helps fight the poison and keep it from coming back. I'm pleased with how well you are mending. I predict that if you have a care for yourself and give the wound time to heal, your shoulder will eventually be nearly the same as it was before."

"How long?" Fawkes braced himself for the answer.

"At least a month before you can lift anything, or use your arm strenuously. Although you must not favor it too much, or the muscles will stiffen and become too rigid to work properly. So move it around, but do so gently."

"A month. I fear I will go mad." Fawkes let out a sigh of frustration. The pain of having his shoulder stitched had worn him out. He wanted desperately to lie back and sleep. But how could he, when everything he cared about was at risk?

To Glennyth he said, "Now that you're finished, I want to see Reynard. We have things to discuss."

Glennyth nodded and gathered her things.

Fawkes leaned back and closed his eyes. He might as well rest until Reynard arrived.

****

Nicola was awakened by shouting. She rushed from the garden. Several knights were headed for the stairs to the parapet. She followed and joined them on the castle wall. A mass of mounted knights, foot soldiers and supply wains were marching toward Valmar.

A weight settled on her chest. Because of her, everyone and everything she cared about was in danger: Her home. Her people. Fawkes. Her son.

Gerard turned to her. "Do you think it's the same force Oliver and Alexander saw at Mordeaux? Does that mean FitzSaer has surrendered?"

"We don't know for certain." Nicola focused on the banner of the man leading the army. His device looked familiar, but she could not place it. What baron went to battle under a gold flag with a black leopard *couchant*? Would any of the Mortimer knights recognize it?

She turned the other direction, her view taking in the village near the river. All was tranquil now, but soon this peaceful scene might be shattered with the strife of warfare. The clash of swords and lances. Shouts and battle cries. The hooves of destriers churning up the grass. Blood staining the fertile ground. The cries of the wounded and dying. She shuddered, wondering again what her foolishness had wrought. Then she turned and started down the stairway.

"Where are you going?" Gerard called.

"To speak to Fawkes."

He hurried to reach her. "I thought Reynard had decided we should not burden him with this until he is stronger."

"The army at Mordeaux was one thing, but an army outside our very walls is another. He must know of this at once."

Gerard followed her down the stairs. "Someone could ride out and meet them."

"And tell them what? How will you explain why Fawkes hasn't come to parlay with them?"

"They could explain that he is injured, but mending."

"That might make them think that this is a good time to strike."

Gerard's hazel eyes were dark with anxiety. "What else can we do? I don't see how Fawkes can sit a horse, let alone ride out and negotiate with these men."

"But that doesn't mean he shouldn't be consulted."

"But what if this is too much for him and the fever comes back?"

"Fawkes has a right to know what's happening."

Chapter Twenty-Six

Fawkes woke to Nicola calling his name. As soon as he saw her face he tensed. She looked as if she was poised on a knife's edge.

"Fawkes. I must speak to you about something."

He nodded, his muscles tightening.

"The army that was at Mordeaux—they're here. At Valmar."

Everything he'd worked so hard for was threatened, and here he was, an invalid, stuck in bed. Or was he? Glennyth had told him to be careful of his arm, but his legs still worked. He tried to sit up.

Nicola reached out to stop him. "There's no reason you must deal with this yourself. Tell me what should be done, and I will do it."

"Nay. *I* will do it." Reynard entered the room.

Fawkes looked at his captain and then at his wife. "I want to see this army."

"I can tell you exactly what we face," Reynard said. "About fifty mounted knights and twice as many foot soldiers."

"Any siege engines?"

"Nay, but perhaps they intend to build them."

"Then we have time. They can't take this castle without siege engines. And that's exactly what I will make certain they understand."

"You can't even sit a horse."

"I can try. If I fail, we'll think of another plan."

"I could meet with them and convey your words."

"You know if I don't show myself, the enemy will assume I'm dead or so badly wounded that I'm no threat."

"You *are* badly wounded. Which is why you can't—"

"Nay! I'm not so badly wounded that I will risk the enemy thinking I'm not a force to be reckoned with. If anyone goes out to parlay with this army, 'twill be me!" Fawkes motioned. "I want the two of you to get me up and help me down the stairs."

Nicola regarded him uncertainly. "If you want to try this, we'll need more help."

Reynard looked ready to explode. "You're going to allow him to do this? You probably hope he will sicken and die. That would be very convenient, wouldn't it? Then you could marry this FitzRandolph bastard who leads this army and reclaim your son."

Nicola froze as she recognized the name of the powerful baron she knew supported John. "FitzRandolph? The man who leads the army is named FitzRandolph?"

Reynard nodded. "Apparently. Old Thomas in the stables recognized the device of the baron's pennant."

"A gold banner with a leopard *couchant*," Nicola said. "I knew I had seen the design before." Then the rest of Reynard's words sank in. Blessed Jesu! She could not let Fawkes think Reynard's horrible accusation was true. She gave Fawkes a desperate look. "I don't want to marry FitzRandolph. Or any other man. I want *you* as my husband. You're the one I love."

Fawkes's dark eyes assessed her. Her heart beat wildly. As usual, she could not tell what he was thinking.

It was Reynard who broke the silence. "Don't let her fool you, Fawkes. Think back to all the lies she's told you already. Lie upon lie. I vow, no one can believe a thing she says, least of all you."

"But I do believe her," Fawkes said. "Nicola told me about this army because she understands me. She and I are alike. We both seek to be in control of our fate, no matter what it costs us."

Nicola let out her breath slowly. "It has cost me dear, as you well know."

Reynard crossed his arms over his chest. "Very well then, Fawkes. What do you propose to do? Have us tie you to your horse and hope you don't fall off in front of the enemy?"

"That's exactly what I mean to do. But first, we need to find out about this man, FitzRandolph."

"He visited here once," Nicola said. "'Twas shortly after Mortimer came back from London. Mortimer insisted I act the hostess at the banquet he held in FitzRandolph's honor. But the two men parted on bad terms. Mortimer was fiercely loyal to Richard. FitzRandolph was John's man, and already plotting what he might gain with Richard off on Crusade."

"What else do you know about FitzRandolph?" Fawkes asked. "Is he a strong leader? Or, merely acting as John's lackey?"

"My impression of FitzRandolph is that he is a shrewd man and a careful one. The very opposite of Mortimer. When they disagreed, FitzRandolph remained calm, while Mortimer argued and raged."

"Having met the man, and knowing what you know, how do you think we should approach him?"

Nicola was stunned. That Fawkes would ask her opinion—a mere woman—'twas unthinkable.

She concentrated, remembering the banquet. At the

time, she'd been so distracted by the misery of being Mortimer's wife, she'd scarce paid attention to their visitors. And yet, she did have a sense of this man, Roger FitzRandolph. "I think you might be able to reason with him. You have the writ from Richard, and you are married to me. Your claim is strong. More importantly, Valmar will not be an easy castle to take."

"That will be my strategy then. I will reason with him."

Reynard looked as if he would burst. His face was flushed and his green eyes bulged. "One day ago, you were deathly ill. Now you propose to arm yourself, mount a horse and ride out to meet an enemy!"

"I can do it. If I take one step at a time. I am weak, but not so weak I can't rally for this, when my whole future—our whole future—depends on it." He looked at Nicola as he spoke. His gaze burned with emotion.

Reynard stared at Fawkes and then headed for the door. "I'm going to get Glennyth. We'll see what she has to say about this nonsense." He slammed the door behind him.

With Reynard gone, Nicola felt much better. Fawkes seemed to understand her, while Reynard never would.

A frown creased Fawkes's forehead. "I wish we knew what was happening at Mordeaux. There are so many unknowns. 'Tis risky to bargain when we don't know what's truly at stake. If FitzSaer has our son, we must stall FitzRandolph while we think of a way to rescue the boy."

Nicola nodded. It was a relief to be talking strategy with Fawkes. "If Temmen was able to get inside Mordeaux and speak to Morwenna, we should soon know much more."

"I don't think we dare wait for Temmen's return. The

longer we delay in confronting FitzRandolph, the more confident he will become."

"You believe you can do this? Don your mail and sit a horse?"

"I have to try. If I don't ride out to meet him, FitzRandolph may decide Valmar is ripe for the taking."

"But it's not," Nicola insisted. "With the grain harvest almost in and the rest of the foodstores, we could hold out for several months."

"What if they bring in siege engines and batter the walls? And what of the people outside the castle? Although FitzRandolph has undoubtedly brought supplies, if things drag out, his army will end up living off the land. How do we stop them from seizing the crops and livestock of the villagers? We might prevail in the end, but what's the point if our villeins end up starving this winter?"

It pleased Nicola to realize Fawkes saw things the way she did. That being a lord meant you were responsible for the people you ruled. "If you are determined to do this, what do you need?" she asked. "How can I help you?"

"First, I must get up."

Nicola nodded. "I will fetch some men.

****

After Nicola left, Fawkes lay back and closed his eyes, thinking he might as well rest as much as he could. What he was about to do would take every bit of his strength and will. He hoped Nicola would hurry. Although he didn't think Glennyth would agree with Reynard in this matter, he didn't want to waste any more energy arguing with his captain. Reynard might have the best intentions, but it was not his decision to make.

He also didn't like Reynard's treatment of Nicola, the way he had accused her of wanting him dead simply because she wasn't treating him like a pathetic invalid. If Nicola had wanted to be rid of him, she could have easily managed it over the past few days. She'd done everything she could to save him.

She loved him. Knowing that made him feel like anything was possible. He imagined himself floating down the stairs, buoyed by the thought that his cool, dispassionate wife loved him. The thought of it made everything he'd endured up until this moment seem more than worthwhile.

But there was another test ahead of him, and he dare not fail it, or all his dreams might still come crashing down. If anything happened to their son, Nicola would never get over it. She might never forgive him if that happened. "One more trial. One more test. If you can make it through this, then you will have finally won your heart's desire."

A short while later, Nicola entered followed by burly Engelard and Ellis the smith. Fawkes motioned Engelard and Ellis near. "I'm getting up. Whoever is on my left side needs to be especially careful. Support me under my arm and don't pull or bump my shoulder."

He eased himself to the side of the bed. The two men stood on either side of him and gingerly helped him to his feet.

Reynard entered the room. "You're a fool," he muttered.

Fawkes had no energy to waste arguing. With the two men half carrying him, he managed to make it down the stairs and out of the castle. They help him to the armory where he sank down on a bench. He sat struggling against the pain and weakness. After a time he motioned for them to bring his gambeson and mail shirt. They armored him and he sat down again. He was out of breath, and the weight of the mail shirt made his shoulder ache excruciatingly. How would he ever manage to ride out of the keep, let alone converse once he met up with FitzRandolph?

He'd told the men to give him a moment. But the longer he sat there, the more he suspected Reynard was right and he truly could not do this. He took long slow breaths, hoping the pain would ease.

"You see?" Reynard swiped the air in a frustrated gesture. "You're not up to this. All you're doing is risking further injury to your shoulder."

"Did Glennyth tell you that?" Fawkes asked. "Did she say I could not do this?"

"Nay, but 'tis obvious to anyone with eyes in their head!"

Nicola stood nearby. So far Fawkes had avoided her gaze. He dreaded the thought of failing her. The idea that he could not defend her home and the future heritage of their son was utterly humiliating.

"Perhaps this is not such a good plan," Nicola said in a soft voice. "For FitzRandolph to see you like this would only hurt our cause."

"Finally, she sees reason!" Reynard exclaimed. He motioned to Engelard and Ellis. "Get that mail shirt off him and arm me instead. Time is passing. Soon it will be too dark to parlay with FitzRandolph."

The knights helped Fawkes stand and eased his mail shirt over his head. Fawkes sat down with a grunt, still wearing his gambeson. He'd never felt more like a failure.

"To me." Reynard motioned to his own mail shirt hung on pegs on the wall.

"You're going out there?" Engelard asked.

"I'm Fawkes's captain. 'Tis my place to speak for him. Besides, there's no one else."

"That's not true," Nicola said. "I'm the lady of Valmar, and FitzRandolph knows me. I will speak to him."

"What nonsense is this?" Reynard turned to her. "You're the prize FitzRandolph seeks. If he seizes you, all is lost for Fawkes. And for the rest of us."

"I'm not going to ride out by myself. I'll take an escort, a dozen knights, all on swift horses. Meanwhile, post archers on the walls. If FitzRandolph knows his own neck is at risk, he won't try anything underhanded. He's a cautious man."

Reynard appeared on the edge of apoplexy. "This is ridiculous!" He turned to Fawkes. "You can't let her do this. She has no experience in negotiating."

"Ah, but she does," Fawkes said. "Indeed, if it were not for her, FitzRandolph wouldn't even be here." He saw her blanch and added, "I have no doubt Nicola is a match for any man when it comes to bargaining. Especially when it involves someone dear to her. She has the most to lose in this. Therefore, it's only right she be the one to confront FitzRandolph."

Reynard shook his head. "I can't believe this. You clearly have no faith in me."

"That's not true. I know you are loyal to a fault and always have my best interests in mind. But my instincts tell me that in this matter Nicola matches up against FitzRandolph better than you do. After all, her lineage as the lady of Valmar goes back generations."

"But she is a woman, negotiating with a man. She may have charmed and seduced you to do her will, but you can hardly expect her to manipulate FitzRandolph so easily."

Fawkes made an abrupt gesture. "I've made up my mind. If you want to be part of her escort, I see no harm in that. But Nicola will speak on my behalf."

"I must change. I scarce look like a lady in my stained work gown with my hair in rough plaits."

"Go then," Fawkes said. "And hurry. As Reynard pointed out, the day passes quickly."

****

A short while later, Nicola rode down trackway from the castle, accompanied by a dozen knights. She wore her gray silk gown with her scarlet mantle over it. Her hair was braided away from her face, but she wore no head covering. She would not go to this man looking demure and meek, like a nun or proper matron. She hadn't listened to Old Emma's counsel in what to wear, but Fawkes's. He'd advised her to ride forth like a queen, her bright mantle mirroring the vivid red of the banner Sir Gerard carried.

The Valmar device—a black hawk on a crimson banner—fluttered in the breeze. *I must think and act like a queen,* Nicola told herself as she steadied her hands on the reins of her white palfrey. She must be like the Queen Mother, Lady Eleanor, who had a will to match any man's. She would remember Eleanor as she negotiated with FitzRandolph. She would also remember the way Fawkes had looked at her before she rode out, his dark eyes blazing with pride and love. He believed she could do this. She would not fail him.

The army was setting up camp, staking out their position in the valley. But a look-out had seen their approach, and as they drew near, a group of mounted knights carrying the gold and black FitzRandolph banner made their way through the mass of men, tents and supply wagons. Nicola and her escort halted and waited for the envoy to approach.

FitzRandolph wore a gold and black surcote over full armor, but no helm. His nut-brown hair was thinning at the crown and streaked with gray, but he looked fit and strong and his weathered features were as bold and striking as Nicola recalled. The troupe of knights halted a few paces away. Nicola saw the flash of surprise in FitzRandolph's dark eyes as he realized she meant to lead the negotiations herself.

"Lady Mortimer." He inclined his head politely.

"Not *Mortimer*," Nicola answered. "Lady *de Cressy*. Mortimer has been dead for some time. I am wed to Fawkes de Cressy now."

"Where is de Cressy?" FitzRandolph asked. "Why is he not here to argue his claim? I had not thought to negotiate with his wife. Or perhaps I am mistaken. Perhaps I'm negotiating with his *widow*."

"Fawkes was wounded, but he is mending. If you look up at the walkway near the gatetower, you will see him." Nicola turned and gestured to Fawkes, standing tall and proud in his crusader surcote, his black hair clearly visible even from this distance.

FitzRandoph cocked a skeptical brow. "Mending? And yet he does not come to meet me? Doesn't he realize what's at stake?"

"Fawkes is healing well, but I didn't want him to overtask himself. He took a crossbow bolt in the shoulder, shot by an assassin on Adam FitzSaer's orders. A cowardly act, to shoot a man on a peaceful mission, especially using such a brutal weapon. If you think to ally yourself with FitzSaer, you should beware of his treacherous nature."

FitzRandolph's tone was scornful. "I'm not allied with FitzSaer, and I certainly do not answer to him. Indeed, the only man I answer to is Prince John, soon to be King of England."

"Ah, there is the crux of the matter. 'Tis all well and good to say John will soon be king, but you can't know it will be so. Richard may be imprisoned, but the terms of his release are being negotiated as we speak. Given that he is strong and fit, there's every reason to think he will be our king for many more years. As you've no doubt been told, my husband Fawkes de Cressy has a writ from Richard giving him Mordeaux and Valmar. For you to try to seize these properties from their rightful overlord is nothing short of treason."

FitzRandolph gave her a grim smile. "You had no trouble plotting treason when you were wed to Mortimer. Or have you forgotten what you told Father FitzAlan?"

Nicola fought to control her anger. FitzRandolph was trying to provoke her. "Mortimer was unfit, both as a husband and as an overlord. I believe Richard learned of Mortimer's failings and that's why he awarded the lands to Fawkes, knowing he would be a much better steward of the castles than Mortimer could ever be."

"Even so, if Richard was ever to learn of your part in Mortimer's downfall, I don't think he'd be pleased. 'Tis ungodly and unnatural for a woman to plot against her husband, no matter his faults. Richard may tolerate such behavior in his mother, but I doubt he would accept it in any other woman. Indeed, I think he would discipline your unwomanly pride and defiance by wedding you to a man who is strong enough to take you in hand and force you to submit to his will. Fawkes de Cressy is clearly not that man."

"These are matters for the king to decide when he finally returns to England. You have no say in whom I'm wed to. And no claim whatsoever to Valmar or Mordeaux."

FitzRandolph's dark eyes glittered. "Such defiance. 'Tis unbecoming of a gentlewoman. You are most desperately in need of discipline, Lady Nicola."

"That is for my husband to decide, Sir Roger."

"Perhaps. Or perhaps not." FitzRandolph turned and started to raise his arm. A second later, an arrow whistled out of nowhere and struck the ground in front of him. Almost the same moment, Engelard and Reynard rode forward, their horses forming a barrier between Nicola and FitzRandolph.

"Go ahead," Reynard jeered at FitzRandolph. "Give the order to seize Lady Nicola. I vow you'll die with an arrow in your gullet ere any of your men touch her."

Nicola let out her breath in relief. The archer on the castle wall must have had his bow already drawn and been waiting for some sign from Reynard to loose the arrow.

If she was startled, then FitzRandolph was stunned. But his look of surprise quickly altered to one of fury. He glared up at Fawkes, who saluted him from the ramparts. Then FitzRandolph jerked his mount around and shouted at his men to do the same.

The troupe of knights rode off. Nicola's stomach churned as she struggled to master her frazzled nerves. "Thank you," she said to Reynard. "I'm glad you came up with this plan to defend me. Otherwise I'd probably be on my way to his tent at this moment."

"Mayhaps now you will realize that while you may be the lady of Valmar, you have no hope of holding it without Fawkes."

"Of course I realize that. I'm not an utter fool."

Reynard's jaw remained stiff and his green eyes frosty. "What do you think you've accomplished in all of this? You've faced down FitzRandolph. Now what happens?"

"I don't know what will happen. But at least FitzRandolph realizes I'm not powerless, and neither is Fawkes. He also knows we stand united. Perhaps he will think twice about attacking Valmar, knowing it is guarded by a seasoned battle commander…and his bold and daring captain." She smiled at Reynard, hoping her recognition of his part in things would ease his anger. His fierce expression did appear to soften as he turned away.

"I wish we knew what was going on at Mordeaux," he said. "If FitzRandolph controls the keep there, he'll see this as only a minor setback."

"Surely Temmen and Alexander will be back soon," she said. "Perhaps they are, and we don't know of it yet. They might have gone through the village to avoid FitzRandolph's army."

Reynard didn't answer, but wheeled his horse around and set off for the castle.

Chapter Twenty-Seven

By the time Nicola and Reynard reached the tower room, Fawkes was back in bed and Glennyth was tending him.

"You were magnificent," Fawkes said, his voice husky with emotion.

Despite his effusive reaction, Nicola could tell from the ashen look of his normally tanned skin that the last hour had consumed every bit of his strength.

"Thank you," she responded. "But despite my efforts, all would have been lost if not for Reynard's quick reaction and planning. Although I knew FitzRandolph might try to abduct me, I thought there would be more warning. But one moment we were calmly conversing and the next he was giving the order to grab me."

"Trust no one, is my thought when dealing with highborn men," Fawkes said. "I certainly had enough experience while on Crusade."

"FitzRandolph is a canny one," Reynard said.

"Which might work in our favor," Fawkes responded. "He will think very carefully about what he risks. If we have convinced him that taking Valmar will cost him time and men, he might well decide there are easier properties to seize."

"I believe we've made a good start of convincing him of that," said Nicola.

"I believe we have," Fawkes responded.

Reynard remained silent.

Nicola stood. "We need to find out if Temmen has returned. If he hasn't, we must send someone after him." She started toward the door.

"Nicola," Fawkes called. She turned, her spirits lifting at the warmth in his expression. "Hurry back."

"Of course." Her body tingled with happiness as she started down the stairs. Many things could still go wrong. But God willing, Fawkes was recovering and it was possible they might have a future together.

She reached the yard to the sound of shouts and cheering. It seemed to be coming from the barracks so she headed there. Inside, Gerard and Engelard were regaling the rest of the knights with the tale of the meeting with FitzRandolph. They were in high spirits, boasting of how Fawkes and Reynard had thwarted FitzRandolph's plans. Then they saw her and quieted.

Gerard stepped forward. "Lady, you were so brave and fierce. I don't know many men who could match you." He bowed. "To Lady Nicola, who faces down her enemies like a she-wolf."

"To Lady Nicola," the other knights echoed. The men all inclined their heads in acknowledgement.

"I'm not certain I'm pleased to be compared to a she-wolf." Nicola smiled at Gerard so he would know she did not really take offense. "But it's gratifying that you see my actions as brave. FitzRandolph told me my boldness was unnatural and unfeminine."

"You could never be unfeminine, Lady Nicola," young John put in. "You are far too comely."

"'Tis true," said Robbie.

Nicola felt a flush of embarrassment creep up her neck. She was not used to being complimented. To change the mood, she asked, "Has anyone seen Temmen and Alexander?"

"Everything was in confusion when they arrived. I think they went to the kitchen to get something to eat."

Nicola started to leave, then stopped at the door and smiled at the boisterous group of knights. "Thank you all for your loyalty."

When she reached the kitchen, Agelwulf told her he'd sent Temmen and Oliver to the hall to eat. Nicola found them there. Temmen's blond head was bent over a bowl as he shoveled pottage into his mouth. Alexander ate more leisurely. Seeing her, Alexander got to his feet and gave a nudge to Temmen. Temmen glanced at Nicola and rose abruptly.

Nicola gestured to both of them. "Please sit down. I need to sit myself." She sank down on a bench across from the boy, thinking about what a long day it had been. "So...what did you learn at Mordeaux? Did you speak to Morwenna the cook as we suggested?"

Temmen nodded. "She tried to shoo me out of the kitchen at first. It took a while to convince her you had sent me. When I told her I had entered the castle through a secret entrance, she finally believed me."

"What news did she give you?"

"She said to tell you that all was well."

"What else?"

Temmen shrugged. "She said everything was back to the way it was before, and you shouldn't worry."

"What about FitzSaer? What about Hilary and Simon? Has she seen them?"

Temmen's freckled face tightened in a look of anxiety. "She didn't mention them."

There must be some reason for Morwenna's

terseness. "Did Morwenna behave as if she was frightened, as if she someone had threatened her if she spoke to anyone from outside the castle?"

"Nay. She behaved as if she was in a hurry. As if she had to get back to her duties as soon as possible."

Nicola released a sigh of frustration. The trouble with using someone like Temmen as a messenger was that he didn't know what questions to ask. He'd gone all that way and learned almost nothing. Although Morwenna's words were reassuring. It was unlikely she would advise Nicola not to worry if Hilary and the children were being held prisoner or missing.

"What about the army outside the castle?" she asked. "Can you tell me anything about them? How many men and horses did you see?"

Temmen looked baffled. Alexander said, "There was no army."

No army? That meant FitzRandolph had brought the whole force to Valmar. His army was smaller than they had first thought. It also brought into question whether FitzRandolph was actually in control of Mordeaux.

"How did the castle appear from the outside?" she asked. "Was the portcullis up or down? Were there men on the ramparts?"

Alexander frowned. "I think the portcullis was down, but I can't be certain."

Nicola sense of frustration built. They still didn't know if Simon was safe. It seemed the only way they would find out was to send someone to Mordeaux who knew the right questions to ask. "Thank you for what you've done," she told Temmen and Alexander. "I'll not forget your loyalty."

****

"So, we still know nothing." Nicola sank down on the stool by the bed.

"Perhaps this is a sign you should leave it for today," Fawkes said. "Have some of the pottage Old Emma brought up and come to bed."

Nicola looked at him questioningly. "Even though we still don't know if FitzRandolph controls Mordeaux, or if Simon is safe?"

"Think about what Morwenna said. She told you not to worry. I hardly think she would say that if Hilary and the children were still missing. At any rate, there's naught you can do tonight. 'Tis time to rest."

Nicola ate a bit of the food Old Emma had brought up, then washed her face in the bowl of water the servant provided. She dried off and removed her gown. Clad in her shift, she sat on the stool and undid her braids. Then she fetched a brush and attempted to remove the snarls from her hair. "I should get Old Emma, but I hate to disturb her. I know she's been up and down here all day, fetching things."

"Why don't you let me brush your hair?" Fawkes suggested.

"'Tis hardly a task for a man. And what about your injury?"

"My right arm is uninjured."

"But I've never heard of man brushing a woman's hair."

"Why shouldn't I? I vow I would take pleasure in it."

Nicola moved the stool close to the bed and sat facing away from Fawkes. She'd expected him to be rough, but he brushed her hair with long, smooth strokes.

"It's probably good for me to do something like this. I've been so feeble and helpless these past few days. I need to get my strength back."

"I scarce think this is the means of doing so. Although I'm not complaining."

His touch was gentle. His movements slow and deliberate. She relaxed, the tension of the day draining away. By the time he pronounced himself finished, she was on the verge of falling asleep. She got up to close the shutters.

"Leave them open," he said. "If I haven't sickened from being exposed to the night air yet, I'm not likely to do so now. Besides, the fresh air smells so good. Almost as sweet as you."

"I can hardly imagine I smell good," Nicola said. "After the challenges of this day, I'm certain I must stink."

"You could never smell bad. At least not to me."

She lay down beside him. He eased closer to her and buried his face in her hair. She'd been concerned her worry for Simon would keep her awake. But in seconds her bone-deep weariness dragged her down into dreamland.

****

She woke to the sound of Fawkes speaking quietly. Opening her eyes, she saw that it was morning and he was talking to Reynard. She felt a stab of irritation. Reynard might be Fawkes's closest friend, but as soon as things settled down, she would have to make it clear he couldn't simply walk into their bedchamber any time he wished.

She sat up in bed and saw Glennyth was also there.

"Reynard brings good news," Fawkes said. "At least it's good in that it finally answers some of the questions we've had."

"What news?" Nicola asked.

"We now know who burned Glennyth's cottage,"

Reynard said. "Henry told us everything."

"Henry!"

Reynard nodded. "I realized Alys had to have an accomplice, and I'd seen her with Henry on more than one occasion. Henry seemed relieved to tell me what had happened. I think the guilt was gnawing away at him."

"What did he say?" Nicola asked.

"He said Alys's resentment of you went back to when you first wed Mortimer. Mortimer had suggested you engage a young maidservant, rather than relying on Old Emma. Alys thought she would be the one to serve you, and she was very eager to be freed from her tasks in the weaving shed. But you insisted on keeping Old Emma."

"Why would I not?" Nicola asked. "She can still do everything that needs doing. Even if it does take her longer these days."

"But most royal women want someone young serving them. Alys discovered that when several of Mortimer's highborn friends visited Valmar and brought their wives. She argued her cause with you. Told you how she could do everything much faster. Help you with the sewing, which Old Emma, with her stiff fingers and weak eyes, is no longer able to do."

"I remember the conversation," Nicola said. "Although not very well. My memory of that time is poor. I had just discovered Mortimer's true nature and I was terrified. Old Emma was all I had. The only person I could trust."

"And so you rejected Alys's offer, and not in a kindly way either."

Nicola bit her lips. She recalled telling Alys she didn't need a young maidservant who would be off flirting with the knights half the time. "Perhaps I should been gentler in my dismissal of her, but what I said was true. Alys has always had a terrible reputation for dallying with the knights. Indeed, I'm surprised she hasn't gotten with child yet."

"Oh, but she has." Glennyth interjected. "Twice I've given her something to be rid of it. But the last time, I refused."

"Why did you tell her *nay* this time?" Nicola asked.

"'Twas for her own good. I thought she should settle down and marry. I believe she would be happier—and get into far less trouble—if she had a husband. This was a little over a month ago, after Fawkes came. Even though he was wed to you, Alys had designs on him. She thought she could get him to make her his mistress. I suspect she intended to seduce him and then tell him the babe—which was already growing in her womb—was his."

"But I wasn't interested in her," Fawkes said. "I'd been with her once when I first lived at Valmar. But now I have eyes for no other woman than you."

Nicola gave Fawkes a fond look. Most noblemen took mistresses. She was grateful he felt differently.

"When you rejected her offer, Alys grew angry and vowed she would get back at you," Glennyth said. "She was probably the one behind the rumors you poisoned Mortimer and caused his decline. When Fawkes rebuffed her, Alys's resentment deepened. She decided to strike out at me. So she seduced Henry and convinced to him to set the fire. Although now that I know Alys was behind the fire, I'm fairly certain she didn't intend to kill me, only destroy the cottage and my livelihood."

"Why do you think that?" Nicola asked.

"Because she knew I wasn't in the cottage at the time, but with Reynard." Glennyth nodded to Reynard.

"Remember? She saw us together at the castle when we went there to get some food to take for our walk in the woods."

Reynard nodded thoughtfully. "Henry says he didn't mean to kill Glennyth. He also had nothing to do with Alys's plot to neglect Fawkes until he succumbed from his injury."

"But why did Alys want to kill Fawkes?" Nicola asked. "Then there would be no hope of him ever taking care of her babe."

"When Fawkes showed no interest in her, Alys decided to ally herself with FitzSaer," Reynard said. "When you sent him away to Mordeaux, FitzSaer saw this as his chance. He would get Gilbert out of the way, and then murder Fawkes. When the crossbolt failed to kill him, he decided to finish him off another way."

Reynard turned to Fawkes. "Once you were dead, FitzSaer meant to seize control of both Mordeaux and Valmar. He would have to wed Nicola in order to solidify his claim. But Alys would still get what she wanted. FitzSaer promised to set her up as his mistress and let her take charge of Mordeaux."

"And what of FitzRandolph? What part did he play in this?"

"Strange as it might seem, it was mere coincidence that FitzRandolph arrived when he did. FitzSaer wasn't pleased to have his own scheme disrupted. He had no choice but behave agreeably with FitzRandolph, but he knew his dream of ruling Mordeaux was over. Unless he was wed to Nicola, the people of Mordeaux would never accept him as their lord."

Nicola shook her head. "The arrogance of the man. As if I would willingly wed a man I despise."

"He believed if he controlled Simon's fate, you would do whatever he wished."

A chill of dread slithered down Nicola's spine. If Morwenna had not helped her escape the oubliette, her worst fears might have come true. She owed Morwenna a huge debt.

"Surely you did not learn all of this from Henry," Fawkes said.

"Last night, when Gerard saw how upset Nicola was when Temmen couldn't give her more information about how things were at Mordeaux, Gerard rode to Mordeaux. He spoke to Gilbert and had him tell the whole tale."

"Gilbert? What's he doing back at Mordeaux? Did he find Hilary and the children?" Nicola felt almost afraid to hope.

"Hilary and the children are safe. They got lost on the way from Rosebrook, but eventually made their way to Mordeaux and took refuge in a nearby villein's cottage. As for Gilbert, he questioned the local folk and they took him to the house where the family was sheltering. Gilbert stayed there until FitzRandolph's army left Mordeaux. Then he entered the castle by the secret entrance. With the help of several knights loyal to him, Gilbert overpowered FitzSaer and imprisoned him in the oubliette. Few people at the castle liked FitzSaer or thought he was fit to rule them, so it was easy for Gilbert to resume control."

"De Vescy is certainly an able fellow," Fawkes said. "It reassures me to think he is in charge of Mordeaux."

Nicola let out a sigh of relief. "So, everything is as it should be. At last."

"Not everything," Fawkes responded. "Our son is still at Mordeaux. He should be here with us."

Our son. Hearing Fawkes say the words made her

throat go tight. "I will go today and fetch him."

Fawkes looked at Reynard. "What if FitzRandolph decides to return with a larger army?"

"It's a possibility. But gathering together more knights will take time. 'Tis not likely FitzRandolph will bother us for a few weeks at least."

"The summer is fast slipping away," Fawkes said. "Already the nights grow cooler."

Nicola got up. "I must dress and ready myself for the journey to Mordeaux." She glanced at Reynard hoping he would take the hint and leave.

Fawkes looked to Glennyth. "We must also decide what is to be done about Alys and Henry. What do you think? You suffered the greatest loss at their hands."

Glennyth contemplated this for a moment. "Alys must be punished somehow. But she is with child, although I'm not certain who the father is. Mayhaps she doesn't know either. Until she has the babe we can do little but keep her under tight control."

"One thought is to marry her off to some man who is strong enough to keep her out of trouble," Fawkes suggested.

Nicola nodded. It seemed like a logical solution. "Perhaps Edwin, the wheelwright in the village. He was betrothed to Maida, but she doesn't want to wed him. And he needs a wife. He lives with his mother now, but she's getting very frail."

"That's an idea," Glennyth said. "Edwin is stolid and hard-working and not much seems to bother him. And if Alys gives birth to a boy, he would be so delighted to have someone to pass down his craft to that he wouldn't care if the child was his."

"And if she has a girl?" Reynard asked.

"Edwin isn't the sort to mistreat a child. And the fact that he dwells in the village would mean everyone there would all be able to keep an eye on Alys."

"That settles things regarding Alys. But what of FitzSaer?" Reynard asked. "Do we hang him?"

"I don't think we have a choice," said Fawkes.

Nicola nodded. "He tried to kill you. I can't forgive that."

"I will take care of it," Fawkes said.

Nicola shot him a look of gratitude.

"Speaking of FitzSaer, do we know who the actual assassin was?" Reynard asked. "I'm fairly certain FitzSaer doesn't have the skill to shoot a crossbow so accurately."

"I think I know," said Glennyth. "I suspect it was not a knight, but a local villein who is skilled archer. His name is Ranulf."

"How can we find out for certain?" Fawkes asked.

"He shot you from the ramparts of Mordeaux," Reynard pointed out. "Someone must have seen the man go up there. Perhaps I should go there and question the knights."

"Gilbert can do that. The garrison there is loyal to him," Glennyth said.

"Finally, there is Henry." Reynard nodded to Glennyth. "What do you think should be his fate?"

"Send him away. Give him a chance to try to find a place in some other lord's garrison. Although he cost me dear, and would have cost me even dearer if Reynard had not rescued Tom. I don't think Henry is truly cruel. Alys told him to set the fire and so he did. But I don't believe he meant to murder me. And I'm certain he never considered that my cat might be inside the house."

"I agree," said Fawkes. "Henry deserves another

chance. But not here. I don't want someone as weak and malleable as him in my retinue."

"Where would you send him?" Reynard asked.

"I'll write to Lord Wazelin, asking him if he will take Henry on. I'll tell him Henry is misguided and foolish, but still has potential as a knight."

"I can write the message," said Nicola.

Fawkes smiled at her. "I forgot that in addition to being beautiful, resourceful and brave, you are educated and literate."

Nicola smiled back. "I think we've discussed our plans for punishing the people who caused us so much grief. Now I'd like to get ready to leave for Mordeaux. I vow, I won't be content until I see Simon with my own eyes."

Reynard and Glennyth got up to leave. Glennyth paused at the door. "Perhaps I will go with you, Nicola. While I was at Mordeaux, before FitzSaer imprisoned me, I met a young woman who has some knowledge of herbs. I would like to bring her back here, if she is willing. I'll need help if I am to replenish my store of healing supplies before winter arrives."

"That's another thing," Fawkes said. "We must rebuild Glennyth's cottage as soon as possible."

"Or she could stay here at the castle," Reynard suggested.

"I'll not wed you, or live with you now that you are well enough to be on your own," Glennyth said. "I must have my home and my freedom, or things will not work between us."

"I feared you would say that." Reynard smiled ruefully. "But I had to ask."

"Go and ready yourself for the journey." Nicola

motioned. "We'll take a cart, so we can bring Simon back. Then there will also be room for this young woman whose help you seek."

Reynard and Glennyth left and Nicola began to dress.

Chapter Twenty-Eight

"No wonder you usually ride to Mordeaux." Glennyth grimaced as the cart bounced over another rut in the trackway.

"'Tis not normally so rough. But having FitzRandolph's whole army pass this way has made a mess of the road." Nicola hardly noted the constant jostling; her thoughts were too focused on Simon. Now that she could finally bring him to Valmar and raise him as her own, she'd begun to have doubts. In Simon's mind, Hilary was his mother and Joanie his sister. Although he was fond of Nicola, it was in the way he might be fond of an aunt or a much older sister. How would he adjust to living at Valmar, away from the only family he'd ever known?

The thought of it dampened her joy. At last she would be able to claim Simon as her son and have him in her life, but was it the best thing for him? And how could she explain her concerns to Fawkes? As a man, he wouldn't understand how difficult a change like this might be for a young child. He would consider only that Simon was his son and therefore should be raised in their household.

"Despite the bumpy ride, there are other advantages to traveling like this," Glennyth said. "We are moving quickly, but not so quickly I can't enjoy the passing scenery. 'Tis interesting to note the differences between this part of the forest and the forest around Valmar. The woods are denser here, perhaps because they cut fewer trees to provide fuel at Mordeaux. Certain plants that I have difficulty finding near Valmar might grow in more abundance in this area. After we get to the castle, if there is time, I'd like to explore a bit. See what herbs I can find."

"I think there would be time for that," Nicola answered. "After all, I can't grab Simon and whisk him away to Valmar as if he was puppy newly weaned from its mother. First, I must get him used to the idea he's going to live at Valmar."

"I'm sure it will be difficult for him in the beginning."

"He'll also be leaving Joanie. They're very close." How could this be, that she'd finally obtained her heart's desire and all she could think of was the challenges and problems she faced? "I can't help wondering if I'm doing the right thing for Simon. He's so young. I don't want to upend his life and make him unhappy. I fear he'll be lonely at Valmar."

"Did you mention these concerns to Fawkes?"

"There were too many other things to deal with. And in truth, I've not thought about much of this until now. I was so focused on my goal of having my son be part of my life that I never considered what it might be like for him to leave the only family he's ever known."

"Perhaps there can be some sort of compromise. You can bring Simon to Valmar to meet Fawkes and spend some time there, then take him back to Mordeaux. Gradually get him used to the idea that you and Fawkes are his true parents."

"Such an arrangement would probably be best for Simon. I could accept such a compromise, knowing it would better for my son. But Fawkes..." She shook her head. "Men don't understand how easily children can be hurt, and how that hurt can change them forever. Simon is such a happy, sweet boy. 'Twill break my heart if I do anything that damages his sunny nature. But of course Fawkes will want Simon to be tough and strong, not sensitive and sweet."

"You never know. So far Fawkes has surprised me. He is uncommonly sensible for a man. Perhaps if you explain these things to him, he'll come to understand your concerns."

Despite Glennyth's attempts to reassure her, Nicola could not help fretting. There didn't seem to be a good solution, other than having Hilary and Joanie come to live at Valmar. But that would mean they would be separated from Gilbert. How could she ask that of Hilary, who had been such good and loyal friend?

As they started up the trackway to the castle, Glennyth scanned the area, as if seeing it for the first time. "There are a few villeins living here." She motioned to the handful of houses near the river. "But you couldn't really call it a village."

"I suppose not."

Glennyth nodded thoughtfully. A few moments later she turned to Nicola, hazel eyes gleaming. "If I am to remain at Valmar, my cottage would need to be rebuilt. What would you think if I decided to build it here instead?"

"But why? There are far fewer people here Mordeaux than at Valmar. There would be much less need for your skills."

"The people here might appreciate my skills more than the people of Valmar do. And it would be a chance for me to start fresh. The other advantage is the area appears richer in terms of herbs and plants. Less of the forest and brush has been cleared away. And there's something about Mordeaux that appeals to me."

"What about everyone at Valmar? How would we manage without your healing skills?"

"'Tis not so far away. You could send someone to fetch me when I'm truly needed. I would make certain you had a good supply of herbs at the castle, and come every fortnight or so to replenish it. While I was there I could see to ailments and problems that need ongoing care. You know how to treat the simple things. I'm certain if you looked around, you could find a suitable young woman to train to help you."

"What about Reynard? He's Fawkes's captain, not to mention his closest friend and companion."

"What about Reynard?"

Nicola gazed at the wise woman in surprise. "I thought you cared for him."

"I do. I'm simply not willing to plan my life around a man. If he wants to share my bed, I'm more than willing. But I'll not be his wife. I've never sought a husband. My mother taught me to avoid such entanglements. They inevitably interfere with the responsibilities of being a healer."

Poor Reynard. He was clearly besotted with Glennyth. He would not take this news well. Unless… A sudden thought came to Nicola. What if Fawkes made Reynard castellan at Mordeaux, and Gilbert and his family came to live at Valmar? Would Gilbert be content to have fewer responsibilities and considerably less power?

Of course, Valmar was a much larger castle. There was a lot to do and many more things to look after. She'd already sensed Fawkes chafed at some of the responsibilities of his position. He was skilled in warfare and defense, but not at seeing to the day-to-day details of the demesne. And Warin was getting old. They would need a new steward eventually. Someone who could help her account for supplies and foodstores.

Gilbert took care of those tasks at Mordeaux, in addition to seeing to the area's defense. Although she was not certain how well he could read and write, she knew Gilbert was good at tallying and keeping track of quantities of goods. Her excitement grew. Mayhaps this was a way to help Simon adjust to his new circumstances, as well as giving Glennyth a fresh start.

"It looks so peaceful," Glennyth said as the castle came in view. "Difficult to believe all the turmoil that took place here in the past sennight."

"There's still evidence of FitzRandolph's army." Nicola motioned to the muddy meadow where the hoof prints of dozens of horses, and the ruts made by the wheels of the supply carts crisscrossed the trampled grass.

"That's not what I was speaking of," Glennyth said. "I was thinking of the day when FitzSaer took Hilary and me and the children prisoner. When I was in the cellar at Rosebrook, I truly thought I would die there. I'm very glad FitzSaer is now enduring similar circumstances."

Nicola shuddered. "I won't feel safe until I know he no longer walks upon this earth."

"Don't think about that," Glennyth said. "Think about the fact that you're finally able to acknowledge Simon as your son."

"You're right. 'Tis a happy day, indeed." Nicola turned her gaze to the castle. "And now that I've thought of a plan to make moving him to Valmar less upsetting for all concerned, I can truly enjoy this moment."

"What plan is that?"

Nicola met her friend's gaze. "A number of things have to fall into place, but I think you will be pleased with my idea."

****

Nicola had been in the solar for some time. After hugging Simon and Joanie and giving them honeycakes from Agelwulf, she'd sat beside Hilary and set to work on the sewing she'd brought—a tunic for Fawkes. Hilary worked on a gown for Joanie. As they sewed, she caught up Hilary on the events of the past few days: Fawkes's recovery, FitzRandolph's arrival with his army at Valmar and Alys's plot with FitzSaer.

Hilary listened thoughtfully, occasionally nodding or making a comment. When Nicola told her that Fawkes knew Simon was his son and wanted to see him, Hilary put her sewing aside and turned to look at Nicola, her blue eyes troubled. "I knew this day would come, and Simon would eventually to go off to live with you. Even so…" She glanced toward the corner of the solar where Simon and her daughter were playing. "'Twill be very hard to say goodbye to him. Poor Joanie will be heartbroken."

"I've thought that myself. And I think I have a solution. What would you think of coming to live at Valmar—you, Gilbert and Joanie?"

A slight frown creased Hilary's freckled brow. "We're happy here, and now that FitzSaer will no longer trouble us, I'd hoped things would return to the way they had been. Gilbert is well liked and respected here. If he went to Valmar, he would be one of many knights in the garrison."

"Not necessarily. The steward at Valmar is getting old. I think he would be relieved to give up some of his responsibilities to another man. Gilbert would do well in such a position. He does a fine job of tallying castle supplies and recording produce from the villeins here at Mordeaux."

"'Tis true that Gilbert has more interest in things like that than warfare. I have often thought it a pity that the only way men of ambition and drive can improve their lot is to become skilled at injuring and killing other men, or at least being in charge of men who do such things." She motioned to Simon. "'Tis very hard to imagine little Simon as a knight. But I suppose that is his destiny."

"I'm afraid it must be. Although, like you, 'tis not my preference. There is always the Church. But I'm not certain I want him to be part of that world either. Then he would never know the companionship and pleasures of marriage."

Hilary smiled. "Much has changed over the summer. At one time you were wary and suspicious of Fawkes, and very discouraged about your future with him. Now you appear content, even happy. I'm pleased to see it."

"I am happy. Fawkes is not like most men. At least the ones I've known. He seems to respect and admire me. The thought of it quite amazes me."

"Once you have your beloved Simon with you, I'm certain your contentment will only increase."

"And yet, I don't want to disrupt his life and tear him away from the people he loves. Which is why I hope you will consider my idea."

"I will, of course," Hilary answered. "But one question I have is, if Gilbert leaves, who would be in charge of Mordeaux?"

"I have a plan for that as well. Glennyth the healer desires to live at Mordeaux instead of Valmar. And seeing as Fawkes's captain is in love with her, he would seem a natural fit for the position of castellan."

"You are clever, milady. I have always thought so."

Clever. Perhaps she was. Although it had nearly been her undoing. "So, you will talk to Gilbert about this? Or do you wish for me to do so?"

"Better that it should come from you, I think."

"But I don't want him to be unhappy. If he objects to my plan, you will tell me, won't you?"

"I will tell you."

Nicola got up. "I should go and speak to Gilbert. I will do that while you get Simon's things ready."

Hilary also stood. "What will he need? You don't want me to send all his things yet, do you?"

"Not yet. Pack only enough for a visit of few days. I will either return with him then, or fetch the rest of his possessions, depending on whether I can convince Fawkes of my plan."

"He does not know of it?" Hilary gazed at her in astonishment.

"Not yet." Would Fawkes see her idea as a means of trying to manipulate him? Would he understand how important it was to Simon to have Hilary and Joanie nearby?

She found Gilbert in the hall going through the tally sticks. Perfect, she thought. He started to rise. She waved him down and sat on the bench across from him. "I have a proposition for you, Gilbert. I don't know yet if Fawkes will agree, but this is my plan." She told him about taking Simon to live at Valmar and her plan to move Gilbert and his family there as well. "What do you think of the idea?"

"'Tis not my place to say. When Fawkes defeated Mortimer, I swore to him as the new lord. He can assign me duties as he sees fit."

"Even so, I want you and Hilary to be happy and content. I'm certain you have concerns. Valmar is a much bigger castle and you will not have nearly the authority there you have here."

"Nor near the responsibilities," Gilbert said. "After what I went through with FitzSaer and FitzRandolph, I would rather not be in charge of a castle's defense, at least not on my own. On the other hand, I truly don't know that much about what a steward does."

"Perhaps we should have you come and speak to Warin and learn more about his usual tasks. We can tell Fawkes that you are keen to improve the record keeping at Mordeaux and that's why you are shadowing Warin."

"Why must we give Fawkes an explanation for my presence at Valmar? Doesn't he know about this plan to move me and my family there?" Gilbert looked alarmed. Nicola reminded herself that most men didn't think it was a woman's place to be involved in such decisions. Most wives deferred to their husbands in important matters. Indeed, that was exactly what Hilary had done.

"I haven't spoken to Fawkes about this yet. But once he realizes how important this is to Simon, I'm certain he'll agree."

"Simon? What's his part in this?"

"I can't bear to separate him from Joanie. He's grown up with her and is as close to her as he would be with a true sibling."

The always-serious Gilbert gave her a glimmer of a smile. "In fact, they are closer than most siblings. They rarely fight or squabble over anything. Although that's probably because Simon is younger, and very sweet-tempered."

"So, you understand my reason for asking you to do

this?"

"I do. The question is, will Fawkes? While my moving to Valmar will solve the problem of your aging steward, it will create some difficulty here. There are a couple of knights I could recommend, in terms of seeing to the castle's defense. But I doubt Fawkes knows either of them. He may not be comfortable with appointing an unknown man as castellan."

"In fact, the man who will replace you is very well-known to Fawkes. It's Reynard, Fawkes's captain."

"'Tis clearly an opportunity for him. Although he did not strike me as a man who likes to be in charge. I thought him the carefree sort, someone who is happy to take orders and be spared the hard decisions."

"There is much of that in Reynard. But recent events have forced him to take charge of things and he's not such an easygoing fellow these days. Besides, if his beloved Glennyth decides to live here, I think he will be pleased to take the position. He would do near anything to make her happy. Fawkes owes Glennyth a boon for saving his life. If she chooses to live at Mordeaux and Fawkes's captain chooses to follow her, Fawkes can hardly say no."

Gilbert still appeared wary. Not only of her plan, but of Nicola herself. She suspected he was very thankful that gentle, accommodating Hilary was his wife, rather than her. Would Fawkes eventually tire of her forthright nature and wish he had a meeker, more biddable wife? But how was she to change now, when she knew that without her bold actions, both Fawkes and Simon would likely be dead or lost to her forever?

"I need to find Glennyth and gather up Simon's things and then we will leave," she told Gilbert. "I assume you would prefer to ride, so you can return to Mordeaux whenever you wish."

"Aye, milady. I will arrange for someone to be in charge in my absence, then get my mount and meet you in the bailey."

Nicola returned to Gilbert and Hilary's living quarters to get Simon. He was still playing with Joanie. When he saw her, he got up from the floor and regarded her with a pensive expression. "Can Joanie come?"

"Next time she will, I promise. Now, do you have everything you want to take—your favorite toys?"

He nodded, his expression solemn.

She held out her arms to him. "Will you come then?" He hesitated, his lower lip trembling. Nicola felt her own throat close up. She had not thought this would be so difficult for him. "What's wrong, sweetling?"

Hilary drew near. "'Tis all right, Simon. You know Lady Nicola loves you as much as I do. She will take good care of you. And there are all sorts of fun things you can do at Valmar, aren't there, lady?"

"Aye. All kinds of fun things. You can explore the castle and ride on a horse with your fath—Lord Fawkes. Get treats from the kitchen." Nicola wracked her brain, trying think of things Simon might enjoy doing.

"Do you have doggies and kitties there?" Simon asked.

"We have both. Glennyth, who you will meet soon, she has a big golden kitty named Tom. And there is another cat that lives at the castle named Gimlyn. And in the stables there are hunting hounds."

"I want Willow." Simon's voice hovered on the edge of sob.

"I'm afraid there isn't room in the cart for a dog," Nicola soothed. "But next time you come to Valmar, you can bring him, I promise."

Simon thought this over. He went over to where Joanie was working on her sewing. The little girl's freckled face was screwed up in concentration as she sought to make her stitches even and neat. "Joanie, you must take care of Willow," Simon said. "Give him food at dinner. I don't want him to go hungry."

Hilary leaned near to Nicola. "I'm sorry, my lady. I know I should have put a stop to it. Simon is so hard to resist."

"Let us hope Fawkes is as charmed by his son as we are," Nicola murmured back. "Time to go," she told Simon gently. He nodded, and seemed reassured that Joanie would look after Willow. He took Nicola's hand and let her lead him out of the solar.

Once they were in the cart, he grew anxious and tearful. Thankfully, Gilbert soothed things over by having Simon ride with him on his horse. Watching the two of them, Nicola felt the familiar longing. Someday Simon would look to her for comfort and reassurance. Although she might have to wait a while.

****

"What the devil are you doing up here?" Reynard strode toward Fawkes as he stood on the rampart walkway. Reynard's green eyes were bright with accusation. "You told me you were going to rest!"

Fawkes braced himself against the crenellated wall. He knew he was overdoing, but he couldn't bear to stay in that room any longer. The bedchamber that had once tantalized him with Nicola's allure had since become a hellish prison. "I needed to stretch my legs. And I want to see them as soon as they arrive."

"If you're going to watch for Nicola and Glennyth, at

least do so from the gatetower where you can sit part of the time."

"You're right. I'll come down in a moment." Fawkes turned for one last look over the valley. He saw a wagon and a half dozen horses coming down the trackway. "They're here."

Reynard came to stand beside him. "Who's that with them? Looks like Sir Gilbert. I wonder why he decided to ride back with them."

"I don't know. I hope it doesn't mean there's been more trouble at Mordeaux." Fawkes strained to see the occupants of the wagon. Nicola and Glennyth. And another woman, but not Hilary. And where was Simon?

Then he saw a young child sitting on Nicola's lap. He looked so small from this distance. So vulnerable. Of course. Simon was not yet four years old. Just barely past babyhood. Fawkes experienced a sudden sense of unease. He knew nothing about children. He swore softly.

"What is it?" Reynard asked.

He let out a weak laugh. "I can face down attacking knights. Whole armies. But here I am, about to meet a small child and I'm terrified."

"Terrified? Why?"

"I don't know what to say to him. How to act." He took a deep steadying breath. "Simon has been in my thoughts constantly from the moment I stood on these ramparts and FitzSaer told me Nicola had borne a babe. For a long time I imagined him as a tiny infant buried in a lonely grave. Then a few days ago I learned he was alive. Nicola has described him to me, but in my mind he was a lot bigger. A lot more grown up. I assume he's talking. But even so... How much can he understand? What should I say to him?"

"Watch Nicola. See how she acts with him. And don't expect too much. Small children are often fearful of new people. They will cling to their mothers and cry."

"How do you know this?"

"Told you before. I'm the eldest of six. I've had more than my share of rocking babies and soothing toddlers."

"Simon is very fair. I can see his golden hair from here."

"Nicola warned you he doesn't look anything like you. Indeed, that's part of what created this whole mess. If he'd looked like you she probably would have told you about him right away."

"Probably not." Fawkes answered. "I don't think she trusted me enough. At least not at first. She thought I was some bloodthirsty ogre who ate small children for breakfast." He couldn't help grinning at the image. "Odd to remember, now that I'm the one quaking in fear."

Reynard squeezed his good shoulder. "You'll do very well, I'm certain. Pretend he's a horse you're trying to gentle. Go slow. Give him time to get used to you."

"I wonder who that other woman with them is. Perhaps she's some sort of nursemaid for Simon, although I would have thought he'd outgrown that."

"I'm more concerned with why Gilbert has accompanied them. What do you make of that?"

"I don't know. We'll have to find out." Fawkes turned. "Indeed, I'd better start making my way down there, if I don't want to appear pale and sickly when they arrive. Both Nicola and Glennyth will give me a tongue lashing if they think I've been exerting myself too much."

Fawkes took his time navigating the stairs and crossing the bailey. He stopped at the cistern by the gate, knelt down and splashed his face with water. Then there was nothing to do but wait.

The riders came in first. The four knights Fawkes had sent as an escort and Gilbert. Gilbert nodded to him as he dismounted. "My lord."

Fawkes was on the verge of asking why Gilbert was there when the cart rattled in. Nicola, looking beautiful as ever—and on her lap, the boy. With golden hair and huge eyes the vivid blue of cornflowers.

Nicola handed the boy to Glennyth, then took Fawkes's hand to climb out of the wagon. He wanted to kiss her in greeting. But he thought that might be going too far, with half of the castle gathered round to watch.

"My lord," she said. "Fawkes." She corrected herself with a smile. Then she turned to the wagon and Glennyth handed her Simon.

To Fawkes's relief, the boy looked more curious than frightened. "Hello, Simon." Was it too soon to tell the boy he was his father? Wanting some contact between them, he extended his hand. The boy regarded him with puzzlement.

"He doesn't know yet about shaking hands," Nicola said.

"Of course not."

And yet he longed to touch this child. Impulsively, he tousled the boy's hair. Simon giggled, grinning in delight. Emotion squeezed Fawkes's chest. A sharp aching sensation.

Fawkes cleared his throat and looked away. "I see that Gilbert came with you."

"Aye. Indeed, Simon rode part of the way with him."

"But why did he come? Is there more trouble at Mordeaux?"

"Nay. Nothing like that. He came because...I have a

proposition for you."

"What sort of proposition?"

"'Tis complicated. I'll explain after we wash and eat."

"Down," Simon said. "I want down."

"Of course, love." Nicola set Simon on the ground.

Fawkes thought the boy seemed impossibly small. And yet he recalled Nicola telling him that Simon was large for his age.

Fawkes glanced at Nicola, wondering what she meant by a proposition. Only a moment passed, but when he looked down again Simon was gone. Fawkes turned, stricken with sudden fear. "Simon!" he called. "Simon!"

"He's there." Nicola pointed. "I told you he loves animals."

In the bailey crowded with horses and people, Simon had caught sight of Gimlyn and was headed straight toward the cat. Although there was no obvious danger, Fawkes's heart jumped into his throat. "Will he be all right? The cat won't scratch him, will he?"

"More likely, Gimlyn will run away," Nicola said.

But he didn't. Instead, the cat rubbed against Simon's legs. Simon reached down to pet the animal and the cat lay down on his side. Simon gave Gimlyn a few awkward pats as the cat rolled around in the dirt.

"See, I told you," Nicola said. "Most children his age would grab at the cat and make it run. But Simon has been taught to move slowly and touch animals gently, so Gimlyn accepts him."

"I don't know what most children do with animals. Or with anything else. I know nothing about children, Nicola."

She touched his arm. "You don't have to learn all at once. In truth, I don't know much more than you. I've only been around Simon for short periods of time. I've never cared for him on my own. I wish now I'd had Hilary come along. But she would have had to bring Joanie and there simply wasn't room in the cart. And I must learn how to be Simon's mother sometime."

"We can learn together how to care for him."

Nicola nodded and went to Simon. Kneeling, she said something to the boy. He reluctantly turned to her. Even as she picked him up, the boy swiveled his head to look at the cat.

"Come on, Simon," Nicola said. "We'll go into the hall and have something to eat. But first, we must wash our hands. Here comes Old Emma. She's going to help me take care of you. Did you know she took care of me when I was your age? Hard to imagine, isn't it?"

Nicola approached the elderly servant, Reynard appeared beside Fawkes. "Should you not go back to bed?"

Fawkes started walking to the hall. "I'm well enough. Seeing my son has revived me."

Reynard made a grumbling sound. "I'm pleased for you, I truly am. I only wish my own life was turning out so happily."

Fawkes gave Reynard a searching look.

"Glennyth is going to live at Mordeaux. The young woman with her, Lyssa, is going to be her assistant. I think Glennyth is here mostly to gather her things."

"Does Nicola know about this?"

Reynard's tone was bitter. "Of course."

"Glennyth is the healer for Valmar and the village. We need her. I can forbid her to leave."

"She'll say she owes you nothing. And she's right. She's not a villein tied to the land."

Fawkes nodded. Even if he had the right to coerce Glennyth to stay, it would be foolish to try to do so. The wise woman was willful and stubborn; she would get her way somehow. He glanced at Reynard, wanting to tell him he should go with her. But if he did that, what would he do for a captain? More important, how would he survive without Reynard's jesting and lazy good nature?

Of course that good nature and humor had not been much in evidence of late. Falling in love had changed Reynard, and not necessarily for the better. Before, he had been carefree and lighthearted. Now that he had something to lose, he was no longer so easygoing and cheerful.

Love could do that to a man. Tie him in knots and make his life a living hell. And yet it could also make a man feel as Fawkes did now: as if his chest might burst with tender emotion. As if he could do anything, conquer any foe, fight his way to any goal. To love was to risk everything, and yet you could gain everything as well: purpose, joy, contentment. 'Twas a hard bargain, but a fair one.

"Let me talk to Glennyth. Perhaps we can work out an arrangement where she visits Valmar regularly to care for those who need her skills. You could visit her also. At least during times when Valmar faces no serious threat."

Reynard nodded glumly.

"For now we should go to the hall and have something to eat. And I need to speak to Gilbert, find out why he is here. Perhaps he's heard something about FitzRandolph. There must be a reason why he felt four knights wasn't enough to escort Nicola and my son safely back here."

They went into the hall. Fawkes sought out Nicola and Simon. Old Emma was seated next to Simon, who

417

was propped on two cushions. The servant appeared to be giving him pointers on how to behave.

Fawkes sat down across from Nicola and met her gaze. She nodded to Simon and Old Emma and shrugged her shoulders. "Apparently, Simon has never eaten in the hall with everyone else. I suppose Hilary hadn't thought him old enough. I would have had his food brought up to the bedchamber. But Old Emma said if he was going to be lord here someday he needed to learn how to behave as a gentleman."

"I would have thought him too young myself," Fawkes said.

"But neither of us have any experience in this. Since I was a girl, my training was different. And you were not a lord's son."

Fawkes motioned to Maida and the servant put some roasted meat on his trencher. When Maida had moved away, he asked, "Does it bother you that I am low-born?"

"I can find no fault with your manners. But I'm certain you learned them slowly, over the years, picking them up from watching men who grew up in castles and fine houses."

"True." Fawkes took out his eating knife to cut his meat. "I suppose you know about Glennyth's plans. Needless to say, I'm concerned. What if something happens to Simon and we need a healer immediately?"

"I don't think we can stop Glennyth from doing this. She promised to supply me with basic medicines and herbs and train someone here at Valmar in how to use them. That's why she brought Lyssa, the young woman accompanying us. So she can train both apprentices at the same time."

"Who does she think to train here?"

"She hasn't said yet. Perhaps she's still deciding. I was thinking of Maida." Nicola nodded to the servant girl, now pouring wine.

"But there was that incident with de Ronay. Her demeanor afterwards was very petulant and childish."

"She dallied with the jongleur because she is ambitious. He told her he would take her away with him and she believed him. She wants more out of life than to be the wife of a villein. Or a castle serving maid. If Glennyth can train her in healing skills, that would give her status, and a sense of purpose. It might be the making of her."

"I suppose so." Fawkes was doubtful, but what did he know about young women and their fancies? "Still, there is the matter of Reynard. If Glennyth leaves, 'twill break his heart."

"Reynard? The Sly Fox? The carefree knight who charms and seduces and then quickly moves on to his next conquest?"

"That has been his reputation. But this time it's different; he has serious feelings for Glennyth. Or do you think it only fair, that he experience the heartache he's caused others?"

"He's undoubtedly caused some heartbreak, but not a lot. At least I've heard he is clear about his intentions and doesn't lead women on. He doesn't pursue the young, vulnerable ones like Maida." Nicola reached over and squeezed Fawkes's hand. "I'm happy enough that I want everyone to be happy, at least the good, honest people who deserve it. I have an inkling how to make everything work out, if you agree."

Nicola had not anticipated she would tell Fawkes about her plan so soon. But perhaps it was better this way.

His worries about Reynard would work in her favor.

He listened quietly, eating steadily while she explained all of it: Simon's welfare. Reynard's happiness. Gilbert's skill at tallying. Warin's failing eyesight. "So, you see," she said. "It works out for everyone. Simon's life is not entirely uprooted. Reynard and Glennyth can be together. You get a strong, trustworthy castellan for Mordeaux. And Gilbert gets a position more in keeping with his skills."

"What of Hilary? She's chatelaine at Mordeaux. How does she feel about leaving her position at Mordeaux?"

"I think she would rather move to Valmar than give up Simon. She loves him and wants what is best for him. At least here she can be part of his life."

"When will we explain things to Simon? Tell him that we are his true parents?"

"I think he is too young to do so yet. And there's no real need. Children don't question it when someone who cares about them comes into their life. It's only when they lose someone that they need answers and reassurance." Nicola nodded to Old Emma. The servant was telling Simon something, and they both looked as comfortable and at ease as if she'd been his nurse from birth. "No one has ever been injured by having a surfeit of doting mothers, I assure you."

"Not injured, perhaps. But what about being utterly spoiled?"

Nicola shook her head. "You don't know Old Emma like I do. She's as strict as she is affectionate. She'll not let him grow up spoiled and selfish. Besides, he'll have two fathers to look up to and learn from." She smiled at Fawkes and again patted his arm.

"And you accept this arrangement? Knowing you

share Simon with two other women?"

"'Tis a very simple thing. I want what is best for Simon. As for you having to share the role of father, I'm afraid fathers aren't terribly important in the early years. You'll have plenty of time to shape and mold Simon to your liking." Nicola felt her smile waver. She feared there would be conflicts between them over how Simon should be molded. But, God willing, they'd have other children, and that would ease the responsibilities that rested on her dear sweet boy.

"It seems you've thought of everything," Fawkes said. "There are times I feel certain you should have been a man. I vow, you have the shrewdness and the force of will to command an army."

"I've not thought of everything," she answered. "For example, I'm not entirely certain where everyone is going to sleep tonight. I suppose Lyssa can bed down in the weaving shed with the other unmarried women. Hopefully Gilbert won't be too offended at having to sleep in the barracks. I doubt I'm going to be able to separate Old Emma from Simon. Yet having all four of us in the tower room is going to be very cramped."

"Perhaps for tonight, Simon can sleep with Old Emma in her alcove and you and I can have the bedchamber to ourselves." Fawkes's dark eyes bored into her, reminding her that this was not only the man she loved, but the man she desired most passionately.

"You're certain you won't hurt your shoulder?"

"There are positions we have not tried." A faint smile quirked his lips.

Nicola suddenly felt breathless with anticipation.

Epilogue

Nicola shut and latched the door to the tower room and turned to Fawkes, who was already undressing. "You're certain no one saw us come up here?"

"What if they did?"

"They might guess what we're up to."

"Who cares if they do? There's no crime in tumbling my wife, even if it is only midday." Having stripped off his tunic, Fawkes sat down on the bed to remove his boots.

Nicola undid the lacing on her gown. "I suppose not. But they might think it strange that we've come here to do it instead of the lord's bedchamber."

"Until only a few weeks ago, this used to be our bedchamber. Or rather, *your* bedchamber. It still reminds me of that first time."

Fawkes dark gaze raked her, making Nicola shiver. "I can't forget that day either. You weren't what I was expecting at all."

"Why not?"

"Mortimer said he'd found a lowly squire to bed me. But then I saw you and you looked like a knight to me. And not lowly at all."

"You would never have seen me if I hadn't insisted on opening the shutters."

"I would still have known you were man grown, and a bold one, by the way your body felt against mine and the way you loved me."

A faint smile touched his lips. "How did I love you?"

She smiled back at him. "Slow and tender. At first I wanted you to hurry. Then I didn't."

"And now? How should I love you this day?"

"Today, I am impatient."

He nodded and finished undressing. When he was naked, he came to stand next to her. He placed his hands on her waist and drew her close, so his magnificent up-thrust shaft pressed hard against her belly. The feel of his hot flesh made a delicious ache spread from her groin to her breasts. She sighed with longing. "When I see you, my body doesn't want to wait." She caressed the tender tip of his shaft until he made an agonized sound.

"I'm the same," he said, breathing hard. "I want you naked. Hurry."

She stepped back and pulled her gown over her head, then swiftly slipped off her shift and loincloth. In seconds he had her in his arms. He kissed her desperately and maneuvered her over to the bed. After helping her onto it, he straddled her and kissed her again. She stroked his shoulders. Her body trembled with need as she raised her hips. Nicola moaned when he touched her between her legs, a quick stroke to open her further. Then he eased himself into position and thrust deep.

Nicola shrieked at the intensity of it. Then she pressed her lips together, letting only low moans escape as he rode her to the heavens and beyond.

****

Wild. Magical. Fierce. She was all those things. His beautiful Nicola, so fine and exquisite, and yet so strong. Fawkes gave into the violent passion building inside him and let the soul-deep fulfillment wash over them both.

Seconds later, they sprawled in a helpless tangle on

423

the bed when there was a knock at the door. "Lady Mama!" a small voice called.

Fawkes let out a laugh. "Jesu, what's he doing up here?"

"Milady. I'm sorry. He wouldn't wait." Old Emma's breathless voice echoed through the door.

"Give us a moment," Nicola called back. She met Fawkes's gaze, grinning. "We must hurry."

They dressed rapidly, Simon's small voice and Old Emma's answering murmurs spurring them on. When they were mostly presentable, Fawkes went to the door and unlatched it. "Where is my young Simon?"

"I'm here, Sir Fawkes." Simon burst into the room. He held up a small gray kitten. "I found her."

Fawkes glanced at the kitten cradled in Simon's arms, and gave Nicola a helpless look.

Nicola bent next to Simon. "Is she old enough to be away from her mother? And how do you know the kitten is a girl?"

"Sir Gerard said."

Fawkes and Nicola exchanged another look.

'Can she sleep with me?" Simon gazed at them with wide, hopeful eyes.

"I suppose so," Nicola answered.

Old Emma waddled over to the boy. "Come, lovey, let's take the kitten to the kitchen and get it some milk. Then we'll see what we can find to make it a bed of its own." The elderly servant shot Nicola a reproving glance and herded Simon toward the door.

Halfway there, Simon turned back. "Her name is Isabella, Joanie says."

Nicola shook her head as Simon and the servant left. "Old Emma certainly doesn't approve. You probably don't either. But I did tell you Simon loves animals."

"I suppose I can tolerate one kitten in our private chambers. It will keep the place free of mice."

"Eventually." Nicola approached him. "Some months from now."

"We'll have to endure until then, won't we?" Fawkes's smile was like a glowing sun. He took her in his arms and kissed her.

Thank you for purchasing
this publication of The Wild Rose Press, Inc.

If you enjoyed the story, we would appreciate your
letting others know by leaving a review.

For other wonderful stories,
please visit our on-line bookstore at
www.thewildrosepress.com.

For questions or more information
contact us at
info@thewildrosepress.com.

The Wild Rose Press, Inc.
www.thewildrosepress.com

Stay current with The Wild Rose Press, Inc.

Like us on Facebook

https://www.facebook.com/TheWildRosePress

And Follow us on Twitter
https://twitter.com/WildRosePress